The Kukulkan Manuscript

by

James Steimle

Technical Data Freeway, Inc.

Author's Note:
This book is a work of fiction. Any references to historical events, real people, or real locales are used fictitiously. Other names, characters, places, and incidents are products of the author's imagination, and any resemblance to actual events or locales or persons, living or dead, is entirely coincidental.

Technical Data Freeway, Inc.,
P.O. Box 308, Poway, CA 92074

First Edition

This book is set in 12-point Adobe Garamond

ISBN-13: 978-0-9841600-0-6
ISBN-10: 0-9841600-0-0

Visit www.tdfbooks.com

For Bruce H. Porter,
no relation to John D., but no less loved

Teacher, mentor, and most of all,
Friend.

Foreword

Due to the controversial nature of the facts presented in this book, the names of the primary universities involved have been altered to avoid legal entanglements.

Despite the many well-published intellectuals involved, the events surrounding the unwanted codex of 1997 have skillfully passed into the realm of the quickly forgotten. While I recognize the dangers that will become apparent to the reader in the following pages, I have recorded, to the best of my limited ability, the only existing record of the ancient American book worth murder to keep buried.

Stratford University will deny everything written here.

The FBI will have no comment, for all related issues are currently under investigation and top clearance is required to validate the bulk of these words.

Erma Alred is more than willing to tell her side of the story, and Porter even more so.

But the voice of the individual is often little more than the cry of a cricket in a gale.

Prologue

May 7, 1997

I, John D. Porter, have done at last that which I thought I would never do.

Who will blame me? Who can be my judge after all the trials that have eaten at me since Dr. Ulman found the codex?

I fear I am trapped at the end of the chase.

No more games.

No more answers.

I honestly believe that no human starts a day with the clear intention of engaging in a crime which is undeniably evil. Even Cain in the Old Testament thought he was doing that which served his best interests. That's the motto of modern culture.

It is an angry mouth chewing on me each minute now, a creature which ignores intelligence while feigning a prudent brow for a reason I have yet to understand.

I know this shall progress no further than today. I may never learn the end of the story.

Who is left to trust? What mortal can I lean on...in this, my final hour?

I wish Alred had never gotten involved. She can't hide anymore behind those strong eyes and her stalwart posture. Alred's a good person. She's the only one who's been with me from the beginning. I'd like to think she even understands....

Now I cling to the only thing that hasn't been taken from me: my painful testimony of the reality of the unwanted codex.

Surrounded by many, I feel...alone.

I pray this is not my last journal entry.

Chapter One

January 31, 1997
10:42 p.m. Eastern Standard Time

"I know they are going to kill me."

New year rains fell like needles from unseen clouds in a black sky, a constant and cruel battery warning him of the doom to come.

But Christopher Ulman had never been more excited!

Automatic gunfire pounded in Ulman's ears as he slammed the door shut and bolted it with a thick piece of wiring. Dropping his papers on a makeshift desk and his duffel bag on the ground, he lowered himself quickly in the dark onto his bed and rammed his fingers into his temples.

The bed was made up of an old sleeping bag with a broken zipper, a sheet that badly needed to be washed, and a beaten pouch of lumpy feathers that he called a pillow, all laid out on a solid board he'd procured from a stranger.

His shaking fingers scraped a match against the rough metal of a Spanish lantern. The flare reflected off the cold glass and momentarily filled his nostrils with sulfuric fumes.

Lighting the wick, Ulman turned off his flashlight.

He tried to smile, but had to squeeze his eyes shut. He forced happy thoughts into his mind of Greenwich, the small town in eastern Illinois which had spawned him. He remembered the white porches and the picket fence that surrounded his boyhood front yard. He conjured up visions of the dry leaves of autumn smashing between his toes, and for a moment he wondered if he could smell the sweet dust kicked up by new rainfall.

But the booming thunder above beat at his forehead, reminding him that his cozy memories were only lies now. His past was gone forever.

Buckets of water splashed down on the roof, which had proudly been made by the son of a roof-mender—Ulman was at last happy for the skill his father had pushed upon him.

And the gunshots started up again.

AK-47, he thought, remembering Vietnam. Painful emotions exploded to life: friends left in the jungle for good; old companions absorbed by a chaotic war, never returning. He wiped his forehead, his mouth gaping and then slamming shut. "How can I be thinking about the war?!" he whispered, digging his fingers into the inner corners of his closed eyes. A taste of salty water laced his lips. It was the same sweat and rain mixture he recalled from the Orient.

He opened his eyes and stared at the ceiling. Would he live to see tomorrow? he wondered. Would they raid his tiny fort, or bomb him without warning? Best to die in a sudden bang than to know you are being killed? Smiling and frowning, Ulman recognized he'd asked the same question on a daily basis in Vietnam.

The gun fired again, hurling waves of bullets from afar. He pinched his eyes closed and thought about the weapons carried in the unclean hands of the guerrilla soldiers. He could picture the short warriors, drenched like he was; black eyes poking out of dark faces; brown skin hiding them in the shadows; Ulman felt the chill of the fear and anger of the *Vietcong*.

Shaking his head slowly, he rubbed his temples as tears slid down his cheeks. He was soaked, but still certain of the tears. With a smile he realized there really were no *Vietcong* soldiers around him. The shots came from the sky; the normal roar of thunder.

His hands trembled, but he wasn't cold.

Ulman knew he was in trouble. He wanted to think about Illinois again, but his exhausted mind failed to comply. His dreams came to life and fought to choke his perception of reality. He didn't want to sleep. He worried that if he lost consciousness…he might not ever wake up again.

Having not rested to the degree human bodies require, Ulman could feel the thick cotton in his brain. It was hard to concentrate on anything. His thoughts slid from dark visions to unwanted memories, from his trapped reality to dream and then back into his haphazard hut again. When his eyes opened, they looked to the soiled papers on his desk.

The table, as skillfully thrown together as his precarious shelter with the nice roof, did not look much like a desk at all. Off-white food-storage buckets with another flat board set on top had become a garden for steadily growing piles of note sheets and worn books. Many of the volumes were open, and a thought rushed through his mind that the spines were being damaged. He didn't care anymore.

His face dropped, and his right cheek pressed against his sleeping bag. Ignoring the men's-locker-room smell of the bedding, his eyes looked to his more important treasure. A small chest, two feet long and one foot wide, held his prized discoveries.

With glazed eyes closing on their own, he smiled again.

As his mind, longing to dream, interrupted his coherent thoughts, he saw James G. Masterson, the chair of the Department of Ancient History and Anthropology at Stratford University, standing behind his oval desk. Ulman watched the old man lean on his desktop with two spidery hands, his brow hard and his lips shoving up into his large nostrils. "Do you honestly think I can allow you to publish this paper?" Masterson's voice boomed. "Don't you realize the ripple effects this kind of report would cause?"

"I don't care what happens!" Ulman heard his own voice reply in dream. "In fact, I'm looking forward to the outcome!"

"Looking forward to it?" the Chair said. "I cannot allow it! I will not!"

"Then I'll publish it on my own!" Ulman said, his voice stern and unwavering.

"I will not permit it!" Masterson said.

"How can you stop me?" Ulman said.

Masterson bent his neck like a buzzard across his desk, his blue eyes bulging out of his wrinkled head. His baldness reflected a lamp somewhere in a corner of the office. "If you publish a work on this find, identifying yourself as a professor at this University, I'll have you dismissed! It will destroy the school! It will ruin anyone who touches it! Take my word! Let it decapitate and bury you if you will, but don't drag the world down with you!" Violently lifting off of his desk, Masterson walked out of his room, his eyes holding solidly onto Ulman until he disappeared. He slammed the large wood door hard behind him.

Ulman jerked and opened his eyes. The crack of the door had been the blasting of thunder again. He looked back at the chest and licked his lips. A small grin turned the corners of his mouth for a fleeting moment. Masterson had only been a dream. He let his eyes close and then forced them open.

No one would believe him. They would all see the evidence and be unable to deny its existence, but no one would take his find seriously. Ulman himself felt that the discovery had to be a mistake, a lie. *Yet there it was in the box.* As an expert in ancient Mesoamerican studies, he knew of few people more qualified in the entire world to judge such a find! And like all the other professionals, Ulman couldn't believe it was real, but he *did.* He had to!

It was *his* discovery! It ruined everything! He almost laughed. What would the world think? Already, Ulman had dispatched letters to some of his more prominent colleagues. He regretted sending a few of the memos. It didn't take a genius to realize that his find would not be something the world would be eager to see. Dr. Masterson in his dream had spoken the truth. The breakthrough posed particular questions for which the scholarly world would be forced to seek answers, though they would despise the necessity of the operation. The results would contradict many of their previously written and spoken statements concerning the early history of Central America. Modern historical textbooks would become as obsolete as all the maps and globes depicting the Soviet Union as a single country.

Archaeologists and ancient historians are interesting people. They seek the truth, but hate it at the same time. They publish a thesis or write their masterpiece—their greatest attempt at eclectic scholarship—and within fifteen years someone overthrows their facts, their theories with new ones. And rather than accepting their previously incorrect suppositions, they spend the rest of their lives attempting to back up what they've already said. Ancient history is a fluid science, ever-changing as new facts and theories bridge the gaps of older hypotheses and mysteries. Of course, no one likes to be proved wrong. History is a constant argument concerning the past.

Both archaeologists and historians would come to abhor the name Christopher Ulman.

Why?

Ulman smiled, shivered, and fought to stay awake.

His find was unbelievable! Would the world accept it at all? *Ulman* didn't want to! Why should the world believe in it? But as Ulman translated what he could from his precious codex, the thing looked up at him and said, *You cannot deny that I am in your hands!* Could Ulman renounce his long years of academic training? Could he shout to the memories of his pushy professors at Yale, "Look at it yourselves! It is here in my hands! You cannot dispute that tangible fact! You cannot and I cannot!" Would they believe him?

He knew that all the dating techniques would work, but they were unnecessary. Anyone capable of translating the codex could see the truth it bellowed to the world! Let them call the document a fake, but they would have to acknowledge that no better forgery existed, for it was flawless.

Besides the writings themselves, Ulman had discovered the city from which they came. The world would shake at the sight of this ancient metropolis!

It was final! These new truths would come forth and make Christopher Ulman as famous as the discoverer of King Tutankhamen's tomb, Howard Carter. His work would be in all the papers and journals! He imagined a smiling picture of his face beneath the red letters of *Time Magazine*. Scholars would argue over it all for decades, as they did with the Dead Sea Scrolls found in the Middle East.

Only one thing could suppress the appearance of these findings: the death of Christopher Ulman.

With a frown and foggy eyes, Ulman looked at the door.

He heard the gunshots again.

Chapter Two

March 21
11:03 a.m. Pacific Standard Time

"Mr. John D. Porter?" Mrs. Welch said in a flat voice.

"Yes."

"What does the *D* stand for?"

"It stands for: *Does That Matter*?"

"Do you know why you're here Mr. Porter?"

Mrs. Welch, a forty-three year old with tight brown curls, which were obviously dyed, and matching color contacts in her eyes, sat behind a neatly organized desk in her pin-striped business suit. Her skin had been tanned too often and showed the splotchy signs of sun and age, but her face wore enough make-up to look almost normal, except where it cracked near the wrinkles around her mouth. She knew her position was high and mighty relative to his, and her relaxed eyes examined Porter's with only an occasional glance to his face.

Porter let his eyes drop to her name plate, Debby-Anne Welch—Degree Assessment, Office of Admissions and Records. Without a smile, Porter asked, "Am I safe in assuming that I'm here for assessment?"

"Do you know what your problem is Mr. Porter?" She spoke again in her flat voice. She really didn't want to bother with this. In her mind, John Porter was just another smart-aleck student who wasn't mature enough to leave the university and step into the real world. Though he never smiled, his eyes were lit with a fire that looked for an opportunity to burn someone.

Had Porter been particularly handsome, Mrs. Welch might have treated him differently. But he had as normal and plain a face as one could get. His eyes were small, his nose average, his lips not too thin, but not thick. A light complexion showing little time spent in the sun. So he was probably a bookworm know-it-all. His brown hair, cut short, neatly fell to one side. He wore no earring, no wedding ring, and was dressed in gray slacks and a white button-down shirt. His features might have appeared attractive in their simplicity on anyone else, but not on Porter. But neither was he ugly—just bland and somewhat colorless.

Most of all, she didn't like his attitude. If he wanted to have a hard time, she'd be happy to give it to him.

"I have lots of problems, Mrs. Welch," his lips curved in a slight smile, and his eyes seemed to sigh. "To which might you be referring?"

Mrs. Welch looked at him for a moment without speaking. There was just something else she didn't like about him. And it wasn't due to her bad-hair day. "Mr. Porter," she said, sighing as she looked down at his record. "Let's see now." Pause. "You graduated with a bachelor of arts in history from Berkeley and went on toooo—"

"Chicago," he said. His face smiled the way it had since he'd stepped into the office, his mouth barely moving, his eyes glowing. A little pride held his head aloft.

Mrs. Welch looked through his file to confirm his words. "An MA in Ancient Near Eastern Studies. And you wrote your thesis on—"

"Semitic temples," he said as she read it.

She took a long breath. "It says here that you graduated in the top of your class, *summa cum laude*, from Chicago University," she flipped backward through the file. "But you didn't do so well at Berkeley."

"It was a real liberal school," he replied, looking at the white walls with colorless Yosemite photos and a matching calendar hanging as if set by a professional decorator. His gray eyes stopped on the framed shot of her father's yellow catamaran in high waves.

"What's wrong with liberal schools?"

She saw the smile as he looked back into memories of Berkeley. "Nothing, as long as there are some rules attached. We had people come to class on a daily basis with barely a stitch of clothes. I got my mortarboard. Personally, I think an anti-conservative theater allows me to do better work. But it can be a bit distracting."

"Berkeley didn't have regulations?" she said sarcastically.

He returned to his normal smile and smooth tone. "Berkeley had rules, but a great deal of the students thought they had the right to rewrite them."

"Maybe they did," she said, her eyes dry and locked onto his.

He smiled again with his mouth, but his eyes didn't shine. "You graduated from Berkeley."

She nodded. "A fine school."

"I assume the students wore clothes in your day."

"We had streakers in my time," she said, getting personal, but keeping her face hard.

He realized that he had walked into a mine field and should back out slowly, but he couldn't resist the set-up. "Was Berkeley an accredited university *way back then*?"

She lifted her eyebrows at the insult and dove into his file. "Mr. Porter, might I assume that you have a problem with *our* liberal university?"

"No, Stratford is a fine school," he said, repeating her definition of Berkeley.

She stopped and stared at him for another moment, squeezing her eyelids tightly together. After contemplating the idea of finding another counselor to advise this John D. Porter, she tossed it aside with the hope that he was stupid enough to get himself thrown out of Stratford University despite her warnings.

Looking back into his file, she said, "Well it seems to us that you have a problem with this university."

"When you say 'us,' I assume you mean the assessment department?" He crossed his right leg over his left, put his right elbow on the arm rest, and leaned his chin into his hand.

"You don't get a Ph.D. until after *we* say you do," she said, pointing at him with her black pen.

"Of course." He smiled again.

"You have been at this university for a long time, haven't you Mr. Porter."

"I have been attending Stratford for close to seven years."

She nodded as she clarified, "One semester shy of seven years. You studied at Berkeley from 1982 to 1987, six years, and then at Chicago from '87 to '89. Why so long at Berkeley?"

"Do you normally ask personal questions while assessing Stratford students?" Porter said, his eyes shifty.

"I didn't realize I was asking a personal question, Mr. Porter. If you would prefer not to answer—"

"I took a two year leave of absence to serve as a missionary in Tokyo," he said, staring at the fake rubber tree in the corner of her office.

"Oh," she said with one raised brow. "And you'd prefer not to talk about it. Bad experience?"

"Not at all," he smiled and cupped his right knee in his hands. "I don't mind discussing my time in Japan, but it was a sacred occasion for me. A special moment in my life."

"I see," she said without looking at the file. Her curiosity was taking her away from her actual duties of student assessment, but he seemed distracted by the subject as well. "You were a missionary. Campus Crusade?"

"Mormon," he said. The fire still danced in the back of his eyes, and the corners of his mouth lifted. She could tell he was attempting to ascertain her response.

Her minister had given enough warnings about Mormons to squelch her curiosity. She looked back to the file. "You speak a little Japanese then?"

He nodded, smiling as if recalling some mental secret. She had heard that the Mission Training Center in Utah was supposedly well known by the United States government as one of the best language training centers in the world. There were also rumors that the FBI loved to search Brigham Young University for returned missionaries who had served in foreign countries. Mormons had the reputation of learning languages better in two months at the MTC and two years in the mission field than the majority of military intelligence agents serving in the US. Mormons and the government—one of her minister's biggest warnings in predicting the end of the world.

He didn't tell her just how good his Japanese was, but grinned, and she had suspicions. He was probably wondering if she knew any of the language and if she'd dare to speak to him.

But his pride wouldn't be gratified today in that way. According to his transcripts, Porter had not taken a single course in Japanese. "You've covered extensive courses in Near Eastern Languages, not to mention German," she said, shuffling through the file. "Arabic, Aramaic, Egyptian, Hebrew...Spanish 101?" She looked up inquiringly about the last class since it stuck out as the only Spanish course he'd taken.

"Four units," he said. "I needed four more units at Berkeley to graduate."

She looked back down with a nod. "You've taken Hebrew 101 four times and both Arabic 101 and 102 twice."

"It's too easy for me to forget one language as I study another," he said, probably wondering about the problem she had referred to. "I knew I couldn't take them for credit. I just wanted to restudy them for myself."

"It's taken you a long time to review all these courses." She said, looking up at him. He was thirty-three, a Mormon, and unmarried. She had known a couple of girl friends at Berkeley who were Mormons, but they had both surprised her by getting married before they were twenty-one. She'd scorned them for leaving school without their degrees and told them they would regret it. But when she'd bumped into one of them only a few years earlier, the friend had appeared happy and healthy. She learned that together, her two friends had more children than she had fingers.

In that way, Mormons seemed forever mysterious. They never lost that cheerful glow, at least not publicly. They faced the hot furnace of reality with hope and a faith she couldn't understand. They gave up everything, only to end up with more than she could gain while sacrificing nothing. Meanwhile, she felt alone and afraid of the world. So she wanted to smile at the young man before her without the wedding ring. To find a Mormon his age and unmarried was something pleasantly unexpected. There had to be something really wrong with John D. Porter.

Mrs. Welch looked back at the file and flipped to the end. She took a single sheet in her fingers, scraped her red nails against the page, and examined it. "John D. Porter," she read his stylized signature at the bottom of the page. "Dated September seventh, 1989." Her eyes drifted to the paragraph directly above the signature. She coughed into her hand and read the words:

> In compliance with the rules of the Stratford University Doctoral Program, I the undersigned do hereby agree to comply with all school regulations and stipulations of the abovementioned university. The attached con-

> tract has been assessed and accepted by the undersigned professor, who will be my advisor and supervisor during the duration of my stay at Stratford University. I understand that failure to comply with any of the above regulations and stipulations will be recognized by the assessment board of the aforementioned university as just cause for immediate dismissal from the university. If I am dismissed, all former contracts will become null and void upon announcement of my dismissal, and all credit work completed for the doctoral degree at the abovementioned university will be forfeited at the same time.

Porter sunk a bit in his chair and knew he was in trouble, though he probably didn't know in what way. No doubt, it was one of those paragraphs that he hated to read. He'd probably breezed over it quickly, said, "Yes, yes, of course," and signed in order to rise to the next step of his schooling.

Mrs. Welch smiled lightly as she watched him squirm. She leaned back in her chair, still holding the paper. "Do you recall signing this agreement admitting you into the doctoral program here at Stratford?"

He opened his mouth, but must have been too busy pondering all the trouble he might be in. He'd violated no rule that could result in his dismissal from the university, but then, what student remembered all of the rules. He had been here for seven years, after all.

"Is your advisor Dr. Kinnard?" she asked with a dart of her eyes to the second signature at the bottom of the page.

"He is," Porter said.

She stood, pulling at the bottom of her blazer, and took a step to a shelf set up as neatly as her desk. She sniffed, realizing that his Old Spice scent clashed with her Liz Claiborne, displeasing her even more. She pulled a thin book from the row and sat back in her chair.

He would recognize the book, though he most likely had not seen it, nor its equivalent, in a couple of years.

"This is the Stratford Catalogue of Doctoral Studies," she said, flipping to somewhere in the beginning.

Surely, he felt humiliation coming on. She was obviously about to show him something in the first sections of the book which he ought to be very familiar with after working on his degree for almost seven years. He didn't have the mission excuse this time.

"I won't read this to you, Mr. Porter," she said, being kind. "But I will paraphrase it."

She turned the book around and flopped it down on her desk with the pages facing him. As she tapped twice the page titled, "The Duration of Your Stay," she said, "As students working on their Ph.D's often need more time than other students, they are encouraged to relax and do their best at Stratford. This is a school of pride, Mr. Porter. I assume that is why you came here to finish your studies on the Near East. However, Stratford wants her students to graduate. Do you see how many years are allotted for doctoral candidates."

He looked through the mess of letters and found the answer at the bottom of the page. Mrs. Welch watched his heart sink into his stomach as he answered in a soft voice, "Seven years."

She sat again in her high-backed chair, confident that his silent cockiness had been squelched for good. "Seven years, Mr. Porter." She waited a minute to let the poison seep deeper into his body, closer to his heart. "May I assume that you understand your problem now?"

He read the page in the book as he nodded and thought to himself, sins of omission have always been my worst problem.

"Mr. Porter?" she called his name as if they hadn't been talking for the past ten minutes.

Porter continued bobbing his head and looked up. The fire in his eyes had turned to a struggling smoke, and the corners of his lips remained flat. His eyebrows relaxed with innocence and vulnerability. She had the knife and was about to stab him dead. Of course, he already knew how the wound would feel.

She went on. "You do not seem to have had any difficulties in your classes, but to our knowledge, your dissertation has yet to be completed. The last day for all papers and presentations is...May 21."

He continued to nod, and his eyes lowered to the desk.

"You have the remainder of this semester to finish it," she said, dropping the fluff, "then your seven year stay will be up, and the conditions of your final agreement paper, which you signed, will go into effect. Do you have any questions?"

"Yes," his gray eyes fluttered. "Do I have the opportunity to apply for an extension?"

"That's taxes and loans, Mr. Porter. I believe the contract is clear." No emotion escaped her eyes, but she obviously enjoyed this. It was her ball-game now.

Slowly, he continued to nod, looking at her desk. "I have two months?"

She leaned forward. "Mr. Porter, if you do not complete your dissertation and present it by the twenty-first of May, you will not earn your Ph.D."

CHAPTER THREE

March 21
5:51 p.m. EST

Slamming the book down, Ulman shouted, "This is *my* find!!!" his throat trembling.

Something was burning. A sharp scent of black smoke thickened the air. Maybe the chimney had been obstructed.

Peterson smiled, pulling the long muscles in his face into view, his eyes thinning. "Of course it's *your* discovery," Peterson said in a voice as calm as sand dunes but as dry as papyrus. "*You* found it, and no one's going to take it away from you."

Ulman didn't look convinced. His eyes continued to bulge from his red face, and his lips puffed moisture. "You can't come here and act as if you're running things!" He waved his hands around.

Peterson remained unconcerned and unbothered by the professor's hysteria. Native Indians pushed past him, speaking Spanish faster than he ever could. The work would progress no matter what Ulman was thinking. Over a table covered with quick notes and ruddy maps drawn with bleeding pens, Professor Albright stood with two other assistant locals dressed in brightly patterned outfits, who did their best to ignore the high-strung English conversation. Numerous tables filled the room, each piled with materials relevant to the study. Rain bombarded the outer walls of the small building, and Ulman seemed strangely determined to be louder than the thunder.

"This is my site, and I didn't invite you!"

"You wrote Dr. Albright. He called me." Peterson walked around the table, stretched forth his bassoon-length arms, and put an aging hand on Ulman's shoulder. "My friend," he said in the British accent he never lost despite his time in the states. "You have no need to worry. We are only here to assist you in this magnificent work. It isn't every day that science has such a wonderful opportunity to look through the doors of hidden history!"

Ulman's red cheeks filled with air which then seeped from his pierced lips. He stormed over to Albright, while Peterson watched him closely.

Alexander Peterson didn't mind Ulman's excitement, nor did he criticize the man for his quick defense. It was very understandable that Ulman would rather work alone on the project, but there was no way he could uncover the city on his own. Actually, Ulman had not really invited Albright in his memo, but merely said, *"Oh, Dennis! You really must see what I have found! It changes everything we thought we knew about Mesoamerican archaeology!"* Ulman's caffeine-fired enthusiasm had become his undoing.

Nor did Peterson and Albright actually intend to steal the discovery of the century from their colleague. Dennis Albright taught as a professor of Mesoamerican studies at Ohio State University, and had been looking for a reason to get away. What better excuse was there than word of a new dig in Central America.

Peterson technically was already on sabbatical. Carving out his new book, *Dispelling the Myths of the History of the Ancient Yucatan*, had grown tedious and dry after a few months. In his slow voice, Albright had read him Dr. Ulman's memo, and Peterson's head filled with new ideas for his literary creation.

Together, they offered their assistance to Dr. Ulman—in person. Having procured funds from Ohio University, the two professors rented a run-down building up the hill on the far outskirts of Kalpa, Guatemala, hired some local help, and magnified Ulman's study ten times. The find was located a stone's throw away from the small Indian village from which they obtained the help.

It shouldn't have been raining, for the rainy season had ended. Peterson listened as the water smashed against the roof. He had learned that Highland Guatemala, especially at Kalpa's elevation of 7,000 feet, was cool year-round, but dry and otherwise bearable during the winter season. The surrounding Cuchumatanes rose above the ground, tall and beautiful. The mountains would be so much better looking without the cumulonimbi, Peterson thought, those giant clouds creating darkness in the day and growling like ancient gods through the night. Peterson couldn't figure out why it was pouring so much. Rains usually came and went between May and November. He couldn't shake the feeling that they were messing with something protected by a higher influence. And he wasn't thinking about the mountains.

Years of experience in the Bible Belt had taught Peterson to decide one way or another concerning religion. While he never bashed on the faiths surrounding him at the time, he had made the scientific decision that God didn't exist. But ever since he'd set his resolve, the subconscious fear that something *might* exist beyond his temporal vision had fueled his fear of the dark, his dread of solitude, his anxiety when contemplating the unknown and the illogical.

He knew that the finds here would turn some religious heads.

Maybe there was no divine connection to the showers. Peterson shook his head and laughed at himself for thinking like a superstitious native. The smile didn't stay.

"I'll call in the law!" he heard Ulman say.

Peterson allowed himself a short laugh. "Dr. Ulman, we are not a threat to your work here."

Ulman spun around and licked his lips. "No?! You've been here four days and you've already sold an article on the place."

"No—"

"I saw you typing it in the room there!" Ulman shrieked accusingly. "I saw you mail the stupid envelope!"

"I am writing a book!" Peterson said. "I've been working on it for months now."

"You carried your great scholarly opus to an archaeological dig?"

"There's no digging going on here," said Dr. Albright.

Ulman swung around and pointed a stubby finger. "Ah! Didn't I say you were in this together? You want everything I've found! And I trusted you!"

"Calm down, Dr. Ulman," Peterson said as the rain beat harder on the roof. "Do you honestly think I've written about this site already?"

Ulman's voice dropped in pitch, then slowly rose, as he turned on Peterson. His hands shook violently, and his eyes filled with tears. "Tell me you didn't. Tell me you wrote your mother. Go ahead! Tell me she lives in an office suite in New York or works for the *Archaeological Journal!*"

"You've been poking around my materials," Peterson said, his eyebrows bending down.

But Ulman's voice rose to a hysterical scream, and he started stalking toward the skinny professor while Peterson backed just as quickly away. "*Your* materials?!? The mail only comes up from Guatemala City once every two weeks! You asked me about that specifically two days ago! Tell me why! I've kept my eyes on you two thieves! Go ahead! Tell me, Dr. Peterson, that you haven't already informed the world about my discovery!!!"

Peterson ran into the wall behind him, imitating a freshly hammered doornail. Ulman pushed his face so close that his stale cheese breath was distinct from the rotten smell of the wooden building. But instead of attacking as Peterson expected, Dr. Ulman slid by him, passing through the portal to Peterson's right and out into the rain.

Sighing, Peterson looked around him. The entire room had grown still. Every eye waited on him until he grinned and looked at the ground. "Dr. Ulman doesn't seem to understand the eclectic nature of our business."

Albright sagged as well. They both knew Peterson's words were lies. But that wouldn't change the future.

* * *

Ulman felt the rage fighting inside him like a million baby spiders struggling to push out of their giant egg sack. The rain was cold, and his hot skin turned the liquid to steam. He was going back to his hut near the site, and he'd walk the whole way even though it was dark. He'd been traveling by foot among the black mountains long before these fly-infested robbers had come to take his glory. He insisted that he didn't need their help.

He knew the truth. They both wanted to share in his find. Or to twist it into something that it wasn't, to protect old reputations.

Ulman wanted the honor of addressing his worldwide colleagues with the information from *his* site personally. He ached to see their faces. He longed to watch their jaws go limp, their fingers tremble, their eyes wander. They would be lost! Years of work would be overturned! He wanted to witness their shock and dismay himself. He would be the new king and Hitler of scholarship, both admired and hated. His finds would put his picture in every archaeological magazine, his name on each professional journal, and his voice in numerous television documentaries throughout the planet. At last, the relatively neglected history of Mesoamerica would become important enough for universities and private parties to fund, just as people had once paid for more and more and more research in Egyptian studies!

He scowled as he rammed his way through the door of his leaking shack.

The chill of the refrigerator room surrounded him, but at least the rain was off his head. A dusty scent of soaked cardboard momentarily choked him, but he wouldn't go back to the main operations building. Not for a while at least. He shook dramatically in the dark, then searched for his lantern.

Peterson and Albright were two fine scholars. Dr. Peterson had studied primarily in Europe, but moved to America to teach. The old man with mint breath saw his knowledge as exceptional when around the other aging professors of the United States. The way Peterson walked and talked reverberated this feeling, but his colleagues put up with him, for his publications gave the university in which he taught the prestige all schools coveted. Nevertheless, he'd danced his way from one academic institution to another, beginning in Louisiana and then curving northward. Peterson knew that no one had a shot at a faculty position before he did, so he skipped from one complex to the next without worrying that one day the simple Americans around him might discover his disloyalty and pride and no longer welcome him in any institution of higher learning. Peterson's only other positive attribute was his reputation as a good family man. He'd been married for almost thirty years and had four children to speak of, all of whom had attended Harvard.

Albright was a much nicer fellow from Los Angeles, and Ulman really couldn't see how he fit into this dastardly duo. Having grown up as an overweight bookworm, Albright had personified scholarship before entering college. Reading and memorizing what he read gave him a reputation that put him in the news—something Ulman never experienced.

It wasn't that Ulman wanted to be on television, but didn't all scholars dream of the limelight from time to time? Every worthwhile professor had found himself at his desk, circling the name of some notable historian. Ulman had written hundreds of papers, citing other historians who were always closer to the facts under his mental microscope. Just once, Ulman thought it would be nice to know that *he* was the one being cited!

This Mesoamerican find would be Ulman's key to the highest heaven. He had been so sure of it! And he still was.

His shoes squeaked with wet leather as he moved to his wooden chest. He set the lamp down and grappled with the lock.

Peterson and Albright may want their fingers in the pie, Ulman thought to himself, but they don't know about *this* dessert!

He opened the box and looked inside.

Within an hour, Ulman was writing his own article. It was all done by hand, and he had no publisher lined up, but that was irrelevant. He may have lost the site, but he still had enough to make him famous... first!

* * *

Dr. Albright looked at the papers strewn across the table before him.

The facts leapt at him as if alive and about to escape the muggy room.

He focused on the map once again. He couldn't believe it was real, and yet there it was. The size of the site was enormous, rivaling Teotihuacan. Surely, an entire mountain must have fallen onto it. With all the volcanic activity that had occurred in the region, he could understand how such a place could be lost for so long. No digging had yet been done. They were waiting for the storm to first subside. In the meantime, there was plenty of work to do on the finds available.

He still couldn't believe it. But all the facts came together. This discovery put Mesoamerican archaeology in a new perspective. It would give fresh reasons to start excavating the many known but heretofore untouched local sites of ancient origin. He just wondered how the rest of the world would take this!

Albright didn't care about Ulman's slow opinions. He chose not to.

Albright had worked with Ulman at Stratford University for seventeen years before Albright lost tenure, due to an incident with a female student that he didn't like to think about. Archaeological departments in universities throughout the states were steadily dissolving, as if digs were growing more scarce. When he'd first read of a university in Arizona closing an archaeological department, Albright hadn't worried much. One scholar went around proclaiming the end of the world for archaeologists, and Albright had shrugged it off until Stratford shrugged him off. Then he'd gone to Ohio, where he'd learned to appreciate his job.

For Albright, this find would renew the importance of the study of archaeology, especially ancient Mesoamerican studies. It would broadcast to the world in every newspaper and magazine, *"We've had it wrong from the start! There is a need to pursue these new ideas!"* His job would thereby steady and affirm itself, and Albright could relax

At the same time, Albright and Ulman had been close enough friends at Stratford for Ulman to contact him about the find. Obviously, Ulman couldn't live alone in the highlands of Guatemala with his precious discovery without others learning of its existence.

There was no telling who else Ulman had contacted, or what he'd told them. That factor alone kept Albright working as quickly as possible. What if others developed the same idea he and Peterson had and decided to duck out of the spring semester to join Ulman in Central America? Albright had to collect all the data he could, following Peterson's dubious example, and submit articles to professional journals immediately, thus tying his name to the project. Then, if anyone else joined the excavation, they would be seen as latecomers. Albright could be back in the states sewing a book on the Kalpa site before the summer began.

Albright recognized that his conscience repeatedly dodged the guilt and compassion he felt for his old friend. Ulman had actually found the site, after all. But Albright didn't care. If it was one thing that historians agreed on, it was survival of the fittest!

* * *

March 22
8:07 a.m. EST

Panting like a lost mutt beaten to the point of exhaustion, Ulman finally made it into Kalpa. He carried the packages under his arm. All night long he'd written the pages he carried. Now it would be a game of strategy and a test of trust.

Ulman's wife would receive one package, with instructions. A more trustworthy friend at Stratford would receive the other. He only hoped they did as he asked in the letters.

Ulman's heavy body slid down a soaked, muddy slope. He turned his head back to see if anyone followed him. Trees and high brush waved at him in the wind. There was no way to spot a tail if there was one. There was no time to cover tracks anyway. He continued into the shabby village, accidentally ramming into a native so hard he knocked him over.

"Sorry! Excuse me!" he muttered, without translating, and kept moving. His legs felt weighed down with the previous night's rain, heavy and dragging in the moss-scented mud. He'd already dropped the packages three times. He had to get one of those peculiar-looking cars headed for the Valley of Guatemala immediately. His parcels needed to be in the mail right away, and he wanted to see to them himself. His own writings would be behind Peterson's by only a few days. They would reach America, and hopefully his wife would contact the names of the editors in the letter. With a little luck, his article would come out at the same time as Peterson's, winning for him the credit for the find.

He needed to make a few more bundles and send them off with the next mail.

But Peterson couldn't find out. Men willing to come thousands of miles, paying good money to do so, all to steal another man's work, might be capable of worse.

Looking behind him again, expecting to see Peterson's dry face with tightened muscles smiling at him from a nearby building, Ulman stumbled a little faster.

The sun was barely rising when Ulman left the dig. Soon, they would find out that he was missing. He figured they would search the camp, then walk around the site for a while trying to locate him.

Peterson and Albright would put their heads together and decide upon one of two things: either Ulman had gone crazy, run off through the woods, become lost in the cold and died, which was unlikely, or he'd run down to Kalpa. They would ultimately track him through the fresh mud to the village and find out he'd gained passage to the valley. And why would he go to the valley unless he planned on going home—thus abandoning his find, which was an absurd idea—or perhaps he'd taken in his own writings to be mailed, with memories of the screaming discussion the three scholars had had the night before.

In which case, Ulman might not be welcome back at the site. Peterson and Albright would wonder what he would have sent—what he could have shipped out of the country—that would override Peterson's work in importance. This might lead them to suppose the possibility that Ulman had sent more than paperwork. Mailing archaeological finds across boarders was illegal, not to mention unethical, when it competed with the work of other archaeologists.

Of course, this was exactly what Ulman was doing.

Nevertheless, Ulman had to return to the site. He had to go back, even if the choice could kill him.

Chapter Four

March 24
10:55 a.m. PST

"This can't be happening." Kinnard sighed into a cup of bitter coffee before putting it down. He put his muscular hands together, blew through his fingers, and closed his eyes.

It seemed that Kinnard was always pulling Ulman out of trouble. But he didn't know what to do with Ulman's latest predicament.

In 1948, Troy Kinnard caught Chris Ulman slyly taking candy from the smooth glass jar on the counter of the First corner store. Kinnard remembered his amazement. He had no idea how Ulman had removed the metal lid from the jar so quickly. There wasn't even the faintest sound. Mr. Hefleiter, the storekeeper, busily spoke to Maria Higgins, which for once was a turn of events. Maria Higgins, weighing in at three hundred pounds, could talk more than a bird could sing! Somehow she and old baldy Hefleiter had come upon a subject Hefleiter had way too much interest in. Hefleiter interrupted her repeatedly, overexcited about the topic. Mrs. Higgins stuttered and wrestled to get a full sentence in as he rambled at high speed. Kinnard didn't have a clue as to the subject of the conversation, and that was when he turned to find Chris with his hand in the candy jar.

Wham—bam! Without a sound, Ulman's hand was out of the jar, the thin metal lid miraculously back in place, and Chris grinned, showing yellow, orange, and green hard candies for a split second before sliding them into his pocket.

They were only ten years old, but Troy had considered himself as intelligent as if he were twenty.

His wide eyes darted to Higgins and Hefleiter, both rotund and still talking like two dogs yipping face to face. Mrs. Higgins's round face flushed red. Hefleiter's glowed as if he was about to win a very long tennis match. But unfortunately for the ten year old boys, both adults slid down the counter toward the candy jar.

The counter had been built right onto the floor, wood against wood. The planking was old, and Hefleiter liked it that way. Someone, before Hefleiter's day no doubt, had put the small building on its short stilts and set the warped wood down over the anciently sturdy frame. The boards had crumbled over the years, so it creaked quite a bit when walked across. Hefleiter appreciated the sounds because he could shout, "May I help you!" from anywhere in the store as soon as someone entered. The squeaky planks did the job that laser lights and bells do today. By listening quickly, Hefleiter could discern the number of the customers, whether they were children or adults, and in the case of Mrs. Higgins, he could even tell it was her without hearing her voice or seeing her face. Hefleiter claimed he knew the sound of everyone in Greenwich who happened to play on his old accordion deck.

But as Hefleiter and Higgins tromped in the direction of the two ten-year old boys, Kinnard remembered glancing with guilty eyes at the candy jar.

The lid hadn't gone on all the way.

The floor creaked and bounced, and the counter rocked just a little.

Ulman turned around. Both boys knew the alarm was about to sound; the metal top would slip clear of the jar and sound their capture. They had seen the jar as it swayed ever so slightly on the counter.

Kinnard watched the metal lid as it barely hung to a lip of glass lining the hole of the bottle. The steel cover rocked and swung as if only held on by a string.

Heavy Hefleiter' and Higgins's feet pounded on the wood. Their arms pushed against the counter as they dueled back and forth with words.

Another step—just one more jolt!—and....

As the lid slid free from the top of the glass, rang against the counter, and spun to the ground, ten-year old Troy Kinnard felt his hands fly to the mouth of the candy jar.

The lid crashed like a cymbal into the planks at Troy's feet. Both his hands locked onto the top of the jar. His eyes darted to the two older people who focused on him like circling hawks without motion.

Kinnard figured he looked like a dog caught messing in the garbage. He couldn't see his friend from his angle, but he froze motionlessly until Hefleiter spoke up.

"Well now," the old man said with his clogging voice, a light smile coloring his dry mouth. "You plan on paying for that before dig'n in?"

Kinnard nodded. What else should he do? His dark brown eyes were huge circles. His fingers gripped the lip of the jar, only white knuckles showing. He didn't smile. He squeezed away the blood of embarrassment attempting to fill his face. Cold swept through his little body. But he managed to say with a weak voice, "Yes, sir."

"How much money you got?" Hefleiter said, prying the jar away from Troy's hands with one quick motion.

Kinnard had to think about it fast, rummaging through his pockets with his mind. "Got a penny," he said with the same shaky voice.

"Let's see it."

Then Kinnard remembered flipping the penny he and Ulman had found earlier that day. Heads, it was Troy's. Tails, Chris kept it. Flip… tails.

It was in Ulman's pocket.

"Well?" Hefleiter said, spotting the hesitation.

Kinnard spun around and Ulman turned to face him. Chris's face lacked the little color he normally had, and Kinnard realized Ulman's eyes screamed, "*Yes I have it, you idiot! But it's in the pocket with all the candy! It's beneath all the sweets!*"

Ulman didn't move.

"Let's see that coin," Hefleiter said. In the past, the old man had given the boys candy for free once in a while. But the two were getting older, and it seemed Hefleiter wanted to teach them the rudiments of business. Once he said he wanted money, he never backed down. That probably accounted for Ulman's impulsive attempt to snag all he could.

Kinnard felt the air point fingers of accusation. He remember the lightness in his head, the swaying sensation. Lies to protect his friend surrounded his mind. Nothing Troy could say would get him away from the crime. His eyes dropped to the ground. He prayed for a miracle—for a forgotten penny to wait somewhere on the planks that had betrayed him....

"Oh, land sakes!" Mrs. Higgins said, "I have a penny! Candy for you both." She promptly produced the funds and jumped just as quickly back into her previous debate with new ammunition spewing from the edge of her lips.

A moment later, Troy and Chris scurried quickly from the corner store with sugar in their hands. Energy surged through Ulman as he bumped again and again into Troy's shoulder, laughing about their stolen treasure, their free food, and the close call.

Finally, Troy shoved back. "I can't believe you, Chris! You stole that candy!"

"He wasn't gonna give us none for free, Troy!" Ulman said, leaning into his friend's face.

"We were dead meat back there! We could've been dubbed robbers and ruined for life!"

"We was fine," said young Ulman. "You want some?" He produced a lint-layered palm full of hard candies.

"I don't want any!" Kinnard said, shoving him away with a wave. "Don't you know stolen candy's got no taste! It's filthy! It's rotten! And it's no good when guilt's fill'n your stomach!"

Ulman shrugged. "I heard untouchable goodies taste sweetest."

Troy stopped walking and shoved his face into Ulman's. "It's a lie, Chris! A fib told you by thieves! You wanna be a looter? You wanna be a no good, dirty rotten, two-faced, lying, cheating, stupid-bag-of-potatoes criminal when you grow up! This is all how it starts, you know! Everyone in prison begins this way, Chris!"

"What's wrong with potatoes?" said young Ulman.

Troy pounded his open hands into Chris.

Ulman lost his footing and skidded to the ground, one leg bending under his bottom while the other stretched out in front of him.

Breathing so hard his shirt felt tight, Kinnard stood with clenched fists over his friend. "You ever do something that dumb again, Chris," his said through labored breaths, "and you can find yourself a new friend."

Kinnard remembered storming off in a hurry.

But that hadn't been the end of their relationship. Relatively, it was still sprouting. Chris had begged Kinnard's forgiveness and told him he'd gone back to Mr. Hefleiter's shop to return the candy. Kinnard never knew that for certain, but forgave him and decided to avoid the store for a few weeks.

The two boys grew up together as close pals all the way into high school.

A similar unhappy experience happened in their early dating days.

Ulman ditched his girlfriend, Lily Ungar, at a dance he'd taken her to their junior year. Kinnard found him hiding around the back of the building with Jennifer Broachman where they were kissing away. Kinnard saved his friend from a near disaster when Lily went looking for her boyfriend. Evidently, Lily and Chris had hidden in the same place to learn how to smooch just a year before, so she knew the spot well. Kinnard had to warn his friend without letting his date wonder where he'd gone. Of course, the chaperons were looking out for stragglers, so Kinnard had to dodge them. And if Lily spotted Troy walking alone in the dark, she'd know for sure his best friend, Chris, would be near.

Kinnard ended up climbing through a small window, or rather a fair-sized one, a little too high for his steadily swelling size. He broke the glass, ripped his jacket, and barely got away without being caught stuck in the portal.

Ulman also escaped, but got a scolding later from his friend. Chris must have known it was coming.

Kinnard had continued to save Ulman throughout his life. They both made unwise mistakes, but only Ulman made such absurd choices that they always required Kinnard to pull him out in the end.

Kinnard grew to be large and muscular while Ulman remained small. Size opened a number of avenues for Kinnard, but Ulman found few and thus sought escape from an unfair world through books. Fate gifted Ulman with an exceptional memory. It was a door to a level of prestige neither of the boys could have expected. In time, Ulman became the example and Kinnard the follower. Ulman wanted to study ancient history, so they both did. When Ulman went to Chicago University, Kinnard stayed close behind. They parted ways when graduate school came along, but both sought higher education in similar fields. Ulman went into the nit-picky study of archaeology with a focus in Central and South America, while Kinnard chose to follow the advice of a favorite professor and examine areas of oriental studies. Ulman graduated with a doctorate in archaeology from the University of Minnesota and quickly joined the staff at Stratford University in California.

Kinnard and Ulman remained close while Kinnard slowly finished his studies in Arizona after a short time at the American University in Cairo. Both became professors at Stratford, where they laughed about the past and murmured together concerning the future.

Well, the morrow had evidently arrived, and the grass wasn't green.

Kinnard rubbed his eyes until they stung, then kept smashing them until the stinging went away.

"What is Ulman doing?" Kinnard said to his wrists.

Three knocks from the door.

Kinnard dropped his hands and tried to focus his bloodshot eyes. "Come in."

John Porter was already standing in the room, but Kinnard couldn't tell who it was.

Porter stepped forward and sat in the chair in front of Kinnard's desk while speaking. "I apologize for not calling for an appointment. If you're busy, I'll understand."

Kinnard watched Porter get comfortable in the chair, slouching a bit. It was obvious the student hoped to stick around and considered Kinnard a close enough acquaintance to freely relax in his small office.

Smiling, Kinnard looked out the window. "I'm always busy, but don't worry about it."

The window was of fair size and hung in the middle of the room on Kinnard's right. The office was cramped and overlooked the married student housing district of Stratford University. At least he had a window. Pine bookshelves without paint or stain covered the walls behind him and to his left, and the tidy desk, a dark wood that didn't fit in the white room at all, stretched nearly from wall to wall, making it difficult to get around. Actually, the contents on the top of the desk were orderly by Kinnard's standards, though it needed serious dejunking in the opinion of the secretary just beyond the wall. Files, open books by Philip K. Hitti, Ibn-Khalhkan, and Kinnard himself, and a large pile of unread papers hid the tabletop calendar that covered two feet by two and a half of his desk's surface. In the center of the heaps sat Ulman's brown package of soiled paper, which Kinnard gently moved to the floor on his left.

Kinnard examined the graduate student sitting before him. John

D. Porter. Fair height, medium build, thin-boned. He wore a white button-down shirt and silver-gray slacks. Nice shoes: the ultimate judge of character. Porter had young skin, which made him look to be in his twenties rather than in his thirties. His thin hair had been cut short and rested like brown silk, slightly parted on one side, but otherwise simple—a commodity not found often in today's society. It made Kinnard think of the far-too-modern Dr. Richmond for a moment. Richmond wore a style like many of the freshman young men: cropped in back, the hair grown out long on top; the result was a constant pouring forth of hair in front, which protruded outward from his face, leaving only a four inch tunnel of dark hair through which to see. Kinnard thought it was ridiculous, but then his own hair had thinned and now he was completely bald on top. Kinnard wore dark-rimmed glasses, a weak prescription, so at least he could take them off whenever possible. And the dark hair that wrapped around the sides of Kinnard's head had begun to gray a few years ago. He didn't consider himself as handsome as he used to be, but then he didn't know why he was thinking about it. He hated pondering his looks.

"How's your paper coming?" Kinnard said, rubbing his eyes again.

Nodding comfortably, Porter said, "Fine. I can have a copy of it to you by Friday."

"That would be nice," Kinnard lied. He had at least twenty-five thick essays to read and couldn't pass them on to assistants because they came from the assistants. All he needed was another anchor to pull him down. He cursed Ulman inwardly and then all who worked for him.

"If you'd rather, I could give a quick oral overview of the project," Porter said. "Stratford has reminded me recently I have other pressing work to get started on."

"What's that?"

"My dissertation."

Kinnard stopped. His tired eyes looking over the tips of his fingers. His mind churned. Porter doesn't have his dissertation done, he thought. How long has he been working at Stratford? It's not seven years yet....

"I have this semester to do it—"

"May twenty-first?" Kinnard said, his eyebrows going up. "Can't be done."

"I appreciate the pessimism, but you know I'm not your regular Joe Bloggs student," said Porter with his best humble grin.

That was for sure! Kinnard smiled. Few students were so comfortable around a supervising professor that they started bragging about their intelligence—especially in light of threatening impossibilities.

"I think I can accomplish the task, Professor Kinnard...but I could use your help."

"How much help," Kinnard said. His voice was strong. He could imagine getting sucked into some big project in order to save a student who hadn't used his time efficiently. Of course, Kinnard also knew he was partly to blame. Instead of directing Porter toward his dissertation, he'd had the assistant running around doing dirty work. Kinnard had too many other jobs to attack.

"Well," Porter said with a weak smile that quickly went away, "I could use an idea for direction."

"You said you'd give me an oral review of your paper?" Kinnard leaned back in his chair. The high back of the seat squeaked.

Porter nodded. Kinnard could see the student fiddling with the dry skin on his knuckles.

Kinnard lifted a hand.

"Well," said Porter. "I think I've found sufficient evidence indicating Nabataean trade with China."

"Something new? Like what?"

Porter licked his lips and looked through the desk as he spoke. "The Parthians regulated the trade of most Indian merchandise—"

"And we know the Nabataeans traded with the Parthians. But that only indicates trade as far as Parthia."

Porter nodded with a grin. "But I may also have found evidence of a Nabataean temple in Tengyueh."

"*You* do. Who found it?" said Kinnard, focusing a little more on Porter.

"Dr. Bertrand from Crispin University in Maryland."

"I've never heard of him or his college," Kinnard said.

"Bertrand's a Berkeley graduate, younger than I am, who's taken the chair of the History department at Crispin. Crispin's the youngest university in the states." Porter straightened his slouching posture.

"Why haven't I heard of it," said Kinnard. His mind floated back to

Ulman's package. He thought he could smell the dusty paper. He tried to regain his declining attention in order to sound coherent. "Where did you say it was again?"

"Still small. You don't have plans to leave Stratford, do you Dr. Kinnard?"

Kinnard didn't bother shaking his head. He nudged away the image of Ulman writing quickly in some beaten box he called a house in the mountains of southern Guatemala. His mind finally clicked back to Porter's insinuations. Evidence of a Nabataean temple site in China was sufficient to alter the history books—something scholars love to do. Relics of Nabataean temple sites had been found in Rhodes in the Aegean sea and Puteoli, just north of Naples, Italy, indicating such a high degree of trade that permanent structures were required so that Nabataean traders traveling afar could still worship Dhu-Shara, Hadad, Al-Uzza, and the rest of their gods.

"Refresh my memory; where's Tengyueh, exactly," he said. Kinnard was a professor of Ancient Near Eastern studies, and regardless of what he may have learned in the past, he continued to recognize areas of his own ignorance—something many of his colleagues refused to do.

He saw Porter smile before speaking. At least someone was happy with Kinnard's deteriorating mind. "In China. Southwest from Yangtze Kiang. Close to the Northeast border of Burma."

Kinnard nodded. "And this Beartrend—"

"Bertrand."

"—thinks he found a Nabataean temple site?"

Porter shifted in the chair. "Not...exactly...but what he describes, the pictures he presented...it looks Nabataean to me."

Kinnard's tense eyebrows relaxed.

In other words, Porter didn't have anything at all. Just another organized example in speculation. Porter was a master at this sort of thing, but plenty of people disagreed with him as a common practice.

"I think you'll agree with me, once you read—or hear—my paper."

"I'm sure," Kinnard said without interest. Porter was in a difficult situation, and they both knew it. He looked at the Near East books on his desk. "Do you intend to continue your study of the Nabataeans for your dissertation? It will definitely give you something to argue."

Porter stuttered a moment, then said, "I was...hoping for—for some advice."

Leaning forward and putting his elbows on his desk, Kinnard looked Porter right in the eyes. "You know, some universities don't even accept students anymore without some idea of their intended thesis. Stratford just hasn't jumped onto the wagon yet. Do you realize the predicament you're in?"

"I am well-reminded," Porter replied without feeling. He knew he was stuck, and it was obvious. But Kinnard could see that the student planned to go out fighting. May twenty-first was still a full two months away.

"I don't think I can help you, Mr. Porter." Kinnard said, leaning back and putting his hands in the air. "I'd love to, but I don't have any ideas for you." He let his hands fall to his lap and sighed. "You really should have come to me sooner."

Porter nodded to the window, squinting his eyes. He stood and put his hands on his thin hips. His lips twisted as he thought. "Then I'll come up with something on the Nabataeans."

The problem was, Nabataean finds were relatively few and didn't say all that much. Besides, Dr. Glueck and a few others had already said it all. How Porter could come up with a new Nabataean idea in the next few weeks, then write, present, and argue a paper about it by the end of the semester seemed impossible. They both knew it. Porter was in real trouble.

"Call me tomorrow," Kinnard said, glancing from his desk to his student, to his desk again, then back to his student. His face showed no emotion. The gravity of the game demanded seriousness. Kinnard's brown skin hardened, and his muscular jaw flexed. He had to think this out. Turning his eyes and hands to the papers on his desk, he said in a low tone, "Pray for magic, and maybe we'll come up with some."

Porter nodded without a sound, without a smile, without a single sparkle in his eyes. He closed the door behind him.

Chapter Five

March 25
11:27 a.m. PST

"What do you think you're do'n here!?!" the old man bellowed. He was lean and tall, but had a hunched back and a mustache that drooped to his chin. All his thinning hair had gone gray. He once said he'd been a huge boxer before old age had settled in, which was why he kept the nick-name, Bruno, and his bar-bouncer attitude.

Porter froze halfway in the glass door frame. "Just came for more fries."

"And all my hot chocolate, right?" Bruno wore a white T-shirt, stained yellow by years of grease and the colored bulbs in the place.

"I'll drink cup after cup 'til you take away the 'free refills' promise in your menu."

Bruno smiled and continued wiping down tables while Porter, wrapped in the restaurant's scent of juicy chicken, took his seat. "So what'll it be?"

"Same ol'."

Porter chose his table by the door. He always did. Bruno said it was for a quick escape, and regularly thought up reasons which might necessitate such a flight. Porter said he might need to make a quick get-away due to the food served in Bruno's cafe. Bruno blamed Porter's choice of food or his uneducated taste buds. Sometimes Porter would actually come and eat a meal like normal people: biscuits and gravy in the morning, a hamburger around lunch time, or some fish or a French dip for dinner. But generally, Porter ordered a cup of hot chocolate, a plate of French fries, and a side of ranch dressing. He'd dip the fries in the dressing and order the advertised free refills of the hot chocolate a minimum of five times before leaving. And he did this at any hour of the day.

Bruno's cafe was open between five in the morning and one in the evening. He appeared to work the entire shift, without vacations. That was a lie, but when people asked Bruno where he'd been the day before, he'd say the same thing, "In the back! Too busy for you!" Everyone knew he was probably resting at home like normal people. But no one knew where Bruno lived.

And Bruno never seemed to sleep. "Old folks don't need sleep!" he'd say. "You young'ns sleep and play all day—don't think there's anything else to life! Completely forgot we've come to this earth to work by the sweat of our brow!"

His customers always wore smiles, and Bruno never lost his energy.

"No books?" The old man said to Porter in his usual voice full of sand and vigor. "What are you in for?"

Though others might argue that a cafe is not conducive to study, Porter found it a pleasant place to do all sorts of research. He often brought in a text, called for the regular, and sat for a couple of hours with his head bent over the pages. He would contort his face and rub his forehead, but Bruno had long ago stopped offering him aspirin.

"Meeting with Dr. Kinnard today," Porter explained.

Bruno's body jerked as if in surprise. "About time you got him back here! You'd think he didn't like my cooking."

Bruno never forgot a name or a face, so everyone loved the cafe—or all the regulars did anyway. Each had been impressed by the place's friendly atmosphere. If anyone walked in a second time, Bruno would shout out their name and offer them something special. It was like each of Bruno's customers belonged to a family they'd forgotten about.

The cafe was warm and usually smelled of fried foods and baked pies. Bruno loved pies. People of all sorts came into the cafe, but mostly those affiliated with the university up the street. Custodians, professors, other faculty, and students came in at odd hours—one often trying to catch another, while avoiding someone else at the same time. Bruno liked the adventure in his shack. He'd seen 241 break-ups, over 300 arguments between students and professors who'd given the former an undesired grade, and the beginnings of over 500 romantic relationships. He'd listened to cops and their cases, without their knowledge, of course. He was familiar with many of Stratford's problems long before the students found out—like the time when graduation seating was reduced due to construction at the university and poor planning on the part of certain people who should've been fired. Bruno knew all the gossip, long before anyone else, and had become the silent key to the success of university journalists.

Porter was eating when Kinnard entered the cafe, but his stomach churned with uneasiness.

"Good morning," Porter smiled as Kinnard sat down. "Try the fries, they're wonderful."

Kinnard slid into the booth by the window, setting his attaché case protectively between himself and the wall. He didn't look at the food on the table. His eyes moved around the cafe, stopping on Bruno, who quickly looked away to clear a few more tables.

Porter didn't notice, or rather he did, but chose to plunge another French fry into the sea of ranch dressing and not think about Kinnard's curious nervousness.

Kinnard barely fit on the seat, or though it seemed. He leaned forward, slouched, and rested his muscular chest against the edge of the table. "I might have something for you, Porter...if you're interested."

Porter stopped chewing. He met the gaze of his supervising professor and felt his prayers answered. Realizing that he'd frozen in an awkward position, Porter swallowed quickly and nodded while doing so. His eyes opened, wide and curious.

Kinnard looked down at the table and touched his fingertips together. "What I have is very...unorthodox...but it might be something up your alley. Now, the only reason I'm bringing you this idea is that I trust you as a student. You're intelligent, and everyone knows it. I've read your work, and you go out on a limb all the time. You're published, and you're brave. You know my colleagues might consider you a little eccentric in some of your ideas."

Porter smiled and nodded. He liked the idea of a being a peculiar person. Scholars—including Dr. Kinnard—could disagree with him, but they had to acknowledge that his arguments were good and worth investigating. A lot of people read his material, even when they suspected it would make them angry. They also knew John D. Porter published well-thought out material which others would jabber about, so it had to be read. No one else jeopardized their future career as frequently as Porter. But at the same time, those who read his stuff knew he had all the facts, and those facts would be presented in a manner which couldn't be shrugged off with the same ease that Porter brought them forth.

"But you're good at what you do."

"I enjoy my studies," Porter said with a smile. He wasn't being cocky, especially because his position currently looked very unstable. He didn't want to blow any opportunities Kinnard might present, and the humility showed in Porter's face.

The smell of cinnamon simmered on the air.

"Do you know Dr. Ulman?" Kinnard said.

"Should I?"

"He's a good friend of mine." Kinnard looked at the table. "Always has been. Ulman has found something you might want to use to finish your work at Stratford. It provides a fixed argument, so you won't have to spend time deciding your point."

"I'll use anything I can get my hands on," Porter said with raised eyebrows.

"What do you know about Mesoamerica?"

"I haven't studied anything in school," Porter said, wondering what American history had to do with his dissertation. "But I've done a little research on my own...for interest's sake."

"I thought you might have," Kinnard said. Porter was an excellent student. More than that, he excelled in his studies. Yes, he was eccentric, but some of the best professors were those absolutely obsessed with their work. So when Porter said he'd "done a little research," Kinnard had no doubt that Porter's grasp on the subject was stronger than his.

"This have something to do with my dissertation?" Porter said, scratching the back of his neck.

"You're in a real fix," Kinnard said, his face hardening. "You realize that?"

"Yes I do."

"My colleagues know what caliber of student you are. It would look real bad on my record as your supervising professor, if you of all people failed to complete the requirements of Stratford University in the last seconds of a long, drawn-out game."

"Wouldn't want to blemish your reputation, sir," Porter said. "I'll do my best to rectify my situation."

"That would be wise." Kinnard said. Porter realized his supervising professor looked as bad today as he had the last time they'd met. Maybe even worse. His hair was askew, his eyes puffy, not to mention his peculiar paranoia.

"So what did you bring?" Porter said. He noticed Kinnard had a difficult time looking him in the eye. Kinnard's hands fidgeted, and Porter wondered if the professor was taking this a little too personally. After all, it was Porter's problem, not Kinnard's.

"Dr. Ulman...my friend..." Kinnard said, "was working on something he found in the southern mountains of Guatemala."

Porter sat up.

"I understand that at first it didn't look like much. Another mound, buried in a Central American forest, but Ulman was led on by an ancient tale told by a few of the locals whose small families reportedly lived in the area for the last fifteen-hundred years."

"A story?" said Porter.

"About a sacred place...destroyed by the hands of an ancient god, or something," said Kinnard. "Ulman said it was a fascinating tale, all of which he would tell me after he returned to the states."

"But he hasn't come back," said Porter.

Kinnard spoke, staring at Porter's hot chocolate. "He found something. Wouldn't even tell me about it at first. He said it was really big."

"What, a Central American Jurassic Park? I've seen movies about lost—" Porter stopped.

With eyes hardening into marble, Kinnard stabbed his way into Porter's gaze.

"I'm sorry. Dr. Ulman," said Porter, "he's an archaeologist?"

"Professor of Archaeology here at Stratford. He was down there for more than six months before he wrote me the first time. A memo." Kinnard looked back at the table. Porter sensed that his professor's mind had left the United States and was heading south. "Ulman said he'd written others as well. Seems he found something no one else would believe. Of course, we all like the sound of that, don't we. But now I realize his words were accurate."

Porter didn't nod. Intrigue and questions colored his gray eyes.

"Ulman sent me more, since that time, and...I don't know how to explain what he's found. Or what he thinks he's located." Kinnard looked Porter squarely in the eye. "*You* might want to explain it."

"Tell me more," said Porter, sipping from his scalding mug.

Kinnard sighed. "Seems that Ulman discovered a book."

"I found one recently in my closet under a pile of clothes I didn't know was there. What makes this book special?"

A red flush filled Kinnard's face and the muscles in his jaw flexed. "I'm trying to save you from your mistakes, Porter, remember that! You may be a smart student, but there's a big difference between intelligence and wisdom. Intelligence will get you through the university, but only wisdom can get you out with a doctorate! Up till now, you have not proven your brains!"

"Dr. Kinnard!" Bruno said, coming to the rescue out of nowhere. Of course the old man couldn't let fights disrupt the cozy spirit of his place. "Can I get you something to drink?"

Kinnard let all the hot air rush out of him before looking up. He relaxed the muscles in his face as best as he could and said, without eyeing the old man for more than a second, "Coffee."

Bruno turned with a smile. "One cup, com'n up!"

Porter relaxed, though he hadn't realized the extent of his building tension.

Kinnard started again. "The book Ulman found appears, according to his analysis, to be a codex dating somewhere around 500 BC."

"What's it written on?" Porter said, intrigue in his tone.

"Paper," Kinnard said without looking up from the fries on which he'd suddenly focused.

Porter waved a hand for him to have some. "A paper book?"

Kinnard shook his head at the food. "It's not that uncommon."

"I know. Two manuscripts made of bark paper were found at Mirador, but no one's been able to separate the fused pages. I believe they dated to somewhere around AD 450. But I am not aware of any other paper codices recently discovered in the Ancient Americas."

Kinnard nodded, gazing at the table as though ashamed of what he was saying. But that was an absurd idea, Porter thought. "Ulman's codex isn't glued together," said Kinnard, putting a fry in his mouth. "The pages are in beautiful condition. But they hold something we never could have predicted."

"What's that?" Porter said. He swallowed the rest of his hot chocolate and put the cup on the end of the table for a refill, never taking his eyes off of Kinnard's bald spot. "How'd Ulman find a book that wasn't cemented together? Was it a scroll?"

Kinnard kept his eyes on the table, only looking up once in awhile. "*You* would come up with that, wouldn't you."

"Excuse me?"

After a deep breath, Kinnard spoke. "You're a...a member of the LDS church, aren't you?"

"I...am," Porter said, his head bobbing with growing curiosity.

As if to divert any awkward feelings, Kinnard asked, "What does that stand for again?"

"Well, the full name is the Church of Jesus Christ of Latter-day Saints. It's that last part which differentiates us from other churches... by name anyway."

"I had an LDS friend growing up in Illinois. Learned it was wrong to call you 'Mormons'."

Porter smiled. "Well, it's not bad. Most people don't understand where the term 'Mormon' came from. You know that along with the Bible we read the Book of Mormon. Evidently, those who didn't belong to the church gave us the title 'Mormons' based on our scriptures. It may have been an insult a long time ago. Some might even have negative feelings toward the use of the nick-name, but I don't really care. It's almost a household word now. Think about it. What do you see in your head when you hear the word 'Mormon'?"

"White shirts and ties on bicycles."

"Right," Porter said, pointing a finger.

Bruno delivered the coffee with a smile and disappeared again. Neither of the customers seemed very intent on eating.

Porter went on. "Mormon missionaries. Clean cut, young, smiling, nice guys that you'd never expect to commit a crime. Kind of the ideal young man." He shifted in his seat. "I don't see any insult in that image. If the name brings to mind an old-fashioned all-American reflection, then I don't mind the name."

Kinnard nodded. "As a Mormon, then, you believe in transoceanic contact between the Old World and the New, prior to, let's say, the

Viking arrival 'round the year 1000."

Porter nodded.

"Well, then you should love this codex."

"Why…does it back up that argument?"

Leaning forward in his chair, Kinnard said softly, "Ulman's codex may be something of a Rosetta Stone. The book is written in two languages on every page. That's a good thing, because Dr. Ulman can barely make out one of the languages. The second he can't decipher at all. But he says it's only guesswork at present."

"You're giving the book to me," said Porter.

"You couldn't be worse off, Porter," said Kinnard. "Not unless you'd been shot and left to die, anyway. Ulman's a good man…and he's my friend. I think he'll understand after he gets back. You will of course need to give Ulman credit for the physical discovery."

Porter imagined the writing on this Mesoamerican 'Rosetta Stone.' All students of Ancient Near Eastern Studies were familiar with the real Rosetta Stone, the big slab of black basalt found in 1799 by an unknown person. The rock contained a text praising an Egyptian king, Ptolemy V Epiphanes (203-181 BC), written in Egyptian Hieroglyphics, then in Demotic, which some termed New Egyptian or Egyptian Short Hand, and then in Greek. Before 1822, scholars had not yet conquered the Egyptian writing system. But in September of the same year, a Frenchman by the name of Jean-Francois Champollion, realizing the message was being repeated in all three languages and finding specific names in each text, presented a paper deciphering the obscure glyphs for the first time to the *Academie des Inscriptions*. The result was a blaze of excitement concerning Egyptology throughout Europe. Champollion changed the world, an opportunity that both Porter and Kinnard could only hope for.

So why was Kinnard giving Dr. Ulman's find to Porter for study?

"A new Mesoamerican script?" said Porter.

"Ulman could read a little of the first set of characters on the page. Maybe the language is just an older version of characters common to the area, I don't know; I don't read any of those languages. But that was the writing Ulman *could* read to some degree."

Porter blinked and thought he misunderstood.

"Ulman couldn't read the second language on the page…" Kinnard said.

They both looked straight into each other. Porter felt the room warm around him. Perhaps it was his own blood pulsing faster just beneath his skin.

"...but...I thought *I* recognized letters of the second script," said Kinnard. "*You* might be able to decode it, Porter."

"But I...don't know any ancient American languages."

"Neither do I."

Chapter Six

April 1
3:00 p.m. PST

Erma Alred closed the door behind her. The room had far too many people in it for a casual discussion between Professor Masterson and herself as she had planned. But as the head of the Department of Ancient History and Anthropology at Stratford University, Dr. Masterson could do what he wanted.

"Good morning Ms. Alred," Masterson said with a bloated smile as he stood to shake her hand, "Right on time as usual."

Evidently the other four men in the room had come early, though she hadn't the faintest idea why. They watched her as she shook Masterson's hand. She eyed them closely, but also casually. She recognized a few faces, she thought, but couldn't be sure.

Masterson raised a hand to the only empty chair around the rectangular table. "Have a seat."

"Thank you," she said, sitting down. The room smelled like old pipe smoke, memories of the professors who first ran Stratford University. Masterson's cordiality confused her. Never before had he treated her with so much respect. She had come to the office hoping to discuss her proposal for her dissertation, which she'd been working on since last semester. She had plenty of time to change it, so she wasn't pressured with that.

But Alred had learned that Masterson, who served as her supervising professor, was a difficult man to sway from his own stubborn opinions. He had plenty of ideas and was sick of being kicked around by other professors who thought they had more efficient or effective plans. Bitterness had swallowed him long ago and kept him boiling in a stomach of acidic antagonism. As he had told her many times, he hadn't climbed his way to the top, he'd fought his way. He didn't expect others to follow his example and rather hoped they didn't.

Alred looked forward to working in a university back east, if at all possible, when her studies ended at Stratford. Masterson said he'd made up his mind to mold her into a killer in the field. She could go far in Mesoamerican scholarship, if she knew what she was doing.

Alred never worried much about her future. Having been raised by a fine instructor of mathematics, Alred found there was a logical side to everything. The anxieties of most people were unnecessary. Those who worried about relationships, for example, usually caused more problems fretting over negative possibilities than would have occurred naturally. Stress leads to self-fulfilling prophecies, Alred told her friends. Most people didn't realize that. General ignorance and self-promoted apathy was the greatest problem in the world, she believed. Thus, Alred didn't cope well with those who were always coming up with excuses. She just shook her head and wondered why people didn't take control of their lives instead of letting others boss them around. Pro-activity led Alred to higher levels of success than most others would be able to enjoy.

Masterson turned quickly to the other men in the tight room. Indicating each with a relaxed hand, he said, "Ms. Alred, this is Dr. Goldstien, Dr. Arnott, Dr. Wilkinson, and Dr. Kinnard."

"Pleased to meet you," she said, maintaining the odd cordiality, and throwing out the idea that she would discuss her dissertation at all today. While pushing back a lock of red hair over her right ear with her fingers, she grumbled inside, but let the feeling pass.

Goldstien smiled—probably at how well Alred's neatly kept fingernail polish, her lipstick, and the red hair blended in a singular color. It wasn't a perfectly red shade, but rather a light auburn. She sensed he was one of those who were amused at how women were able to play with make-up to enhance what was already there; a typical low-class man who couldn't get married or had been, but quite unhappily so. He liked her, and didn't hide it well. But she figured Goldstien didn't care if she knew it. He projected himself as one who found the rule prohibiting professors dating students a little juvenile and old-fashioned.

Alred avoided further eye contact with Goldstien. She could feel his gaze easily enough, and sat with determination on her face. But again, she wasn't worried. Her passive guardian—her Uncle Alan—had enrolled her in a martial arts class at an early age. She'd grown up with the reputation of beating up the boys in her Junior High school. Alred had the peace of mind of knowing she could break a man twice her size, were he to try something, no matter how dark it was and no matter what alley they were in.

With his big smile, Masterson sat down, slapped his hands on the ends of the armrests, and sighed. He looked happy, and Alred knew it was all a front. She suspected everyone else saw the same picture, but couldn't be sure. She scanned her eyes over the other three men.

Dr. Arnott smiled with his thin lips, but it really did look fake. His eyes sagged and looked too much at the table. The fingers of his left hand played against the knuckles of his right as he rested both elbows on the lightly varnished wood.

Dr. Wilkinson, dressed in a brown suit dating to the early nineteen-seventies, kept his eyes on Masterson. It was obvious he was waiting for something.

Dr. Kinnard stared seriously at the table, and as far as Alred could determine, he hadn't looked up since she'd entered.

Underneath, they all trembled with seriousness, she thought, and the subject obviously dealt with her.

"How are things?" said Masterson.

It felt as awkward as it sounded.

Alred decided to get right to the subject and spoke honestly. "I thought we were going to discuss my dissertation."

Masterson nodded. "That's the plan."

"With all due respect," she said, "what do these gentlemen have to do with my thesis. Am I in trouble?" She knew she wasn't, but felt slightly agitated and didn't want to admit it. She was used to being in control of her life, and this situation was highly irregular.

Masterson continued to nod. Then quite suddenly, he leaned forward in his chair and clasped his hands together. "Ms. Alred, we've come up with a great idea for your dissertation."

"I was...was under the assumption that the student chose the subject of her final argument," she said. Her face remained relaxed, though all her muscles grew firm.

"Oh, absolutely!" Masterson said.

Alred knew he was lying and recognized that everyone else in the room had a better grasp on the truth than she did. They'd obviously planned this meeting from start to finish. She'd made the appointment, and they'd set it all up. Question was, what were they pushing for?

Without losing the smile, Masterson said, "You have complete control over your dissertation. All we would like to do is present an option."

Alred wanted to squint at him, to scowl, but she relaxed her face and remained outwardly unmoved by his words. "An option," she said. Was it really a choice, or a threat? Did she have control, or were they really saying, *If you want to get your doctorate at Stratford, you will complete this project!*

Masterson's smile did not sit well with him, probably because he rarely smiled. He was a kingpin in scholarship, and Alred was smart enough to recognize it. Masterson made the rules, knew he did, and liked it. His options were not alternatives, but demands. Those possessing wisdom learned to do as he said. He'd been the Chair of the Department of Ancient History and Anthropology for far too long, and there was no way he'd let anyone else in his seat.

Alred inwardly confirmed to herself, I've lost all control over the end of my academic career.

Her muscles started to feel unusually tense, but she tried not to show it. She kept her hands under the table so no one would catch her scratching her fingernails together. She sat like a rabbit before headlights, without motion, without breath, as the explanation continued. She even fought the urge to look at the shielded window in the corner of the south side of the empty room

Masterson lifted a hand, indicating the end of the table, "Dr. Kinnard?"

Kinnard lifted his head slowly and began immediately. "Ms. Alred, you studied under…Professor Ulman for how long?"

Alred pulled her head back. "I've worked with him since I came to Stratford two and a half years ago. He's an excellent man." What was this, some sort of secret board of inquiry?

Looking back at the tabletop, Kinnard swallowed, and his face hardened. His eyes appeared to be closed, but were only squinting behind his glasses. Both his hands locked together in a firm grip. Alred almost thought he looked like he was about to scream out in rage. "Dr. Ulman…has disappeared."

Alred waited in silence for a moment, then said sincerely, "I'm sorry to hear that."

"I understand you were close," Kinnard said, shooting a sharp look at her.

She suddenly felt as if she were being accused of some odious crime involving her favorite professor, the one she'd wished had become her supervisor of studies, but had already taken on too many graduate students. Smoothly, she clarified, "We worked on one of his books together, *Ancient Man in Modern Mesoamerica*. It's due to come out in five more months."

Kinnard didn't nod.

Alred looked at everyone before saying, "How are you connecting me with professor Ulman?"

"Ulman and I were good friends," Kinnard said. "He praised your work. Said you were quick and possessed a strong initiative."

"What's happened to him?" Alred said, not realizing she was leaning slightly forward.

"We don't know," said Masterson. "But we are sure there is nothing to be concerned about."

"Do you have any idea where he is?" Kinnard asked Alred.

"If you're not worried," she said, looking back and forth at the two professors, "why are you asking me where he is?" She tried to keep her voice controlled, and succeeded, but her actions revealed her concern.

Masterson's smile faded momentarily, but quickly returned. "Dr. Kinnard is more concerned than the rest of us." He hit Kinnard with a glance, which Alred assumed she was supposed to miss, and it looked as if Masterson was doing his best to send some dark kind of telepathic message to the muscular professor opposite him at the table. Masterson resumed his smile.

Kinnard seemed to ignore the gesture. "What is your knowledge of Ulman's current whereabouts, Ms. Alred?"

"Am I being accused of something? I thought we were discussing my dissertation," she said.

"You're not being accused of anything, dear," Goldstien said with a grin, revealing his poor dental work. Like an actor making sure he was sticking to his lines, he looked at Arnott, but only for a moment.

"Ms. Alred, are you aware of Dr. Ulman's most recent project?" Masterson said with gray eyebrows smashing his bald forehead into wave after wave of wrinkles. "Did he send you any letters? Memos?"

"I believe Dr. Ulman has been working on something he found in Highland Guatemala," she said, a little hostility in the back of her throat. "He wrote me sometime last semester, but I had assumed he was too busy to write me a second letter. We are not working on his new project together."

"Did Dr. Ulman invite you to join him in Central America?" said Kinnard.

"No."

"Did Dr. Ulman send you anything other than a letter. Say, some artifacts, anything he may have found in Guatemala?" Masterson said.

"That would be illegal," said Alred.

"But did he send you anything other than a letter?" Goldstien said.

"No," she said, but she could tell by the look in Masterson's darting eyes that he didn't believe her. "Why do I get the impression that I'm being interrogated?"

"We don't mean to give you that feeling," Wilkinson said over a cough as Kinnard put his face in his hands and sagged.

"You're accusing me of a crime, aren't you," Alred said, her muscles hardening.

"Not at all," Kinnard moaned from behind his hands.

"Why are you so suspicious?" said Goldstien with a big grin, repulsive to look at.

"I'm not being suspicious," she said, her eyes rigid in her head as she turned it from side to side. She did her best to keep her voice calm, but there was too much energy in her lungs. "I came here to discuss a dissertation proposal with Professor Masterson, only to find you four in the room circling me like vultures. Now, what do you want."

Masterson leaned back in his chair, at ease in the room. "Ms. Alred…I didn't mean for these questions to get you all rallied up."

"I'm fine," she said, but instantly sensed her forward-leaning position, the tension in her face, her tightened eyes, and realized that everyone would recognize all of these signs for what they were. She relaxed and allowed the steam to rush out of her overheated muscles.

"We just wanted to know how suited you would be for the project we're about to suggest," said Masterson. "It is unorthodox enough to be exciting and give you the opportunity to make quite a name for yourself. It is also something we thought you might find particularly interesting since it is based on Dr. Ulman's recent discovery. Unfortunately, little is known about the find so far, except for what letters he has sent to the states. We were hoping...that you already had your hands in the work; that Ulman had informed you of his theories. It would have provided you with a greater advantage than starting with nothing."

"I see," she said.

"Ulman sent me...some artifacts," said Kinnard.

"We know it's not exactly legal," Masterson said, putting up a hand, "but it could also be something important enough for all of us here to drop what we're doing...and investigate."

Everyone stopped to examine Alred's expression. But where they seemed to have expected to find awe and curiosity, she kept her face stone-like and unaffected. "You're saying Ulman found something so revolutionary that everyone here is considering a sudden sabbatical to study it?"

Masterson nodded, his grin intensified by the signs of her growing interest.

Wilkinson said, "Of course we're all engaged this semester and can't just run off."

"At a major university like this? Sure you can. You all have assistants, don't you?" Alred said. "They could take your classes easily enough, couldn't they? There's more to it...isn't there. You don't want to drop everything and risk a bad reputation on sketchy finds. You want me to take the risk, to get my hands dirty first. Then, if there really is something out there, you'll gladly jump in. But only after I've had my shot."

Goldstien smiled. "Very good!"

Masterson nodded, "That's right."

"But you also want me to clean up this mess and present my finds first...in the case there *isn't* really anything there."

No one nodded, and that meant yes.

Kinnard rested his thick chin on his clasped hands. His eyes told her he wasn't as interested. In fact, he looked exhausted and trapped in the room.

"And what about you?" Alred said, pointing at Arnott with her chin. "Why don't you have anything to say?"

He smiled. "It's all been said."

Everyone waited, but she wasn't sure for what. Finally she asked, "So what's the catch."

"There isn't one," Masterson said with his false grin.

"Actually—" Kinnard started.

"Ah!" Alred nodded, sure that she knew everything a step ahead of the play.

"There is something, but it's not exactly a catch, *per se.*" Kinnard looked up at her. He touched the black rims of his glasses, but didn't remove them. He looked at Alred's tight little mouth, her straight brow, and her slender nose. She got the feeling that he was looking inside her, asking questions she couldn't hear. "There is already another student working on the project."

"A joint dissertation?" said Alred, looking again at Masterson, with disdain on the back of her tongue. How was that going to help her shoot up the ladder as Masterson had repeatedly promised?

"A *counter* dissertation!" said Masterson.

"I've never heard of a counter dissertation."

"Well maybe you have," Masterson said. "Many times when a dissertation is argued, the student is countering a previous study, sometimes someone else's dissertation."

"So what are you saying," she asked.

Wilkinson smiled, and she could see a lot of thought behind those old lips. The words about to come out had been well-discussed. She held her breath as he spoke. "Ms. Alred. What do you know about the Mormons?"

She breathed. That wasn't a question she'd expected, and she let it show on her face. Her brow bent, and her eyes squinted.

Wilkinson waited.

She looked from Masterson around the table to Kinnard on the end. "Mormons," she said, her eyes accessing the dictionary in her mind, "I believe they are a Christian sect founded in Utah, aren't they?"

"Whether or not they are Christian is debatable," Wilkinson said, rubbing the side of his nose. "They say they are. They also believe they have a special tie to ancient South and Central America."

"*The Book of Mormon*," she said.

"Right," Masterson said, looking through eyelids that had long ago grown into thick layers of skin which now almost cut off his vision entirely. "Have you ever read their holy scripture?"

"No," she said and saw the sigh. "Never."

Masterson took over. "The Mormons believe a group of Jews built an ark, sailed across the Pacific, and settled somewhere in the mid to lower Americas. Of course, they don't have anything to back up this claim."

"That's right," Alred said, looking at the ceiling. "Don't they believe the Amerindians to be the descendants of these Jews?"

Masterson nodded.

"So how does this fit into my dissertation?"

Kinnard answered. "The student I brought into the project is a member of the Mormon church."

"I...see. And I'm supposed to debunk the pronouncements you expect him to make." Alred pushed her hair over her right ear and kept her face at ease. "Why did he get the project before me?"

"I'm not technically a professor of Archaeology or anything that has to do with Mesoamerican studies," said Kinnard. "I teach ancient Near Eastern history. Porter is my student."

"Do you know John Porter?" Goldstien said with a suspicious smile, as if suspecting that the two had dated secretly or she was a Mormon and was hiding the fact for some reason.

"Should I?" she said, shaking her head. "He's an archaeology student?" she asked, confused. Why would this John Porter be studying under Dr. Kinnard if Kinnard has nothing to do with American archaeology?

"Only wondering," Goldstien said, leaning back in his chair.

"Porter's an analyst of ancient Near Eastern studies," Kinnard said. "Ulman sent me the package, because he thought *I* might be interested. I shared it with John Porter before discussing it with Dr. Masterson, which I shouldn't have done. But it's done. Porter's been working on the project for a few days now."

"How could he be working on an archaeological find from Mesoamerica if he has no knowledge of Mesoamerican studies?" Alred said, feeling offended and assaulted.

"The find," Wilkinson said with a pause, "seems to draw...a connection to the ancient Near East."

No one said a word.

"So the Mormons are *right*?" Alred said. She saw the smiles, but didn't change the shape of her face. Her question was both sincere and sarcastic. She didn't believe any religion had logical bearing or any integrity. They helped people be morally and ethically better than they might otherwise be, but the rest was a fill-in-the-blank to lessen the fear of death—look at Heaven's Gate, the thirty-nine human-inhabiting "aliens" who committed suicide at the end of last week! She smirked and looked at Kinnard who sat still with his hands in front of his mouth.

"If the Mormons are right, we are all in grave spiritual trouble," Masterson said with a chuckle.

The room rumbled lightly with laughter before Wilkinson continued. "If you look hard enough, you'll see what you want to see. That's an old idea historians must deal with daily."

"Of course," Alred said, hoping this was all some huge April Fools joke.

"Porter is a keen student," Kinnard said. "He is very skilled in what he does and loves it when everyone disagrees with him. He thrives on argument—"

"—But then so do you!" Masterson added, jabbing his finger in the air, grinning at Alred. "That's why I knew you would be the best student for the project."

"John Porter will give a wonderful analysis of the find, though his time is extremely short," said Wilkinson.

"And therefore so is mine," Alred replied with a sting at the aged scholar.

Goldstien squinted at Alred, "But Porter will also have a resolute Mormon bias."

"What we want from you is an unbiased study of Ulman's discovery," Masterson finished. "While Porter quickly presents his dissertation, which will no doubt excel in the field, you will present a counter dissertation just as briskly, which will be the first objective view of the discovery presented by Porter. The scholars of the world will love you, and you will soar to the top of all the most recent doctoral graduates. You will then gain access to any university in the world and be set for life as a well-known scientist!" He grinned, and it was his real smile: one full of greed.

Alred shot a quick and curious glance at Kinnard who continued to silently stare into the tabletop.

Masterson added, "You and John Porter are assigned to work together, and that you will. At the same time, you shall be fighting head to head with him. Only…Porter must never know it!"

Chapter Seven

April 10
9:54 a.m. PST

"Well it's about time you showed up," said Porter with a smile on his face and fire in his eyes.

"Good morning," Alred said as she slid through the tight portal. The door wouldn't open all the way.

"Sorry about the mess," Porter said without enthusiasm.

The stuffy air choked Alred almost as badly as the tension she felt from her fellow student. She thought she smelled forgotten lettuce and bologna sandwiches and wouldn't be at all surprised if a few hid beneath the disordered piles of papers, the open files, the scattered heaps of books.

"Need a bookshelf?" she said, only to regret it. The walls were naked and white, but there definitely were enough volumes in the tiny room to carpet at least two walls. Obviously, whole cases wouldn't fit in the room. If Porter lined each wall with independently hanging shelves, his books would practically be falling on him. His desk wasn't a desk, but a common four foot by two and a half foot classroom table, and some of the stacks on top of it stood two feet high. Florescent lights shined from behind a rectangular plate in the ceiling. There was no phone that she could see. His ergonomic chair squeaked with every movement.

"I'm fine, thank you," Porter said, bending around his desk to remove a one-foot high mountain of pages from the only extra seat in the room.

Alred stepped carefully wherever she could see the floor. She really couldn't believe it. "Nice office," she said. If it sounded sarcastic, she didn't care. Porter's response would probably be bitter no matter what she said.

"I realize the room is disguised as a closet," he said, landing noisily back in his chair. A pencil dropped from behind his ear, and he bent to pick it up while speaking. "I won't be offended if you try to hang your coat on the door."

Alred sat.

"How'd you manage to get an office?" she said, trying to see what he was doing. His back and shoulders shook quickly as he erased some unseen mark his stylus must have made on one of the open files on the floor, and the jiggle made the chair squeak like a captured rodent.

"Oh," Porter said getting up. His short hair fell like the fur of a long-haired dachshund after hanging upside down. "I'm a research assistant."

"I know plenty of research assistants without offices," she said, measuring him with her eyes. He looked tall, but that may have been due to his thin bone structure. His face also looked thin and awfully plain. There was nothing attractive about him, but nothing unattractive at the same time. Well…his hair did look soft, but it caused no emotional stir. If only he could clean up his attitude.

Porter smiled again and sighed. "It's who you know in the world that counts, they say."

"Yes, but who is *they*?"

"The cause of all good and bad; the blamed in every society," Porter said as she smiled. He stood and gave her his hand. "John D. Porter."

She took his hand without getting up. "What does the *D* stand for?"

"Desirable," he said, sitting down.

"I guess you…already know who I am."

"Erma Alred. No middle name. Been with us at Stratford for…five semesters now? And you're in the same position I am in."

"What position would that be?" said Alred.

"The desperate need for a dissertation, of course," his smile faded slightly.

"If I understand things correctly, the *D* in your name deserves the word *desperate* far more than I do."

He scratched his head with one abrupt movement, focusing his eyes on his desk. John *Desperate* Porter. Why did that have such a natural ring to it?

"Why aren't you married?" she asked suddenly.

"Why do I get the feeling everyone's asking me that?"

"I thought Mormons were supposed to wed and have lots of little kiddies like the Catholics," she said matter-of-factly.

"You know I'm Mormon."

"It sounds like we know a lot about each other."

He smiled at her. "And still so very little." She watched him examine her medium-length auburn hair, green eyes, and fair, unfreckled skin.

"Just enough to get the job done," she said.

"What?"

She tilted her head. "Mind wandering, Mr. Porter?"

"I'm sorry," he said. "You have green eyes."

"You always this perceptive?"

"Lived in Japan for a few years. Green eyes are highly praised there. If you were half Japanese and kept the eyes, you could make it big in the *Nippon* entertainment industry."

"That's good to know in case this dissertation ruins me."

"You don't want to do this?" Porter questioned as her eyes wandered down and over the papers throttling her chair.

From the floor, she lifted a thick pad of pages bound by one heavy paper clip and said, "Frankly, I was hoping to do a dissertation on early Athapaskin settlements."

"Who are they?"

"The Athapaskins?" She looked up at him, her eyes wide and wondering if he was joking. "The ancestors of...many North American Indian tribes. Tell me, how is it that you are leading a study on an ancient Mesoamerican find without knowing the rudiments of American archaeology?"

"Just lucky I guess," he said. "You already know I have religious interest in Mesoamerican history."

"Yes, but I hardly believe someone's religion validates a worthy academic assessment of an area outside one's expertise." She looked down and dragged her eyes over the paper in her hands. "This is written in Spanish. What is it?"

"Nothing you'd be interested in. Solid evidence of the authenticity of the Book of Mormon. It's an ancient Indian history compiled by a

Aztec prince."

"Ixtlilxochitl?" she said, trying to find the first page—an impossible task.

Porter waved his head in what might have been a nod. "Seems his curiosity about the white, bearded god revealed some finds so disturbing that after the book was shipped to Spain, it got buried in the archives of a church until only recently. Of course, now that it has been so long since the original writing, scholars can say the man made the entire thing up based on his own religious system. But it does back up facts already in our grasp."

"The white, bearded god," Alred said. "And who would that be?"

"Don't you know?" Porter said, glowing with his quirky smile.

She waited a few seconds before answering, her eyes examining the titles of stapled articles and worn books ganging up on her chair. She saw the words, "The Canaanite Text from Brazil" by Cyrus H. Gordon and "Who Discovered America First" by William F. Dankenbring. Some of the words leapt at her in Germanic, Arabic, and other languages that left her feeling like she didn't belong in this office.

Looking again at Porter, she said, "Mormons believe Quetzalcoatl, Kukalkan, Tohil, or whatever one might call him...is none other than Jesus Christ, don't they?"

Porter's face didn't change. "Some do."

"Don't you know Quetzalquatl was represented by a feathered serpent? The serpent in Bible stories represents the Devil, if I understand the symbolism correctly. How do you get Jesus in there." She put the document back from where she'd snatched it, sorry she'd picked it up.

"You're forgetting the caduceus," Porter said, leaning back in his small chair. He crossed his arms and looked completely at ease.

"I beg your pardon?"

"The symbol of the medical profession?" he said. "Two serpents wrapping around a pole with wings? It was the staff of the Greek god Hermes."

"I know what you're talking about, but I don't see how that has anything to do with Quetzalquatl or the Devil."

"It is quite arguable that the caduceus is also based on an often forgotten Biblical story found in the book of Numbers," said Porter.

Alred pursed her lips and raised her eyebrows.

"While the Hebrews wandered in the wilderness after Moses freed them from Egypt, the Torah states that they encountered *ha-nechashim ha-seraphim*, fiery or poisonous snakes."

"Torah," said Alred, "I thought you said this was in the book of Numbers."

Porter nodded, shutting his eyes momentarily at her biblical ignorance. "Many were bitten by the serpents and needed serious medical attention, death being the alternative. Moses constructed a pole with a serpent made of brass on the top of it. He told the dying all they needed to do was look at the brass serpent, and they'd be healed."

"That's it?" Alred said, disappointed.

Shaking his head, Porter said, "But too many of the afflicted children of Israel wouldn't believe they could be healed that easily…even after all the miracles preceding the experience. Some looked up, following the admonition, and were healed.

"Now the snake Moses made obviously didn't represent the Devil. On the contrary, both 2 Kings and 2 Chronicles recount the sins of the children of Israel in worshipping the pole with the bronze serpent, many years latter.

"Now, Christians compare the brass serpent, which was 'lifted up,' to Jesus Christ, who was put up in like manner, and forever after all followers of Jesus have professed to the world that all anyone need do is look to the man on the cross…and live."

Alred squinted her eyes. "So you're saying the serpent on the pole of Moses was Jesus, who is also Quetzalcoatl." Doubt laced her tone.

"Can't you see why some people would make the connection?" said Porter.

After swabbing the inside of her dry mouth with her tongue, Alred said, "I once had a grammar school teacher who played a game with us wherein we compared different kitchen utensils to aspects of learning. I remember a spoon related to a teacher in detail, a piece of paper to our brain, and a knife to our principal. But I—I don't think abstract or arbitrary connections should be taken seriously. Rhetorics can show how any two unrelated things are connected."

Porter wiped his eyes. "Yet wouldn't you agree that finding logical connection is the center of scholarship? What else is a dissertation?"

She chewed on the inside of her lip. "As scholars we can only do our best."

Leaning suddenly forward in his chair, Porter said, "I wish other scholars were as honest as you! You're right, of course. None of us are as enlightened as we'd like to believe. The problem with the Enlightened thinkers of Rousseau's day was that they *thought* they saw the truth. Not just reality, but absolute truth! They chose to believe that there was nothing more than what they were seeing. It's...a problem we all have...to some degree or another. We focus on paradigms we've collected over the years, without acknowledging the *existence of paradigms*. You and I might know what paradigms are—a pattern or model of reality defined by our own thoughts and observations—but we go on living with them, without consideration of the other paradigms in the world. So who's right? No one. Who thinks they're right? Everyone. What's right? Will we ever really know—that is what we should ask ourselves."

"But that's a philosophical question, not a historical one," Alred said.

"Right. And I'm not implying we should do away with historians... I'd be out of a job!" Porter said, throwing up his hands. "What we *are* forced to deal with are...*possible*...truths based on all the finds in our possession."

"*Possible* is the key word," Alred noted. "Scholars don't want to deal with possibilities that are so improbable as to be defined as near impossibilities."

"Of course," Porter said, his chair squeaking again as he leaned back. "The only thing that has greatly bothered me is that most scholars only acknowledge possibilities they like. Some possibilities grind against their feelings.

"You can't mix business and emotions, they rarely work well together, no matter your office or profession. If you and the rest of the planet are inclined to believe that the world is flat, for example, and you worry about what your friends and associates will feel if you were to acknowledge the possibility that you might think the world is *round*, you'll be wise to keep your mouth shut until everyone believes the same thing."

"Of course, there's always someone who likes to stand out," said Alred.

Porter agreed with a raised hand. "Shouting their beliefs even if they *know* few will receive them kindly. The majority is always slow to change opinions, and only does so when the populous of scientists begins to move toward the idea that the world *might* actually be round. At that point, you wouldn't have as large a problem in telling everyone that *you* might believe the world round as well. But you see, emotions—worry in this case—really get in the way." Porter folded his arms.

With one eyebrow rising, Alred said, "That's why most conservative religious people refuse to recognize archaeological discoveries which say their Bible might *not* have been the original source they thought it was."

"Exactly!" Porter sat up like a startled cobra. "Most old-fashioned religious folk have mastered the doctrine of *believing* and *having faith* in place of facts. When new artifacts turn up…they flat out don't want to see them, because they fear what they *might see.*"

"I agree with you there," said Alred.

"Truth is, they often don't recognize how the new finds *do* correspond to their old pious ideas. The problem lies with their belief systems. A lot of religious people believe things that have been passed down from person to person, but have no valid backing in their scriptures."

"Really," said Alred.

"Someone once told me the Leaning Tower of Pisa and the Tower of Babel were one and the same."

"Are you serious?"

Porter shrugged. "He was a nice guy…but obviously no scholar. Someone a little more respectable probably told him that—it may even have been a joke!—but the guy believed it and related it as fact."

"Did he know what specific area you study?" she said, wondering who could be so naive, so presumptuous.

"Well, it was a long time ago. I don't remember. But he was sincere. I just nodded, and let his delusion continue. Arguing with a fool is like wrestling with a pig, they say. You both get dirty and the pig likes it."

"That's an oldie—" Alred said, pulling her red jacket around her.

" but a nice one!" Porter finished with a smile. "As far as scholars go, the biggest hang-up can be found in their general lack of interest in things that would be embarrassing to believe."

Pause. "Like the idea that what the Mormons profess is real?" Alred said carefully, no malice in her voice. Of course she needed to validate Masterson's warning of a Mormon bias in the project.

Porter nodded without a word. He sat forward, slowly this time, and rested his arms on the table. "I like you, Erma. You're all right. The number one concern I have with most scholars in your field of Mesoamerican Archaeology is…they choose not to acknowledge the possibility *of a possibility* that what the Mormons say about the ancient Americas is true. I'm not talking about dealing with truths here…but possibilities. You said yourself it's short-sighted for religious scholars to conclude that secular scholars are automatically wrong when their papers contradict biblical themes."

Alred nodded, but kept her face and all emotions hidden behind tight skin.

"Why then would secular scholars automatically assume papers written by religious scholars…unworthy of a thorough reading based on the premise that religious academics are 'Old School?' To tell you the truth, I know a good number of very talented Mormon scholars who have published numerous books and papers in the secular realm. But few in that society recognize their existence. Is anyone reading their papers, or do they see the name, the title, the thesis, and quickly turn to the next essay."

Alred closed her green eyes and opened them again. "I can see why you are praised for your work. You've obviously thought out your arguments."

Nodding, Porter added in a soft voice, "I look forward to working with you, Erma…though I admit I was steamed when I found out I had to share Dr. Ulman's codex. I know it will be a challenge—it is whenever I work with someone else. My ideas are often extreme, but I'm sure *you'll* keep me in line," he said in a sarcastic tone.

"Count on it," she said with the same voice.

"But, Erma, let me say one more thing." He licked his lips and said slowly, "I will have a great deal more respect for you as a scholar if you admit the possibility…that there is a possibility…that what I present is true. I'm not asking you to believe me. Everyone follows their own paths, and no outside individual has a right to change another person. You are in charge of you. I am only asking you to *not* be an *enlightened* scholar who presumes to already have the answers. After all, we're moving into new territory—case closed. I'm asking you…as a scholar…to keep an open mind. Come to your own conclusions, but don't shrug off others because you're worried about what reviews your dissertation will receive."

She nodded and stood. "We'll see." Her voice was hard. Turning to the door, as Porter leaned back in his chair and scratched his head with a clawed hand, Alred said, "Oh…Porter?"

"Yeah."

She pushed the door open and faced him. "Don't ever call me Erma again. That's my aunt's name, and I'd prefer not to think about her right now. I hate the name, but out of respect for my parents I will not change it. Understand?"

* * *

April 10
6:18 p.m. PST

He was late, and he knew it. But there wouldn't be a problem.

Checking his $4,000 watch, snug on his wrist, he waited as the elevator flew another fifty stories. He brushed away a white spec that had landed on his thousand dollar, dark navy suit. With a flash of his eyes, he made sure the white cuffs of his shirt protruded exactly one quarter inch from his jacket. One glance at his Italian shoes made of black leather, and he knew the tone and the shine couldn't be more perfect.

He never once let go of the briefcase, even though it was much heavier than usual. Standing in the rear of the elevator, he let his muscles relax as he examined the heads of all those standing with him.

Two red heads.

Partly bald man, who smelled of spent cigarette cinders.

Purple old woman.

He listened to the music, a cheap rendition of Vivaldi's "L'inverno", saw the digital number soar quickly upward, skipping ten floors at a time, and glanced at the three lightly gossiping secretaries with brown curls in the right corner.

Everything was fine.

He sighed silently at peace.

He looked down at his hands again. They weren't shaking, which was good. He moved his mouth, licking his lips. No stuttering motions. Excellent.

Holding his breath, he peered at the black leather briefcase in his right hand, held slightly away from his pant leg as if it carried the Ebola virus.

He imagined the elevator cable snapping.

He pictured the car rushing at the ground.

He saw himself in an ambulance, just about to die, realizing the whole world as everyone knew it would shake and perish if he passed away.

He'd never been so important....

Closing his eyes slowly, and opening them just as slow, he was back in the elevator car. And all was well.

Bong!

The door split in two and disappeared into the walls.

"Excuse me," he said with the voice of a shadow as he pushed his way through the small crowd.

He walked down two halls and opened a door.

The secretary looked up, but he didn't hear her if she spoke.

He went straight into the conference room as if he owned the place, though he'd only been there one other time.

He fought the urge to check the hour, the minutes, the seconds....

The room was long with florescent lights recessed into the ceiling. Portraits of important people lined the room in expensive frames. Large windows covered one of the two long walls, but hid behind thin white drapes. The oblong oval table seated at least fourteen people, but he chose to remain standing.

From the high-backed chairs, the faces turned to greet him. No smiles. Only gray eyes. Fine leather portfolios and expensive computer notebooks were open in front of them all, and papers filled many of their wrinkled hands. Each wore a tie that could have fed an Ethiopian child for ten years.

The talking stopped like a sudden cold current.

"Good of you to join us," one of the old gentlemen said.

Putting his Ebola-virus briefcase on the table without a word, he inserted a small key. The case popped open. Then, round the table he went, passing out one manila envelope to each person in the conference room. He was the youngest man present, but didn't want anyone to notice it. His face remained as stern as everyone else's. As he lifted each envelope, he made sure it did not quiver in the air. Not once did he breathe through his mouth.

One elderly man stood as the circle began to open their packages. In a raspy voice he said, "I assume you've all read the brief and understand the nature of the codex." He shot the younger man a look as the briefcase locked with a snap.

Silent and listening, the young man waited at the far end of the table. He wore a face without emotion. The smell of lemon spray scented the air.

"You have before you a similar paper written by a Dr. Dennis Albright of Ohio State University," the old man said as everyone but the young man standing at the opposite end of the table scanned the words in the file. "News of the find seems to have spread to a greater degree than we realized." He looked up at the young man and said, "Peter."

With his fingers firmly attached to his briefcase so he wouldn't flinch, Peter said in as bland a voice as he could manage, "It appears that Dr. Ulman sent a codex to another professor, a Dr. Troy Kinnard of Stratford University. Within four days, Professor Kinnard passed the ancient record on to a student by the name of John D. Porter."

"And what do you know about this Mr. Porter?" the old man said, still standing.

"Everything," Peter said. "Mr. Porter has been at Stratford for almost seven years. His focus is Ancient Near Eastern studies, and he is praised for his research. He is single, lives alone in a dusty apartment adjacent to the University grounds, has a small hole of an office on campus, and is a member of the Mormon church." Peter waited a minute, looking over everyone's grim stare. "Mr. Porter was evidently in need of a dissertation topic and has chosen Professor Ulman's find on which to focus. He's both bound and driven by a time limit. If he doesn't complete his written dissertation and present the argument to Stratford by the twenty-first of May, he will fail to gain his doctorate and will be evicted from the institution. That means he will be working fast."

"Current developments?" the old man asked, though he already had a pretty good idea, and Peter was aware of it.

Nevertheless, Peter spoke as if he were the only one understanding the situation. "John Porter has now been joined by a young lady, another student at Stratford University. Her name is Erma Alred, and she also is renowned in what she does. Liberal, intelligent, lives alone, has no religious affiliation and is unlikely to join any church whatsoever.

"Alred was Dr. Ulman's prized student for a little more than a year and a half, until he went to Guatemala. An archaeology student specializing in ancient America. She is a hard-nosed woman with a mighty flame inside, so she won't be pushed around by Porter. She's wise and intelligent enough not to be taken advantage of.

"The two students together, complemented by Porter's pressing time schedule, will mean quick and efficient work on their part. But they will formulate separate opinions. While Ms. Alred has an excellent reputation and is destined for success in her field, Porter is making a questionable name for himself. He's clever but eccentric."

Waiting a moment as Peter stood motionlessly, breathing through his nose, the old man at the far end of the oval redwood let his associates mull over the information before speaking. "Gentlemen…I think it is time we inform other interested parties."

Quickly, Peter said, "I have already prepared a meeting."

All the bones in the room chilled in silence as thought-filled eyes looked on the young man.

But Peter stood like a work of marble in very expensive attire. His skin was cold and white. His dark hair, short, slightly receding, was sprayed into immobility. He paused, letting the world push its stressful hands past him, and looked calmly to the old man standing on the other side of the table.

Unmoved by the words, the elderly figure was little more than a reflection of Peter set far in the future.

The air hung icily throughout the room, but no one shivered.

"Good," the old man said at last. "We have no time to waste. We all have work to do now…so I suggest we adjourn until this evening."

Chapter eight

April 11
9:07 p.m. PST

The glass door slapped against the door frame when it closed, and for a second Alred was sure the pane would break and rain razor-sharp shards all over her back.

A few heads turned then turned away, but the owner, a thin old man who she assumed was Bruno, called from behind a counter in his gruffest voice, "Don't worry about it! Been meaning to get it fixed anyway."

She looked back at the door, which was fine.

Walking into the depths of the cafe, Alred found herself a booth away from the bar. From here she could see most of the restaurant, but wouldn't easily fall in the path of everyone else's eyes. Bruno came to her quickly, wiping his hands with a yellowed rag. "What can I get you?" he said with enthusiasm.

"Coffee," she answered, taking papers out of her bag. She opened a copy of *LOGOS, The Journal of Archaeology*, which Porter had called her about. "Better read Dr. Albright's paper," he'd said, and there had been no levity in his voice. She wasted no time tracing down the table of contents.

But she looked around as Bruno left.

The cafe had the air of being safe, like the kitchen of one's childhood home. Sure that she'd heard of the place from other students, Alred wished she'd found it earlier in her career at Stratford. There seemed to be a number of individuals from the University, but at this hour, most sat tired and relatively quiet, save those laughing over hot mugs and dinner at the bar.

Booths tightly lined the walls of Bruno's cafe, which bent like three halls around the kitchen in the center. Tables filled all the extra floor space. Red and white checkered cloths draped over every tabletop, and the floor was a simple gray color with a battered shine. Rafters could be seen in the brown ceiling, and the walls were also wood brown without insulation. Evidently, the kitchen produced enough heat in the winter time that no fiberglass padding was needed. The warmth and smell of cooking smoked the inside of the cafe, and it was hard for Alred not to think of her mom.

She hated being reminded about her parents. Alred shoved the thought away.

During the warmer months, there was probably a fan above Bruno's kitchen to vent the hot air and delicious aroma outside.

Happy not to return to a chilled apartment, she preferred to be hugged by the cafe and its friendly fever. Bruno brought the coffee and asked her if she wanted something else. She shook her head, and the old man ran off, yelling at someone who only laughed in return.

Alred's eyes found the beginning of the essay Porter said she *had* to read:

THE MESOAMERICA MIDDLE-EAST CONNECTION
Codex KM-1 and Related Finds
by
Dr. Dennis Albright, Ohio State University

She squinted, attempting to understand how this Dr. Albright could have come upon their project. If others scholars were involved, especially those with their Ph.D's, her dissertation would quickly lose importance.

After reading the title three or four times, Alred finally decided she couldn't push through it. She couldn't do any of it. Or rather, it was possible, but she didn't see the project with Porter as being as profitable as Masterson had described.

Her mind wandered to Professor Ulman.

What did they mean when they said Ulman had disappeared? People didn't vanish. There was no logic to this. Why would Ulman choose invisibility after making such a fantastic discovery, after working in Guatemala for so long? Alred couldn't come up with any reason at all, but wrinkled her brow and pressed her knuckles to her lips. She stared at the patrons of the cafe for a while, as irrational thoughts darted through her head.

She had to focus.

How many others were involved in Dr. Ulman's Guatemalan discovery? If Dr. Albright was able to write a paper on the find already, he must have had detailed knowledge of Ulman's work long before she'd learned of it.

The thought of murder flashed like a memory from a movie in her mind. Could someone have killed Professor Ulman? She didn't want to consider that absurd possibility. After all, who would do it? Another scholar? Dr. Albright?

Staring again at the title before allowing her eyes to gaze out the window, Alred drank her coffee and ordered another.

Two more coffees later, she ordered an ice tea.

Alred had turned to other articles in the journal and fell entranced in their ideas until there weren't any more.

The snuggling heat of the cafe and the thoughts that continued to jumble her head at every pause made her very uncomfortable. She pictured Ulman running for his life from thugs hired by jealous scholars, and other such nonsense. She knew it was all absurd, but she was exhausted. Every time she looked down at Albright's article with the silly title insinuating early transoceanic contact between two separate worlds, her mind began to run away. She watched her favorite professor passing through customs, only to be mugged, kidnapped, tied, gagged, and thrown over a bridge. She shook her head and imagined him getting inside his car, turning the ignition, and—

"Something else to drink," Bruno said, wiping a glass with what looked like the same rusty towel he'd been using for over an hour.

"Water," she said, trying to ignore the washcloth.

She went to the bathroom. She had to stretch before attacking this essay. Her blood had slowed too much, and she looked at her watch: 10:12.

When she returned, the water waited for her next to her magazine. She took a sip and set the glass down before noticing…words, quickly scrawled next to the title of Albright's paper.

In blue pen the letters read,

Can you believe this?!! Figure it out Alred!

Alred stopped thinking.

She read the words again without realizing she was holding her breath.

Standing quickly, Alred looked around the cafe. She scanned over everyone's face as fast as she could.

Looking down, she read the short sentences again. Again. Again. She touched the words. The blue ink came off on her dry index finger.

She jumped to the front door and pushed it open.

"Hey!" Immediately Bruno was behind her in the doorway as she took three steps into the dark wind. "Not thinking about taken off before pay'n, are you little lady?"

Alred looked through the blackness, but didn't find anyone. Few cars pushed by the cafe on the two-lane road. Three empty automobiles waited against the curb, one of those across the street in front of an out-of-business donut shop. Yellow lamp lights painted everything a dirty orange color.

She kept her feet still, so as not to panic the old man, but her eyes went through every car window, ducked under every tree pushing out of squares chopped in the sidewalk, cut left and right through the shadows, searching....

"Little lady?" Bruno said, watching her wisely.

"Did you see anyone at my booth after I went into the restroom?" she said.

Bruno shook his head beside her. "Was keep'n my eye on you and my work. Someone take your purse? No one steals from my place! I'll—"

"No, no. I just thought..."

Slowly she turned back into the warm cafe, and Bruno left her alone, though she felt his eyes following her.

She went back to her table and read the words again, written just to the left of the title. She sat and stared at the two sentences and Albright's title for a full minute. "What's going on here?" she asked the air in a whisper.

Catching Bruno watching her from a distance with a concerned look on his face, she closed the scholarly magazine and gathered everything in haphazard order to leave. Freezing, she thought about all the people who could have written the words. Why? What did they mean? She opened the magazine again and read the message.

Can you believe this?!! Figure it out Alred!

Bruno appeared again, looking busy and just conveniently in the area, though Alred had seen no customer near her booth for the past hour. "Everything all right, ma'am?"

Her face wouldn't change shape. She pictured other students she knew writing the message. What would they know about it? How did they know this was her booth when she wasn't present? She pictured Professor Masterson scrawling out the message with his thin fingers holding a gold pen, his face smiling in a twisted knot of tight flesh. Or Professor Kinnard, or Wilkinson, or Arnott, or Goldstien. She had seen professors pop into the cafe twice since she'd arrived this evening. Both had been from the Math department. Why would any of these instructors write these words?

Perhaps Porter had come by, seen the journal, and deduced it to be hers!

But Alred had the nagging feeling that this was what Ulman's handwriting would look like in a hurry. He'd written her from Guatemala when he first thought he was close to finding something.

Porter or one of the other professors wouldn't have seen her journal since she sat so faraway from everything.

She crushed her eyelids together, not wishing to ponder the question any longer. She moved to pack up again, but saw the old man with the wise blue eyes. "You wouldn't know anyone by the name of John Porter would you," she said. But realizing how silly that must have sounded, she quickly looked away, amending the question with the words, "No, of course you—"

"John D. Porter? Know him good and well! The tall skinny Mormon boy who gets a grin when he knows he's make'n other scholars sweat under their collars? Just haven't learned what the *D* stands for!"

"Have-have you seen him? Has he been in at all this evening? Maybe just now?"

"Not today," he said with a grin. She could see the wheels working behind his gaze. This Bruno was obviously one of those fellows who thought twice as much and three times as fast as common folk. He looked more regular than anyone else, but could likely solve all the world's problems from right here in his cafe.

But Alred didn't want his help.

"Thanks," she said. "Another water please."

"Haven't finished your first," he said, indicating the one by her left hand.

She looked across the cafe to the glass door and the darkness beyond. "Yeah," she said, with her mind searching the street again for someone leaving the place. She hadn't been in the bathroom that long! No matter how many times she went through the possibilities in her mind, she couldn't figure out what had happened. There were more questions than there were answers.

She nodded at the old man, and he smiled and left her with the journal. She opened her notebook and prepared to read what looked like a waste of time, but was now tied to…to what? Blue ink?

If there were answers, Alred had to find them. More now than before. If it was a race to study the new find, then she'd burn the oil of all ten virgins. She'd stand on the shoulders of Albright *and* Porter. She would succeed and benefit. But most of all, she would find the answers to her new questions. And she'd figure out what had happened to Ulman.

With new resolve, Alred looked down at the page.

THE MESOAMERICA MIDDLE-EAST CONNECTION
Codex KM-1 and Related Finds
by
Dr. Dennis Albright, Ohio State University

Introduction

When I first arrived in the Valley of Guatemala, I was surprised by the intensity of the beautiful surroundings and the simple humility of the native people. But surprise is too shallow a word to describe the immense shock I felt when I walked around the new archaeological site just outside of the small Indian village called Kalpa in the Cuchumatan mountains. One point solidified in my mind when I beheld all the facts for the first time. I would have scoffed at the thought only hours before![i] There *is* an ancient Mesoamerican connection with the Middle-East. The academic world can have no doubt about it anymore.[ii]

When my companions expressed their impressions, I simply couldn't believe it. In fact, I refused to! Then I saw the codex which we have come to term KM-1 (Kalpa Manuscript, One).[iii] Part of a larger library, KM-1 and its apparent home illustrate three points which I shall illuminate below.

First, Kalpa sits on the outskirts of an ancient city far greater than any metropolis previously discovered in Central America. That fact alone demands years of investigation.

Second, KM-1 contains both words and pictures correlating directly to certain localities of the Middle-East, suggesting more than arbitrary evidence of the transoceanic contact discussed by a small number of recent and heretofore relatively unrecognized scholars over the last twenty years.[iv]

Last of all, I suspect KM-1 is the most complete and detailed codex of the ancient inhabitants of Highland Guatemala c. 700 BCE.

I do not wish to mislead the reader. The aforementioned finds are completely new and require a thorough study, which will surely tax Mesoamerican archaeologists for at least the next fifty years.

I acknowledge certain flaws involved in our present study. We have found so far no definitive name for the ancient center, nor are we unified in supposing exactly who lived at the site. Dating has been assumed from the language of KM-1 alone, and the writing has been a tremendous point of argumentation for the few of us at the Kalpa dig.[v] No part of the manuscript has been interred into a lab. KM-1 is unlike anything we have found in the past, and is subject to numerous questions that we have no time for in this paper.[vi]

The first and foremost argument against this paper might be an attempt to show that KM-1 was planted at a later date by evil-designing persons bent on fame or religious prestige.[vii] But the codex, coming forth from a small library tightly sealed from the outer world, speaks for itself. It exists! It is tangible evidence of the study presented below. We shall soon see the day when KM-1 will meet every conceivable scientific test, all careful scrutiny, and each critical eye, revealing to the public the fluidity of the past as we know it.

There *is* an unquestionable relationship between Mesoamerica and the Middle-East. Allow me to be your guide!

Alred tossed the magazine to the far edge of the table and slammed her eyelids shut. There is no connection whatsoever between ancient America and the Near East, she told herself.

Figure it out Alred!

Who'd written these words in blue ink by the paper's title?

Where was Dr. Ulman? And what *had* he found?

Worth ruining his life for?

Hers?

She dropped her head until it thudded against wood.

Chapter Nine

April 15
6:48 p.m. PST

Dorado went insane.

That had to be the reason.

Running mad into the dark, brave Dorado, now deranged.

Alred tried not to think about it, but the feelings, the memories came like a tidal wave…forty-two feet above the shoreline and hovering….

He escaped when everyone thought him securest. Somehow he bypassed the massive birthday celebration. Everyone was present. Alred couldn't believe Dorado went unnoticed. His black hair on end like Mr. Hyde. His mouth dripping with hot saliva.

He got away.

Someone stumbled upon the hole in his cell.

So as not to disturb the party, the word was spread in secret, and the necessary people stepped out.

They ran to their vehicles and scoured the area.

Alred knew where he went. The same place she would go, if she could run from this mad world into greater madness: the highest building…it had to be climbed. The edifice existed for that sole challenge.

Dorado fled to that holy point.

He bypassed the security guards.

He slid into an elevator…and flew.

To the roof.

With the stars shining down, he called to the night in a painful wail. Only the constellations knew Dorado's lost madness. Like silent gods they stared down on the sacrifice.

Crying one last time to the moon that never gave comfort, Dorado jumped...into empty space. Gravity caught him with selfish hands, yanking him to the ground so far below.

They didn't find him until the next day.

Alred's father wasn't even sure it *was* Dorado. But he had to tell his little girl something.

They'd get a new dog, he said.

Staring at the night sky, at the star formations, she knew somehow she'd cursed her best friend by naming him after the stars in the southern hemisphere. She'd trapped him in eternal darkness, which had become his destiny. The scourge had something to do with the night, but she couldn't figure out the rest.

Weeping, Alred wondered if her father had lied.

Dorado...was flat as a bunny on a highway, her Dad said.

So...what if it really wasn't Dorado? Wasn't it unidentifiable? Black fur? It meant nothing.

Alred shivered as the wind scratched her arms in passing. Was Dorado still out there...?

Forever after she heard the cry of her dog...faraway.

The question was never answered.

The darkness took her father within a year.

Did she ever hear his voice?

Now...what about...Dr. Christopher Ulman?

The wheels of Alred's car squealed in pain as they rubbed against the cement curb in front of the Ulman's humble place.

Alred pulled on the emergency break, which sounded for a second like a chain saw trying to start without gasoline. "You must be mistaken with this."

Porter laughed, but ran out of energy. "You've seen my translation!"

"But I still haven't seen the codex itself, Porter, and I was told we were both working on the project. I have no way of validating your words, and frankly, you are really disappointing me!"

Porter pulled his head back. "You're...afraid it's true."

"I am trying to make an accurate study of something I can't even see." She wouldn't look at him.

"And I'm protecting you the best I can. You never *asked* to see the book," he said with a weak smile.

"You're stealing the work!"

"Possession of this codex is probably illegal, Alred. You *don't* have it. You can't be implicated." Porter stared at her right ear.

"I was assigned to work *with* you on this project," she said, shooting him a stinging glance. "Ulman's codex belongs to the University, or at least to the department heads. If anyone is implicated, it's Masterson and maybe Ulman."

"Okay," said Porter, "I'll show you the book tomorrow."

"That would be fine." Her face was quiet marble and colder than Antarctic ice.

The doors of the brown Toyota Celica opened like bat wings.

Alred made it to the top of Mrs. Ulman's steps first and stabbed the doorbell.

"I really don't think she'll have anything for us," Porter said. He looked back at the street and the rest of the neighborhood in the late afternoon sun.

Alred didn't bother with a reply. She had other motives.

The door swung open.

"Professor Arnott!" Alred shivered. "What are you doing here?"

Arnott stood in the doorway in a dark suit. He smiled, the muscles in his face at ease. He stood tall like he owned the place. "I've been concerned about Dr. Ulman," he said. "Still no word."

"I...see," Alred said, nodding, feeling her cheeks flush and her lipstick drying in the Eastern breeze.

Mrs. Ulman's worn face appeared in the door frame. "May I help you?" she squeaked.

Porter stared at Arnott, the nicely dressed man with the handkerchief in his breast pocket.

Arnott only glanced at him.

"You won't find anything here," Arnott said, looking down with ebony eyes into Alred's jade circles.

She stood her ground, though inside she trembled with confusion.

The professor turned to Mrs. Ulman and said, "Thank you for your time. Please call me if you learn anything." He took her hand with both of his and shook it lovingly. With a nod of his head, he walked quickly down the steps, entered a dark sedan across the street, and drove away.

With his hands in his pockets, Porter watched him go. "Nice car. You know that guy?"

"Mrs. Ulman," Alred said in a kind voice with a smile, extending her hand to the lady in the doorway, "My name is Erma Alred. I'm one of your husband's students. Could we have a word with you?"

The skin around Mrs. Ulman's brown eyes sagged. The black hair running straight to the bottom of her neck seemed terribly to need a wash. "Why not," she said without enthusiasm, turning into the house.

They entered and sat at two facing love seats offset by an coffee table of oak and glass, Porter and Alred together with Mrs. Ulman opposite them. An old molasses smell hung in the room, which made Alred wonder what was rotting or perhaps growing in the kitchen.

Porter nodded with a thin smile, trying his best to shine happiness from his otherwise wandering eyes. "John Porter." He extended his hand. "Pleased."

"We wanted to ask you a few questions about your husband," Alred said. Her mind flirted back to Arnott's appearance.

Mrs. Ulman sighed long and weak.

"Is that a problem?" Porter said with concern in his voice.

Mrs. Ulman looked up, but never met eyes with the students. She whined slowly, "I just don't know any more!" Exhaustion killed any possibility of crying, though she looked like she needed to release a few thousand tears.

Porter and Alred glanced at each other with confused faces.

"Mrs. Ulman," Alred began again, "We promise not to stay long."

Ulman sniffed. "That's what the FBI said before drilling me for an hour."

Porter leaned forward with interest but no one spoke for a moment. Alred's face remained impassive as she ran the words through her head again. Mrs. Ulman's eyes traced the shape of the coffee table.

"They came two days ago, asking questions, just like you," Ulman said, her voice sounding lost. "Look, I don't know where my husband is. I have no idea what he was working on. There is nothing I can show you or give you. The FBI has it all."

"Mrs. Ulman," Alred tried to start a third time.

Porter quickly put two fingers on Alred's arm and said, "The FBI *took* things from you?"

"It was illegal for him to mail artifacts out of a foreign country, they said. How do I argue against the government? I don't know why Chris mailed things to *me*. What could *I* do?" Mrs. Ulman said with her eyes closed.

Porter spoke quickly. "FBI? Not Customs agents? What exactly did your husband send you?"

"A package, that's all," she said shaking her head. "A couple. He sent something else to our mail box downtown, though I didn't know it. The FBI made me fetch it for them," she said, her voice straining. Her face shifted with discomfort, her eyes darting every direction except at her guests. "I just wish everyone would leave me alone, is all," she sighed again.

Alred raised her eyebrows. "The FBI knew Ulman mailed something to your post office box?"

"How would they know that?" said Porter.

"Well I definitely didn't tell them!" she said, throwing up her hands, looking at the walls and the ceiling. She shivered and said, "Now, I'm sorry, but as I told Mr. Arnott, I don't have anything to give you—"

"Arnott wanted something your husband sent home?!" Alred sat forward, a gleam of anger in her eye.

Mrs. Ulman stopped moving. She looked at Porter. She turned her head to Alred.

"Just like the FBI," the older woman continued. "Just like you, I assume. Wanted anything Chris sent me. Artifacts most of all, but also letters, notes, or journals he may have sent home. Papers. That's what they asked for. Everything."

"I don't want those things, Mrs. Ulman," Alred said. "And I'm not here for your husband's notes. I just want to know what happened to him."

Mrs. Ulman pulled away, falling against the well-cushioned back of the orange couch. She closed her eyes and shook her head without speaking.

Porter gazed at his companion, bewildered.

Alred ignored the movement, but focused on their unspeaking host.

When Mrs. Ulman stopped shaking her head, she stood, sighed, and said without feeling, "Can I get you a drink?"

The two students waved the offer away politely, while Mrs. Ulman went to a short bar, pulled out a nearly empty bottle of vodka, and poured herself a glass. She swallowed and dropped her head.

"Mrs. Ulman," Porter said, "truth is, we need to find out what's... going on. The only way I can figure of doing that is by studying your husband's work."

Alred knew Porter was playing along with her own words, probably supposing them to be a ruse. He had only one thing in mind, obviously. If Mrs. Ulman had more to contribute to Porter's dissertation, he needed it. Alred had told him about Ulman's purported disappearance, and even mentioned the message written on the front page of Albright's essay. Porter simply shrugged it away and continued his single-minded work on his peculiar translation of the codex. How could he translate it anyway?!

Mrs. Ulman's reply was barely audible. "Third time I've heard that."

"Mrs. Ulman, your husband was my favorite professor," Alred said. She slowed her speech and reset her tone to a calmer note. "I studied under him before he went to Guatemala, and he's written me since then. I hoped to continue his work. And now we've been given an assignment to do just that."

Porter said, "In my case, this assignment is the last chance I'll get to succeed at this university. If I fail, Stratford kicks me out. If there's anything you could do for us, something you know about his work...it would be priceless. I really could use your help, Mrs. Ulman."

Alred stared at him as if examining his weakness behind a magnifying glass. He wasn't being very diplomatic, she thought.

Mrs. Ulman nodded, bracing herself up against the counter. As she turned, her arm hit the vodka bottle, and the liquor splashed over her clothes and poured into the carpet before she could catch it. She sighed, but it was almost a groan.

Alred chewed on her lower lip and looked at Porter, who met her eyes.

"I think," Mrs. Ulman said with a pause, "I need to be alone."

Porter and Alred nodded, stood, and thanked her for her time.

She led them to the door while Porter scribbled on a pad. Tearing out the paper as the door opened, he said, "This is my—"

"Right," Mrs. Ulman said. "Dial you if I learn anything. I'll just have to call everyone who came before you first. Hope you don't mind."

She smiled a bitter smile which disappeared quickly.

Porter didn't reply.

Once outside, the door closed behind Porter and Alred.

Opening the door to the bark-colored Toyota, Porter shot Alred a glance. "How did the FBI know Ulman mailed something to his P.O. Box?"

"Intimidation, probably," said Alred. "Scared her to death. When they asked about mail, she probably mentioned the box. They would have seen the mail box hanging by her front door as they entered and assumed the rest. A logical guess. A housewife with a mailbox at home wouldn't check a separate post office box regularly. And as a professor, Ulman would get mail at the university."

"Why would he have an extra post box?" said Porter.

Alred looked at him across the top of her car. "Side projects, most likely. People get post office boxes for different reasons. Maybe it was a money-making scheme only the Ulman's knew about."

"A scheme?" Porter said, tilting his head at her as he climbed into the passenger seat.

"Doesn't have to be illegal. Just some project where you'd get mail, but didn't want people to know your home address. Something like that." Alred looked up and down the street, then to the fuchsia sky.

In a shallow voice, Alred said as she fell behind the steering wheel, "I want to know what Arnott thinks he's doing. Creep!"

"D'you just call me a creep?"

"No. The professor here before us." Alred shook her head. "He's trying to figure it all out before we can." She lightly bit the inside of her cheek. "I'm going home."

Scratching his five o'clock shadow, Porter looked back at the Ulman home.

The curtain in the window fell closed.

"She's hiding something," he said, not turning away. "She wouldn't look us in the eye."

"Yep," Alred said, shifting her gaze back to the house. "But why?"

10:59 p.m. PST

Dear Stan,

Don't die on me!

I know, you're shocked I'm writing. The worst reputation I bear has to be my irregular letter-writing pattern. Truth is, I've written you a number of letters! Most of those even went into envelopes. But by the time I got close to putting a stamp on them, they were at least a month or two outdated.

Yes, when we served as missionaries together in Japan you taught me to purchase a number of spare stamps to have on hand. Well, we all have our weaknesses.

But this letter, you have to get!

I'll jump to the point. You've been a field agent with the FBI for at least eight years now, haven't you? Ten, maybe? Anyway, I've got a question that needs a quick answer: I'm working on something right now that would fascinate you. But I've just learned the FBI may get in my way.

I really need this!

I figure there must be a file or something. Most likely it's all out of your reach. But if you can tell me anything about a Dr. Christopher Ulman and his work, I'd appreciate it. Word has it Ulman has recently disappeared.

Ulman found something in Guatemala that's going to cause an uproar in the intellectual community. See the irony? He's a professor with a gold mine—and he's vanished! Yes, my imagination might play games with me from time to time, but if I know archaeologists—which I do!—they wouldn't throw away a discovery of this magnitude—the type of thing they hope for all their lives.

I know I haven't really said anything about what he found, but I have to make sure this letter gets in the mail. I'll tell you more later.

Kiss your wife and kids for me.

The Church is still true.

Your friend,

John D. Porter

(P.S.—The D *stands for* Dr. in Training *of course)*

(P.P.S—Write back quick! You guys at the FBI might want him for something illegal, which may soon tie to what I'm doing. Actually, I doubt you really want him at all—not your department, if I'm right. But what do I know. If the FBI confiscates my project, I'll fail out of Stratford University in a big embarrassing way. I really have to hurry. Too much to do. Sayonara!)

Chapter Ten

April 16
5:23 p.m. PST

Porter's heart beat like a race horse just in sight of the finish line, like a medieval bellows loaded with metal and coal growing hotter and a brighter red, like a baby taking its first breath of the new world.

He drew his fingers from right to left across the rough paper.

With his right hand, he scribbled English words into a spiral notebook of sheets that had been turned too quickly and smashed together.

"No," he said like an exploding light bulb. His eraser hit the white page with faint blue lines, and he scribbled the correct word.

A constant whisper came from his lips as he translated. He repeated words and parts of words in both his native language and the foreign tongue before writing again. Eight facial tissues soaked with sweat and wadded into twisted balls lay around the ancient codex, his notes, and the other piles of lexicons, histories, and atlases on his desk. He wished he had a handkerchief, a towel, or something. He couldn't afford to get the document wet with the salty water running nonstop from his face.

With a clamor, Alred entered the sweltering office. She dropped her bag and gasped. "You have the heater on in here?!?"

"The date's all wrong," Porter said, his eyes wide and ferocious, concentrating on the words scrawled on the codex. His unprimed voice left his mouth with a growl as if he'd been sleeping for the last twelve hours and not working. He needed rest.

She could hear the vent, pumping hot air into Porter's tiny office. But she couldn't find a thermostat on the wall.

"Heating's controlled from a central system. In all my years at Stratford, I have yet to find the controls," Porter said without lifting his eyes. "What perfume are you wearing? Polo Sport?"

"There's gotta be a way to turn this down," she said, using a chair to boost herself up to the vent. Almost sacrificing her nail and the tip of her thumb, she successfully pulled the little lever on the metal grating, shutting the duct. Looking at it from the ground, however, she realized the aperture would only close halfway.

"We could go to Bruno's," said Porter, dropping his pencil. He stabbed both his tired eyeballs with his fingers and smashed them as if they were trapped cockroaches.

"What did you say?"

"Where the temperature sustains human life. Sorry, I—"

"No," said Alred, "about the dating?"

Porter looked to the right of his chair. From amid the high stacks of indiscernible files, multicolored volumes, and stapled papers, he pulled up the last issue of *LOGOS, The Journal of Archaeology*. "In Albright's article." He flipped it open to a well marked page.

"Did you memorize it?" she said, looking at his yellow and green highlighting, blue, red, and black underlining, and the masses of notes he'd scrawled in the margins.

"Right here in the introduction Dr. Albright says he's dated the KM-1 codex to 700 BC."

"BCE," said Alred. In the modern world of scholarship, there was a big difference between the terms *Before Christ* and *Before the Common Era*, though the years were essentially the same.

"Whatever."

"He said he dated KM-1 based on the writing. He talks about that later in his paper," Alred said, leaning over Porter and pushing red hair behind her ear. Porter realized he smelled a little too well-aged today and knew Alred recognized this also as she pulled back to a standing position.

"He's guessing. And these footnotes?" Porter looked up at her. "They look like they've been added by someone else, an aid or something. I think Albright hadn't returned to the states before writing the article."

"You're saying Albright raced to get his paper published?" Alred said, taking the seat opposite the desk. She couldn't even stand by Porter, he stunk so bad. It came with not showering. His exuberance and panic at completing the task would make him a social outcast, she deduced.

Porter's hair hung wet to his eyebrows. If he'd had Fabio-length locks, the sweat probably would have repulsed Alred out of the room. Nevertheless, Porter nodded and reached for another magazine. "I missed this. Too busy with my dissertation, I suppose."

Alred examined the periodical as he flashed the front of it. Bold letters in a black cover read: *Archaeological Journal.*

Flipping to another spot devastated by his rainbow markings, Porter tossed the open journal onto Alred's lap.

She looked down.

THE NEW MESOAMERICAN MYSTERY
Guatemala's Hidden Treasure
by
Dr. Alexander Peterson, Ohio State University

"Ohio State University," she read out loud.

"An obvious connection to Dr. Albright."

"But this was Ulman's discovery," said Alred. "Why haven't there been any essays by him?"

"Maybe there *have* been," Porter said, leaning back in his chair, which squeaked with the sound of a thousand tortured mice. He put his hands behind his head and closed his exhausted eyes. He didn't want to think about Ulman. Frankly, he wished Alred would go away. Porter preferred working with solitude, his quiet lover these past years.

Alred saw the codex on the desk. Porter weighed the volume through her eyes. She recognized it instantly, once she saw past the piles of other academic junk Porter had put there as if to hide it. The artifact held the same tan color of the other ancient Central American books she had seen.

The manuscript was thick, but the pages were surprisingly thin. Each page of the bark paper had years ago been attached to the page beside it until it looked like an unrolled scroll of great length. But instead of being rolled together, the pages had been bent toward each other to make it look like an accordion or an oriental paper fan that could close into one solid form. The codex was opened now, not unlike the way books open today.

Numerous colored glyphs washed across the pages. Different inks and paints had been used, and pictures were interspersed among the lettering.

Alred squinted as if to decide what language the codex had been written in.

Porter eyed her closely.

She had read and reread Albright's paper by now, but still couldn't come to grips with the possibility that Near Eastern devices were found in KM-1. But then, she didn't know exactly what she was seeing right at this moment.

Porter held his eyelids parted only slightly. He smiled. That the terrible thing was on his desk would be enough to throw her logical mind into emotional chaos, he figured. He'd wait a bit.

Alred saw him appraising her, however, and recreated her unfeeling face with contemplative green eyes. "You don't think these professors killed Dr. Ulman to get to his find."

"Well," Porter said, dropping his hands into his lap, "I didn't say it. You seem to be more concerned about Ulman than the manuscript on my desk."

"What is it?" she said nonchalantly, as if it didn't matter as much as it did. All this time she'd done her work in her apartment, checking out books from the library and ordering others through the inter-library loan system. She'd kept her work quiet. Her prerogative. But in the end, she would need to face the archaeological evidence. Well, here it was.

"In tradition of the great scholars who wrote articles before we knew it was a race, I call this KM-2," said Porter with a hand presenting the object like a new guest in the small room.

"Ulman's codex."

"The one he sent Dr. Kinnard, yes." Leaning back to his card table, resting his elbows thereon, Porter looked at the bark book and at the notes he'd hoped to finish before she arrived. "I've been translating—"

"You don't know Spanish," Alred said, "how can you translate a Mesoamerican document?"

Porter looked up at her. "Why are you making this so difficult, Alred? We've talked about this. Can you be so obstinate concerning science vs. religion as to not see the facts before you?"

"Religion isn't an issue," Alred said, sitting back in her chair.

With unbelieving eyes, Porter said, "I'm glad to hear that. Be a scientific judge then." He lifted a hand again to the codex.

"KM-2," she said, carefully picking up the ancient book.

"Hope your hands are clean," Porter said as he dived back into his notebook. He flipped through the pages to review his work. It really was a mess and needed to be rewritten. But he was really wondering with all his mental faculties what his companion was thinking. "Ever see a volume like that? Looks a lot like a scroll someone decided to press flat and open differently, doesn't it?"

"I saw one in a museum in Mexico City. They are rare, but not unheard of. This codex was very well-preserved." She looked at the writing on the top half of the pages. The characters were very square-like, while the figures on the bottom of the pages resembled organized chicken scratches written in black and red.

"You translated some of *this*?" she said, shooting her eyes up.

"A little over halfway through as you can see," Porter said, motionless.

"Halfway. When did you start?"

"As soon as I got the codex." Porter jumped to his feet. He took two books from his desk and added them to an apparently orderless pile against the wall on Alred's right. Immediately he started fishing for another volume. "I couldn't make a bit of it out right away, but Kinnard thought he could read some of it." He found his book and sat back down with an explosion of metallic cricket sounds.

"Kinnard's an Orientalist."

"So am I, Alred." Porter couldn't understand why she wouldn't accept the Mesoamerican connection with the ancient Old World as Albright had described in his paper. "You know that."

"And you can read ancient Mayan?" she said, lifting a brown eyebrow.

Porter looked at the codex. "Is that what it is?" He opened the book he'd found and started rummaging through the pages with two wild hands. "I suspected a correlation with the Maya, but when I looked up their script, I thought it didn't match well enough."

"You're not a Central American archaeologist," said Alred, turning the delicate pages of KM-2.

"Please don't lose my spot," Porter said, one of his hands leaping from his book.

Alred found an envelope on the edge of his desk, which she gently used as a bookmark. Before turning the page again, she glanced at five hand-written letters above the address on the envelope: FARMS. She held up the white paper for a moment. "What's this. You're a farmer on the side?"

"Forever harvesting new levels of knowledge," Porter grinned as she put it back and turned the page. The word was an obvious acronym, but he didn't want to explain it at present.

Alred tightened her eyes. "I thought you said you'd translated—"

"The bottom half of the codex," said Porter, standing up again, one finger jammed in the volume he held. "What language might that be?"

Alred squinted at the letters, as if it helped her to think, and tilted her head to the left. "Mmmm...proto-Mayan, maybe? The language of a sister group small and fortunate enough to have evaded archaeologists until now?"

"Possibly," Porter said. He came to her side—pushing her away with his smell—and opened his book before her eyes.

"That looks different," she said.

"Only as different as the Mayan on the top half of the codex pages and the Mayan I found in the Stratford Library."

Alred examined the letters in the hard-bound volume, comparing them to the characters on the lower half of the ancient page in her hands.

"This is a facsimile of a document written in a language scholars now call *Meroitic*. It dates to approximately 600 BC, and is closely related to Egyptian *Demotic* from the same time period," Porter said.

Alred forgot about his odor. "You can read this *Meroitic*?"

"Well," Porter said, setting the book on his desk and returning sluggishly to his seat. He landed in his chair with a thud and another irritating squeal. "I'm a little slow going, but...yes."

"Would you please stop doing that," Alred said, closing her eyes. Her head was obviously throbbing. Either that, or the ideas she was hearing made her want an excuse for a pain reliever.

"What," said Porter, trying to prop his feet on his desk. He didn't have much room between his table and the wall and so had to rest the heels of his running shoes on the corner of the desktop.

"Never mind," Alred said.

"You know…reading KM-2…is easier than translating *Meroitic* Egyptian."

Alred stared at him. "It should be *C*M-2."

"What?"

"Kalpa should be spelled with a *C*. I know of no village that starts with a *K* in Central America," she said.

He dropped his heels to where they belonged and leaned forward, still unaware of his screaming chair. "Meroitic was developed by a group of people fleeing Jerusalem around the year 600, as I said. The language is a mixture of two Egyptian scripts: Demotic and its mother, Hieratic. Hieratic is simply a shorthand version of the famous Hieroglyphs everyone thinks of when picturing Egypt."

Alred pointed at the bark page. "You're saying this is a form of Meroitic?"

Porter shook his head. "Not really. It's a twist on a Demotic/Hieratic style; kind of a sister to the Meroitic language."

Alred sat up. "If I'm following you correctly, Porter, you're saying these ancient Mesoamericans living in Highland Guatemala wrote in an Egyptian language."

"Of a sort," Porter said.

"That's why Kinnard could read this," she said.

"Well he could and he couldn't."

"That sounds scientific," said Alred, reaching up to wipe her brow. The stickiness was probably growing under her arms as well, and whether or not the headache had ever truly come, Porter could tell she wanted to leave. "You know, Porter, I hate to say this, but it sounds like you're not proving your Book of Mormon true. I understood you believe Jews settled in Central America."

"Kinnard had difficulty understanding what he was reading because while he recognized it, he didn't." He realized that sounded stupid so he rubbed his mouth with his wet fingertips and started again. "The writing is clearly of Egyptian origin…but it has distinctly *Hebraic* attributes."

"What?"

"Moses Maimonides, one of the greatest rabbis and Jewish philosophers of the late twelfth century, worked for a time as a court physician in Cairo. He recorded his thoughts in what may seem to be a peculiar way. His book is quite famous: *The Guide for the Perplexed.*"

"Sounds like the book we need," said Alred.

"The language was Arabic," Porter said with a sniff, "but he used the Hebrew alphabet."

"He mixed up his languages on purpose?" said Alred, unsure of whether she understood Porter right. Of course it wouldn't make sense to the casual student, but this was business, so she had to understand.

"Actually, it is not uncommon to find such crossovers in history," Porter said.

She lifted her eyebrows.

"I have read of Arabic texts scribbled in Coptic characters. There is also the *London Magical Papyrus*, and then *Papyrus Anastasi I*, and then other Hebrew works penned in Arabic writing. *Papyrus Amherst 63* confused Egyptologists for years until they realized the demotic script formed sentences in the Aramaic language. There are plenty of examples from the earliest times to this very day!"

"Give me an illustration outside of the Near East."

Porter lifted a hand. "You are probably aware that there's a lot of French-Latin out in the world—I don't mean French *derived* from Latin, but a form of pseudo-Latin. It was written by people who tried to use the language of the well-schooled, but ending up blending their own speech with their writing. Like the folk in the middle ages who wanted to write in illustrious Latin, which was seen as more prestigious than their own language. Whoever wrote our codex, scribed words in the characters of the learned Egyptians while most of the lingo was Hebrew."

Silent, Alred let it soak in.

"In other words," Porter said, "KM-2 was written by someone schooled in Egypt, who was a native of Palestine…or one of this man's descendants. It is well-known that distinguished people studied in Egypt during in the fifth and sixth centuries BC. Many famous Greeks did it. I could start dropping names. Socrates, Pythagoras—"

"Please. Don't," Alred said with an uplifted hand. "I read a year ago that Rameses III was the Father of Ancient America. The book was full of evidence suggesting connections between Central America and Egypt."

"What kind of connections?" said Porter.

"Architecture, art forms, symbols...but I don't believe Rameses had anything to do with America. Some things just *look* alike."

Porter smiled a wry grin.

"You don't think—"

"No, I doubt there is any relation between Rameses III and Mesoamerica," Porter said, closing his eyes. "But some of the facts cited in the book might be valid."

"Two Egyptian figurines were also purportedly found on the west coast of El Salvador. Roman coins dating back to the year 200 have been discovered in North America. but those things could have easily been transplanted."

Porter nodded.

Alred put KM-2 back on his desk. "I'd like to examine the codex in detail when you can take a break."

"Sure," Porter said. He felt the back of his teeth with his tongue.

"So why do you think Albright's paleographic dating is incorrect," she said, a sigh in her voice.

"Just a hunch," Porter said, realizing it was pointless to continue the discussion. Alred's mind stood solid. She wouldn't listen. If he said anything else, it would only make her regret her participation in the project more. It was obvious she wasn't enjoying this. If he was going to work with her, he'd have to be more amiable.

"I see," she said with a light nod. "I say we subject the codex to carbon 14 dating. We can get Dr. Atkins to do it with little hassle." She stood. "Unless you have a problem with that?"

"In my first archaeology class," Porter said, "we...talked about different dating processes. When my professor, Dr. Jacob Noble, told us that many scientists argue the date of a find or question the validity of the year concluded by the tests, I pursued the idea of arguing archaeologists with a string of questions which probably made my professor sorry for writing up the lecture that day. I just couldn't understand how *science* could bicker with itself. If the carbon dating's done, I naively figured...the date had to be right. If it wasn't, how could scientists continue to use that dating procedure. I asked Noble what would happen if I removed my right ear and had it carbon dated? What year would the process present? He shocked the class by telling us...my ear could be 150 years old."

"That can't be true," Alred said, shaking her head, her eyes drawn into thin slits.

"Right! I would have *just* cut it off. Two opposing truths cannot exist at the same time. And yet in science, they often do! When I came to Stratford, Kinnard told me that the problem with scholarship is that about fourteen years after you write a paper on a given subject, some other scholar formulates a paper proving what you said to be false. It's all a big game, with new truths forever overriding old ones. But then, if the discoveries had really been true in the first place, no one could debunk them at any point in the future. So we are not necessarily dealing with truths here, but *the redefining of reality*. Every scholar wants to make a name for himself—"

Alred frowned.

"—herself," Porter smiled. "In order to do that, we have to write something that stands out. The best way anyone has found of doing that is to find something new in all the old material; stand on the shoulders of past scientists, and say they were wrong, and we are right, and here's why!"

"What does this have to do with carbon 14 dating?"

"After my archaeology professor informed us that my recently severed ear would register to be older than my great grandfather, he gave us examples of numerous artifacts which have been dated far older than they could have been. A cola can found in Germany on the side of the autobahn weighed in at a hundred plus years. That particular can was obviously a recent invention."

"So all the scientists are wrong?" Alred said, folding her arms tightly.

Porter caught a sudden whiff of Alred's pleasant perfume and felt moisture run down the small of his back. "Not at all."

"You're saying all the dating archaeologists have been doing is completely useless. I understand your facts, but wouldn't scientists recognize these peculiarities? Or is this knowledge yours alone?" Wise sarcasm colored every word.

Porter turned his chair to the left, stared for a moment at one pile of books, withdrew a red hard-bound copy, and flipped into the pages. "Robert Eisenman and Michael Wise write of the problem in carbon dating the Dead Sea Scrolls, stating clearly that 'the process is still in its infancy, subject to multiple variables, and too uncertain to be applied with precision to the kind of materials we have before us.' Of course scholars see the problems with dating procedures we use today."

"So why do they continue to use carbon dating...if it's faulty?" Her voice was sharp and almost demeaning. She squinted her eyes and looked down on him as if he was nothing more than an arrogant child arguing against the existence of the wind.

"Same reasons chemists, biologists, and physicists use faulty ideas in their experiments. Until someone proves the world is round, we are forced to accept that the world is flat! It may not *be* flat, but we can only use evidences available to us...in science. Someone always comes along and changes the system to one degree or another. As far as archaeologists know, there is at least a fifty to a couple-of-hundred years potential variation on anything we date. And that is what we *know*. But then *that* truth could change any day now! In the meantime, we can only work with what we have."

"Then we'll send KM-2 in and let them cut a piece from it," Alred said.

"Soon as you're finished with your analysis," Porter grinned.

Alred left without saying good-bye.

Porter leaned into his leaning desk and stared at the cracked door. She hates me, he thought. She didn't stay, as planned, and they were in a rush. She even forgot her bag. Would she return for it?

He put his fingers to his lips and rested on his elbows.

He knew he had a reputation for being overbearing. His eccentricities had gifted him with a lonely life. And here was someone willing to share some time with him...he hoped. He had to straighten out, be helpful.

Porter slapped himself in the forehead and returned to his translating.

They would know within a few days when the manuscript had been written.

* * *

Alred stomped away with one thing in mind. She only needed a few major pieces of the puzzle to give her counter dissertation power. Other scholars had already set the foundation for her argument. KM-2 would prove to be the final key to destroying the theory of ancient transoceanic contact as Porter described it.

Soon, those points would present themselves.

But on the way to her car, she couldn't help but scan the darkness… for Dr. Ulman.

Chapter Eleven

April 17
11:53 p.m. PST

Polaski's breathing seemed to echo off of the office walls as his good fingers flipped quickly through the file. Wilkinson gurgled his last breath from the floor. Polaski dropped the papers with shaking hands. They spilled over the desk, the chair, the carpet.

"That's it, I'm out'a here!" he said, running to the door.

He reached the street and looked around, driving thin fingers through his thick hair. "Great!" he said, remembering his car parked two blocks away. Sprinting, he crossed the quiet road, his heart thundering. Mutts barked somewhere in an alleyway. With a sigh, he swung around the corner and spotted his gold Mazda hatchback.

Figeroa leaned like a gargoyle against the door on the driver's side. His dark skin frozen in the cold air, his black goatee shifted like porcupine spines as his eyes met Polaski's.

"What are *you* doing here?" Polaski said to the brute, who glanced at his misshapen hand. Polaski hated it when people did that.

"Was the parking lot filled behind Wilkinson's office?" Figeroa said. He shook his head. "You did it, didn't you." He came around the side of the car, his voice icy. "You murdered him!"

"You know what would have happened if I didn't!" Polaski said as Figeroa shoved him. Polaski's lanky body stumbled backward, his scarecrow arms waving in the air until he steadied himself.

"I can't believe you killed him! Don't you realize you've pinned us down? There's no hope now! None!" said the gargoyle with dark eyes.

Polaski caught Figeroa by the shoulders. They pushed against each other as he commanded, "Quiet down!"

"What does it matter?" Figeroa said, his shadowy eyes wide, his hands locked on Polaski's shoulders. "We're dead men, now! They're gonna fry us!"

"Get in the car," Polaski said, keeping his voice down. His eyes cut up to the dark windows on the buildings around them. The street smelled of exhaust and oil.

"You have ruined my life!"

"I said sit!"

Forcefully, they pulled away from each other. Figeroa threw himself into the passenger seat as Polaski started the engine. Within minutes they were in Polaski's apartment, packing a large Samsonite suitcase.

"We'll go to your place next. Get your things," Polaski said.

"No way, man. Can't go back there!" Figeroa said, looking at each wall as if they hid police cameras.

"Fine!" Polaski said, flinging his closed bag at Figeroa's chest.

Figeroa barely caught the bag. Its weight stabbed the snaps of his black suede jacket into his ribs. "What are you do'n?!"

"Get out of here!"

"What?!"

"Take the bag and run. There's six-hundred dollars stashed in the bottom corner."

"Huh?!"

"You heard me!" Polaski went into his closet, pulled at a shoe box on a high shelf, lost his grasp on it, and watched the .38 spill out with the bullets when the container hit the floor. "I'm staying to make sure the carbon dating doesn't happen."

"Oh, man," Figeroa said, watching Polaski load the gun, "You're crazy. You killed Wilkinson and—"

"So?" Polaski shot him a hard glance. "I told you to leave! This is no longer your concern." He slid bullets into the black revolver with shaky fingers.

"What did ya do to him?"

"Stabbed him with his letter opener," Polaski said with a dry voice.

Figeroa shook his head, ran to the window, and peered out through the crack in the drapes. He almost laughed, but his voice trembled with nervousness. "Don't suppose you wore gloves, did ya?"

"Shut up."

He turned back to Polaski and shouted in his face, "Then your *prints* are all over the place! You probably left the murder weapon in Wilkinson's back!"

"So what?!"

"Polaski," Figeroa said, easing his shaking voice when his eyes stopped on the gun again. "You lost your wallet in the building earlier today, remember?"

"I was pick-pocketed!" Polaski said, sitting on the edge of the bed. "Some student's got five dollars more than he had yesterday. He'll toss the wallet in a dumpster, and no one will ever see it again."

"You don't know that! It might'a slipped out when you poked around Wilkinson's office this morning! What if Wilkinson found it and put it somewhere safe, left the building for his meeting across town, returned this evening just in time to run into you and get killed?! Man, the cops will be storming your place before noon tomorrow!"

"Never committed a murder before," Polaski said to himself, looking down at the gun. "Didn't think I was capable."

"You never will again!"

Polaski looked at Figeroa and slowly lifted the gun. "I told you to get out of here."

Figeroa froze, silent for a minute. Then he said, "You fire that weapon and cops'll be here instantly."

"You'll be dead," Polaski said with wide eyes.

Without another word, Figeroa nodded slowly, bit his upper lip and went to the door. "You're insane, man. Cops'll get ya."

Polaski didn't lower the weapon until Figeroa had closed the door behind him. He sighed and looked at the window. In a low voice he said, "It's not the police I'm worried about. If I don't work fast, I'll be dead by the time they find me."

* * *

Porter's covers were already on the floor. He turned hard enough to wrench off the mattress sheet.

No nightmares.

No sleep!

He stared at the bare wall for a while. The codex, its delicate pages covered in words that would stun the world, flashed again in his mind. He thought of the smell of the paper breaking into a fine mist of pepper, different from old books but so similar to Egyptian papyrus.

He closed his eyes in anger.

He knew he was going overboard with the subject, but he'd never run across something so exciting. The guys in Utah who worked for the Foundation for Ancient Research and Mormon Studies (FARMS) would kill for this document…in a manner of speaking.

But its very existence in America wasn't exactly legal. The thought burrowed like a tick into his brain.

He rolled again.

Alred was about the most uptight woman Porter had ever worked with. She was spending fewer hours with him as time went on. He'd caught her in the library two days before, volumes stacked neatly around her, pads of used paper open and piled under her busy hands. When he'd tried to find out what she was doing, she'd nearly bit the tips of his fingers off.

She was pretty.

Porter tossed on the bed.

Red letters of the clock glowed with a growl: *2:27*.

April 18

"Hear the news today?" Porter said, catching Alred in the parking lot behind the Dover building. He'd waiting for almost an hour in the cold, hoping she'd show up. It was past noon, but the fog hadn't subsided.

"I'm surprised you have time to watch television," she said. She carried a black portfolio twice the size of a briefcase but only two and a half inches thick. She also wrestled with her bag, which she'd retrieved the day before.

"It was on the radio. Dr. Wilkinson was found stabbed to death in his office this morning. His own letter opener."

"Professor Wilkinson—here?" Alred said, shooting him a glance, then staring off into memory-ville.

"Don't suppose you want some help," Porter said, looking at her full hands. The black overcoat she wore crowded her person and made her look like she carried more weight than she could have been. She was big-boned, so her outfit also seemed to give her an added fifty pounds around the waist.

"No thank you," she said. "Any word on the dating?" Striding tall, Alred held her head up. Her relaxed eyes scanned the rear entrance to the building with Porter's office. Porter tried to keep up.

"Not till tomorrow," Porter said, still looking at her bags. "Dr. Atkins says she's drowning in assignments. What'cha got there?"

"Are you always this persistent, Mr. Porter?"

His feet slowed, but he skipped forward, turned his eyes away, and said, "I'm not offended by my first name."

"I didn't mean to hurt your feelings, *John*," said Alred without emotion as they climbed the few steps to the glass door, "but I have a single streak of relentless conservatism." She opened the door and looked at him. "Formality."

"After you, *Ms.* Alred," Porter said with a happy grin.

She slid by him, banging her packages into the sheet metal door frame.

"Tell me, Porter...do you think the world will convert to your religion if your dissertation's proficient enough?"

Porter's eyebrows rose. "To tell you the truth, I think you are right."

"Really," Alred said, coming to the elevator. She rubbed the tip of her nose with the back of her hand.

He sighed and said, "I asked you not to discount the possibility of a *possibility* that my findings were true...and then I threw out any chance of believing I was wrong."

DING.

The door slid open.

Alred didn't move, but looked into Porter's gray eyes.

"Not very scientific of me," he said.

The portal started to close, but Porter threw a hand against it.

Looking at the elevator floor, Alred lifted her eyebrows. "Hmm." She entered, and Porter followed, unable to read her thoughts, unsure whether he'd made ground or hit another heartless wall. He didn't know what else to do. Liberal women loved men who admitted their mistakes, especially when it was true.

Before the door closed, a tall man walked by and looked in. His dark eyes shot fiery darts.

Chapter Twelve

April 18
10:23 p.m. EST

Albright would die if he didn't run. That's what the doctor said, at least.

He panted in the dark, wishing he'd been exercising as much as his physician recommended. It would be easier then, wouldn't it?

Only circling three blocks.

Halfway around, he knew he'd do the same as always: stop running and start walking!

His lungs were filled with smoking acid, as was his heart. He could smell the burning. He lifted his fists higher, hoping it would relieve some of the stress on his body. He didn't know anything about proper running form.

Just to the next stop sign, he told himself, then walk.

He'd heard on television that whether one ran or walked, one would burn the same amount of calories. He supposed it would be the same with his cardiovascular system; he'd burn the energy, sweat a couple liters, and keep his pulse rate high. He couldn't say his heart *wasn't* going!

It was under thirty degrees, but warm for an Ohio night in April. Thunderheads hid in the dark overhead, but the pavement his feet beat upon looked dry as concrete in a desert under the yellow street lamps. All the snow had disappeared, but there would probably be more by midnight tomorrow.

So why was he sweating?

Didn't exercise but once in a week.

He could see the stop sign…relief!

Wiping away the sticky moisture on his face with his gray sleeve, Albright slowed to a gentle stride. His arms fell to his sides. His lungs sagged, waiting for his heart to rest.

He had a good excuse for not running. He'd been out of the country. The doctor couldn't expect Albright to run in the mountains of Guatemala!

But why tell his physician he ran every night? For more Fenfluramine and Phentermine! They were supposed to lower his appetite. It wasn't easy shaking thirty years of carefully acquired excess weight! Besides, he wasn't supposed to get more than two weeks of the prescription at one time (which he *did* take regularly, and *couldn't* do without), and Albright was going into his second month.

Nice doctor. He got his check.

Running fingers through his wet hair, he held his breath as a blue Chevy passed, vomiting invisible smog.

He'd left the Kalpa site in a hurry to get back to the states. It was very peculiar, he thought, passing the stop sign. Peterson had taken off the day before him, and Albright had no idea what had happened to Ulman...though he had suspicions.

A colorless Ford Taurus with bright lights rounded the corner.

With a snarl, Albright lifted a hand to protect his eyes.

He dropped it and listened to the car pull to the curb and die some twenty feet behind him.

So why had the University requisitioned KM-1, Dr. Albright's codex?

Made him too famous, he figured.

That was fine. His first article was published, and a more thorough paper would be finished tomorrow morning.

It wasn't illegal, his possession of KM-1. Not mostly.

He'd passed through channels...bribed, his way, that is. Wasn't too hard to obtain the necessary paperwork. Easier to purchase than he'd thought it would be!

But the University had frowned on his measures and said they would keep it, "For legal purposes."

Right.

Okay. Albright had plenty of notes and a complete set of photographed facsimiles of the manuscript and a great deal of the ancient library where KM-1 had been found. He'd already made plans for the publication of a set of volumes tentatively entitled *The Hidden Library of Ancient Kalpa*. But Dr. Peterson argued that they could not yet conclude that modern day Kalpa had any relation to the lost city, so the title would have to be amended after they'd learned more.

Peterson had decided to focus on the site itself, which to Albright's knowledge still didn't have an accurate mnemonic distinction. But Albright suspected that Dr. Peterson had smuggled a manuscript of his own into North America. His colleague was not beyond such actions, when necessary. Not that all professors of Archaeology and Ancient History would do such things, but…no one had found something so feasibly controversial as they had.

Or Ulman, rather.

Whatever. It didn't really matter anymore.

Albright suspected Ulman had never left Guatemala.

There were reasons.

Was Dr. Ulman's body rotting under a bush crawling with Mesoamerican spiders? Most likely. Unless the larger animals had gotten him.

Albright shook his head. He shouldn't think about it.

Death.

He'd read in the *Tribune* that a Stratford University professor of History had been murdered. Why would anyone want to kill old Dr. Wilkinson? No taste for his archaic clothes? The paper said it may have been done by a convicted felon named Raymond Polaski, presently sought by the authorities. Red hair, short beard, blue eyes, Caucasian, medium weight, withered left hand, 35-40 years of age. Why did Albright remember the description so well?

Albright gazed behind him.

A shadow leaned against the stop sign he'd passed seconds before. A yellow light behind the figure solidified his silhouette. The phantom looked at Albright, but didn't move. Albright thought he saw breath release like cigarette smoke into the cold air.

The professor turned away.

Now growing paranoid, Albright thought. Need a good ten hour nap!

Why would someone kill the professor? Angry student? It wasn't unheard of.

Ulman was dead.

Wilkinson executed.

Where was Peterson?

Okay, Albright admitted to himself. KM-1 and the site might be worth murder…to some people.

Albright's heart pounded. But for all the wrong reasons.

How would he get the manuscript back from the University? He thought of three ways to steal it. None of them would work. He wouldn't make it as a criminal. There had to be a bureaucratic way.

He looked back.

Death moved in perfect stride with Albright's feet.

It's nothing.

A withered hand? Of course not. But the shadow's flanges rested within coat pockets. There were no eyes either.

Albright kept walking, his feet involuntarily doing double-time as the ghost followed.

Sweat trickled into his right eye and stung as if two parts alcohol.

Albright wiped it away and thought about Peterson. Where was he anyway?!

Buried?

No. On sabbatical…of course, hidden from the world, trapped in his big house shrouded by empty night. Dr. Alexander Peterson, proudly writing his great archaeology text, no doubt centering on the newest and most outstanding of all Central American finds!

Still could be dead.

Albright glanced back.

The guy was closer.

Well what-d'-ya-know! Second wind!

Albright started jogging again, pounding the asphalt with cheap tennis shoes as he crossed to the end of the last block.

Down to the next stop sign, then left. Almost home.

He turned back.

The shadow jogged with him. Same pace? Just a little closer.

Albright made for the end of the block at top speed. It had been years since last his legs felt the strain of sprinting. They'd forgotten the correct coordination.

Throwing himself forward, feeling the killer puffing with poison white breath on the back of his ears, Albright let his mouth hang loose.

Had to get home!

He didn't care if anyone saw him flying like an out-of-shape fool.

He hoped someone did!

He heard the feet slapping the ground behind him.

He felt the shadow overpower his mental energy; a ring wraith from Tolkien's world, commanding his feet to stop.

Albright refused to listen.

Running mad. He pumped his fists from his hips to his cheeks.

The weight of his body bounced.

But I'm not that fat!

Toes pointed. Heels kicked against the thorns behind him.

The power of the sprinting shadow reached at him with giant hands.

The air chilled.

The hands grabbed Albright's left forearm.

Albright screamed, but kept running.

The black beast, the murderer, the dark assassin had him, but didn't.

His head swam with a white mist.

Albright didn't stop screaming.

He turned the corner, ignoring the claws, the knives, stabbing his arm.

The shadow commanded the ground.

The curb lowered beneath Albright's feet, then rose abruptly.

Concrete hooked Albright's right toe.

The dark sky disappeared.

white lightning flashed inside his eyes.

Albright rolled on his back, dropping into the gutter. His head roared with pain as if run over by a truck. He felt cold wetness in his hair.

The shadow stooped over him, breathless.

The streetlight behind the being created a halo of fire around the black hole in man shape. An alien. A spirit. An executioner. Death himself!

Talons tore at Albright's left arm.

Albright grabbed his chest with his right hand, opened his mouth more widely than his watering eyes…and never closed it again.

April 18
8:33 p.m. PST

"Thanks for coming, Porter," said Kinnard, looking out of his drapeless window into solid blackness. "I've gotta meeting I'm already late for, but I had to talk to you before you went home today."

"If I had a phone in my office, you'd be to that meeting right now," Porter said, casually taking a seat. The white walls of Kinnard's room and the soft color of the bookshelves contrasted the window and the cherry wood desk. "I think you need an interior designer."

"To make my office looked as stripped as your own?" Kinnard said, forcing a small smile. He moved to his chair, took off his glasses, and rubbed his eyes. "You won't need a phone, Porter."

"Well, I figure—"

"You won't be in the office long enough."

Porter's playful grin froze. His eyes went dead.

Kinnard looked at him for a moment with sobriety in his telepathic words. But, of course, Porter couldn't understand. "I suggest you simplify your dissertation. Cut all the corners you can."

"I thought I was already doing that. I only have a month left," said Porter, sensing an unrevealed weight in the room.

Kinnard felt a immense surge of emotion. He could see Porter's predicament better than anyone else. Including Porter. He knew how much this doctoral candidate needed him. But what could Kinnard do? He didn't have the strength to say what needed to be said, and he didn't have the power to alter the situation.

Porter let his eyes drop as he waited. He scanned the scattered papers and books on Kinnard's desk, as Kinnard shot him short glances. A bent copy of *American Archaeology* with a female figurine on the cover, rested on top of a number of other magazines. Stacks of unread research papers choked one corner of the table, threatening to topple and roll off. A copy of *Newsweek*, hidden just under Truman H. Campbell's, *The Atlantis Bridge: The Egyptian/ Mayan Family*.

Porter picked up the book. "Not your regular reading," he said to the professor of Near Eastern Studies.

"How is it going with Ms. Alred?" said Kinnard, straightening his briefcase in preparation to leave. In reality, he was just hiding the nervousness in his hands.

"You actually taking this seriously, Dr. Kinnard?" Porter said, lifting *The Atlantis Bridge* and flashing the glossed cover at his supervising professor.

"I don't know what to take seriously anymore."

With a shrug, Porter said, "As well as you probably would have guessed. I know it wasn't your idea to put me with a partner. No one's ever liked working with me!"

"That's how it is?" Kinnard said.

Porter, who had pushed his way to a grin, let it slip away. He nodded.

"I've enjoyed working with you." Kinnard pulled a stubborn file from his leather bag, tearing the card and warping the pages in the process.

"You know, you'll subconsciously give those papers a lower grade because they're hashed?" Porter said, eyeing the manila folder.

"Alred's a great lady. Top of her class. Excellent woman," said Kinnard, letting the folder hit the floor to his right. "You should marry her; tell her your middle name."

"Always looking out for me," Porter said.

Kinnard looked at him with sober eyes. His eyebrows high, his eyelids drawn together, he bit the inside of his bottom lip and said, "I don't like this."

"Still fighting with your wife."

Kinnard sat and leaned back in his chair.

Porter lifted himself to the desk. "I'm kidding with you. Who wouldn't feel the tension in this room?! It's like cigar smoke from six card players trapped in an office the size of mine without a vent."

Kinnard nodded and gazed at the edge of his desk.

"Don't worry," Porter said through the silence as heavy as iron. "I'll get my dissertation done."

"I've already left a message on Alred's answering machine," Kinnard said.

"I've heard of those contraptions! Setting up a date for me?" Porter said, sitting back again. The chair groaned beneath his weight. He put his hands behind his head and tried to close his eyes, which were laced with red streaks in a shattered glass pattern. "I'm really not interested in *Erma* Alred. I just wished she'd *like* me a little. The *D* in my name is starting to mean *Discord*, I think."

"I've told her everything, so she won't yell at you when you spill the news."

"Good!" Porter said. "Whatever it is, I don't think I can stand looking into her cold green eyes again. Albeit, they are kinda nice—"

"They've changed the date for dissertations. All papers are due on the fifth of May," said Kinnard.

"I was baptized on that day," Porter said.

"You and Alred will also argue your material on the fifth."

The air chilled.

"But...you said...I have till...the twenty-first," said Porter.

"They've moved it up," Kinnard said without looking up.

"It says so in the schedule," Porter continued, "I read it! I have five weeks!"

"I'm sorry, Porter." Kinnard put his dark-rimmed glassed back on.

"That's an implied contract! They can't change it!"

Kinnard stood, the light gleaming off the top of his head. He kept his face hard. There was nothing he could do. There was no point in wasting breath and any more emotion over it.

Porter got to his feet, realizing he was wailing at the wrong person.

Kinnard walked him to the door. "You have a little more than two weeks. Don't waste your time making formal complaints. They'll only add to your ruin."

Chapter Thirteen

April 21
10:36 p.m. PST

"Where've you been?" Porter said with his best smile. He had pistachio bits in his teeth, which he tried to clean away quickly with his tongue. The result was an unplanned comedic grin.

"Thought I'd find you at Bruno's," said Alred leaning against the library table. "You came to a place more conducive to study."

The library overflowed with books. The volumes, piled high and jammed in the rows, waited under layers of dust for a new building to hold them. A maze of tight shelves, reaching for the ceiling, choked all four floors, promising students an adventure if they dared to enter.

The sun had disappeared and darkness spilled across Porter's back from the large window overlooking the employee parking lot in the rear of the building. Cold air blew freely through the vents as if someone had turned it on to freeze the students out. Porter worked under the brightness of a florescent lamp. He had spread his books beneath the single light, pulled others from the shelves, opened them and started stacking. Only for a moment did Alred think the pages of one of the books might catch fire if it got too close to the light. Porter had scribbled his thoughts and flipped through indexes. According to Bruno, many of these books he'd either read or poked through before. That's what made him a good scholar; he'd studied all or nearly all the books of his interest the library held.

Alred'd had enough of Stratford's Michael H. Weiss Memorial Library a year ago when she'd lost herself among the stacks as a research assistant for Dr. Ulman. She loved working for the man, but disliked doing everyone else's dirty jobs. That's why she had put her trust in Dr. Masterson, before he'd betrayed her. The more she progressed with Ulman's find, the more she disliked it. She wanted to throw up every time she saw Porter's codex.

It wasn't Porter's anyway. He was hogging it.

No matter. Alred was good. She didn't need the manuscript in her possession to succeed. She used it often enough and took adequate notes.

But she hated it anyway. The codex and everyone attached to it were ruining her life. She had to conquer the project.

Porter seemed to recreate his office wherever he went. From the many opened and discarded volumes, he had one book open before him, a number of his fingers stuck in the pages he'd passed.

"Since you didn't show up," Alred said, "I decided to ask Bruno about you. Then I read for a while."

"Were we meeting there?" said Porter.

Alred smiled a little. "You'll make a great absent-minded professor."

"It is my highest aspiration," Porter said with a growing grin as he leaned back a bit, shadow dribbling over his face as he pulled away from the only light in the room.

"5:00," said Alred, checking her watch to see exactly how many *hours* ago that had been. She leveled him with a dry gaze.

Porter's glow dulled. As if just remembering his small bag beside his book, he jumped, "Want some pistachios?"

"Food's not allowed in the library. I thought Mormons were supposed to be perfect."

"Ah. 'A city that is set on an hill cannot be hid...Let your light so shine before men, that they may see your good works, and glorify your Father which is in heaven.'"

"Shakespearean all of a sudden?"

"Matthew 5:14 and 16." Pulling a legal pad from beneath two others, he flipped through the sheets and handed it to Alred.

"What am I looking at," she said, examining a chart without lines.

"On the right side we have the English," Porter said, interlocking his fingers as he relaxed.

"*This* is English?!?" Alred squinted at the scribbled words.

Porter cocked his head to the left and wiggled a finger in his ear.

"My second grade teacher said I was doomed if I didn't practice better penmanship. Thank goodness for the personal computer! Anyway, I feel a little rushed."

"This supposed to be Mayan?" she said, looking at logograms drawn in the middle column of the sheet.

Porter leaned forward, snatched the pad from her, and pointed at one Mayan glyph on the page. "What's this?"

"I don't know. You said this was supposed to be Mayan? Looks like a hand."

"Right. How do you pronounce that?"

"If this is your best attempt at Mayan, I'd say this character is *man-ik*...pronounced *keh*."

"Look at this letter," Porter said, sliding his finger left to a more simple squiggle.

"Is that supposed to be a hand?" Alred said. "Let me guess. You pulled it off the codex."

Porter shook his head. "It's the Hebrew letter *k*. It is *kaph*, a hand. Tell me if I'm mistaken, but doesn't the Yucatec Mayan *kab* have the same meaning?"

Alred looked up, scanning her memory. "It does, if I recall."

"The West-Semitic word for hand or palm, represented by the image of a hand in ancient times, was also pronounced...*kap*. As far as our current study goes, these connections shouldn't surprise us. There is a link between the Middle East and Mesoamerica. Both Dr. Albright and Dr. Peterson have publicly noted it."

"I recently found a paper from a professor of the University of Calgary who supposes a connection between three letters of the Mayan calendar to the Hebrew alphabet," said Alred.

Porter lifted a finger. "I have some of those here! The Hebrew *lamed* and the Mayan *lamat*. A similarity so obvious, one might suppose it to be complete fraud created by those desiring to prove relationships between the Old and New Worlds. Yet here it is, solid fact. Tell me it's a coincidence."

"But these correlations are not proven." Alred pulled a chair from a nearby table and sat on it, looking around at the quiet library. Was anyone else here? Most of the lights had been turned off. She smelled moist carpets and shifted the points of her heels on the wood floor running from the window behind Porter to the stairway some thirty feet behind her. "Are they trying to conserve energy here?"

"These logographic systems sound too much alike to go unnoticed. Did you know the Chinese character for *boat* is made up of three pictures with distinct definition? The first meaning a *vehicle*, the second is the number *eight*, and the third, a clear depiction of a mouth. A vehicle with eight mouths?"

"Does this have an application to Mesoamerican languages?" said Alred, wrinkling her brow.

"Both have connections to Biblical tongues," said Porter, lifting an open hand. "Noah's ark had eight mouths: Three sons and their wives, and also Noah and his wife."

"Doesn't folklore school us that Noah brought two of every kind of *mouth* on the planet?"

Porter smiled, but his excited eyes didn't waver. "More, actually. But…there were only eight humans on the ark. All ideograms, like Egyptian, Mayan, and Chinese—in fact all letters!—originate from preconceived mental images. Why did the ancient Chinese, when desiring to write the word *boat*, describe such a detailed picture that has no reference to floating or even water? Why was a vehicle with eight people on it so clearly representative of this particular word?"

"You're shooting in the dark," Alred sighed.

"Isn't that what all scholars do, followed by an analysis of facts explaining their assumptions?" said Porter.

"What's the rest of this?" Alred said, looking at the pad full of foreign figures and badly scrawled English.

"Ever heard of the *Popol Vuh*, a Mesoamerican codex written not long after the Spanish conquered the area?"

"Did you forget my area of expertise?" Alred smiled. "*The Book of the Council.* I've quoted it. It was created by American Indians of the Quiche tribe, the most powerful nation in the area and also a branch of the Maya."

"Right, in 1524, a general under Cortez forced the Quiche to surrender, burning their capital city, Utatlan."

"You know some American history," Alred said, her eyes relaxing. "The *Popol Vuh* was one of the few books that survived the period. Most of the native libraries were decimated by the Spanish inquisition, ruining our chance to obtain a detailed history of the Maya."

"Some Mayan codices survived the Conquest," Porter said quickly.

"Most are fakes." Alred crossed her legs. "The *Popol Buj*, or *Popol Vuh* as you call it, was only one of four authentic works we know of. What about it?"

"Well, you know it is a collection of oral tales recorded by the Quiche nobles," said Porter.

"I am well aware of the book's background, Porter. Do you also know that we don't have the original?"

"Is that supposed to preclude what I'm about to say?"

Alred paused. "I'm the Mesoamerican scholar here."

"I…realize that. That's why I think you'll appreciate this. Especially in light of our new study. I have the book right here." He picked up an English copy from under a thick lexicon of Hebrew words. "Listen to this: '…*they* planned the creation.'"

"Is that why we're talking about the *Popol Vuh*?"

Porter looked at her, shock on his face.

Was she supposed to understand something in all this rhetoric?

"It says the same thing in the Book of Genesis."

"I thought the Bible defines *one* god as the creator," Alred said as Porter reached into his briefcase and pulled out his scriptures.

He put them on the table and Alred's eyes widened. The black book with worn gilding was at least three inches thick, and as he opened it, she could see the onion skin pages. "Here. Genesis 1:26. 'And God said, Let *us* make….'" He shot his face up at Alred's.

"What happened to Judeo-Christian Monotheism?" said Alred.

"*Vayomer elohim vaaseh adam btsalmenu kdmutenu.* The Hebrew word for God in this verse is *Elohim*. As in Cherub*im* and Seraph*im*, the *-im* implies plurality, just as *-es* in the English language. And the gods in this scene are obviously *planning* to come down and create. Here: chapter 2 verse 4 and 5: '…in the day that *the Lord God made* the earth and the heavens, and every plant of the field *before it was in the earth*, and every herb of the field *before it grew…*'

"'Thus it was created in the darkness and in the night by the heart of heaven,' says the *Popol Vuh*." Porter looked up from his books.

Alred nodded. "Is that the Mormon in you speaking, or the scholar." She didn't know why she listened. She was sure she could find a Jew capable of explaining why their monotheistic religion had a deity with a name implying plurality.

"The scholar, actually!"

"You'll bring up *The Books of Chilam Balam* next," said Alred.

"You know I can find Semitic relations with the name *Balam*, but I wanted to point out the *Popol Vuh*. See these names?" he indicated the pad again. "I'll read them for you."

"Please." Alred closed her eyes.

"This one, *Vucub Cakish*, a main character in the book," he said. "Did I pronounce that right?"

She nodded.

"And this…*Xbalanque*."

"Small Jaguar," Alred said, opening her eyes and folding her arms.

"What?"

"That's what the name means."

"Well," said Porter, "both correspond to…names in the Book of Mormon. But neither *Vucub Cakish* nor *Xbalanque* were available to scholars let alone anyone else until Carl Scherzer translated the text in Vienna from the original language into Spanish in 1857…many years after the publication of the Book of Mormon."

"Really," she said, skepticism in her voice. "What Book of Mormon names exactly."

"Well in a section called the Book of Ether, there is a person by the name *Akish*. That's not a stone's throw from *Cakish*."

"But ambiguous enough for debate," said Alred.

"True. The second might take a deeper dive, but look. Break up the name *Xbalanque*. Of course the *x* in older Spanish and Portuguese languages is pronounced *sh*. And you know vowel shifts are common enough that rarely can we trust vowels at all in etymology."

"Okay, you've effectively turned *Xbalanque* into the word SH-B-L-N-Q," said Alred. "Where's your correlation."

Was she humoring him? Or just hoping he'd get it over with.

"Do you believe the *q* with an *n* preceding it could fall off the end of a word?"

"Why not."

Porter tightened his lips together, then softened. "And an *m* is interchangeable with an *n*?"

"Are you patronizing me?" she said lifting her brow. "We all know *p* and *b*, *t* and *d*, *k* and *g*, *l* and *r*, and other such combinations can be found in the evolution of languages. *Balam* and *Balan* are essentially the same name. What's your point."

"There is both a Shiblon...and a Shiblom in the Book of Mormon. Incidentally, the Hopi Amerindian tribe professes even today that they come from the 'great red city of the south.'"

"Oh, really," she said, relaxing with the realization that the further Porter babbled into American anthropology and philology, the more he left behind his area of scholarly specialty.

"Yes. There is a similar mention in the Book of Mormon about groups of people departing a city they called Zarahemla. By a strange coincidence, in Arabic, *dar* or *zar* is one word for settlement, and *ahmar* means red. *Zarahamra* and Zarahemla," Porter tilted his head. "Could be nothing, but seems enough evidence to at least warrant serious consideration of transoceanic contact with the Old World even without Ulman's codex."

"Did our conversation just leave the *Popol Vuh*?" said Alred.

"The Mayan Indians possess plenty of proofs of Near East connections if you ask me," said Porter.

"All long shots?" said Alred. "Give me one."

Porter raised a hand and let it flop as if he'd already spoken his thought. He grabbed his copy of the *Popol Vuh*, flipped the torn up pages, and read a line. "'In this way they carried Avilix to the ravine called Euabal-Zivan,' pardon my pronunciation, 'so named by them, to the large ravine of the forest, now called Pavilix....' Pavilix, in Mayan—"

"Means *in* Avilix," said Alred. "Tell me your amazing fact."

Porter didn't speak, his face shining as if it was obvious. "The Mayan prefix *p* can be defined *in*?"

"That's right."

"The letter *b* is simply a voiced *p*."

"Are we back to sound shifts?"

"The Hebrew mirrors the Mayan in this case. *B* is the prefix used at the very beginning of the Torah or the Old Testament: *B-reshit bara Elohim et ha-shamaim vet ha-aretz. B-reshit, in* the beginning....See it?"

"And what does this have to do with our precious KM-2?"

Alred realized she was sitting in a tight ball, limbs wrapped together like tape, strapping her to the chair. Her eyes had found their usual hard stare. Her skin had paled in the dim library light. Her auburn hair had turned to dark gray.

Licking his lips, Porter visibly debated his response. "I…found something even better while translating. Something I know…you won't believe."

"I'll believe anything less subjective than the ride you just took me on," she said. "What."

Porter scratched his forehead and gazed at the shelves around him, holding volumes of their own secrets. "I probably shouldn't…say… yet."

"Because we're at war?" she said, leaning forward and propping her hands on her knees as if about to spring at him. She tried to loosen at least her shoulders. "Or because you're not sure about your facts?"

Porter sagged in his seat. The fire in his pupils dimmed. "Alred… I'm not trying to fight you. I really wish we could work together on this. That's what Kinnard wanted us to do."

So little he knew, she thought, squinting with her eyes and her lips.

"Do you have the codex here?" she said.

"I do," he said.

"You go everywhere with it?"

"No," he said, before holding his breath. "I hide it in the vent in my office. The heat's not too bad for it."

"We should trade off," said Alred, thinking him foolish with the manuscript, "a day at a time."

Porter made his mouth into a tight line and nodded.

Alred stood.

"I guess you got the carbon dating results," Porter said.

"That why you *forgot* about our meeting at Bruno's?" Alred drew a manila envelope from her portfolio.

"Are you asking me if I'm insecure about the results?"

Alred stood in silence, waiting, the envelope in her hands.

He stared at it. "Tell me, when was the Valley of Guatemala populated…according to the facts?"

She said nothing.

Porter listened.

The delicious smell of dry paper moistened the air around them—

the splendor of all good libraries.

"Archeological evidence suggest 600 BCE," Alred said.

He smiled. "Then I'm not worried a bit!"

Taking a breath, Alred looked at her package. "There's been a delay. Dr. Atkins wants to take another cut of the codex."

"She'll burn it all if she has the chance." Porter took KM-2 carefully in his hands and slipped it into a brown paper sack. "What's that," he said, looking at her envelope.

Alred pushed her lips to one side of her mouth, looking at it. She pulled at the manila flap and withdrew a folded sheet of newspaper. "Dr. Masterson wanted me to give this to you."

Porter stood and took the gray paper, the ink smudged all over it. The obituaries stared at him. Highlighted, he found the name Dennis GEOFFREY Albright, Ph.D.

"What?!" He scanned the words too fast and had to back up to figure out what had happened. "A heart attack?"

"While jogging," said Alred. "Some at the University...seem to think he was murdered."

Porter slumped back into his seat. He touched the corner of his mouth with a couple fingers and stared at nothing. "We never found out what happened to Dr. Ulman...Wilkinson."

Her right eyebrow lifted and she frowned. She came close to the table. "Porter. Albright died of natural causes."

"I bet Kinnard doesn't think so? He knows Albright personally, if I remember right." Like a hypnotized bug, Porter gazed at the florescent light on his table. "What's their...connection?"

A flash of memory hit Alred like a two-by-four. She saw Kinnard slumped on one end of the table, his hands rubbing his temples; Masterson standing as she walked into the room; Goldstien smiling at her... too much; Arnott, quiet like a little devil with sharp eyes; and Wilkinson in his dusty suit....

She shook away the image and said, "You think someone wants Dr. Ulman's KM codices."

Porter said nothing for a moment. He looked at Alred with a serious grin. "Scholars are human too. Mankind has this nasty habit of doing things they really shouldn't...including genocide. Question is, where does that put two doctoral candidates working a hundred-miles-an-hour on the same task as dying professors?"

Alred pulled her head back.

* * *

She looked troubled when she left. Porter couldn't blame her.

But he had too much work to do. And if someone wanted to kill him over it, he had to do it even more quickly. Time to figure things out. All the implications.

His eyes stung with lack of sleep. He didn't dare look at his watch.

He glanced for only a second at the manila envelope with the edge of the obituaries poking out.

The library would be open all night. The same every weekday. It was a new policy the students had fought for just last year. A bit revolutionary, but Porter took advantage of it. Librarians dimmed the lights after 10:00, probably as a tactic to dissuade students from coming after that hour. If no one came, the managers could fight the board for the right to close at a decent hour again. They'd win.

Porter rubbed his face and looked around.

He knew someone was on the lower level, but the fourth floor was devoid of life, save himself...and a cricket he thought he'd heard half-an-hour earlier somewhere beyond the stairs. Fourth floor! What a feat that must have been for a little black insect that couldn't fly! He thought about it until he saw himself as the insect, climbing the cream-colored walls, the naked stairs, the bookcases, not knowing where he was going.

Lost among the stacks, Porter the cricket dug his way through the volumes. Skipping from one title to the next. Hoping he'd find some direction, a clue to the way up or out.

Whisper.

What was that? He spun around too fast. His cricket legs rubbed and a chirp erupted.

Cats weren't aloud in the library. But he could sense them sliding through the bases of the shelves.

He couldn't outclimb the creatures. He couldn't hide motionless forever. If the felines didn't see him, they'd hear him, smell him, track him down by following his droppings....

"Shhhh!"

Porter lifted his head from his books and note pads.

He'd dropped to sleep.

But he heard the whisper again.

In his mind, he replayed the shush shouted in silent breath, like a wind let loose among the catacomb halls of manuscripts. Yet, he knew no sound escaped anyone's lips.

He thought about Albright, running....

Footsteps on the stairs.

He pictured Wilkinson with the letter opener in his back.

Closer now, but slower...more careful...quiet....

Dr. Ulman....

Silently, Porter stood.

Wailing metal against wood, the chair betrayed him. The sound echoed from each shelf to the wall to the stairs.

The codex.

Porter took it, still in its brown bag. The paper whispered to the cricket.

Sleep choked Porter's brain. He tried to shake it away. Now was a good time for adrenaline. Gazing with wide eyes at the stairs, he saw the shadows of people rising from below.

Had the librarians gathered to mob the one student who dared to stay all night?

Unlikely.

Imagination.

But on his mission in Japan, Porter had learned to trust his feelings.

He took up his briefcase with one hand, slipping his notes into it quickly. He bit his lips with his teeth. He grabbed the paper with Albright's death notice and dived into the shelves.

Through the volumes, Porter saw the men in black. Nice suits. Turtleneck shirts under the coats. Very stylish. But why all dark?

The guns weren't hidden. Nine millimeter. Silencers?

Only two of them.

Had Porter served as a Marine, he might have opted to fight and find out who these men were.

But he was a scholar.

The pen may be mightier than the sword, but books don't deflect bullets.

Chapter Fourteen

April 22
1:40 a.m. PST

The ghost appeared that very same minute.

Alred couldn't see it directly. It was a shadow in a raven black room. Standing. Breathing. Watching her rest.

She knew she'd been asleep, for a moment earlier she was in the grand Victorian house of her great aunt who lived in Peru, Nebraska. But the house wasn't the same as it had been when she'd visited as a child. She was quite young again, but that didn't matter. The walls were whiter than she remembered, the ceilings higher. The house swayed in the wind on a hill of green that hadn't been there. And she wept deeply, seeing the grave stone bordered with pansies and other flowers, pink and yellow, which she didn't recognize. Carved in the granite were the words, JACQUELYN ALRED.

Alred loved her great aunt. No relative had been so kind, making sweet cookies with peanut butter or chocolate chips on the rare occasions when she'd come over. She'd only seen the woman as many times as she had fingers on one hand. But Alred cried when she saw the stone. And tears covered both cheeks as she wandered round the mansion—three times bigger than she remembered it—with the soon-to-be new owners.

The house no longer belonged to the family. There was no more family. She had to leave.

Standing on the grass which leaned and relaxed repeatedly in the comforting breeze, Alred said her good-byes….

And was in her room again, awake and aware that something else phased in and out of the molecules of darkness around her.

She looked...but didn't turn on her light.

Of course there was no one—

"Alred...."

The apparition stood where it didn't, oscillating like a mirage of shadow, there...but not there...then....

"Alred, can you hear me?" said the fiend, the monster that shouldn't be.

The door was closed, locked, the window sealed.

"I've come...to speak to you."

She smashed her pillow with the back of her head.

Alred could smell sulfur in the musty air.

The phantom looked at her, waiting for a reply. It had no feet she could see, no facial features but those it created to look human, no hands at all for they were too complex to mimic well. It was a cold breeze holding still in the tepid room.

"What do you want?" she said.

"Alred...can you hear me?" said the ghost.

"Of course I can hear you," she said before realizing the mouth of the monster didn't move in conjunction with the words that came out. It was like an old film from a foreign country, poor black and white, with the actors shifting their tongue behind bobbing lips while no sound worked with them. Even now, the vaporous man opened his mouth and beckoned with unheard words. He spoke for nearly ten seconds before she heard anything.

With his arms at his side the shadow with features said, *"I don't dare touch you."*

"You got that right!" she said, realizing if she turned on the light he would cease to be.

"But I've...brought you something. And I need you to listen."

"Go away," said Alred, tears still in her eyes from her dream. But the words had no force by the time they left her throat.

The ghost stepped forward. Or was it a slide more than a gait?

Shrinking in the mattress, Alred couldn't move.

Clink.

She looked at the oak nightstand to the right of her bed. Was something there, by the clock where nothing had been before? It looked more like a stain...a mark...of the ghost.

She could feel the apparition behind her now, close to her ear. Spinning her head around, she saw the ghost near enough to kiss.

"Just..."

She saw his mouth moving, saying words that didn't reach the mortal world. Petrified, she listened.

"...tell...my wife...I'm...okay....She'll know what this is for."

Closing her eyes tight, she bit the inside of her cheek and tasted salt. She knew the voice now. She knew what the face was supposed to look like.

"I have to go," said the spirit.

She watched the shadow, staring at her from the wall hidden in the darkness.

"Keep looking over your shoulder, Alred," he said, passing into nowhere, but visibly going away. *"You're in danger...and so is your friend...."*

Alred awoke with an ache to speak in her throat. She let the words out in a whisper. "He's not my friend." Rubbing the sleep from her eyes, she sat up and looked around the room.

Just another dream.

Of course. How could someone who was such a stickler for scientific process have failed to see her experience for what it was while it was happening?

She felt her quick pulse running through every part of her body.

She heard a whisper.

From the dark, the phantom lashed at her.

Alred screamed.

She caught the beast and scolded it quickly.

Just Samantha. It rubbed against her and meowed as she caressed the soft fur. "Don't do that again."

The cat jumped from her bed and went after the ghost that hadn't been there.

Flopping back to her pillow, Alred moaned and closed her eyes. The lids opened to peek once at the clock, though she didn't want to know the fiendish hour.

What she saw made her sit up.

On the nightstand, a small key waited like a child squirming to be lifted.

She leaned forward and swiped the cold metal.

Her light went on, and she traced the markings with the tip of her fingernail: 0417-2105.

It was difficult getting back to sleep.

* * *

Porter's fingers felt their way through the books like blind moles climbing through underground caves. The cricket inside him wanted to chirp for help, but he knew the cats would hear him first. And they would only need a moment to strike.

He couldn't shake the thick fog of dream from his head. Porter knew he was awake, but still saw himself as a tiny insect running from Halloween cats with sleek fur and shining fangs. After all, *this* couldn't be happening!

For once he was thankful for the labyrinth of bookcases making up the fourth floor of the Stratford University Library.

The hunters were perfectly quiet.

They *did* slide forward like cats.

Before running deeper into the shelves, Porter saw the shadows of two of them, but he worried there might be a third man.

He thought he heard whispers as rubber soles touched down on dark vanilla-colored carpet. The silence rang like a non-stop train whistle in his ears. He heard his breath as if amplified by a microphone and a thousand dollar stereo system. Trembling hands stroked the book shelves. Wide eyes stared through the holes in the stacks, trying with no success to see the newcomers.

He'd already spotted the guns. The barrels were too long. Silencers were illegal in the state of California. These weren't university personnel, police, or even customs officials looking for the codex.

Maybe they'd tracked down the wrong man. But there couldn't be anyone else in the library. Porter knew he was lucky they hadn't shot him through the window.

It needed to be cleaner.

They probably had a car outside, a van. Three other men, dressed in the same expensive black attire, waiting for the body to be brought forth, prepared to haul it to an unmarked grave….

What am I thinking?!? Porter thought. He rubbed his face and told himself he had to see clearly. Drop the dream state and reevaluate this new reality.

In his mind, he saw Wilkinson face down on the floor of his office with the letter opener in his back. He watched Albright die. He imagined Ulman chased through the tall trees in the mid-highlands of Guatemala until *they'd* caught him.

No. Who can *they* be?

There was no *they*. These guys had the wrong man. Perhaps there *was* someone else hiding in the building. They'd climbed all four floors and already checked the basement levels. They had to be sure he wasn't hiding among the books on the last story. If Porter didn't watch out, he'd probably bump right into the man they hunted! Porter'd be taken hostage. They wouldn't care. Bullets would zing. He'd fall....

Porter bit his lip until he tasted salt. He had to focus, or he was a dead man. It was instinct. These men were too quiet. If they communicated at all, they made no noise of it. They were good, and he didn't want to know how well-trained in the art of killing they were.

Rethinking their entrance, he wondered if they'd really made any sound at all.

These weren't lowly thugs. Their black suede shoes, their leather gloves of the same color—these men didn't fear the act of killing. They didn't do it for the rush an amateur might feel. And there were too many of them.

Two? Three?

Yes, too many...for one miserly bookworm, professor of ancient history wanna-be.

There would be more outside. He slid to the wall and looked through the window at the parking lot.

The kill would be silent. Unless they intended to leave the body, they had to carry him to another location.

To disguise the death? To make it look like natural causes?

Porter was sweating. He wiped it away and kept moving. He knew he was thinking irrationally, and his fear mixed with anger at himself.

Albright's body had been found.

Wilkinson hadn't been moved.

Ulman....

Turning a corner with caution and eyes large enough to roll out of their sockets, Porter thanked himself for putting on his leather Rockports, the black soles of which were comfortable and thick. He made no sound other than the involuntary snare drum of his heart and the growing thunder of his swelling lungs.

He was running out of places to hide.

They were moving.

He had to get to the stairs or the fire door, and if they expected he was here—if they'd been watching and already knew he was hiding among the bookshelves—they would be waiting for him to sprint.

The fire door would be covered at some point by another gunman, if they were as professional as they looked. And there was at least fifteen feet of open space from the main stairway to the nearest wall of bookshelves.

He tasted sweat in the corner of his mouth. The remaining bits of flavorful pistachios turned to gray moss in his teeth.

Holding his breath, he paced from one aisle to another, covering ground in the direction of the main stairs.

He had no idea where they crept now, bent like panthers ready to strike. He knew they'd sniff the air with their ears. They'd stand still, waiting for whatever slight murmur of sound Porter made as he rolled on the balls of his feet as best he could in his dress shoes.

He tightened his hands on the handle of his heavy briefcase and felt the wetness between his fingers, his palm, and the brown leather.

The shelves grabbed his shoe.

He looked down.

The lace on top of his left foot had unraveled itself from his poor knot. He hated penny-loafers, but was now wishing he had a pair.

Glancing up, he saw a shadow on the ground appear from around the side of the bookshelf.

He backed up quickly, eyes moon-shaped, but not watching where he was going. His free hand did the seeing.

The shadow became a man of the same color.

But Porter had stepped out of sight.

He held his breath again and could hear the assassin's air leave his lungs, catch, and slide inside to silence again.

Porter put a bookcase between them, striding fast.

Were the other men just around the next bend in the shelves?

The guy behind him would turn the corner before he would reach the next break in the great bookcases.

Porter spun around and saw the man's subtle shadow hit the shelf as he neared the far end of the bookshelves. The man in black would do the same as Porter had: come to the turn, make a left, swing around and—bang! Porter would hit the ground more loudly than the bullet would when leaving the gun.

There was nowhere to go.

The young scholar looked to heaven, but only saw the ceiling. And the top of the old wooden bookcase.

Only a second now.

Porter climbed the shelves like a ladder, kicking the books in with his feet. No time to think about the damage, the signs he'd leave behind. He only hoped he could make it to the top before the man appeared again. He had to have faith in the impossible chance that the rest of the men wouldn't see him pressing his hands on the ceiling, which floated five feet above shelves. No.

Porter rolled quickly onto the dusty summit, his eyes looking at the ceiling that hung five feet up with cold lights waiting for morning to illuminate them. He clamped his briefcase to his chest and stapled his lips together with the muscles around his mouth. He shut his eyes.

His ears didn't pick up the feet of the aggressor in the alley beneath him. He couldn't sense the breathing he'd heard when the books stood like a wall between them, though they'd been only three feet apart. But he felt the man's rippling presence in the dark light.

Turning his head, Porter could see the florescent light of his desk hitting the ceiling thirty feet away. The beams from the lamps along the stairway walls shined a bright square on the roof twenty-five feet away.

He rolled his head to the side where he felt the assassin…stop. Was the man looking at the books smashed into the shelves…as if someone had used this part of the bookcase as a ladder? Was he feeling the spots were Porter had put his feet and may have left some aura of warmth? Did he point his gun and his eyes at the top of the bookcase and see the faint outline of a human shape?

Porter…waited.

Porter had to find out if the man knew he was there.

He bent his head…to the edge…and he peeked.

The hair was dark and slicked out of the way with gel. The assassin hadn't gone far, which meant he *had* stopped. But with his weapon at waist level, he started walking away.

Porter knew he had to get down. Trapped on the fourth floor, he had to exit the Library.

Lifting himself, Porter swung his leg off the safe side of the bookcase.

His hard rubber heel caught the edge of the wooden shelf with a sharp *crack!*

Porter swung his head back to the assassin.

The man whipped around with his gun raised, his fiery eyes blown wide, his cold mouth in a tight frown.

As Porter launched his weight to the top of the next bookcase, away from the man in black, the gun went off with the chirp of a bird. The bullet struck one of the hanging lights, shooting sparks for a millisecond as metal passed through metal.

Smashing his briefcase into the top of the second bookcase, Porter gripped the wood with his hands, one leg falling off secure ground completely. He pulled himself up, his ears picking up the sound of silent running.

Porter looked at the stairs, so close from here, but so far through the weaving shelves. Such an old fashioned library.

The men were almost around him, however many there were.

Hugging his package tightly, Porter twisted his bottom and top lip together and climbed to a squatting position. Immediately he crouched upward and jumped to the top of the next bookshelf.

Peripheral vision spotted two other men closing in on him.

Landing on the top of the bookcase, his legs kept going, springing him to the next case. Faith screamed *Go, go, go!* And he sprinted, dragging the fingers of one hand on the ceiling for balance, shoving the cheap hanging lights aside with his briefcase as the bullets came.

Three guns went off as he ran, but he soon hit the floor. The stairs were in sight. He dove for them, panting breath he'd forgotten to let out.

Bouncing off the wall, his feet cleared three to four steps at a time before he touched the third floor landing. He kicked his heels high behind him as he leaned forward, running, almost falling into the staircase that made for the second floor.

There's a car out front. It's waiting for you.

Porter toppled down those stairs as a bullet ticked the wall above him.

Then a quick right into the shelves of the second floor.

Fiction. The sign fell over when he hit it.

Great trail you're leaving them! he scolded himself.

But he knew he couldn't go to the first floor. Who knew how many men in black waited at the front door.

He threw himself into the far wall when he reached it and made a left, scraping the plaster with his elbow.

The men behind him moved like flying shadows. They uttered no sound. But he knew they were there. How close behind?

It didn't matter.

There was a window on the second floor that overlooked nothing but a rooftop. Porter had always thought it an architectural stupidity. But what did he know about twentieth-century buildings? Porter had told his friends once that if a thief ever wanted to break into the Stratford Michael H. Weiss Library, they'd need only climb the east side of the building to the window, cut it, and walk in. There were no alarms to his knowledge. The library was open all night, so why would there be? It was an unnecessary window, which didn't even give much light, as the J.T. Fowler Building rose right in front of it.

Porter shattered the glass with his briefcase and slid through. He dropped onto the first story roof and grimaced as the speckles of sharp glass cut into the palms of his hands. Jogging like an old man who'd drunk too much throughout his life, he came to the edge of the roof.

He jumped without a pause.

Chapter Fifteen

April 25
8:51 a.m. PST

"None of you will like this," said Peter as he reached for the play button. "You are listening to a telephone conversation. Ms. Alred, specifically. I'm sure you'll understand the rest."

The room was cold, the way the old executives liked it. They each wore dark cotton suits and leaned against leather backrests, eyeing the young man with his marble skin and perfectly pressed attire. They squinted and glowed with suspicion, distrust, and hungry curiosity. Resting their hands together beside their five-hundred dollar pens and their black computer notebooks, they reached into the tape recording with their minds, analyzing the words for double meanings, worrying they'd hear their doomsday announced in forms the rest of the world weren't even aware of.

The room smelled of age, though the building had stood for less than thirty years. The carpet was gray, the pictures on the walls featuring mostly dead people. They dealt with death daily, when necessary. Very little frightened them. No one knew who they were and no one would ever find them.

Like the fluctuating wind, they always existed. Never seen, but forever felt, even when the populous didn't realize it.

"Yes," said the voice through the unseen speakers set somewhere in the walls.

"Dr. Kinnard?" said Alred.

"Present."

"I don't mean to disturb you," she said.

Peter pushed the pause button on the remote. "She is bothering him of course. We taped this conversation just after midnight this morning."

Click. "Dr. Kinnard?"

"...I'm here."

"I don't know if you'll remember me. Erma Alred. You spoke with me in a meeting with Dr. Masterson concerning my dissertation?"

Pause. "Hello Alred." Cough. "Excuse me. You're not calling about the change in dissertation dates, are you?"

"The fifth of May?" she said, "I heard about that—"

"—cause I have no—"

"I'll deal with it. Dr. Kinnard, I need to ask you—"

"That bad?" he said.

She waited for a minute. "Sorry?"

Sigh. "I'd really like to assist you, Alred—"

"I'm not asking for assistance."

Pause. "Masterson's your supervising professor? You'll have to go to him to get out of the project. Porter doesn't have the same luxury."

"Dr. Kinnard, I believe I have sufficient evidence to stand against Porter's dissertation. I need to compose the data into a formal paper, but I'm not worried about the time shortage."

Pause. "Porter's going to love you."

"On the fifth?" she said. "I'll need armed protection to leave the building! Porter's a fanatic. He finds supporting facts in everything he looks at."

"He presents them well. And he is my friend, Alred."

Silence. "Sorry if I offended you, sir. I don't know quite where I stand on this project."

"You didn't want it in the first place," he said.

She said nothing.

"I saw it in your eyes," said Kinnard. "You're a strong woman, Alred. Composed. You'll make a fabulous professor someday, if that's your goal. Masterson knew well to pit you against Porter. But I admit...I was against your involvement."

Again, silence.

"Alred?"

"I'm here....This was Dr. Masterson's idea?" she said.

But Kinnard didn't answer.

After a moment of unspoken thought, Alred's voice came again through the speaker. "There is a...problem."

"What's that," said Kinnard.

"Forgive me for saying so, but...I've suspected for some time that Porter's been holding out on me. Hiding something he found in the KM-2 codex."

"KM-2?"

"That's what he's dubbed the manuscript."

"Porter seeks brain fights," said Kinnard. "He devises polemics just to get your attention. Then he reels you into his hooked net."

"I've learned that," she said.

"He doesn't hold back information from the battle. He's open about everything. Even lets you argue your side if you've devised a good thesis with impressive facts. The essence of his arguments lies in the many evidences he dumps at you. I think he overdoes it, but...keep something back? Last thing I'd expect."

"I was supposed to pick up KM-2 per an agreement we made a few nights ago. I haven't been able to find him. I figure he's buried himself with the book and his notes where he can best be left alone. I know he needs all the time he can get. While I'm proving current archaeological suppositions he's the one doing his all to say we've been wrong from the beginning."

"Is that what he's doing?" Kinnard said without surprise in his voice. Did he smile as he spoke?

"You're not a Mormon, are you professor?" she asked.

"I'm not. Have you tried Bruno's? Porter's one of their best patrons."

"Mmm. The old man hasn't seen him. It's as if Porter's died or something."

Kinnard said nothing for a time, and Alred's voice also evaporated in thought.

"Anyway, I think he's run off," she said.

"He'll be back," said Kinnard.

"My dissertation, as a refutation to his paper, depends on it! I need KM-2, and he's got it."

Pause.

"Dr. Kinnard?"

"Yes," said the exhausted professor.

"I understand you were friends with Christopher Ulman?"

Silence. "That is right."

"You...haven't heard from him...have you?"

Nothing.

"Dr...Kinnard?"

The tape clicked off.

With eyebrows high, but relaxed, Peter stood upright and said, "Gentlemen, this leaves us with a number of obvious questions."

"I have only one," said an old man with a voice that reverberated in falsetto off the walls. "Peter...did you have Dr. Wilkinson killed?"

"What does that have to do with Alred's call," Peter asked without flinching.

"Answer the question, Peter," said a man from the other side of the long cherry-wood table.

Peter looked at their faces, all wrinkled stone, unmoving Halloween masks that they'd forgotten to remove. Their eyes were dry and deadly. He refused to let them break his peaceful facade. "I wouldn't do that."

"Sure you would, and I think you did," said the first gentleman. His face was as chilled as his voice. "It was sloppy. There were better operatives for the job. Even Polaski should have been smarter than to stake such a crude homicide. The authorities know he's guilty.

"Has he left the states?" said Mr. Smith.

"We authorized nothing. I want to know who had the professor killed!"

Peter did not move.

"At any rate," the old man told Peter, wiping a hand down his silk tie as he leaned back in the red leather seat, "the mess is now yours to clean up. You've done a poor job so far it seems."

"Where is Porter now?" said Andrews across the table.

Peter swallowed, but kept it silent. "I was informed before I came in that Porter had been located. We are moving in. We'll have him in moments."

"Peter, the matter is yours. It results in your success or your death... do you understand?" said the gentleman at the far end.

"I have other measures that can be taken," Peter said, unshaken outside, heart palpitations within.

"Sure."

* * *

Porter's leg was wet, which meant he still was bleeding.

The glass had done more damage than he had thought. For hours, he'd held the wound with his hands as he briskly walked through the night. In the parking lot he'd found someone waiting in black clothing not far from his car, which meant no ride home but a long walk instead. Only when he reached his apartment a couple of hours before dawn did he realize someone would be waiting there as well.

How did they know who he was? How did they know he was in the library? Who were *they* anyway?

No answers came that night, and the light brought no comfort.

He walked six blocks south of the campus and found a motel to sleep in. They wouldn't give him the $29.00 room until after eleven o'clock that morning, and he suspected they were calling the owner to tell them about the beat-up college student who'd come for a room just after sunrise. Admittedly peculiar, but he had to hide out. He had to sleep. Even if it was only for a couple hours. Even if it cost him nearly thirty bucks.

But he couldn't rest.

He washed the glass out of his palms and removed his slacks, thankful that the navy color had hidden the blood. The gash on his leg really was minor, but deep enough to require medical attention. It could have been much worse and ten times more painful. He showered before sitting on the bed. Under the covers, he found his head turning involuntarily to the rotary phone made of cream-colored plastic under the lamp on the nightstand.

He needed to call someone. The police? Yes. But what would he tell them? Who was after him? Why? It would only delay his work, and he had too much to do and less than thirteen days to finish it. A formal investigation would mean...Porter wouldn't graduate.

He'd rather amputate his leg.

But he couldn't stop looking at the phone.

Call Kinnard, he thought.

But what could Kinnard do? How would it help? What was Porter looking for, sympathy?

He couldn't call his family...that would cause more stress to everyone.

Alred? She'd probably serve him up to the men in black saying at the same time, "Would you like something to drink with this?" She would grin and sigh as they hauled him into their black van and shot him in the back of the head.

He had to sleep.

In the drawer he found a green Bible. He turned to Leviticus, but found the law too interesting. He flipped to Isaiah, but saw too many similarities with his own time. He hit himself in the head with the book. Reading wouldn't help. He'd read all night before running, and was now beyond exhaustion.

But he did fall asleep without realizing it.

It was 5:07 in the evening before he woke up to go to the bathroom. His leg burned when he moved, and the wound opened. He needed butterfly bandages at the very least. What would they say at the main desk if he asked for their first aid kit? He couldn't find one anywhere in his room.

He crept out of the motel like a mouse poking his head out of his hole in the wall checking to see if the room is clear. Scurrying, he went to the front desk and gave them the key. Before they signed him out, Porter took it back. The $29.00 he'd slammed down in cash gave him privilege to a full twenty four hours, which implied eleven o'clock the next morning. He might need a place to sleep. Porter decided against asking for bandages.

That was days ago. It seemed like weeks.

Taking a route behind the buildings, Porter came to his apartment and slid through the rear entrances into his room. He smelled sour milk and an opened vacuum cleaner bag.

They'd already been here. His books were off the particleboard shelves. The file cabinets were open and files carpeted the hardwood floor, the coffee table, and his short couch of gray tweed that should have been thrown away a long time ago (and actually had been before he'd acquired it). All the closets had been emptied. Clothes, memorabilia from Japan, even the Jerusalem pictures from the wall had been tossed to the ground. Light from the open refrigerator spilled over the vomited contents. There was no place to walk.

If they were watching the apartment still, expecting him to come back, they'd move in now. The thought jolted Porter like electricity. He'd been foolish.

Grabbing his black jacket of suede, which was mostly rubbed away and turning green because of the many times he'd left it in the back of his car, Porter left his room and went for the stairs to climb to the roof.

He heard the elevator ding.

He heard the people behind him.

It didn't mean anything for certain, but he wouldn't take the chance. In his youth he'd seen too many adventure shows not to have a thousand ideas streaming through his head.

But he was trapped on the roof.

A twilight fog filled the air, transparent enough to see the thunderheads twisting above it, thick enough to feel as it brushed against his arm as he put on his jacket,.

That's when *they* moved in. He saw them from the top of the building. Multiple new sedans with beautiful shines screeched into the parking lot. He pulled his head away from sight when they looked up. They knew Porter had arrived. Why had he returned? Was his life supposed to go back to the way it was or something? His head was clouded and he knew they would figure out he'd gone to the roof.

Porter ran to each side and looked down. It was twenty feet and one story to the closest building. No escape.

A tree reached for his height. The top of the swaying Eucalyptus stretched to four feet from the reach of his fingers. Porter could probably jump and hit the tree, but Eucalyptuses were notorious for their brittle branches. Every storm with a heavy wind cut a major limb away. And they had to be trimmed regularly for they grew five times faster than most trees. If he jumped, he'd touch the limbs and they'd crumble into kindling beneath his weight.

But leaping off a building was idiotic!

Porter's leg began to throb, a wet drizzle running for his toes. He knew the wound still hadn't sealed. He'd stretched too much. He was ruining his chance of losing the scar. But that mattered little all of a sudden.

Black nine-millimeters. Silencers. The image of them in the library froze like master works of marble in his head, firm testimonies that they wanted him dead.

Why?!?

Porter looked at the door. He could look for something to pin the portal shut. But with their weapons? Their boldness and fearlessness of consequences? Their silent attack? They'd break through and have him in three seconds.

What was Porter to them?

What was Ulman?

What was Wilkinson?

What was Albright?

He didn't know. How did Wilkinson fit in at all?!? Porter only figured the old man had to be involved.

There was something going on that Porter didn't understand. And it had something to do with…

He dropped his eyes to his briefcase.

… the codex…?

Question: How did it enter the country? Illegally.

Question: Did it rightfully belong to someone? It had to.

Question: Was it worth killing for?

He pulled KM-2 out of the leather case and hefted it in his hands as the cold wind picked up. A priceless artifact—more priceless to him as his entire future rested upon it! And what secrets had he yet to uncover? What religious ramifications did it have?

They killed Albright, Porter said to himself, thinking of the KM-1 codex the professor had written about and most likely possessed. Albright didn't own it anymore.

He heard Alred's scolding, *Albright died of natural causes!*

Porter took the codex out of the brown sack he'd wrapped it in. He stared at it, barely able to fit in its wrappings.

He shot his eyes to the door repeatedly.

What was he doing? The world went gray. His hands moved on their own. He zipped up his jacket to the collar, feeling the tightness in his chest. He gazed at the precious notes still in the briefcase. Could he hide them? Come back for—

The door blew open with an easy push.

A long overcoat of black wool covered the first man Porter saw. The rest of his clothes were the same and very expensive, the turtleneck, the slacks, the shoes. His eyes were cold and just as dark, though Porter didn't see the color. They locked gazes instantly.

"Stay away!" Porter said, holding up the stuffed grocery bag of brown paper. "I'll throw it over!"

"Of course, John," said the man in black on this haze-covered rooftop, his voice comfortable as ice is in the arctic. "Set it down nicely... and you can walk away."

Porter froze at the sound of his first name. It was the same sensation he'd had when the first girl he loved had called his name in the halls of the Junior High. But instead of his heart swelling with light, it imploded into a darkness he didn't know he could feel. "No chance!"

The first man walked casually toward him, but not slowing, a second man only footsteps behind. Both drew their poisonous stingers, silencers ready.

With his briefcase in one hand and the sacred package in the other, Porter turned to the edge of the building.

They would execute him either way.

Don't think. It was the key he'd learned when leaping off of high dives. If you think at all, you won't do it.

His feet left the solid building and his arms waved in open space.

His hands instinctively reached for the weak top of the Eucalyptus tree.

He grabbed.

His fingers held as his weight yanked on the green wood.

His briefcase dumped away from him, his wrapped treasure left in the wind.

He glanced down as the tree bent.

The papers scattering. His pads, his translations, his many notes flew like yellow birds and white rain down, to the right, and in one direction which he couldn't see.

Too late for all that.

The tree crackled as it leaned.

The Eucalyptus popped like illegal fireworks, and the limb tore free, immediately hitting other branches as he went down. His arms flailed about in the air. His legs kicked, and the tree slapped him until his eyes shut. He latched onto the cold wood, but didn't feel it. The ground was coming.

He heard his briefcase crash into the empty parking spaces below.

He caught a glimpse of the codex landing flat, creating its own thunderclap as the paper exploded to a degree Porter couldn't determine.

Pain erupted from his fingers as branch smashed branch with his appendages caught in-between. He cried out, but left the tree and hit the ground hard enough to knock the wind out of him.

Bullets hit the black asphalt as Porter fought his way to his feet.

Landing nowhere around his belongings, he commanded himself in the direction of cover and flew as fast as if the bullets were tagging him in the back, shoving him along.

If he was hit, he didn't realize it.

They had it all, now. He could only hope the chase was over.

The cold wind danced in circles over the brown paper bag sighing with the pages within, waiting to be picked up by the men in black.

Chapter Sixteen

April 26
3:57 p.m. PST

"So you've decided to rise from the dead!"

Porter leaned against Alred's door frame a different man than the one Alred had met two weeks earlier. His slacks sagged, two rips in his right pant leg. The shine in his black shoes had been put out. His simple hair hung, unwashed and sticky. Both eyelids were welts through which he peered at her, and white bandages wrapped around both hands.

Alred didn't even know he owned a leather jacket. She never would have guessed Porter could dress himself in something worn so badly at the shoulders and the elbows. What did he do, sleep in it? The building was well-heated, but he kept it zipped to his collar bones anyway. She imagined his conservative button-down shirt fit the rest of his nasty attire.

"The zombies walk," he said. "Are you alone?"

"I hate zombie movies. How did you find my address?" She walked into her tidy room while Porter closed the door behind him. Her dissertation would be ten times better with the codex in her hand, so she played along, preparing for some ecstatic lie explaining his costume and more pointedly, his crime.

"Followed you home yesterday," he said.

She looked at him, huffing silently that she was right. He'd been here all along.

"Anybody looking for me?" said Porter, looking at the glowing twenty-gallon fish tank on his right, three half-dollar sized crabs wiggling their small legs beneath two diving goldfish with bulging eyes.

"Dr. Arnott came by yesterday," said Alred. "He said he had some information for your ears alone." She didn't hide the suspicion in her eyes. "What would that be?"

Porter fell onto her heavily pillowed couch just past the fish tank. "Mind if I sit down," he asked, staring at something many dimensions away with concentrating eyes. The room smelled of rose potpourri. Pink, dusty rose, and burgundy colors dominated.

"I went by your office every day," she said, getting a glass from the cupboard. She opened the refrigerator, pulled out a pitcher, and poured.

"I never went to the office."

"One of the secretaries let me in," she said, handing him the glass, sitting beside him, watching as he examined the translucent brown liquid. "Thought I'd…take a look at KM-2."

"You brought a screwdriver then," he said, smiling a tired grin and smelling the drink. "Wasn't in the vent, was it. What is this."

"Iced tea."

Handing it back to her, Porter said, "Can't drink it. Water?"

Alred felt her muscles clench. She took the glass, stood, and went to the sink where she dumped the mixture and rinsed out the vessel. She refused to let loose the irritation she felt building. Redirecting the energy, she pondered what to ask next. Where had he been? What did he think he was doing hoarding their precious book? Didn't he know she could get him into further trouble with the university if he thought he could—

"Someone tried to kill me," Porter said. "I think they were after the codex."

She handed him the new drink and sat on the pillowy lazyboy chair opposite the couch. "You…expect me to believe that line?" The words just came out. Oh, well. She'd take responsibility for them and find out what was going on.

Then a voice, a vision, a memory, spoke where the brain meets the spine. *You're in danger…and so is your friend.* Her back bone reacted involuntarily, sitting her upright with an icy touch.

Porter told her what had happened after she'd left the library.

He explained it all: the bookshelves, pushing the lights out of the way as he skipped across the tops of the cases dodging bullets; breaking through the glass on the second floor; hiding in the hotel. When he came to the experience on the roof of his apartment, Alred was amazed at the detail in his story. He jumped to the tree? Dropped everything? Escaped professional gunmen? From which movie did Porter steal these pictures?

"I think you have a very active imagination, Porter," she said.

The shock on his face froze like cooling clay. "Go look, Alred, the Eucalyptus on the side of the building is busted in two places! They still haven't cleaned it up!"

"There's been a storm the last few days," she said in a flat voice, pushing the hair behind her right ear.

"What does that have to do with anything?" he said.

Alred leaned back in her chair. "Eucalyptus trees on campus always drop a limb here or there when the winds pick up enough. I don't doubt there are branches in the parking lot next to your apartment, but how can I believe everything else you said?" Her voice was strong, and she meant it to be. She wanted him to know she wouldn't be pushed around anymore. This was turning out to be her least favorite semester at Stratford, her only consolation being the knowledge that she'd be done in two weeks.

Porter stared at her. A single flickering light hid deep inside his gray eyes.

Alred watched him close. What was this look he gave her? Abashed hope? Abandonment? He looked like her last dog, Vespucci, that gaze when she'd left him with new owners. She saw those dark eyes looking at her through the screen, watching her say good-bye for the final time. There was no way the animal would know she'd never return. But she felt Vespucci's confusion, happy hope, questions, worry…sadness? Or did she project all those feelings.

Porter was human.

He looked into her for almost thirty seconds before reaching down his right side.

Alred looked at his busy fingers, working up the soiled and torn pant leg.

Close to the knee she saw a cut, taped up poorly with medical tape. No bandage. The wound had a thick black scab glistening with hints of red which had already assimilated portions of the white tape.

"I don't know…it might need stitches. Real glass doesn't shatter like it does in the movies. I thought it best to do it this way to help seal the gash."

Alred looked at his bandaged hands, then up at his face. She felt the blood leave her head and her tension release. Her mind went into overdrive, running through his story, collating the hard pieces, the ones that mattered. She heard the whisper of the ghost who had visited her the night Porter started running. Her unpainted lips parted. She pictured the smashed codex on the pavement and the men in black apparel sprinting for it, and Porter scurrying away like a maimed animal.

"You...left...KM-2?" she said, eyes gawking, but only seeing the image of the ancient book shredded on the asphalt.

He nodded, fixing his pants. "For them. I lost all my notes."

"Who cares about your notes! Porter?! How could you give them the codex?!"

Relaxed, he said, "I think I can still remember the bulk of the important things. I'll have to find it all again, to be sure I'm citing correctly."

Alred's brain did a somersault and then a few more tricks. Her heart beat like a runner's as she put all the insinuated pieces together, all the parts of this jigsaw with too many holes.

"You didn't have the codex, so you weren't in danger," Porter said, lifting a finger to remind her he'd insinuated this point before.

In danger, said the ghost in her head.

"What?" she said, staring at the fish tank radiating a blue light on Porter's left, then at a painting of two Eskimos boarding an *umiak* on a cold river.

"That's what I think, anyway. I stayed in a motel while they no doubt tore up Stratford trying to find me," he said, unzipping his jacket.

"But you said—" her eyes locked onto the bent book he removed from the hot cavity between the black suede and his stomach. The bark paper crumbled in front of her, small pieces dropping to the floor.

"I need a bag, a box or something, before this is completely ruined," Porter said, looking at her kitchen.

Like a hawk high in the air, she imagined herself viewing the codex on the black asphalt days before. She dived straight at it, and like a microbe went instantly through the brown grocery bag to reveal the notes and newspaper he'd stuffed in place of the codex.

Jumping to her feet, she pulled open a drawer to the right of the oven, whipped out a large freezer bag with the handy plastic zip-seal, another brown paper bag from the side of the refrigerator where others were stuffed, and a disposable hand towel from the roll hanging to the left of the stove. When she returned to her chair, Porter had carefully placed the Mesoamerican document on the glass coffee table.

They mummified it gently but firmly with the paper towel, placed it into the plastic bag, and slowly pushed the excess air out before sealing it and putting it into the brown bag. They wrapped the bag into a tight book shape before looking at each other again.

"I have something...that might give us a few answers," Alred heard herself say. She didn't know why she was opening up to him all of a sudden. Because he was honest? Because he came to her *with the codex*, while he still suspected his life in danger? Or because she knew she had to have KM-2, which, if his suspicions were correct, meant she was in as much peril as he had been the past five days. "We've gotta meet again with Mrs. Ulman."

"How can she help us?" said Porter.

"Trust me, Porter, we have little to go on!"

"All right," he said, putting up his hands.

* * *

5:02 p.m. PST

A moment later, Alred knocked on the door of the Ulman residence while Porter scanned the street with a grimace on his face, fearful of seeing anyone.

"Mrs. Ulman?" Alred said to the door after hearing movement. "It's Erma Alred."

"Go away!"

It was an exhausted shriek which turned Porter's head.

"If you don't let us in, you're going to have two dead students on your doorstep when you open to collect your morning paper," said Alred. She looked down at the unpruned rosebushes, spiny vines about to take over the small concrete porch while letting loose a seductive scent from its pink flowers. She tried to push her gaze through the door to see the trembling woman on the other side, but all she saw was crumbling white paint and the hunter green paint from years past peering back at her.

Porter smiled, stunned.

"I said—"

Alred cut her off with the words, "Mrs. Ulman, I have some information I think your husband needed to give you." She spoke quickly. "And I have something you need to see. We're not leaving!"

Mrs. Ulman opened the door and stepped back as if she expected an attack.

Alred closed the door behind them, locking the bolt.

"We're not going to hurt you, ma'am," Porter said, "We just have a few questions, and it's imperative that you answer."

Alred followed them into the front room, but they didn't sit. Boxes everywhere overflowed with personal belongings. Mrs. Ulman was moving by the looks of things. She looked terrified, her face melting with sorrow, her eyes vibrant, touching the windows, the halls, the closed doors visible from the room.

Alred widened her eyes. "Is he here?!"

"No one's here, and I'd like you to leave!"

"Is *who* here," Porter asked to Alred.

"Have you seen your husband," Alred said, trying to relax. Her eyes skipped to every point Ulman glanced to.

"I told you last time you came. I don't have any more information," she fell into her chair, tears racing down her cheeks in two lines.

Porter frowned at Alred and put a hand on her arm as if to hold her back. He looked at Mrs. Ulman and said in a quiet voice, "I'm sorry if we've frightened you. Someone's been trying very hard to steal our work on your husband's find."

"Like you stole it from him?" said Mrs. Ulman.

Porter pulled back. "We were assigned this project."

Alred knew that was an exaggeration of the situation, but didn't feel safe enough to play games.

Alred reached into her pocket. "Do you recognize this key?" She held it up.

Mrs. Ulman stared at it with drying eyes.

"Look closer," Alred said, handling the metal carefully so as not to scare the woman. Mrs. Ulman had been through a lot the last few months. Who knew what she'd been crying over before they'd arrived.

0417-2105.

"It looks like my husband's post office box," she said. "But it can't be, there's only one key." She stood and went to her bedroom while they waited. A moment later, she appeared with a similar key with different numbers. There was no air in her voice. "You're not trying to tell me he had more than one box."

Alred eyed the dark-haired woman for a moment in silence, considering. "I had a visitor a few nights ago. Someone whose face I didn't see. Actually, I wasn't sure anyone'd been in the room at all. But the man gave me this key…and I thought it was…your husband, Mrs. Ulman."

She stood like a woman with a gun shoved in her back.

"I don't…know anything," she said in a lonely voice.

"I accuse you of nothing, ma'am, I'm only trying to find out why someone is trying to kill John here and why your husband would visit me under cover of shadows in order to give me a key and a warning," said Alred.

Porter stared at his companion's energized eyes, which never flinched, though she could feel his attention. He had a lot of questions, no doubt, but she'd answer none of them now.

"Who knows what I saw; I thought it was a dream, but here is the key," Alred said, snatching it, and holding its solid form between their faces. "*This* is real."

"I can't help you," Mrs. Ulman said, sitting slowly on the couch, crowded already with the boxes and a menagerie of photo albums, fake plant parts, worn holistic books, and a fallen stack of novels with bent spines. She stared at the fireplace with blank eyes.

"*He* said…to tell you he was all right," said Alred looking at the carpet.

Porter squinted at her.

"And that you would understand what this key is about."

Did Mrs. Ulman hear her? Her eyes ran up and down the cracks in the cement under the mantle, measuring the stones set in the wall. She listened to the birds singing in the leafless oaks outside the glass door, watched them with the corner of her eye, dancing down to the porch, searching for spilled seed. Clouds still grayed the sky, shaking the glass pane with a rumble of thunder.

"It's...not a post office box," she said through the quiet of a storm miles away but closing in. "Go to the West Federal Bank on Cedar Parkway. It fits the safe deposit box there."

Licking the inside of his mouth, Porter looked at the two of them, one at a time. His voice was as calm as he could make it. "Mrs. Ulman, a bank won't let anyone into a secured box without identification. That person also has to have preapproval on a signature card created when the box was opened for the customer."

Alred looked at him.

He shrugged his shoulders. "I worked at a bank while studying for my undergraduate degree."

"There's more," said Mrs. Ulman. "My husband has a friend... at West Federal. Jack Bean. He opened the box for Chris...under the name Jonothon U. Swift. My husband must have mailed something to Jack directly. I'll have to call ahead. Ask for Mr. Bean. He'll be waiting to let you in."

"Do me a favor, Mrs. Ulman," said Porter, touching her arm as they stood to leave. "Give us twenty minutes before calling."

Mrs. Ulman stared at him in silence.

Outside, Porter tried to get the key from Alred.

"We're going to stay alive, right?" she said, keeping the key in her pocket and a hot fist over it.

"I've done okay so far," he said.

"Keep doing it. Write all you can for your dissertation. Father Time is dying early this year. Besides, they'll still be looking for you. With some luck, I won't be followed. Let me take care of KM-2. And I'll get to the box."

Porter wisely didn't argue.

Chapter Seventeen

April 26
6:03 p.m. PST

"We intercepted this letter this morning," said Peter, passing out copies. "It's important to realize that Porter never received this, but it does indicate the direction he's heading. You'll notice the letterhead of the Federal Bureau of Investigations."

The gentlemen lifted the paper and squinted through glasses that didn't reflect the florescent light glowing above the table.

"The letter accompanied portions of a file I didn't feel inclined to copy…because we already have it." Returning to his briefcase, open at the end of the long table, Peter lifted the file and read the name on the top: "Christopher Eugene Ulman, Ph.D."

"A file from the FBI on Dr. Ulman?"

"As you will find in the letter, Porter has a friend in the bureau," Peter said.

With their noses to the paper, they read.

To: John D. Porter
RE: Christopher Ulman, Ph.D.

John,

I wondered what it took to get you to write? The last time you contacted me, you sent a postcard of a Southern California Christmas. That wasn't a real Christmas, you know. The holidays and beach sand are contradictory in my book.

Anyway, I didn't get your letter until it sat in my box for a few days. I've been a little busy out here. You'd love to know what I'm doing! But you also know I can't reveal a thing.

I can tell you Jennifer is pregnant again. She's never been sicker, and you know all I can do is back rubs and fetch things…when I'm home!

—Sorry, you wouldn't know about that yet. Get married, Porter. I won't bother trying to convince you to drop your scholastic emphasis again. But you'll still finish, you know, it just might take a little longer. Look at me! Then again, I suppose you know what's best for you. If you don't, I sure do!

Well, that will be four for us. Cameron is doing fine in kindergarten. He's a little peeved that he has to do homework—can you believe that? Not even in the first grade yet! If you ask me, television is the bane of parents when it comes to a child's education. You probably don't agree with me, but I think it's on the screen that homework receives a bad rep. Cameron's a smart kid. He's been tested at a third grade reading level, and he downs books like you drink hot chocolate! They're elementary level books, of course. Jill can't get enough of them from the library! The other tikes are wonderful. You don't know what you're missing.

Take a look at the file.

I took the liberty of noticing Ulman's connection with your university and his focus on ancient American archaeology. It didn't take Special Agent training to figure you have more than a professional interest in his work.

According to the database, it seems your old friend, the professor, is being sought by the United States Marshals and the Customs office. Most of our file contains details of a missing person.

If you know where he is, John, I'd talk him into coming in.

Well, I've done my work now. You owe me one, and

you can start by telling me your real middle name. Be thankful I let you play this game. I could gather data on you, you know, and tell everyone the truth at the mission reunion next October.

Call me sometime.

Ato de, hen na yatsu,

Stan Clusser

"What does this mean at the end," said one of the old men concerning the words before the typed signature.

"Japanese," said Peter. "The best translation I found was '*See ya later, weirdo.*'"

"Porter's link with the FBI is too close," said the old man on the end, laying the paper down, perfectly square on another manila file. "This thorn could jeopardize our entire project."

"Actually," said Andrews, leaning forward and smiling with gray teeth, "This thorn will bring forth roses. Nothing could be more beautiful."

"How so," said Smith as other quiet eyes waited like silver balls ready to fire from black cannons.

"Porter is doing our work for us." The old man didn't need to say anything else.

The minds in the room stormed in silence, churning possibilities and probable outcomes.

A light went on behind Peter's eyes, and his faced warmed, but he struggled to keep the sight hidden. With calm hands placed on the edge of his closed briefcase, he said, "We give Porter slack—"

Everyone turned their gazes on the presumptuous man whose years were merely half their own.

"Just a little," Peter added, raising a relaxed finger. "The faster Porter flees, the more he'll kick up the dirt around him. The dust will choke all those looking on. Porter is a fanatical Mormon with enough eccentric energy to become a sore thumb in his church. He'll bring the whole world pounding down on him."

"Or...break it all to pieces," said Andrews with slow words, quoting the line from Shakespeare's *Henry V.*

Peter took a breath that made him stand even more upright. "Porter is one…and when his use is up, he will die."

* * *

8:48 p.m. PST

Porter shifted in his seat as if a million termites under his clothes thought he was made of wood. He felt like a spy…or a fugitive. Thank goodness for the rain!

With the collar of his coat up, no one would recognize him…he hoped.

He'd already been to the library to get the books he needed, slipping in and out without a word or a glance of his eye to anyone. Where to then? Another motel? He couldn't afford it. He was already dead and buried in loans. And he wasn't used to studying in such tight quarters. His mind spun a hundred tales of men smashing in the door and filling him with deadly darts from silent guns. He had to hide in public. Bruno's was out. If they'd found him in the library, they'd probably find him there.

But Porter couldn't toss the feeling that they'd come after him by mistake. So why hide KM-2 and drop what the codex had been wrapped in? They wouldn't know what snugly waited in the brown bag. He'd gotten away as they scurried like Japanese cockroaches to the bait.

Why hadn't Clusser replied yet? Porter thought, rubbing his face. Or was Porter simply out of touch. Alred had checked his mail, but told him on the phone she'd found nothing important; no personal letters at all.

This was no matter for authorities.

It would all go away…in time.

He didn't have the minutes he needed to read the papers to see if anyone had noticed what had happened in the library a week ago. He had to study.

Looking up he examined with red eyes the dusty cafe around him.

Certainly was quieter than Bruno's, but too far from the university for any students to frequent. That's why he'd decided to hide out here. He'd stay, eating and drinking amid the heaps of books and growing mass of notes, until they pushed him out.

George C. Richter's *Tales from the Amu* stared up at him from beneath four yellow pages of his scribbles relating three parallel stories Porter had found. With a brown copy of *Von den Bedouinen des Altertums*, by Walther Molin, Tha-labai's *Qisas al-Anbiya*, and of course John L. Burckhardt's, *Notes on the Bedouins and Wahabys* (an oldie, but…you know), Porter wondered if he was heading up the wrong ladder. He had theories only, and as often was the case, none of the scholars agreed with him, which really didn't matter. It was the essence of scholarship: to break traditional ideas in favor of the truth. Unless of course the truth existed in the old conclusions.

"Can I get you anything…else, sir?" said the waitress.

Porter looked at her as if he'd never seen her before. A gold tag read: Michelle. Black hair with a shine. White teeth and auburn skin that would be prune texture in about fifteen years because of sun exposure.

"No," he said, unsure of her message until he mentally played it back. "Yes! Do you have pretzels?"

"To go with your hot chocolate?" she said, leaning with her hip cocked. He'd already had a full pitcher's worth, and she'd seen him go to the bathroom twice, leaving his table hidden beneath a flotsam of falling papers and dirty volumes. He'd buried his mug once and taken at least fifteen seconds to find it when she'd come about the twentieth time to see if he wanted dinner. He'd ordered fries. And ranch dressing on the side.

"Please." His head bobbed back to his books as if she'd already left. With a shake of her head, she disappeared.

Porter didn't worry about her, or what the manager might hear. He had to make positive the links he already supposed he'd found in the codex. If he couldn't prove the relation between the Kalpa Manuscript and the Near East, which Albright and Peterson insinuated strongly, his dissertation would be seen as a flop. He had a certain distasteful, but respected, reputation to keep.

And Alred? Porter couldn't figure her out, but suspected she wasn't all with him in the project. For example, what was her thesis? Why weren't they writing the same paper? Yes, yes, they were separate Ph.D's, but why all the secrecy on her part. She didn't try to hide anything from him, but her constant defensive posture confused him. And her offensive stance against the chance that Ulman's find had a relation to the Book of Mormon? Perhaps she hid a religious fear and not an academic one.

"My father died that way."

Porter heard these words. He couldn't help but be quick to hear anything related to death, since it seemed a horrible possibility at present.

Over the bench in front of him, Porter could see an old man in a suit sitting alone with a cup of something hot. The eyes, aged with the wisdom of the Greeks and surrounded in similar wrinkles, waited patiently on him.

"I'm sorry, are you—"

"Talking to you?" said the fellow, glancing into his cup. "You're the only one who heard me!"

Porter looked down at his notes. It seemed that an ant farm had broken open over his papers and ceased living; all the words were unreadable, a mess only. His heart skipped to a start and pounded like a newborn's.

"Don't have to listen," said the old man, sipping loudly. "Didn't mean to push my emotions on you. Sometimes they rise to the brim and can't be contained, I suppose."

"Know what you mean," Porter mumbled.

"Worked himself to death," said the stranger. "Just stayed out, away from the family, forming regrets he wouldn't have a chance to remedy. He drank, but not too much. Some people hide in bottles. He hid in books."

Taking a breath, Porter looked up at the old man and relaxed a little. The guy was probably just lonely. He didn't look drunk, and his well-pressed Brione of dark Italian fabric meant he was a man of wealth and possible importance. So his head was on somewhat straight. Why wasn't he home with his family. Like father, like son?

The doctoral candidate went back to work, and this time the words on the pages made sense. He needed to rest. He dropped a pad to one side and scanned the index of Molin's volume with hungry fingers and furious eyes.

"He was a attorney. But you look more like a student."

"You also a lawyer? You're very perceptive," said Porter without looking up.

The old man chuckled lightly. "I may be foolish, but...I learned not to follow the path of my forefathers."

"How untraditional," Porter said, scribbling on his pad before sticking his mechanical pencil in his mouth.

"Sometimes tradition is a bad thing. Old things die, and they must. Things in the past should be left alone."

"I'm a historian and therefore have to disagree." Porter said through the pencil. His eyes never left his books. Peripheral vision told Porter's brain that the old man hadn't moved, but continued to sip the steaming liquid. "Simple point. Elementary, my dear Watson."

"Doyle never wrote that, you know," said the fellow.

Porter looked up with honest curiosity coloring his face. "Really?"

The old man nodded, but didn't make eye contact with the student. "Created later in what I would call *The Further Fabrications of Sherlock Holmes*."

"Has a good ring to it," Porter said, returning to the index.

"I can think of no job more difficult than yours," said the old man

"I can think of many more difficult jobs!"

"Columbus."

"What about him," said Porter with little enthusiasm in his tone.

"The most hated man in America, and the only hated man we celebrate once a year."

"Depends on who you talk to," Porter said.

"I speak with *Time*."

Porter looked at him. He pointed at the old man with his pencil, "An English teacher, right?"

A gentle shake of the head.

"Back to your father, are we?" said Porter.

"I watch the years come and go. Same as everyone else, though *time* usually gets in people's way. They hate it and try to paddle against it's mighty current. That's what you're doing. Don't have much time, do you. That's only because *time* is your enemy. If it were with you, you would always win!"

"I've beaten time before," Porter said, working faster because of the conversation, but gaining little ground.

"You have won battles, like many of us. We win a fight with Time and call ourselves *successful*, when in reality we are but shortsighted oafs afraid to face the truth."

"*We?*" said Porter, looking up again. "You lump yourself in with the miserable?

"I meant *you*, in the plural of course."

"Sure. And what's the truth?" Porter returned to his work, expecting nothing profound.

"That *you* are losing the war. A few battles to speak of, but in the end…stress, unhappiness, bad health…death."

"You always such pleasant company?" Porter said, scratching behind his ear with the mechanical pencil, but not lifting his focus.

"I prefer to be grave only when I must be."

"And this evening you feel you have a divine calling to be the bringer of bad news to me?"

The old man stood, leaving a couple dollars protruding from beneath his mug.

Porter looked up as the man put on his black gloves.

The man's face was the same off-white of the moon in a Halloween haze. His mouth, a ridged crease. His eyes the same. He stood perfectly straight; a gentleman, a model magnate, just what every young lawyer would hope to look like in old age; power in his blood, dignity for a skeleton behind his face, posture…perfect.

"Relax a little. You'll live longer," said the old man.

"I have a deadline that will shatter my life if I fail."

"No one has what you describe. Each man and woman has just what they wish for. Everyone is bound to get what they really *want*. Some people want to lose a little weight, but they want to rest in front of the television after work more than they want to exercise. Or in other words, they want one thing, but want other things to a greater degree. So they get what they really search for. Your life is no exception. No matter what crucial moment is coming, you can always rise again if you land on your face."

The philosopher picked up his heretofore unseen briefcase from the side of his booth while Porter watched.

"Make time your friend. Use it to gain knowledge. Don't fight for what you cannot have right away."

Porter pinched his eyes tight. "What are you saying?"

The old man smiled, and his whole form became human for an

instant. "Don't rush things. You can always get into another university." He turned and went for the door, leaving Porter with his dazed eyes fixed on the spot where the man had just been sitting.

As if the manager had hit the ejection button, Porter flew out of his seat and through the door, chasing after the gentleman.

In the shadows, he saw the man's pristine stride. No swing, one hand in his pocket, the other on the briefcase.

"You know me," Porter said, walking up behind the man, "Don't you." He kept a good fifteen feet between them, realizing he may have just been lured into the open for a reason. His eyes scanned the dark street, the ebony windows of the shops across the wet road, the other pedestrians strolling in the cool drizzle.

The old man stopped. He turned. He stared through the blackness filling his eye sockets. But he said nothing.

"What do you want with me!" said Porter.

The old man considered the words. "You're contacting the FBI. Don't meet with them."

"Why not," Porter said, feeling the icy moisture from above slowly seep through his cotton shirt.

"I realize there is no way you can understand, *Mr. Porter*. You'll have to believe me."

"Got a reason?" said Porter, his heart running mad in his chest.

"You trusted your mother didn't you? When you were a child and she told you not to touch the frying pan on the hot stove? You'd burned yourself on things already; children do. You took her word for it and saved your fingers."

"That happens to every kid."

"But *this* doesn't."

"We going to talk about your father again, or was that just a fabrication." Porter was serious.

"You've fallen into a rat race," said the old man who seemed to smile in the shadow. "There is only one...way...out."

"Your way." Porter's lungs pumped as if he were being chased again.

"The eccentric school boy in you has been able to say and do many things the world didn't appreciate because there are ethical boundaries to which all scholars must submit. You've gained a name for yourself among those in your field, and that's admirable. Gain a reputation with those in my business...and you're dead."

"How do you know about me?"

"Oh, Mr. Porter! I know more than you think! You were born in American Fork, Utah in 1963, and you *are* a Mormon. Oldest of seven children, you hated your father until he died while you served your church in Japan. Your sole motivation has been to prove your father wrong...because he always shot down your aspirations."

Porter swallowed hard.

"Your mother...is still alive, as are your siblings, who are *all* married. You know you've been a poor example to them, which is why you rarely if ever contact them. You are six-one, one hundred and sixty-eight pounds, and have a stork-bite on the back of your neck that never went away. I've studied your profile for some time. *I even know your real middle name*, Mr. Porter, that which you so carefully hide from everyone you meet. I already said you're in a rat race. That makes you the small animal everyone's watching. You're in trouble, and I've no more time to waste with you. Don't meet with the FBI."

"That's like telling a bank teller not to call the cops when you're robbing him."

"Do it, Mr. Porter...and you *will* see blood spill."

"I'll follow the path I think is best."

"Exactly what they expect, Mr. Porter. And that is how the race will end. You'll fail any chance to graduate from Stratford, the opportunity to prove your church true will slip away, you'll lose the codex you *still* have hidden, and your friends will die. No need to panic about them of course, because you will meet them in Paradise yourself!"

The old man nodded once, turned, and walked away.

Chapter Eighteen

April 28
4:31 p.m.

"Bernard Heidenstam, you old traitor, I see you've finally made captain!"

Bruno turned around and faced the infidel leaning against the bar. He wiped a wet hand on the front of his Corona Beer T-shirt and squinted his eyes at the old man in the dark suit of gray tweed. "Benjamin Andrews? So you didn't die after all!"

"I've been dead since the war, Bruno. A vampire bit me behind enemy lines. I've been walking the dark for almost fifty years."

"Decided to see the light," Bruno smiled. He slapped the old man in the arm. "It *is* good to see you," he said with fake emphasis. "Let me buy you a drink."

"You owe me at least that, traitor."

"You still harping on my name, Andrews?" said Bruno, pouring the most toxic liquid he could find. He'd kill this vampire, if he could. A band of seven math students pushed by Andrews on their way out, jabbering loudly as if no other humans existed on the planet around them.

"You're a German, *Heidenstam*," said the man, taking the fat glass when it came. "You always were a spy, and we all knew it. It's the only reason you boxed so well."

"Well, I can still take you out any time you're ready, Andrews! Don't call me by my real name. I've got a reputation here I don't want changed."

"Ah!" the old man in the suit said, leaning on the bar. "That's how you keep your new company in order here! Terror techniques." He took a swig and grimaced. "What *is* this stuff?!"

Bruno grinned and said in his best growl. "You don't wanna know, Andrews!" He wiped down the bar, smelling the sour odor of the wet rag in his hands. "We missed you at the reunions, old man."

"I missed the invitations." He braced himself with one hand on the counter and took another swallow.

Watching him from the corner of his eye, as two girls entered the cafe laughing, Bruno said, "coming up again in November. Driskel's putting it on, I think. Means it's in Nebraska this year, if you're up to it."

"Well I am a busy fellow," said Andrews, slapping the glass down as if he were twenty-one and proud of it.

"At your age? Doing what!"

"Look who's flapping his naked gums!" said Andrews waving a finger. "Oh, you remember those days? Soaring over India in the dark? Not a sound! Even the wind, hushing for us!"

"I remember praying we wouldn't be noticed," Bruno turned his eyes up to the dead fan hanging above his old...acquaintance.

"Silent birds diving through enemy skies. 900th Airborne Engineers. Bernard, I knew the wheels on those gliders were useless. Without the skids, we'd all be buried behind enemy lines."

"You knew nothing," Bruno said with a huff and a chuckle. "You'd never touched down in soaked rice patties 'fore. You were ignorant as the rest of us!"

"They told us to land there!" said Andrews. "Besides, you couldn't land a glider if the ground was smooth and a hundred beautiful women waited for you."

"There weren't no woman," said Bruno.

"There were in our company."

"*They* weren't women."

"Jen sure looked like one," said Andrews, tapping his glass.

"Jen's danced through three husbands since the last World War. And I never needed to pilot those gliders. I was only along for the ride." Bruno poured the toxin.

"We got those runways built in no time."

"We did our job. Then I beat you into a ball," Bruno said with grit in his voice.

"I've...given up boxing," said Andrews, drinking.

"For what," said Bruno, turning his back to the man in order to look casual.

Andrews pinched down the alcohol. "FBI, my good man. That's why I'm here."

"Isn't there a law against working for a government agency when you're passed eighty? There should be! The world's going senile, and if you're running things, it's no wonder why!" Bruno grabbed a dry cloth from under the bar and wiped his hands.

"I've retired," said Andrews with a grin. His eyes were tight, dry, and as serious as they had been in India. "But I still work...as a Special Informant."

"Counter intelligence? You're spying on Americans for America, eh? Back-stabbing your brother and that stuff? You gone communist on us, Andrews? That why we haven't heard from you in so long?" Bruno said with a laugh, but the questions had meaning, expecting straight answers. Andrews had carried a dark soul inside his living corpse during the war. No one at the reunions debated how much blacker he'd become since then.

Andrews looked at the remaining liquid in his glass. "You wouldn't understand what I do, traitor."

"How do you know I didn't go work with the CIA before retirement?" said Bruno, turning away.

"You're a fist, Bernard. Not an intelligence officer," said Andrews, scratching the side of his nose.

"Hundred and twenty men and five officers in our division. You were the traitor all along. Here to check up on me, Andrews? You're not here to catch up on lost memories, are you."

Rubbing the rim of his glass in an attempt to get it to hum, Andrews said nothing.

"What *can* I do for you then?" Bruno said to the businessman, as customers waved good-bye, heading out the glass door.

"I'm looking for a student from these parts."

The door slapped into the doorframe with a crack.

"Wait here then. Get about three hundred of them in a day," said the man in the T-shirt.

"Name's...Alred. First name, Erma. Know her?" said Andrews, his pupils dry as natural glass in the Sudan.

"Nope. Said yourself, I'm not a brainiac, I'm a grunt. What's up with her." Bruno kept his chin up, his old trick for inviting punches. He did his best to look vulnerable. That way, Andrews wouldn't defend against Bruno's mind-probing jabs.

"Green eyes. Light auburn hair. Big-boned, but not overweight. Twenty-seven." Andrews pulled a black and white photograph from a leather briefcase he lifted onto one of the stools.

Bruno examined the picture. Immediately he rumbled through the files in his mind, collating the data, searching....

"Hey Bruno!" called a customer.

He shouted without looking up. "Hold your hairy horses!" Bruno remembered the girl. She'd been in a few times. The one who looked like she'd seen a ghost. Had some connection with...John Porter, the hot chocolate, French fries, and ranch dressing man. Asked questions about the young man, if Bruno remembered right. "Don't recognize her."

"No?" said Andrews, obviously sensing the lie.

"What'd she do?"

"She may have stolen something," Andrews said, sliding the glossed paper back into the briefcase. "But I think she's innocent. I can help her, if I find her. What about...this guy."

The picture of Porter made Bruno's blood speed even faster through his well-aged veins. The snapshot looked as if it'd been taken within the month.

"Been a student at Stratford University almost seven years now. Kinda plain looking, I realize, and the black and white doesn't help. Brown hair and gray eyes. About thirty-three, little over six feet...seen him?"

"Not at all," Bruno said too quickly.

"Worth a shot," said Andrews. He smiled and put the photo away. "Well it was good to see ya...you old traitor." His eyes were sharp as old-fashioned razor-blades.

Bruno nodded, eyeing the straight-standing geezer in the suit, wondering who was the real defector. Andrews was a weasel from the beginning, strategically selling his soul—or rather, anyone else's—for a filthy buck. "You take care, now. No dying of old age, hear?"

"I told you," Andrews said heading for the door, "I'm immortal now."

The glass door swung closed, another thunderclap.

"A bloodthirsty killer, I have no doubt," said Bruno.

* * *

8:59 p.m.

"This is a rotten idea. It's going to get me killed," Porter said.

"You don't know that," said Alred, leading the way. "Besides, Kinnard said he needed both of us right away."

"What if he's being cajoled. Gun point or something," said Porter, bumping into the wall as they pushed down the white corridor.

"Porter, you have to trust somebody."

He decided to say nothing else for fear of sounding any more like a child. But still, he looked behind him repeatedly. Almost to Dr. Kinnard's office, Porter sneezed, panicked about giving himself away, and turned around again—doing his best to look as if he'd simply slowed to admire the modern art depiction of a fifteenth-century German pavis, the shield used in medieval times to protect the entire body.

Porter figured there were at least twenty doors on either side of the corridor. He pictured men in black waiting for them to pass before shooting them in the back.

He was examining the closed portals again—pretending to examine the pink and green lily pad in oils—when he heard Alred's knuckles hit Kinnard's door frame. His skin cooled.

"So you did get to Ulman's security box?" Porter said under his breath.

"I'd better tell you about that later," she said as Porter locked eyes on her. Alred wore an attracting perfume he didn't recognize, and for some reason his stomach felt empty.

Kinnard opened the door. "Come on in."

As the professor took his seat in silence, Porter entered and stared helplessly at the wide window to his left with no shade to shut out the night. It was a black hole in the white wall. With florescent light brightening the room, anyone could see them from outside. And if a sniper waited…he wouldn't even need a scope to kill Porter in that small office.

The only other decoration was the silver expansion bolt Porter always glanced at when entering, wondering if there would be a screw in it some day. He looked at it out of habit, but also hoping it would bring some sense of comforting normality. He had to shut off his emotions; they were getting in the way. He felt like a small child on a playground full of bullies hiding behind big trees.

"Thanks for coming so late. I needed to talk to you as soon as possible…before you got much further," said Kinnard, sitting, leaning forward, and clasping his muscular hands together.

"Why," Alred said, taking a seat.

"You'd be impressed, Dr. Kinnard," said Porter. "With all the… opposition we've faced in this project…everything is still progressing well." It was the truth, but did it make him feel better?

Kinnard examined Porter as if he were a caterpillar in a cocoon. "You've found positive links between the ancient Middle East and Mesoamerica?"

"The KM-2 substantiates facts I've already been gathering for many years," Porter said, sinking into the other hard chair before Kinnard's desk, glancing at the window from time to time.

"Like what," Kinnard asked Porter, shooting Alred a quick look.

"Mesoamerican historians professing isolationist's theories have attempted to explain away the existence of the coconut, cotton, and the bottle gourd in pre-Columbian America by saying it simply floated there," said Porter. "Their arguments for the sea voyages of pineapples, maize, and tobacco have proven more difficult. There is evidence for chickens, with weak evolutionary explanations, in America long before Columbus.

"Mesoamerican cultural traits in parallel with the ancient Near East may have come into existence by a means of logical coincidence, but it's hard to invent a chicken, or the sweet potato, or the red-flowering hibiscus which had to be transplanted. In KM-2, I'm finding a slew of patterns brought by visitors from the old world to the New. I'd prefer to publicize them during my formal argumentation."

With his lips together, Kinnard looked again at Alred, who simply waited. "You're an ancient Americanist," he said.

"And I have plenty of explanations for the things Porter has mentioned," said Alred.

"Ah," said Porter, "but your replies are simply the facts taught you by other ignorant authorities on the subject of Mesoamerican history and pre-history. Secondhand knowledge. The KM-2 is *history*, by definition of the word, and—"

"I studied under Dr. Ulman, Porter. You forget that. He was a fine *authority* and the discoverer of the Kalpa site from whence we have KM-2," she said.

"He and his finds will validate our arguments that there is a connection between the Near East and Mesoamerica," said Porter, raising a finger.

"But *he* is dead," Kinnard said, his face flushed by heretofore unspoken excitement. "*He* was my friend...and now....Dr. Albright has also passed away."

"And you think there's a link," Porter said, studying Kinnard's hard face for silent messages.

With a jerk, Kinnard looked out the window.

Porter snapped his head to the glass as well, expecting to see....

"Seems you both suppose the same conspiracy," Alred said to Porter. "But we don't know what's going on. I suggest taking a breath and getting to work."

"I—," said Kinnard, but he didn't say anything else.

Porter sensed the heat radiating from the professor's flexing muscles. Was he having second thoughts? Why would that— "Dr. Kinnard...do you know what is going on?"

Kinnard looked at his desk and reached up with his right hand to rub his bald forehead. He removed his glasses. "Porter, you...are really in a lot of trouble...with your dissertation. I know how terribly consequential these last few days have been—"

"Why was the deadline for dissertations moved?" Porter said. "I suppose there are a vast number of other Ph.D. candidates complaining."

"I had nothing to do with it—"

"Was it Dr. Masterson? Is that who I need to talk to?" said Porter.

Alred closed her eyes.

"Porter, will you stop cutting me off?" said Kinnard, struggling to maintain a peaceful face. His naked head was turning white, and his lower forehead red. He pushed his glasses against his face.

"If I didn't need to write it all out, I could give my dissertation tomorrow," Porter said.

"You could not," said Kinnard.

"I have enough data to speak for a day on the aforementioned connection."

"Porter," said Alred, putting a hand over his.

Porter jumped from his seat, glanced at the window, found a safe location in the corner of the room, and faced the professor again. "Did you know Cortez wrote in a letter to his king that the things he found were so...unbelievable...Cortez knew the description he was about to write down would not be easily trusted? He gave a written warning to that effect before his report." Porter lifted a finger and pointed as he spoke. "Cortez feared-feared no one would go along with his story about the Old World because even he and his men, who *saw* the things with their own eyes that he was about to relate—and no doubt witnessed things he didn't write down!—Cortez and his men couldn't comprehend as actual reality? There is so much that we as Americans have forgotten or lost since ancient times. Not even the natives agree on the old tales. Don't tell me we should give up—"

"Porter," Alred said calmly, turning around in her chair, "sit down. We don't know why Kinnard asked us here. You're jumping to conclusions and...not acting very scholarly right now."

An embarrassed statue, Porter stood in the corner until his legs carried him back to the chair. His eyes shot out the window on their own for a second. No bullets so far.

"I'm sorry, Dr. Kinnard," said Alred, still sitting with her hands neatly settled one atop the other, her folded legs relaxed, her back straight, and her head up. "It's been a stressful semester."

"I'm the one who should be apologizing," said Kinnard, looking back at her. "Ms. Alred, this won't affect you as much...as it will Porter, but it won't make you happy either."

Kinnard stood and looked down at his desk, attempting to collect himself and breathe more easily.

Porter shoved his focus to his own knee-caps, as if the action would hide him from whatever Kinnard was about to say. He still suspected a gun in Kinnard's back...somehow.

"KM-2," Kinnard said. He looked at Alred. "Wouldn't Kalpa start with a *C*, Alred, if it is a Central American—"

"That is my understanding," said Alred. "I can't explain Albright's choice, nor the reason other scholars have perpetuated—"

"Was there a reason we came here?" said Porter as innocently as he could, though the emotions were pouring invisibly from every orifice.

"I think you should forget about this project," Kinnard said looking straight at Porter.

Gazing through the silence, Porter felt the blood to his brain shut-off. "Why?"

"We might be wrong, Porter, but I think you agree with me. This isn't a simple dissertation you're working on anymore. I fear…illegal actions may have been taken, and icy waters are stirring which we should leave alone."

"That," said Porter, "is…it? Thank you, Dr. Kinnard," he said with a smile, "but I would rather present my argument to the board!"

Alred sighed.

"We only have six days left! Six!!! You can't pull the rug out on this one," Porter said.

Kinnard kept his eyes on the desk. "I really feel for you—"

"But…not *that* much, eh?!" Porter huffed and flung his hands, standing again.

Alred got to her feet. It was over.

"Look," Kinnard said as she turned quietly to the door and Porter threw his hands a second time, flopping them against his sides. "I know the vitality of your predicament, Porter, but I can't do anything about it."

Porter froze his arms in midair and looked at his supervising professor. "Wait." He pointed again. "You *can't*. You mean you tried to.…*You* didn't make this decision?"

Alred turned slowly. "What? Dr. Kinnard, you're *not* shutting down the study because you're worried about—"

"No," he said.

"It was Masterson, wasn't it!" said Porter approaching the desk. He felt the acid rain in his lungs.

Kinnard lifted a signed paper from his desk. "Stratford is terminating your research and the applicable dissertations."

"Can the University *do* that?!?" Porter asked Alred.

With eyebrows lifted at Kinnard and arms folded, she said, "Stratford can do anything she wants."

"Especially when impending lawsuits are suspected," said Kinnard. "I'm sorry."

Porter turned like a rhino for the door, bumping Alred aside and yanking the portal open. This was worse than being shot through the window.

Before he could make it out, he heard Kinnard's voice. "We will need KM-2 back…of course."

Black smoke clogging his heart, Porter looked at his supervisor.

Alred thanked the professor and put a hand on Porter's shoulder as she went by him. "That's it, Porter. We're done."

Chapter Nineteen

April 28
9:18 p.m. PST

Alred followed Porter out of the building.

A white T-bird almost hit him as he stepped onto the parking lot.

"I'm not giving up the codex," Porter said without turning.

"That's a good way to make sure you never teach in a university," said Alred under the yellow lights hanging from high poles over the sparsely filled lot.

Porter stopped and jabbed a finger into her face. "You don't care what happens to me! You lost your dissertation, but so what?! You know you can start something else from scratch; you have plenty of *years* left to complete it!"

"That's true," she said, raising her eyebrows, her face calm stone. "I plan to do exactly as you outlined." She folded her arms. "But we—"

"You've been against me from the start," said Porter coming up close to her, "don't deny it."

She nodded. "I was assigned by the faculty to debunk the assertions you would attempt to make. They knew your work would be good."

"They pitted you—"

"And I wanted nothing to do with it," she said, pulling her overcoat tighter as the frigid wind blew through her clothing. "I told you when we met, I already had other plans. I'm done with my schooling. I just need my dissertation, which I saved for the end in order to concentrate all of my energy. Now—"

"Did you even take the codex to get dated, or were you trying your best to keep it from me to slow down my work?" said Porter, turning away from her and stepping into a deep puddle.

"John—"

"Oh, don't get casual on me now, *Ms.* Alred! This has just been a game for you. Well I'm not relinquishing KM-2 to anybody—I especially can't trust you!"

"If you had any brains at all, Porter, you'd see I'm the only one with you on this!" she said pressing herself forward.

"How can you say that?!?" he said, his eyes wide, his hands spread as he gawked at her. "Every time I tell you what's in the codex, you turn to ice! You'd rather be in a mortuary than in my presence! You know my arguments are valid, my proofs are sound, and that rightfully disturbs you! But instead of opening up to the facts, you've been looking for holes, haven't you!"

"You sound like an infant who's had his candy stolen," she said, leaning back. "Listen to your own words."

"You hear me," he said slowly, poking himself in the chest. He took a deep breath to calm himself before starting. "There is an old Arabian tale about a poet named Maymun ibn Qays, who I'm sure *you've* never heard of. Al-A'asha is his more common name. This man, living into the days of the prophet Muhammad wished to see the holy man. But in his time, a poet in a royal circles had great power to turn the heads of political courts. He could change the balance of power if he sided with the Prophet. So on his way to the Prophet, Muhammad's rivals, the Quraysh, met Al-A'asha and tempted him with reasons to *not* join the prophet's party."

Porter spoke in rapid fire, spitting out the story.

"'He won't let you mess around with women,' they told him.

"'No skin off my back,' Al-A'asha said.

"'Muhammad forbids gambling!' they told him.

"'There'll be other benefits,' he said.

"'The prophet doesn't allow you to make loans with interest!' they said, trying to appeal to al-Asha's financial needs.

"'Never borrow or lend anyway!' the poet replied.

"'You can't drink alcohol!' the Quraysh shouted.

"'I'll drink water!' Al-A'asha said."

Alred shook her head. "What does this have to do with—"

"I found *the same story* in KM-2!" said Porter.

"Correct me if I'm wrong, but didn't Muhammad live about a thousand years *after* you think the Kalpa codex was written?" Alred said.

"These stories are eternal. This one is *attributed* to Al-A'asha, but it could very easily have been based on an earlier tale told by Bedouin for millennia. The version in Ulman's codex is different, but basically—"

"Ambiguous," said Alred. "You're the king of Ambiguity."

Porter dropped his hands against his sides and huffed. "Okay," he said and paused. "I *have* been hiding something from you."

Alred lifted her head, her red lips tight, her eyes attentive.

"Remember I'd found something—"

"Are you going to tell me?" she said.

"It won't matter to you!" he said, turning to her old Celica.

"Porter, I have to—"

"All right, I'll give it to you," he said, spinning around, "just to get it off my chest. I found a word—"

"You're being irrational," she said.

"—in the codex that I figured would lead me to harder evidence of a Near Eastern connection than anything else. But without KM-2, I'll never have all the evidence I wanted."

With her arms folded again, she demanded, "What is the word."

"Letters, really: Y, X (Sh, really), A, and Y, H. Recognize it?"

She thought for a moment. "Expect me to?"

"Not really. What letter is linguistically interchangeable with a Y?"

"An I. You could have spelled it that way initially, why didn't you?" she said.

"Dealing with transliterations here, remember?" said Porter.

"Isha-ih?" she said, putting the bits together.

Porter turned his voice into a whisper. "Isaiah! He was a Hebrew prophet from a little more than two hundred years before the date I gave the codex. It's the same letters in old Hebrew."

"And the Arab story? Do Jews often tell the tales of their enemies? How does that fit in?"

"The Book of Mormon clearly has connections with the ancient Bedouin. Names, cultural attributes, social organizations—"

"You're stuck on this, aren't you," said Alred.

Porter caught his breath in the back of his throat. He heard the high cries of a red- tailed hawk lost in the night. He listened to the brisk wind, which evidently had forgotten the meaning of 'spring.'

"Your dissertation, your schooling...all tossed away because of your religion? You'll go to jail, Porter, and die a martyr for your church someday...and they won't even realize it, because there won't be anything to back up your babbling." Alred walked to her car as she spoke, gathering her keys quietly.

Porter lagged behind.

Unlocking her door, she said, "I really hope it's worth it. I heard you were an eccentric...but you used to be a respected one. Your ideas were far-fetched, but even I was impressed by your scholarship. Regain your cool, Porter—"

"What do you care, Alred," said Porter with water rising in his eyes. Her words were true, and they stung deeply. His life was a capsized boat with little hope of flipping upright. He was thirty-three and unmarried, no good at anything but scholarship, no future to speak of with his current plans. The old stranger in the cafe was right.

But he had to do it. He had to translate the rest of the codex. It must go public...and he had to be the man that brought it forth.

Alred pinched the bridge of her nose. "I have to—"

"I know you don't believe me, Alred. Don't bother...speaking to me anymore." He turned from the Celica and headed away.

"Porter," she said, behind him.

"It doesn't matter," he called back. "Good-bye Alred."

"Wait!"

He didn't.

* * *

10:32 p.m.

Porter was walking blindly, and he knew it. He staggered like a drunk man down the hallway, and if someone waited with a gun, he didn't care much.

Three doors from his office. Three doors till he reached the closed vent concealing the codex and his remaining notes.

The door was unlocked when he turned the handle. Everything looked normal: piles of volumes lining the walls and scattered over the floor and desk; sheets of forgotten papers, files, translations, and essays on the chairs or wherever he'd found foot room. *But nothing was the way he'd left it.* It had all been moved, rummaged through, kicked aside and forgotten.

He looked at the vent.

Two screws held the metal grating in place.

He reached over the heaps on his desk, knocking over two books with titles worn off the blue covers, and pulled his pocket knife out of the top drawer.

Slowly, he worked the screws.

The cover came away from the wall…only to reveal a dark hole blowing hot air that smelled of dust.

He threw the grating onto his desk and banged the wall with his head.

* * *

April 29
7:51 a.m.

"Come on in, Ms. Alred," said Professor Masterson, looking down at the bag in her hands. "You got my message."

She entered the room with the rectangular table and looked at the faces staring up at her. Here it had all begun, here it would end.

"I thought I was to—"

Arnott was the first to smile. Then she saw Goldstien who looked even happier to see her.

"—to give it to Dr. Kinnard," she said.

Porter's supervisor sat farthest away, his hands together, his elbows on the table. He watched her with intense silence.

"You've done good work, young lady," said Arnott. He sat like a black scorpion ready to strike, perfectly still.

"Oh, the silent one," she said to him without reservation. "Why haven't I taken any of your classes, Dr. Arnott? Come to think of it, I've never heard a thing about you, and I was unable to find your name in this semester's schedule. Are you *supposed to be* new here?"

Goldstien's smile died and he shot Arnott a glance as if she'd blasphemed against the school deity.

But Arnott's cold grin only relaxed more. "Did you bring the manuscript as requested?" he said glancing at the package in her right hand.

"It's been a difficult semester, and I think I'm entitled to a little clarification on this matter." Alred looked up at Masterson, who only smiled and rubbed his thick lips with the tips of the long fingers on his left hand.

"Excuse me," Masterson said, nodding at the manuscript. "That document should be returned to the authorities in Guatemala." His raised hand opened.

"That's it?" she said, lifting the book in the brown paper. She smelled wintergreen Certz on the old man's breath.

"Sorry gal. This turned into a terrible catastrophe for you, didn't it." Goldstien smiled again as he drew her attention.

"Only a waste of my time," she said as Masterson took up the codex. She watched him open the bag and take a long look inside. "I think Porter was the one really hurt."

"That is too bad," said Masterson with falsified feeling in his voice. "We can still make it up to you at least. Choose anything for your dissertation, and I'll help you along." He moved slowly, like a ship on the horizon, as he rounded the table without lifting his eyes. He handed KM-2 to Arnott. "May it be a difficult task," Masterson said to her, "yet I'll do all I can."

"You're all on top of things here, aren't you," Alred said to the group. She bit the corner of her mouth. The air in the room didn't move at all. "Well...perhaps I can take the rest of the semester off. Begin again in the fall."

"Excellent idea!" said Goldstien as Masterson and Arnott nodded.

Kinnard said nothing.

As she nodded and made for the door, her eyes slipped back to the codex one last time.

* * *

8:01 a.m.

When Alred turned the corner, her heart stopped.

Porter was right there, a wall in her way, a forgotten watchdog, waiting for her.

"Porter!" she said. She lifted a hand as if to calm the fury she knew she'd meet. "I'm glad I bumped into you."

"The codex is gone," he said, "and so are my new notes." She looked at him, an exhausted man, leaning against the wall, suspicion in his eyes. She wondered where he'd spent the night; if he felt he was still being hunted by men in black; what he planned to say to her when she told him the truth. Oh well.

"I took it."

He nodded, wiping his tongue over his lips. His silver eyes were bullets.

"I met with the staff just a few minutes ago and gave it up—"

He spun around and stormed down the hall toward the exit.

"—so we wouldn't get in trouble with the authorities!" she had to say in a louder voice. "Porter!"

She saw the back of his hand rise by his shoulder to wave her away.

"John," she said again, immediately regretting it.

The glass door banged when he hit it. He was gone a second later.

Alred shook her head and went to the restroom.

* * *

9:39 a.m.

"Trying to get yourself killed?" said the voice behind Porter as he drank hot chocolate at Bruno's. Porter knew it was the old man he'd met at the cafe across town. His feet hurt from walking everywhere. Apathy continued to whisper in his ear like a little devil, telling him to just go home and shout the truth to the killers when they came. He didn't notice the spicy scent of roasting chicken filling the small restaurant.

"I don't have it anymore, and I haven't met with the FBI. Happy?"

"I know you don't have it," said the voice. "But you're one of those who has to keep working once your hands are dirty. You're not going to set this aside easily. You'll stir up waves until they are powerful enough to crush you. I told you to relax."

Porter sniffed up the chocolate. "I've been meaning to get my hearing checked."

"Everything all right here?" said Bruno, his voice sharp like a weapon.

Porter looked up at the old hunchback with the Texan mustache. Bruno's eyes flickered to the man behind Porter and back to the student, as if ready to dispel whatever foul thing may have wandered into his cafe if it disturbed the customers.

"I'm fine," Porter said, sucking on his mug. His eyes went straight to the dark bottom of the hot mixture and stayed there.

"You call me *if you need anything*," Bruno said before walking slowly away.

"Old man wants to protect you," said the voice.

"He's a fighter," Porter said in his cup.

"But old, nonetheless. You need not fear me, Porter."

"Who are you," said Porter, not expecting an honest answer.

"Feel free to call me Joseph…Smith."

Porter growled in his mug. "I don't find that humorous."

"But it will be an easy name to remember. You'll have worse things to worry about in the future. Do you have money?"

"Planning on mugging me?" Porter said, joking, but expecting the cold metal of a barrel in his neck at any moment. Did it matter?

"There is a man I know who has more information on Dr. Ulman's find than you've been able to collect," said the old voice behind him. The deep falsetto dimmed its power so as not to be overheard.

Click-click.

"What's that," Porter said, imagining a gun, but knowing it wasn't.

"This…is the…address…of the gentleman you need to see." Smith stood and appeared at Porter's side.

A napkin fell from his hand, slid over the red-and-white-checkered tablecloth, and folded on Porter's lap. Porter saw the writing with a glance.

The old man put his gold-lined pen in the inside pocket of his elegant overcoat. "He won't be interested in sharing with you. In fact, he will soon change his mind about working on the project at all."

"Pardon me?" Porter said, questions filling his insides enough to spill from his eyes. He didn't look up at this Mr. Smith.

"Incentives, Mr. Porter. They are already on their way to see him.

He will be given two choices: drop it…or die."

"Who are we talking about," said Porter, forgetting the hot chocolate.

"Dr. Alexander Peterson of Ohio State University. He's on sabbatical right now, staying in his summer home in the mountains." The old man pulled the skin around his eyes into a thousand wrinkles, smashing his pupils, as Porter looked at him at last. "If you intend on continuing this investigation, you will need Peterson's material. You had better hurry."

The hot chocolate in the forgotten mug, tilting in shaking hands, spilled onto the table and splattered on Porter's right wrist. He hissed and looked down to wipe away the burning liquid.

When he glanced up the old man was already outside the door only one booth away.

The glass door slammed into the doorframe like pounding teeth.

Chapter Twenty

4:54 p.m. PST

Polaski wanted to lunge at Peter's throat, but he only shifted his weight onto his right foot and examined the elderly gentlemen in tight suits sitting around the long redwood table. His eyes jumped to the strangers framed on the wall to his right.

"Nice of you to get here," said the old man at the far end from behind his raised wristwatch.

"I've been busy," said Polaski. He checked to see if Peter, standing quietly beside the nearest window, was still smiling at his withered hand.

"Working for who, I wonder," said another old fellow. His hands worked together like a spider climbing a mirror. "Your work has proven unfruitful, Mr. Polaski. The authorities will trace us through you if you remain in the country."

"Time for retirement," said another gentleman, his voice old and cracked by too many cigarettes in his younger years.

"I did what you would'a wanted, what you needed!" Polaski said, the only slouching person in the richly laden conference room.

"Peter, would you ask Deseree to come in?"

The youngest member of the committee went to the door and stuck his head out.

A tall woman with strong eyes entered. She wore a royal blue business suit with a short skirt, fake glasses, and a hypnotizing perfume. "Yes sir."

Raising his voice as if she was hard of hearing or he was too faraway, the man at the end of the table said, "Ms. Russell, this man needs to visit Europe inconspicuously. One way. Will you make the arrangement."

She nodded.

He raised a hand. "Go, Mr. Polaski. Be a good man…and disappear."

Polaski's eyes darkened, his mouth twisting. He knew the policy. He'd heard it before and participated in the exercises. But the last thing he wanted was dismissal. "The carbon dating never happened! I've taken care of it!"

"That is hardly relevant anymore, Mr. Polaski. Peter?"

Peter stepped forward with a dry smile and an affirmative nod. He placed his black briefcase on the table. Polaski could smell the well-tended leather.

The codex was tattered and large pieces looked ready to fall off the bark pages. With careful hands, Peter set the ancient manuscript on the glossy cherry wood. Polaski thought he could smell the book's rotting age. He hadn't seen it until now, and he hated it more than before. It had already complicated his life. No longer a nuisance, its existence in this room meant all his labors were worthless, resulting only in the end of his career…and a little more.

With the blood slipping from his face, Polaski looked up at all the eyes focused on him. He glanced at the faces on the wall. Even their eyes were alive.

"As you see, the chase is over. The threat has passed," said Andrews.

Polaski licked the dry insides of his mouth and punched his brain into overdrive. "What about Peterson in Ohio?"

"What do you know about him?" said the gentleman at the end with a start, sharp eyes glancing with untrusting bitterness at Peter. "Put it out of your thoughts, Mr. Polaski. Everything's taken care of."

His heart pounding, Polaski looked at one of the gentlemen who sat like a clam-skinned, troubled lawyer in his red leather chair. "Mr. Andrews—!"

Eyes on the table, Andrews waved a quick hand with a minimum of wrist action, brushing Polaski off as if he were an unwelcome fly.

"Have a good vacation," said the old man at the end. He nudged his forehead in the direction of the door. "We shan't see you again, I trust."

Polaski stood in silence as the rest of them waited.

"That's all," Peter said, touching Polaski with the tips of his fingers, nudging him toward the exit.

"Don't push me!"

Peter stepped back and put his hands together at waist level.

Hot breath shooting through his teeth, Polaski looked at all the hard eyes watching him, tracking him like laser sights atop powerful guns.

He pulled at the bottom of his black shirt, drawing it tight around his puffed up chest, then stamped out to the patient secretary.

* * *

The man at the end of the table looked to his left at one individual in particular. "See that Polaski is executed immediately. I don't care who does it. We will not waste our money funding him anymore."

With a nod, the gentleman on his left stood, buttoned his navy blue blazer, and left the room.

Calm eyes looked on the younger fellow standing over KM-2. "Peter, what is Ms. Alred's status?"

"She's finished with the project. After giving up Porter's codex without resistance earlier this morning, it seems she had an argument with her fellow graduate student resulting in their permanent separation. I have transcripts of their conversation. She appears uninterested in pursuing the matter and rather excited about continuing her doctoral research in a different area."

"Can you be sure she doesn't have other reasons for interest. Dr. Ulman was Alred's most preferred professor."

Peter didn't even blink. "Ms. Alred will no longer research the Ulman find."

The man at the end turned his head to Mr. Andrews.

Andrews nodded. "I concur. We had her followed to a West Federal Bank, where she does not possess an account. We concluded there to be a connection with the Ulmans but it seems to have led her nowhere. We found no reason to assume she learned anything of relevance. And she is repulsed with those things relating to the find."

"You're investigating behind my back?" Peter said, his face flushing, but his body unmoving. "You question my competence."

"Not at all, Peter," said the man at the end. "We only want to be sure nothing is overlooked. We need to be." He looked down at the table. "And John Porter?"

"Porter seems furious," said Peter, "but he has no more leads. He can run around and say all he likes, but he'll become a disreputable scholar and lose himself in the back of libraries."

Smith, across the table from Andrews, spoke without leaving his restful position. "Then why has Porter boarded a flight for Columbus… Ohio."

The man at the end looked from Smith to Peter with hard eyes. "You thought this unworthy of mention?"

"I…didn't see that it mattered where he went at this point. As long as he didn't head for Central America."

Andrews wrinkled his brow. "How did he find out about Dr. Peterson's connection?"

Smith closed his eyes and opened them again as he spoke. "The April edition of the *Archaeological Journal* contains the article written by Alexander Peterson, aforementioned."

"The April journal was catalogued as one of Porter's possessions when we first closed in on him and the codex," said Peter.

"Andrews," said the man at the end, "make sure Dr. Peterson expects Porter's appearance. We don't want Porter catching any loose ends. Peter, I think your work is finished for the day. Go home and rest."

Peter would do that, he said with an emotionless nod. He only wondered if he'd wake up the next day.

* * *

8:09 p.m. EST

The young lady closed the door and Porter was thankful; it must have been only ten degrees outside, and the Ohio wind was blowing harder than he thought it could when carrying snow. He'd already stepped in a gutter full of slush, so his right Rockport was soaked and the tips of his toes stung.

The house was very large, and undoubtedly more expensive than anything he could ever hope to own. Porter figured the structure had been built in the early part of the century before the depression. The wide staircase to the second floor suited a historian. From the high ceiling hung electric chandeliers of twinkling crystalline shapes. Ornate rugs depicting a deep forest of twisting trees and scrambling bush covered the entire entry hall. There were at least six doors Porter saw along the walls of the hall and at least two at the top of the stars. Paintings as tall as six feet, depicting Mesoamerican warriors, kings, and ball games, and mirrors at least five feet wide took up the rest of the brown wall space. Of course the elaborate carpets were predominantly red.

"What did you say your name was again?"

"Oh," Porter said with a fake laugh, "John. Peterson will know who I am. You work here?"

"My father does," she smiled, young and pretty but as skinny as a mortal girl could become. She was literally a skeleton with an epidermis layer, one of those girls who saw fashion models as both unreachable and ideal examples of female figures, but tried to attain their supposed weight anyway. The anorexic result was unfortunate. Porter couldn't help looking at the skinny poles with tendons and knobs halfway up which she used for legs as she climbed a few steps. The site repulsed him. Porter felt like a child with a cut on his hand that would heal if he'd leave it alone...and of course he couldn't. He kept looking at the white corn stalks contrasting the candy-apple red carpet on the stairs and kept wincing until she looked back.

"Better wait there," she said. "You're not another student from the University, are you? Dr. Peterson's already sent a number of them away. He is on sabbatical, you know. That's why he's not in his Columbus house."

"No," Porter said with a smile. "I'm from out of state. Only here for a few days." He looked up the staircase at the bookshelves all along the top landing walls, trying to read the titles, which were too faraway. How could any professor afford all of this?!? Porter had no idea, but thought it best not to ask.

"So he *is* expecting you?" said the young lady with sky blue circles around her pupils and frosted brown hair. She'd be gorgeous if she put on a little weight, he thought.

"These students come unannounced?" Porter said.

"He shows them away when they call. They think he'll help them out if they appear in person." She pointed at him with a needle for a finger. "John?"

"That's right." Porter watched her go up the stairs and pass left and through a door he hadn't seen.

He had no intention of waiting for the professor. If scholars had one thing in common, he figured, it was a degree of selfishness if the product was new enough. Ulman's sure was! And Peterson probably wouldn't be that keen on sharing it all with an eccentric Latter-day Saint.

Cutting quickly through one doorway, Porter started scanning for stairs. "Where would I study if I lived in this house?" he said. It had to be on the second floor. Maybe the third. This house was bigger inside than it looked. Places this size always had more than one staircase.

Weaving past other servant and doing his best to act as if he was a guest, and hoping his calm silence worked, Porter went up the stairs in the east wing and slid with quiet feet through the halls. Unless Peterson was prompt, Porter expected to have a couple of minutes to find what he needed and get out. If the professor was working on his book, he'd either tell the young lady to get rid of the visitor, or he'd come after ten minutes of making 'John' wait. Porter was betting on the latter.

Porter peeked in rooms and dodged mumbled conversations made by shadows striding by him without seeing anyone else until he poked his head into what had to be a den.

Closing the door behind him, leaving it slightly ajar so he could hear anyone coming up the hallway, Porter scanned the room. Beautiful Victorian wood curled under every table and over every bookshelf. There was plenty of light from the brass lamps hanging about. A fire cooked the Ohio air, giving it a sweet incense odor and filling the study with blankets of warmth.

"I'd fall asleep in here!" Porter whispered to himself. His eyes examined the heavy desk in the center of the room. Massive. Bright lights beamed over the piles standing in perfect order. Rolls rested together like sacred scrolls waiting to be opened by the pious. Two stacks of hand-typed pages stood on the right side. Three books hid beneath a fourth Porter found open and unfinished. They were handwritten journals.

He drew closer and saw the words: *Kalpa*, and *KM-1*, and *buried site*. Porter remembered the article Peterson had written for the *Archaeological Journal*, "The New Mesoamerican Mystery: Guatemala's Hidden

Treasure." He took one of the scrolls made of modern paper and pulled off the rubber band.

The air in his lungs evaporated, and he stopped breathing.

It was a hand-drawn map.

It had to be Ulman's site in Highland Guatemala. A small scale at the bottom implied the enormity of the find. The buildings, the towers, the canals, the streets...it was hard to fathom. Porter's brain seemed to roll inside his head as dizziness set in.

He shut his mouth, closed the roll and grabbed the others, jamming them all under his arm. He'd examine every detail once he was safe. His eyes glanced at the door, still unmoved.

He looked at typed pages, tempting him. His eyes darted to the journals, which he closed and gathered in a scramble.

Porter came around to the front of the desk, knocking the black leather chair aside.

The fire popped behind him, and he spun to face it.

Nothing but hungry flames. Again he smelled the sweet wood burning.

He looked back at the claw-footed desk, at the dark wood drawers running down the front.

Good antique contraption. No working locks.

He checked the door. No one.

One of the rolls fell from under his arm.

But his free hand was already pulling a drawer open. Envelopes, pens, a small tape recorder.

He slammed it quietly and grabbed the next drawer. Wrenching it open—

He almost fell backward at the sight. He swayed, but his free hand caught his weight on the sinking leather of the chair.

Warm leather.

The pages in the drawer were the same. Crisp, but malleable.

Someone had been heating the seat only a few moments ago.

It was definitely bark paper, just like KM-2. And it was real! And it was in the states! And it was right in front of him! He saw the letters. All of them less Mayan, more pseudo-Egyptian.

Instinctive hands grabbed the codex, took up the fallen rolls—

Crack!

Porter turned his eyes to the fireplace again.

Only the flames.

Cold metal gently touched the back of his neck.

"John D. Porter…I presume?" said a British voice.

Nickel-plated .44 Magnum, Porter's subconscious said as he raised himself slowly. He hadn't heard the professor enter and couldn't see him now—it had to be Dr. Peterson. Porter looked down at the ancient manuscript in his hands, unable to believe its reality, unsure there was really anyone in the room with him at all. The blood drained quickly from his head. "I'mmm…going to pass out," his voice slurred.

"Well then, think boy!" came the British voice through a cloud. "Put your head at knee level."

Trapped, caught, subdued, and losing the real world as he stood there, Porter lowered himself away from the cold barrel of the pistol until his head sunk below his waist. His throat made a weird sound, and he felt tears rising in his eyes.

Dad'll be proud of me now! Porter said to himself sarcastically, considering his situation. "I can explain why—"

"I already know the reason you are here, John," said the Englishman as he walked around the desk into Porter's peripheral vision.

The doctoral candidate (turned madman) lifted himself to his full height. He looked into the professor's squinting eyes, realizing the man didn't hold a gun at all.

inlaid with silver, a brown cane with a steel tip pointed at Porter like a spike. "Put it down."

Porter swayed as if he didn't understand the words. His eyes glanced at the door on the other side of the desk.

"Unless you have a metal plate in your head, I doubt you would stand a single blow of this blunt weapon, Mr. Porter, now put my papers down!"

Porter dropped all of it carefully onto the desk and backed away as Peterson examined the attempted theft. Everything was present, though a little crushed and out of place in this organized room.

The fire spit sparks.

"They said you would arrive, but I didn't expect you so soon," Peterson said with life in his voice, as if he were addressing one of his students and not a thief.

“I know why the others were killed,” said Porter. “I know the truth, and I’m not turning my head.”

“There is nothing for you to see,” Peterson said with eyebrows raised, flipping the cane under his right arm. He took up the codex and inspected a new tear with his fingers.

“You know there’s more than ten years of investigation on that desk and you say—”

“That’s all behind us now,” Peterson said.

Porter stood breathless. “What?”

“Do you play chess, Mr. Porter?” said the professor hanging his cane on his arm. He took up the maps.

Porter didn’t say anything.

“Sometimes…you have to sacrifice a piece,” said Peterson.

“They’re pushing you, professor. I know about it. I can vouch—”

“You don’t have a clue as to what I’m saying,” said the professor. Dr. Peterson smiled, his skin tight as if he’d had a facelift or two. “Sometimes it’s…best to play a game that way. Keeping the end in mind, of course.”

The professor looked back at the fireplace.

His hand shot away from his body.

The codex dropped.

Starving, the fire attacked like golden hyenas over a sick wildebeest. The bark pages arched in pain, but the fire kept coming, biting, chewing. The ancient characters on the cover disappeared in mists of darkness. The book melted and began flying through the chimney to heaven in chunks of floating ash as Porter and the professor watched.

“Stay where you are,” Peterson said, lifting his cane as Porter took a step.

Porter stopped, his mouth loose, his eyes sagging out of his skull, his fingers trembling.

The maps went next, burning entirely and then soaring away in pieces.

“You’re…a…scholar,” Porter said in disbelief, his eyes still on the fire. “*Who* could make you do *this*?!?”

Peterson smiled, but Porter sensed pain behind his eyes as the professor took up his journals and set them neatly inside the overheated hearth. “Oh, my dear Mr. Porter. We probably would have been friends one day, you and I, under different circumstances. For you to come *all this way…so quickly….*"

"Who is making you do this!" Porter said, keeping his voice down so as not to draw any more attention.

But the door had already opened again, and the young lady stood looking at the professor. "Everything all right in here?"

Peterson gazed at her with his eyes unfocused, the typed pages in his murdering hands now screaming to the world's subconscious for help. "All is well, Cerina. Please give us some time together."

She closed the door as Peterson tossed the pages of his manuscript into the raging torrent of heat.

"*They* have no name," the professor said.

"That can't be true. I want to know who's behind all this. It's illegal!" Porter smelled the smoke of the sour bark.

Peterson grinned, his face flickering with yellow and orange firelight. "It's all been against the law, Porter, you *have* to know that."

"Is it the FBI?" Porter said. "Why would they be involved?!"

"They aren't, to my knowledge." He chewed his molars together. "You would do well to forget about them, young man."

"I never will," said Porter, his cheeks trembling.

"If *they* had a name, it would be a metonymic displacement for professional obfuscation," said Dr. Peterson. "You will never find them, for they do not exist. Erase your name from their blackboard, Mr. Porter….You'll live longer."

Porter stared at the professor. "You're letting me go?"

"At your age," said the professor with a look upward as he thought, "I may have worn your shoes and matched your footsteps. I have nothing against you. But if you do not look away, *they* will ponder what reason you *should* remain on the planet….Get out."

"I—"

"The conversation is over, Porter, I have been cordial enough." Peterson pulled on the handle off his cane revealing a long blade of thin metal no longer hidden in the wood.

He pointed the short sword at the student.

"It's an antique," said the professor. "Handy. Its forgotten existence in this modern world makes it priceless for someone like me. Do you like it?"

"I won't stick around for it," said Porter, his face cold limestone. He felt numb in the warm room.

"Bad joke, Mr. Porter."

"Not much left to do," he said, leaving the room. "Everyone's made sure of that."

"On the contrary," came the British accent behind him. "If you're *that obsessed*...I'd start looking for Dr. Ulman. He sent me an unfriendly e-mail last week."

Porter turned slowly. "Ulman's...alive?"

"Unsigned, of course, but I know the fool too well."

Porter stared at the professor who glanced at the fire with aching eyes.

"Question is," said the Englishman quietly, "can you find him... before *they* do?"

Chapter Twenty-One

April 30
9:40 a.m. PST

Click-click-click-click-click.

* * *

Alred shoved her way through the glass door into Bruno's cafe. Whether or not Porter wanted to see her, Alred would tell it all, even if she had to slap him to get his attention.

There wasn't anymore time.

She didn't understand the reason why, but her intuition, her female sixth-sense that something hung out of balance, raised her blood-pressure.

Tapping the old man in the thin T-shirt, she said, "Bruno, I need some help."

* * *

Click-click-click-click.

* * *

Rubbing the ends of a mustache reaching for his beardless chin, the boxer turned and said, "My pies are the answer to everything!"

"I need to find John Porter."

"Hasn't been in today," said the owner of the cafe, cleaning the table again. "Why should I be doing this stuff?!? Where's that girl!" he said to the kitchen.

"Someone has tried twice to kill him," said Alred. "He's hiding out, and he'll want to speak with me." A little exaggeration. She meant Porter would be glad by the end of their conversation. Well, she hoped Porter would feel that way. But it was too complicated to tell Bruno.

The old man laughed a gritty chuckle, but his eyes jolted when she insinuated attempted murder.

Someone shouted, "Brussels sprouts, *Brassica oleracea*!"

"You'll eat what I give ya and like it!" Bruno said to the student with the friends and about two-thousand flashcards.

They laughed.

He looked at his task of wiping down the next table. "Running from you, eh," Bruno said to Alred. "Don't sound like he's *that* interested!"

"Do you know his whereabouts? Porter said you had the up-to-date facts on everybody who frequented your place."

"I've the stomach of an elephant," he said, taking up a black tray of filthy dishes and turning to the kitchen, "not the memory of one."

* * *

Click-click-click-click. Click.

* * *

Outside of Bruno's, Alred sucked in the salty air of morning. She stared for some time at a wooden telephone pole papered with cheap advertisements and pictures of lost dogs, cats, and kids. The storm had not subsided, but allowed the presence of a silent marine layer of high fog from the coast. Stratford wasn't that close to the water, but few hills stood to block the recent chaotic winds.

She looked at the brown portfolio in her right hand.

* * *

Click-click.

* * *

Where would Alred be if she were a crazed Mormon who'd just lost all chance of graduating after seven years of worthy work?

She *had* to talk to Porter.

* * *

As Alred got into her faded gold Celica, which by appearance seemed to have more years than mileage, Bruno looked with sharp eyes through the glass.

"What've I gotta do to get some service 'round here?!?" said a customer. A rumble of laughter from friends followed.

Without taking his eyes off the graduate student, Bruno said, "You wan' me to stick someth'n down your throat?! You wait right there!" He popped the knuckles in both hands and the chortles continued.

The man across the street sitting in the dark blue Volvo put the camera with the telephoto lens on the passenger seat. Bruno watched him hit the ignition as Alred pulled into traffic. The spook stayed three cars behind her until both vehicles drove out of Bruno's sight.

A drinking glass shattered in the kitchen.

Everyone laughed.

Except Bruno.

* * *

11:37 a.m. PST

Dr. Christopher Ulman kept his back to the bench in the covered bus stop while he peeked at the Volvo sedan with the cameraman inside.

It was drizzling again in front of what was informally called the Stratford Science Square. The center had really been named after Krishnamoorthy Ramanujam, which most students refused to pronounce.

Ulman would see his wife tomorrow.

If he guessed right, they didn't care about her anymore.

But first he *had* to tell Alred not to—

The bus pulled quickly to a stop. Ulman bowed his head in the high collar of his new hunter-green raincoat. The door folded open.

John Porter stepped off the bus.

Ulman glanced up, and his skin suddenly chilled like a snake's in winter. He pushed his eyes down the sidewalk.

As expected, Alred finally appeared through the tall, spired gate made of dark metal.

The professor had set himself between the public parking lot and the science buildings, waiting for his prized student to stride by when her business was complete.

He hadn't expected the cameraman, who worked as feverishly with the black contraption in the cab of his car as he had when Alred entered the quad by foot.

The long lens focused solely on Alred. The spy turned his body slowly as Alred pressed toward the bus stop. A car driving by hit a puddle, which splashed the concrete in front of her. She gave the pilot a dirty smirk, then reformed her face to faraway thought.

The camera would catch Ulman in a moment if he stayed put.

"Are you getting on?" said the bus driver behind Porter, Alred's graduate-student friend standing close enough to kick.

Ulman stood, his chin down. He didn't know if Porter would recognize him, but he couldn't chance it.

Porter saw Alred before she saw him. Ulman heard him growl as Porter turned and started off in the opposite direction.

"Buddy!" said the driver, his hand on the door lever, itching to pull it. "Let's go!"

Ulman eyed the bus driver, then watched the camera in the Volvo twist in his direction the closer Alred came. Her eyes concentrated on the sidewalk hard enough to crack the cement with the pressure.

Ulman *couldn't* get caught by the camera.

"Yo!!!" said the driver.

"All right!" Ulman said, his hands trembling as he reached for the railing. He looked at Porter not ten feet away, at Alred not twenty, at the camera in the blue four-door. Almost on him.

Ulman moved one foot onto the lowest step in the entrance to the bus.

Ulman's pinching eyes zoomed in on Alred as his throat grew tight.

He cleared it with a bark.

Alred looked up.

The camera focused.

Ulman grit his teeth and slipped into the bus, which instantly rolled from the curb.

He would have to wait…until it was safe.

* * *

As the county transit vehicle slipped its long body by her, Alred frowned, wondering….

Then she saw, "Porter!"

He didn't turn around.

Alred shuffled up behind him.

"We've already decided against correspondence," Porter said for them both.

"You'll want to listen to this," she said.

Porter whipped his flushed face into hers. "In all my—"

"Be quiet, Porter!" she said, her words a fast flurry of machine gun fire. "I've had enough of your Junior High, tough-boy pouting. Your life's going down the rat holes as long as you choose defeat."

"Easy for my Nemesis to say."

"If you'd open your eyes and take a second to breathe you'd see I've done what's best, considering where we fall at present!" Her pupils spat fire. She stood with shoulders squared, her feet staggered, her left hand swelling red around the handle of her leather bag.

Thick exhaust passed around them from the road.

"We have nothing to talk about," said Porter, keeping his ground.

She cocked her head. "Guess I'll just take *KM-3* to someone who really wants it!"

Silence smacked them both like a cold wind. The sound of cars driving on the wet road came from every direction, echoing inside her head, her heart humming like an overheating engine.

She'd gotten through.

He was listening.

"I tried to tell you after I turned in KM-2," she said, running a hand through her breeze-blown hair. "No one at all knows about this manuscript. I had a scrap of it carbon dated."

He said nothing.

"I just received the results," she said, glancing back at the science square, then quickly into his eyes.

Porter's empty mouth gaped powerlessly.

"450 years Before...Christ."

His brow turned to putty.

"None of the words are Mayan, as far as I can distinguish. It's all written in your 'Reformed Egyptian Script,' I believe. There are Mesoamerican characteristics all over...of a sort. Pictoglyphs. But I haven't had much time to study them."

Porter's shoulders melted beneath his beaten suede jacket.

"Too busy looking for you," she said. She smelled blossoms but had to be mistaken. Who smelled flowers on rainy days?

"Atkins did the dating?" said Porter.

"I didn't trust her. Not after everything with the KM-2 codex. I talked one of her doctoral candidates into doing it for me."

"Do...you have it here?" He eyed her portfolio.

Alred unzipped the top and drew out the ancient book, folded like a fan, so similar to the codex they'd recently lost. The shade of the paper was slightly darker.

Porter took it with slow hands, sliding it out of the plastic bag protecting it.

* * *

The man in the Volvo jolted forward, ramming the telephoto lens into his windshield.

He swore and fumbled with the instrument before banging it on his face where it should have stayed.

Pinching his lips together, he held his breath.

Click-click. Click-click-click-click-click-click-click....

* * *

Porter turned the pages while his tongue dried between his parted teeth.

The marrow of every bone in his system froze in waves. First in his hands, then from his arms to his shoulders, and quickly down his back.

"This is what we got out of Ulman's secret security box," said Alred, "I was waiting to tell you, but circumstances never permitted it."

His fingers and wrists shivered with building emotion. His voice came out as a whisper. "You gave Stratford KM-2 to throw them off."

Alred nodded.

"I...could kiss you!" he said in the same hiss, his eyes great ovals with pupils aimed at the dusty record.

She shook her head.

Three manuscripts all from the same find. Four, counting the one Peterson had cooked! This...the last....

"The bank box also contained a paper of Ulman theories and observations at the Kalpa site. *That*, I have read. It's enough to stop *your* heartbeat."

Breath escaped Porter's lungs as if he'd been punched in the sternum.

"He wanted it published," Alred said, "but-but evidently decided to do it himself when he got home from Guatemala. Of course I'm guessing. His wife has no academic blood in her whatsoever and would rather hide in a corner than shake a man's hand, so sending her the essay would only add further stress to matters. I get the impression Dr. Ulman sent previous works to other parties for entering into professional journals or magazines, but they never made it."

"Mrs. Ulman said she'd handed everything over to the FBI," said Porter.

"Must have given them other things Ulman mailed home. We'll never know what those artifacts were. I still wonder what the Bureau—"

"They weren't FBI," Porter said, putting KM-3 back in the bag, while his eyes scanned for unfavorable persons.

The sky hung gray and wet, turning the whole world a dim color.

He never looked at the blue Volvo down the road.

* * *

Click-click-click-click-click.

* * *

"How do you know?" Alred looked into his squinting eyes.

Porter grabbed her arm. "Ulman *is* alive! *We* have to find him… before he gets killed."

Chapter Twenty-Two

7:51 p.m. PST

"Porter, we have to talk…now!"

The ex-doctoral candidate turned to see Dr. Kinnard holding himself firmly in the doorway of the little office. The professor had 8 x 10 inch photographs in his hand.

"You don't seem like one bearing gifts to lift my burden," Porter said placing his copy of *Sumerian Ostraca* in a brown box on his desk. With one hand he took three gray volumes with the title *Hebrew Eschatology* off the floor and put them on top of the first book. His black copy of the Tanach followed. He eyed the other filled containers, all four with the familiar word 'U-Haul' in bold letters on the side.

Kinnard lowered his voice and his brow. "I don't care how you got it, but you'd better hand it over to the University."

Porter glanced at him with a wiry smile. "My new Stone Edition of the *Tanach*? Are the Aryans persecuting the Jews again?"

Kinnard flashed the pictures.

"What are those supposed to be?" said Porter unworried. He stopped loading to look anyway.

Three shots. All details of Porter examining KM-3 on the street where Alred had caught up to him. But she was outside every frame. Who had taken the pictures? Who'd doctored the prints to show only Porter with KM-3?

"Where should I go, you think," Porter said, returning to his packing. From the corner of the white room, he grabbed eight old Loeb Library books with red covers. "I admit my ignorance when it comes to applying for a Ph.D.—after failing the first. Suppose any school will take me? I can't believe I waited so long to get it done," he laughed to himself, because there was nothing else to do.

"You hear what I said?" Kinnard came into the room as Porter went to the far side of his desk, keeping his eyes on the papers and books on the floor. He carried two volumes by Michael Grant, one from Joseph Campbell, and an old E.A.W. Budge book.

Shuffling through the menagerie, gathering files in semi-organized fashion, Porter stuffed the rest of the box. He held a copy of Wardarcher Tiel's, *Merenptah*, in the air and eyed it as if he'd never seen it before. "Whoops. Bet I have a major fine to pay for this baby." With a smile, he looked at his supervisor. "Disagreed with the old man anyway." He set it on the corner of his desk as Kinnard shook his head.

"In order to be successful in the world, Porter, you need to learn the rules of the game!"

"You know I don't play sports, Kinnard," said the student. Porter pulled on the roll of packing tape, and it screamed like a mugged woman in an echoing alley. The box sealed, he grabbed another and taped the bottom before loading it.

"I want the book!" said Kinnard, slamming his hand on the table.

Porter looked up, his face as bland as it could be. "*You* want it? What would you do with it?"

Kinnard's tongue stuck to the bottom of his open mouth.

"Let me know one thing," Porter said, packing as fast as a bank robber would if stashing money into his duffel bag. "I thought I saw sincerity in your eyes when you first gave me KM-2. Were you really helping me…or just giving me something to run around with since I had so little time anyway? Did you have any intention of letting me do a dissertation on Ulman's find?"

"I tried to assist you," said Kinnard taking off his dark-rimmed glasses.

"And then what happened," said Porter. "When did you lose heart? When the other professors shoved you in a different direction?"

"It was a race that couldn't be won."

"Were you blackmailed? Coerced?" Porter said, looking at him with stabbing eyes. "Was there someone involved…that wasn't Stratford staff?"

Gazing at Porter as if his mind had been read, Kinnard shut his mouth.

"Then I hold no blame on you." Porter went back to packing, finding papers written by other students which he should have read and corrected by now. He left them next to the library book.

"You're in a lot of trouble," said Kinnard, his voice low and serious. "Where is the codex."

"See it here?" said Porter waving an arm but not turning up his eyes.

"You are not listening to me, are you." Kinnard leaned on the card-table desk, which rocked beneath his weight. "You could go to jail for this. You could be killed."

Grinning again, Porter said, "Oh is that all? I thought you'd say something that would get my heart going. I'm already desensitized to those things, you see. Well, maybe you don't. We're driving on different tracks now."

"I gave you Ulman's manuscript," said Kinnard, "I'm responsible."

"You're afraid they'll kill you?" Porter flopped in his screaming chair to be closer to the stacks on the ground to his left, which he immediately reached for.

The heater came on.

"You don't see how serious this is," said Kinnard.

"Better than you realize!" Porter almost chuckled, tossing *The Dead Sea Scroll Companion* into the box, followed by *Civilization Before Egypt and Mesopotamia*, and the new one volume edition of the *Oxford English Dictionary*. "So who are *they*?"

Kinnard put his glasses back on his face and stood straight.

Porter stopped and looked at his teacher. "You taught me yourself that throughout history there have been shadow parties, gangs who have operated in the background, people who started small, but through secrets and careful planning rose to prominent power until they ran the government alone. Pharaohs, Roman Emperors…they've all been oppressed by these hidden sects built up for power and financial gain." He lifted his eyebrows. "I agreed with you, remember? Great discussion we had that day. Lasted way into the night."

"Give me the manuscript," said Kinnard.

"How do you know I have it? Who took those photographs?"

"Where is the document, Porter!" Kinnard said, trembling. "I know you have it—everyone knows you have it!" He slowed his words but the energy stayed. "Shrapnel will fly until you hand it over. A lot of people will get hurt. I hate these people. I had to deal with them in the war, and I thought they were all gone."

"'Those who fail to learn the lessons of history are doomed to—'"

Kinnard wiped his hands on his blue slacks. "I'm through running around! I already told you this project is terminated. If you still don't get it, Porter…you can consider your time at this university finished."

"There's a threat!" said Porter with a relaxed smirk. "That mean I get credit without the dissertation?"

Kinnard slammed two fists into the desktop. "It means you're done, Porter! The University doesn't know you anymore!"

* * *

Knocking on his forehead as if it were a door, Porter moaned and stared at the computer screen.

He typed the e-mail address, cocking his head, hoping it was right. If it wasn't, there wasn't anything else he could do.

Date: Wed, 30 April 1997 8:45:19 -0500 (PST)
To: Clusser@alexandria.va.gov.fbi
From: Tomodachi
Subject: Immediate assistance

Stan,

I'm in the computer lab at Stratford University. Don't reply to this message.

I need your help.

I don't know if there is anything you can do. You're a busy man but you are in the FBI so maybe you'll have some ideas.

I've fallen into a very messy hole out here.

About three months ago, Dr. Christopher Ulman found a city in the highlands of Guatemala. Somewhere inside, he came upon a library with books written in some early form of Mayan. One of the codices has both this proto-Mayan and, though you won't believe it, Reformed Egyptian.

One of the books fell into my hands. I translated half of it before it was taken from me. Albeit, the document came into the country illegally, that's not what worries me. Someone else has been hovering around me like a silent cloud ready to snap out lightning.

I've already dodged bullets, if you see what I'm getting at.

I'm sorry, I can't stay here and type.

They are after me again.

This is worse than I thought, but you can see the implications. This is a solid link to the Book of Mormon. I can't put it down. Even though they are kicking me out of the University because of it. What would my father think....

They won't give me my Ph.D.
If you can come to California, please do. I need to talk to you in person.

Gotta go.

John D. Porter

(If you don't come, the D might stand for Dead. I'm serious. You won't be able to contact me, so don't try. Use your oh-so-special FBI skills to find me. I'll be watching for you.)

* * *

9:21 p.m.

With the funny feeling that he shouldn't, Porter left the motel room to see if the liquor store two buildings away had pistachios. He would dream they came from the Near East and relish the days when he'd pondered entering the exciting life of a professor discussing ancient texts in a squalid room.

The shadow in the alley had a familiar voice, crisp like autumn leaves, clear like a train whistle far up a valley, old as mummy's breath. "Living in motels will break you."

Porter stopped and looked into the dark, lifting a hand to block the obstructing light from the street lamp attached to the wall of the brick building. "My card isn't maxxed yet."

"Easy to track you down when you use plastic to pay."

"I'm out of cash, old man. It's either the card, a bush, or back to my apartment," said Porter stepping into the shadow to see the gentleman.

It was the same one at Bruno's, the same guy in the nice suit of gray tweed at the other cafe across town who'd called himself Joseph Smith. Seemed to have a knack for catching up to Porter. He hadn't realized it was such an easy job. He had to check his back more often.

"Oh, you're a smart person, Mr. Porter, you learn quickly," said Mr. Smith as if he could read minds or was cruelly sarcastic. "Tell me, young man…is there really such a thing as *truth*? Or is it just a word describing an abstract idea that doesn't exist?"

"It's real," Porter said.

"Then why doesn't anyone see it?"

"*You* do," said Porter, trusting his instincts. The scent of short trees in the sidewalk blossomed around them. Some plants were determined to force spring upon the world, whether or not the sky cooperated. But it was still cold.

The old man nodded with a quiet grin, his white hair moving like grain fields in the breeze jetting between the buildings, an unconsciously created air tunnel.

"So what's the truth?" said Porter, his heart quickening.

"You…already know."

"Mormons…"

"—have told the truth since they first came upon it," said Smith.

He stood tall, like a sycamore unnoticed in a park. He leaned slightly to one side, standing with his cane. He was merely a shape and little more.

A discarded cup imitated a rodent and ran down the alley.

"Are you LDS?" Porter said to the dark, afraid to move for fear of scaring off the old man. He had questions....

Smith shook his head. "I have no interest in religion."

"That's a lie. People who say they have no interest are only hiding the fear that something out there *might* be real. Something they don't understand."

"You're wrong," said Smith, tilting his head back.

"Or they're so far in denial they wouldn't realize it if all the facts tripped them to the ground."

The old man kept his grin.

"And yet you insinuate the Mormons have the truth."

"I deny nothing," said the man in the wind. "I also proclaim nothing. No one wants to hear the truth. You must realize that, Mr. Porter. No one except Mormons, who are hardly relevant, and then only as long as it corresponds with their beliefs."

"When wouldn't it?" said Porter, the chill of the evening tightening his skin.

The gentleman's face paled as he came into focus, then lit up again, warping one way then changing like a child's clay; optical illusions. "Come now, John. We are talking about *reality*, remember? Do you claim the members of your church to be perfect?"

Porter waited before answering. "No."

"Do *all* Latter-day Saints believe the same truths?"

Porter wouldn't answer this time.

"Ever hear one of your members say something you know does not concur with Mormon doctrine?"

"What would *you* know about our beliefs?" Porter said. "I don't know a single non-Mormon who understands our faith."

"Nor do I. But over fifty years ago, I did intensive research in LDS beliefs for the committee."

"What...committee?" said Porter, his lips quivering.

"I must tell you only what you *need* to know."

"You're saying you thoroughly investigated my church...and you never joined?"

"Shocked?!" Smith said, smiling widely and lifting his eyebrows. "Don't be." His mouth turned into a straight line. "I have my reasons."

"How do I know you really understand anything about Mormons? In all my college classes when someone mentioned the church, both the students and the teachers made assumptions which weren't true. 'Mormons have more than one wife;' 'Mormons kill animals in their temples;' 'Mormons get married naked!' They never *knew* anything about my faith. Just lumped us in with Protestants and gave us overactive imaginations."

"Of course," the man's old voice eased from his beaten throat. "I thought we already established that no one wants to hear the truth. If the truth has anything to do with Latter-day Saints, do you think people will be more motivated to study it?"

"Most will shun it entirely."

The gentleman nodded slowly. "Your professors and classmates, while perhaps well-meaning, have not *investigated* your church. Naturally they would assume Mormons to be like other religious institutions they know something about or hear about on the news. *Assumption*, my friend, is a drug to which the world is addicted. We see all things through drunk paradigms—yourself included. So of course no one has a grasp on LDS beliefs. The world simply goes on living delusions of happiness, steering clear of what is real if it looks remotely hazardous to their complacent lives.

"Your religion insinuates change, something most people find revolting. Even the intellectuals, who know better. Oh, yes. I understand your church doctrine. I probably know it even better than you do, my friend."

"Oh really?" Porter twisted his lips into a knot off to one side of his face. His feet still ached from walking everywhere, but he didn't notice.

The old man tilted his face toward the light shining only on the sidewalk and the student. "The Mormons possess five books of scripture as opposed to two like other Christians."

"Am I supposed to be impressed?" Porter said. "You probably dug that out of your encyclopedia."

"Besides the Old and New Testaments of the Bible, Latter-day Saints read out of the *Book of Mormon* on a daily basis...or at least they are supposed to."

"Sounds like a logical conclusion," Porter said.

The gentleman kept his face as calm stone. "The two remaining books are The Doctrine and Covenants of the Church, and the Pearl of Great Price. The former is a compilation of revelations produced by the founder of the church, Joseph Smith...Jr. The latter is primarily made up of the Book of Moses, *translated* through revelation by Joseph Smith out of the King James versions of the Holy Bible, and the Book of Abraham, which your prophet translated from Egyptian records which fell into his hands prior to his martyrdom. Am I doing well?"

"Very. You're even getting everything in the right order," Porter said though he wasn't convinced Smith really understood his beliefs.

Slowly, the shadow man said, "John, I have held in these hands the original Egyptian papyrus Joseph Smith found. I doubt even you can make such a concrete claim. I *know* it is real."

"The Joseph Smith Papyri was described in newspapers in the seventies," said Porter.

"I know the Lachish Letters, found in Palestine in 1935, wouldn't have been released to the world had scientists realized how much the records supported the Book of Mormon. Most scholars still don't notice the connection, because they've never read your scriptures. Ordinary folk have never heard of the Lachish Letters. Ignorance of archaeological data is the most common error in supposing the Book of Mormon does *not* meet with evidences that have been found."

Porter nodded, squinting his eyes.

"For years *non-Mormons*, as you call them, were able to laugh at the feminine Latin name *Alma* given to certain men in the Book of Mormon. An obvious failure by Joseph Smith when he wrote the book. Then the Dead Sea Scrolls came out of the caves in 1947. Without realizing it, the Jews published a scroll describing one Alma *ben* Jacob—"

"Alma *the son of* Jacob," said Porter.

The old man lowered his chin. "We've scoffed at the southern hick name *Josh* that Joseph Smith put in the Book of Mormon, until the same name was acknowledged in the Lachish Letters. And scholars have already identified from the Letters that the Jewish King's—Zedekiah's—final and only surviving heir may have escaped with a party between the years 590 and 588 BCE, when the Jews were captured and taken to Babylon."

Porter listened, the chill biting the tips of his ears.

"The Book of Mormon has been describing that same historical scene for over one-hundred and fifty years, hasn't it."

Porter couldn't say anything. In disbelief, he stood in the dark, wondering what more this man knew but wasn't saying. The facts were accurate. "And you're…not…a Mormon?"

The thin man in the Italian suit shook his head. "If I were a Latter-day Saint because of what I know, wouldn't I share that information with my fellow Mormons?" The wind pulled at his buttoned coat. "Knowledge is a dangerous thing. *People will kill to keep some things buried.* Becoming a Mormon…could slay me, Mr. Porter. You can understand why I work in the shadows."

Porter shook his head, his eyes growing weak. His heart beat like a tiger's in a chase. "No…no, I can't. You know about archaeology proving the validity of what the LDS church has said for so long…but you remain separate from the faith?"

"It is *faith*, Porter. I realize what you're saying and how you feel. But archaeological evidence should never be the basis for a man's belief in a divine being or choice of religion. You can own a rock with ancient writings on it, but no one can own a real god."

A car rolled slowly behind Porter, catching Smith's eyes.

Porter turned around but it sped up and was gone.

"You said the Mormons possessed the truth," said Porter. "You mean the Book of Mormon?"

The old man nodded. "For a long time, I've known the book wasn't *written* by Joseph Smith as enemies of your church often claim."

"How's that?" Porter said.

Smith's eyes turned into black slits in the dark. "Do you *really* think Ulman's codex…is the *first* one found in Central America proving the authenticity of your beliefs?!"

Porter touched his throat in silence. His eyes glazed over. He stopped breathing. But this time he didn't pass out. He snapped back, licked the wind against his mouth, and said, "Why are you telling me all this?"

The old man reached into his coat.

Porter could see the shine on the black semiautomatic pistol with the silencer extension.

"My life is near an end." Smith held his cane in his free hand. "I think it's time to shift the balance of power."

"Do you need the pistol to do it?" Porter said, his voice possessing twice the force, but already buried in a grave.

"No, Mr. Porter." The old man smiled. "Only you."

There was a flash.

One *bang* of solid thunder. A second immediate echoing *BANG* followed.

Porter spun with the impact of the bullets.

There was no pain. Even when his head hit the ground, creating a blinding light inside his eyes.

Then the candle went out.

Chapter Twenty-Three

May 1
1:03 a.m. PST

Porter opened his eyelids, the fuzzy world rocking left and right. Nothing he did helped him to focus, so he tried to keep his eyes shut.

They opened again.

There was too much talking.

Faces looking down and then leaving him.

The motors of cars.

Something over his nose.

A constant hiss coming from just outside his mouth.

He couldn't move.

Beeping sounds.

He needed to cough, but as soon as he started the voices intensified, the scrambling increased.

What were they saying?

The light disappeared.

A blinding whiteness followed, and Porter blinked and thought he saw green exit signs, monitors, and ceiling tiles. Where was he?

He smelled plastic and…mild chemicals? He wanted to cry, especially when he thought he smelled his own bowel discharge.

More faces appeared, then disappeared. Hands brushed his shoulder. Moved his arms. He thought he heard someone talking to him. Something about St. Mary's Hospital. "Where do you hurt." Some question about previous medical problems.

Something tugged at him slightly, and Porter tried to lift his head to see what was happening.

They were cutting the clothes from his body.

He wept, realizing his nakedness, and tried to move to cover himself, but they held him down.

The air blew warm over his body, but the tips of his toes and fingers felt chilled.

He saw another monitor, then shut his eyes as they moved him onto what had to be a hospital gurney.

Porter hated hospitals. He despised them when he was the patient, at least, which really hadn't ever happened until now.

Someone moved his arm. He glanced at the IV as they set it. Nausea rippled through him, and Porter slammed his eyes shut.

He looked down when he realized they were poking a second time for a new IV and again to draw blood.

A new voice materialized, more forceful than the rest, but slow and in control. "What's his pressure?"

Someone answered.

"Good evening Mr. Porter, glad to have you with us. What's his heart rate?"

Another sound from another side.

"What's his rhythm?"

The world spun, and Porter realized he'd stopped crying. He couldn't start again, though he wanted it.

He shuddered when a number of the beings around him went to his left side and log-rolled him onto his right.

Pain jolted his insides, and he needed to cough again badly. He needed to rest. He was hurting, but couldn't understand where or why. He just wanted to sleep.

"Get respiratory here stat!"

"Putting in the foley," said a different voice.

It was all nonsense. The words meant nothing. Porter only—

They were doing something below the belt, and he felt a burning sensation and knew he was being utterly violated.

He had to trust the hands of the doctors. Porter hoped he'd pass out. This had gone on too long already.

Someone put gentle clips on his fingers, but he couldn't look anymore.

"I want a med. blood panel and a type and cross for four units!"

A woman disguised as an Egyptian mummy in bright-colored cloth looked down at him.

They moved him but he didn't care, he didn't pay attention anymore. Would he die? If so, why?! Because of the man in the shadows, the man who spoke of truth and reality and knowledge? Because Porter was *important* to the stranger? It was hopeless to understand.

Porter listened to the hiss from the plastic mask over his mouth and nose. It was soothing…goodness amid the chaos.

"I want X-ray for a stat C-spine, chest and abdomen. Move your legs sir," said the dominant voice, a woman with power—how exciting!

But Porter didn't realize she spoke to him.

"Move your legs," she said again, touching his skin with her cold rubber-laced fingers.

He lifted one leg, only slightly. Then the other and coughed.

"Move your arms. I've got two entrance wounds. Looks like close range, left-upper quadrant, one or two exit wounds."

Porter shut off his ears. She wasn't talking to him anymore.

Porter felt more liquid in his lungs and had to cough again. Weakness crushed him, and he thought for a moment they were slowly packing gold-bullion on his chest. Breathing grew difficult under the pressure. He wanted to tell them to get off, but—

"He's becoming more tachypneic!" said a different voice with serious concern in his tone.

Porter opened his mouth to draw more air.

"I hear a lot of wheezes."

"Respiratory give another treatment," said the doctor. "Get me a gas!"

"O2 stat's falling."

"Specifics!"

"Only 86."

Porter felt fingers poking up his abdomen, something jabbed at his rectum, other hands shoving in points along his chest wall.

What was it?!? he worried. Don't ask questions! he told himself.

The cold disc of a stethoscope on his breast opened his eyes.

The world had grown white. Porter knew he could see—had the ability to focus if he desired—but he pinpointed all his energy on breathing…

From the other side came the doctor's voice. "Let's give him some SUCC to paralyze him."

Was time passing, or was everything happening at once? He counted breaths, but lost track after eight.

Porter had to cough once more, but felt the need to sit up. His arms and legs wouldn't budge. Could he even feel them? What had they said? *Paralyze?*

Why would anyone paralyze a patient in an emergency room!?!

Behind closed eyes, Porter saw the man who called himself Smith. The man who'd shot him...because Smith *needed* Porter—isn't that what Smith had said before the flash?!

Did Smith stand in the room now, watching Porter suffer. Would he watch Porter die?

"He's having more trouble breathing."

"He'll need to be intibated."

"Mr. Porter," said the doctor.

Porter didn't want to have to move again. He realized he couldn't. He knew he was immobilized and it was Smith's fault and the doctors would realize he was dying and he'd perish right there on the gurney in another minute.

"A tube is going to be placed down through your mouth and into your airway. We are hooking you up to a breathing machine...to release the pressure you feel."

They moved things on his face; Porter wasn't sure what number of plastic and rubber contraptions clung to his head.

But he felt the rubber tube pass down his throat. He still couldn't move, but saw the tears building in his upturned eyes. How horrible this was. How unreal and terrible. Porter wished they would just finish him off so he—

"No need to worry, Mr. Porter," said the doctor.

How could she tell what he felt? Was he rigged to some emotion meter or something? He was dying!

"Your belly is looking soft. The x-rays look good." Her voice fluctuated as if she busily worked with other devices and was talking to herself. "Your blood pressure is good....Your oxygen is getting better."

But Porter's throat hurt. It was the tube—he didn't want to imagine it, there in his throat. So uncomfortable...unnatural. They had to take it out. Porter wanted to reach up and remove it himself. He wanted to tell them to…but how could he speak?!

He was moving again. Upstairs and down a hall. Into a room. Someone told him something, but all he heard was "Intensive Care unit."

Intensive. What a frightful word.

He listened one last time to the person speaking. He wanted to throw up, but concentrated on her voice. "You've been shot in the left upper abdomen, and you've had a severe asthmatic attack. The tube that is helping you breathe will probably come out in less than a day…."

The gray clogging his vision turned steadily to white. In seconds, it all disappeared.

* * *

On the outskirts of Yaizu, Japan, there were few houses interspersed between wide tracks of wet rice fields. Porter walked along the edge of one of the patties beside a straight road as he looked at the sky.

The thunder heads had turned away. They danced and waved their mountainous forms in the otherwise blue air. They transformed into orange masses as he stared at them. No telling when they'd return to shower again.

Porter smelled the passing rain and the sweetness of the fields as he tightened the grip on the strap attached to the bag over his right shoulder. He eyed layers of soaring and dipping hills to the South. Mountains leapt up in the North. Touching the ground, a brilliant sun, red as hot coals, blazing trails of light to the East, West, and straight up, reminded Porter of the origin of the Japanese flag. The beams turned everything in the world to gold: the acreage full of glistening water, the skinny road, the distant housetops.

The scent of faraway forests, mirror lakes, and pink blossoms from forgotten lands caressed the missionary in the warm wind.

Porter turned around as he walked. "*Hayaku!*"

Stan Clusser in a white shirt with short sleeves continued wearily with a smile. He lifted a hand to indicate he was still coming. A fast breeze caught the tip of the Elder's blue and burgundy tie, tossing it over his shoulder. He pulled it back into place and grinned. The color of his teeth matched his shirt, contrasting his dark skin like the keys and body of a grand piano.

Porter stopped and stared at the sun, fire lighting his face as he breathed in the wet air. His chest heaved and burned. Goose-bumps grew over his naked forearms. "Have you ever seen anything like this, Elder?"

Stan touched his arm with cold fingertips. *"You'll be fine, Porter."*

* * *

May 2
8:25 a.m. PST

When his eyes opened again, Porter's vision wasn't any better.

Immediately a buzzer came to life to the right of his head.

Hard heels banged the floor as someone came to his side. "All right now, Mr. Porter," said a woman's voice, "I need you to take a deep breath."

The sound didn't dissipate. Porter only wanted to rest. His throat ached. He took a little breath.

"Deeper, Mr. Porter," said the woman, whose face was unclear. "One, two, three—deeeeep breath!"

Porter sucked air hard…his lungs wouldn't operate for some reason, and he really wanted to go back to sleep.

The squealing went away.

Porter thought something and made himself say it with shivering lips. "W-w-what…h-happened."

Was that *his* voice?

"You were shot twice in the stomach. Do you remember getting shot?"

Porter didn't say anything. He was suddenly too cold to speak.

The buzzer went off again.

"Take another breath."

Porter took a breath, but knew it was shallow. The sound didn't stop.

"Come on Mr. Porter, we need to get you breathing on your own again."

He forced his chest to swell, feeling with his mind for the bullet wound. Nerves signaled to his brain a sensation of tightness and depth. He didn't want to move anymore.

The sound ceased.

"This alarm is tracking your respiration," she said, though for some reason he didn't believe her; there was nothing on his face that he could feel. How could the machine know when he was breathing? "It will go off whenever you are not drinking enough oxygen."

Porter closed his eyes as they grew wet.

"We didn't know your medical history, and consequently used anesthesia that we now see you are allergic too. The planned extubation, the removal of the tube, was delayed, but you continued to improve. Your blood count remains good. No blood in your urine. We took the tube out of your bladder and removed the tube from your mouth and airway. You were kept another twenty-four hours for observation in the intensive care unit. You'll be okay. But concentrate on your breathing. Take long breaths. Open your lungs. You've been on a machine and need to draw air on your own now. Do you understand."

The alarm went off, screaming.

Porter heaved his chest, sucking as if it were the last time he'd taste oxygen. He couldn't fill his lungs though he tried. He sank when the speaker sang silence.

"I don't think anyone should see him," she said, walking.

Porter replayed the words in his mind and realized the nurse wasn't speaking to him just then.

There was another voice...a man in the room.

Picturing black turtlenecks and revolvers with silencers attached, Porter kept his eyes closed, hoping the world would go away.

"FBI?" she said. "I guess."

FBI, Porter thought, right!

"Hey, *hen na yatsu*," said the man in his ear. "You awake, Porter?"

Porter lifted his heavy eyelids and moved his head like a newborn's, weaving in the direction he wanted to see. He made out the dark figure.

"They said you've taken a couple bullets. Hurts, doesn't it."

"Clusser?" said Porter, shivering out a sigh. He fluttered his eyelids, but couldn't clear his vision. "I'm freezing."

"Can you get this man another blanket!" Clusser said to the nurse. His voice was powerful, deep as a growling steam engine, fueled like a volcano made of endless burning stone.

"He's reacting to the anesthesia used in surgery," said the nurse. "It'll go away. He's not cold."

Porter reached up with imploring eyes, though he couldn't get them to latch onto his old missionary buddy. He already had weighty blankets over him, but…"P-p-please?"

"He's in a hospital for heaven's sake," said Clusser. "Appease the man with another blanket!"

Porter stared at the floating ceiling, thankful for Clusser's powerful voice. He sniffed cleaning chemicals and new plastic.

He heard the nurse storm across the room and pull a blanket from a cupboard, mumbling under her breath.

She put the blanket over him, and Porter made a frail smile.

"There's a policeman outside your door, Porter. Try to relax," Clusser said.

"Unless h-h-h-he's working for G-Gadianton. Than-nks for coming, Stan." Porter tried to put his left hand on Clusser's, but it went aimless until his old missionary companion took it and gave it a squeeze.

"Well, he's making the nurse nervous."

Porter tried to focus on his friend, but confusion mixed with his dancing vision, so he closed his eyes. "How's the w-wife."

"Porter…I came after I got your e-mail. But I am here on business."

"Convenient. Just-just like you to find a way to b-bring your business with you. You said FBI agents don't jump state to state like in the movies."

"You're wanted by the Bureau and Customs, John," Clusser said, looking down.

Porter made his face point at Clusser's. "But the FBI…isn't in-involved," Porter told himself.

Clusser's foggy face jumped, a shadow against the white walls behind him. "We are now."

Feeling a hand touch his left forearm again, Porter closed his eyes. "I've made the want ads."

Standing, Clusser said, "You don't worry about that. Relax. I've got some things to do. I'll take care of everything." He went to the door.

Porter gazed at the rippling figure against the light background. "The guard…he's to keep me here, isn't he. Not p-protecting me."

Clusser turned in the haze of the open portal. "He'll do both, Porter. Hang in there."

"Right." No wonder the nurse wasn't quick to fetch a blanket.

The alarm wailed....

* * *

6:50 p.m. PST

"You have another visitor, Mr. Porter," said the nurse with a flat voice.

Porter opened his eyes. He could focus, now, so he examined his surroundings. He saw the IV tubing first, which didn't please him. Baby-blue flowers lined the white wall close to the ceiling, and light pink hills rolled three feet from the floor around the room. There was an open curtain between his bed and another, but no one else slept there.

The nurse was beautiful. Solid black hair, sharp eyes, and lips that needed no liner. Too bad she looked at him with so much disdain.

Two men stood behind her. One, he recognized. "Mr. Porter, we've met before," said the fellow without putting out his hand. He wore a dark blue suit, a Nick Hilton most likely, with a slight pattern Porter couldn't make out. His tie was bloodshot red sprinkled with transparent paisley. His tight eyebrows were so perfectly shaped, Porter figured he plucked them. There should be a law against masochism, he thought. Women can have their own rules; Porter wouldn't understand anyway.

"Arnott, right?" Porter said, relieved when he heard his natural voice. He rubbed his eyes with his free hand while his nose drew in the sterile smell of Lysol. His brain was working again.

"You have something that belongs to us."

Porter pulled his fingers away from his eyes and looked at the man behind Arnott. Brown suit with a matching mustache. Slightly balding. "To both of you?"

"Are you calling it KM-3?" said Arnott. "You know we *will* get it in time. Question is how much you intend on hurting yourself before it happens."

Porter looked at the IV. He couldn't leave the bed, though his first thought was to run. But to where? The window?

The man in brown tapped Arnott. "You sure he's all there upstairs? Nurse says he's been out of it."

Arnott never took his eyes off Porter's. "Oh, you can see the life inside his head. The churning. He's with us."

Porter's heart began to speed. He could tell his lungs were back to normal. How long had he been in the hospital?

"You have to make a choice, Porter," said Arnott standing tall and immobile like an obelisk, his lips looking cold. "Put the most important things first. You wanna raise a family, John? What about finally finding a wife. Keep the end in mind. You'll do what's right then. Where's the codex."

"So you can burn it with the rest of the library?" Porter said. "Cover Ulman's find and hope it goes unnoticed for another hundred years?"

Arnott kept his mouth a simple slit as he stared at Porter like a judge over a criminal found guilty.

"Let me take care of this guy, Peter," said the man with the mustache.

Porter kept his lips closed.

"Your choice, Porter. We can ruin your life forever, you know that?"

A tear slipped from Porter's closed eyes. He pictured Pontius Pilate standing in his judgment hall, listening to the accusations made against the man called Christ. He saw Jesus there, tall but unspeaking. He heard the voice of Pilate as he marveled at the silence: *"Speakest thou not unto me? Knowest thou not that I have power to crucify thee, and have power to release thee?"*

Porter said nothing. He knew it could kill him. But he also knew Clusser would be back. Stan had a gun, if that meant anything. And if Porter was wanted by the government now, Clusser would be obliged to protect him. So would the guard outside.

He looked around for a buzzer to call for the nurse in the case he needed her. But what could she do?

Arnott turned to the man behind him. "All right," he said, leaving the room.

The man with the mustache said to the officer beyond the door. "Would you come in for a minute. I don't want any problems with this guy."

"Yes, Detective Mercer."

Porter's heart sunk through the bed. His limbs went limp.

The detective returned with the policeman in a dark blue uniform behind him.

"John Porter," said the balding detective.

"Yes," he said with dread.

"I'm placing you officially under arrest for possession of stolen materials and artifacts from a foreign country. You have the right to remain silent. If you give up the right to remain silent, anything you say can and will be used against you in a court of law. You have the right to speak with an attorney and to have the attorney present during questioning. If you so desire and cannot afford one—"

"I understand my rights," said Porter, having heard it a million times on TV while growing up. "I just have one question. How much did it cost to corrupt a cop?"

The detective tightened his face. "If you so desire and cannot afford one, an attorney will be appointed for you...."

Chapter Twenty-Four

7:23 p.m. PST

Stabbing her middle finger into her left temple, Alred fought against the throbbing in her head. She squinted her eyes and kept reading her written dissertation.

> *I have come to the conclusion that KM-2 does not as yet contain enough evidence to substantiate the underlying theories of Dr. Dennis Albright and Dr. Alexander Peterson that there is in fact an Old World connection with this newfound Mesoamerican culture.*
>
> *As has been explained, the relative ambiguity of Dr. Ulman's discovery may conclude many factors, insinuating possible ancient sea voyages or validating our old Bering Strait suppositions. When we think of how nearly impossible, or how highly improbable, our very own existence is—that we as human beings evolved one plane at a time from minuscule compounds of unorganized matter in a primordial swamp to the super-complex mass of genetic machinery making up our modern forms—one may easily devise the polemic that the apparent similarities between the Kalpa Culture and the Middle East are more than spontaneous aberrations, which we as scientists with pre-programmed paradigms may tie together and term as a new scientific discovery for fame and fortune. But is our ultimate and all-compelling goal to gain greater scholarly status?*

Though spectacular researchers they may be, I believe the aforementioned professors who have insinuated and outwardly professed relations between the KM manuscripts and the lands of ancient Egypt, Arabia, and Palestine have only proven the power of rhetoric and the amazing and dangerous ability to link two unrelated things by means of perceived similar attributes.

The KM-2 document suggests the same—

Alred slapped the paper into her lap with a groan.

None of this mattered anymore.

Staring at the walls of Kinnard's silent office, she rubbed the tip of her tongue between the molars on the right side of her mouth. She closed her eyes and waited, but no one walked up the echoey hallway. Her jade eyes looked at the partly open door. Then they turned to the uncovered window, letting in the twilight darkness. It was the gaping hole she'd seen Porter glancing at as if it hid a beast about to spring. But there was something...the feeling she was being examined from afar by unseen eyes. She imagined Kinnard, Masterson, and the other backstabbing professors standing in a building across the way, watching her with a telescope and binoculars, laughing as she waited for advisors who wouldn't come.

Rubbing her moist palms against the navy skirt wrapping her legs, she looked again at her nearly completed doctoral thesis. Yes, they said she couldn't turn this in. KM-2 was gone.

There was nothing in her notes about KM-3 or Dr. Ulman's paper. Ever wary of the thought police, Alred didn't dare reveal the existence of the new codex. But surely she could still petition to present a version of the paper in her hands, omitting the illegally procured codex. Albright and Peterson had already published their thoughts on the matter. Why couldn't she adjust her work to counter theirs? Porter would still publish something, no doubt. He was a froth-mouthed dog gone mad long ago.

What was she thinking?!?

Alred just couldn't see this semester go completely to rot. All the time she'd spent tearing through ancient documents. All the stress working with John D(etermined) Porter. Listening to his moanings and constant arguments for why the codex had to be valid and why everyone was trying to kill him....

And what were her convictions about the project? What did she *really* believe?

She'd toss it all. It was the only conclusion.

Kinnard hadn't asked her here to discuss anything more about her dissertation anyway. In fact, Alred had the peculiar sensation that she wasn't supposed to be waiting in his office at all, that she should stand and sneak out of the building immediately.

A secretary had left the professor's message on her answering machine. But what if the secretary had called the wrong person...no, that was silly.

So why had she brought her dissertation?

She refused to answer the thought.

Standing, she went to the window and stared at the parking lot smashed between the buildings below. She saw shadows move among the Datsuns, mini-vans, Ford trucks, and cars with the letter Z hidden somewhere in the shadows on their bodies.

From the voice inside her head, she heard new words: What if someone else had asked her to the office?

One of the shapes in the blue light below stepped away from a red Ford van.

Alred's breath went solid in her lungs.

His hair had grown longer than she remembered it. He walked a little more hunched over than she recalled. His large nose and balding brow, and the way he looked in every direction as best he could, like a textbook paranoid case—it all gave him away with a scream: It was Dr. Ulman, striding quickly toward the office structure's rear entrance, three floors beneath Alred's feet.

She pressed her hands, her nose, her forehead against the glass as her heart doubled its pulsing pace. Ulman looked so small, standing far below in a woolen coat made of varying green threads.

The professor moved with determination, leaning slightly forward, driving his toes ahead of him as sensors while his eyes looked behind, to the left, the other side, forward, and back again....

Alred rapped on the window pane four times. She swallowed back the urge to shout his name, a useless gesture considering their distance and the obstacles between them. The window was locked permanently in place.

But there he was in the twilight. And he was alive! And no doubt *he* had called her! The secrets he could tell! The answers!

Her eyes touched quickly on the horizon, where the sun was now gone but firing yellow beams which the dark blue abyss overhead absorbed.

An almost black Crown Victoria stopped between Ulman and the office building. The rear doors opened on either side of the car.

What was this?

The man closest to the professor looked directly at Ulman, who froze like a rabbit weary of predators.

Alred watched words pass between Ulman and the stranger, though neither of them moved. She felt ice moving through her arteries. Both of the men who had exited the car stood within a footfall of the door that sprouted them. They wore dark suits, it seemed.

FBI? she thought, considering their possible involvement with Mrs. Ulman. Had they tracked him here?

Ulman had to get away from those men. Alred hit the window with the flat of her hand before remembering to control her emotions. The glass was cold.

Ulman waved a finger at the man nearest him, his body shaking as he spoke. He moved to turn away, speaking quickly words Alred could never possibly discern.

She watched the man nearest him nod once, twist his head away, and then duck back into the car.

Alred wasn't paying attention to the other man in black, who stood with the car between himself and the other two, until the first flash.

Her forehead hit the glass pane as her eyes blew wide.

The second blast of light also wasn't followed by a sound. Had Alred not seen the outstretched arms aiming the tightly held gun over the roof of the Crown Victoria, she wouldn't have realized a silencer was in use.

Such man-killing paraphernalia were against the law in this country.

These weren't agents of the FBI.

And Ulman was on the ground, torquing his body painfully.

Alred banged her shoulder against the window as she spun and shot out of the office toward the stairs. The elevator would take too long, she figured, and Ulman might be in critical condition...perhaps taking his last breaths.

She rammed Goldstien in the hallway.

"Whoa!" he said, but Alred heard no more before she hit her destination.

The door to the stairs slammed into the wall as she pulled on it and threw herself down the cement chasm. Down, her feet slapped the hard floor until she came to the landing, leaning her body and hanging onto the railing in order to whip around back the other direction, and down the steps, down, only to swing around again, and down....

On the first floor, Alred thumped the door like a battering ram. The door exploded aside as she sprinted to the rear entrance. She pushed the glass door out of her way and skidded her heels on the asphalt only when she came to the spot where Dr. Ulman had dropped.

But there was no body.

The Crown Victoria had vanished.

Her lungs burning, Alred looked up and scanned the parking lot.

Oaks waved and glowed in the dim yellow lamplight. The darkening blue sky growled.

She heard lost dogs barking and howling and chasing one another somewhere under the cloudy sky.

She squatted and touched the ground where she thought Ulman had landed. It was cold, with no memory of a shooting.

These men were masters. They hadn't wounded the professor. It was silent. Their movements, balanced like one-legged cranes in shallow puddles. They'd killed him and left nothing to be found. Especially a body.

There was oil...barely visible in the light.

Alred touched the warm wetness. It wasn't oil.

The air escaped her lungs as she stood again, examining the parking lot exits, the quiet streets beyond them, the night birds...they would tell no tales.

The moisture in her mouth evaporated.

Ulman had disappeared months ago.

No one would ever find him now.

* * *

7:40 p.m. PST

"You shot Porter, Mr. Smith. We'd like to know what you were doing with him."

Smith sat tall in his leather chair. "Who here understands Mormons better than I do?" He looked around the dark table.

"You have been our lead operative on LDS studies for the last fifty years. What does that have to do with Porter."

"Our young troublemaker does not fit the cultural norm in the Mormon society," said Smith without moving. The air, a cool broth of sweet roses, stirred around him. "Porter is what Latter-day Saints deem a fanatic. His decisions would be condemned by most members of his faith. He intrigues me."

Andrews cleared his throat. "Your personal interests could jeopardize our careful and long existence."

"On the contrary," said Smith with a scarecrow grin, "my actions could preserve our investments for another century. You know the Mormons believe they live in the last years of the Earth's present existence. Their long-awaited Millennium is near, according to their own living prophets. John D. Porter is an abnormally unsociable member of his church. We see how endlessly and powerfully his fire burns.

"Now what if a man *arose* among the Latter-day Saints who possessed the same inner strength, unstoppable endurance, and passionate intelligence John Porter exhibits before us. Add to that description... popularity."

Smith waited a moment to let the old committee stew over the disturbing vision.

"A *Porter* who is highly esteemed among his spiritual colleagues... could crack the Earth and change Mormonism in the eyes of the public forever. We need to understand John Porter. *I* need to comprehend him fully in order to recognize other prodigies when they are still in embryo."

"You put two bullets into him," growled Andrews.

"And the men behind Porter were not about to do the same? Porter thought he knew me to some small degree. A polite old man was I. I have given him...paranoia. He will trust no one from this day forth."

"We wanted KM-3," said the man at the end of the table.

"That's why I shot him. Porter would not reveal its location. I did not kill him, however, but immediately summoned an ambulance...an anonymous maneuver. He has been chased, so he's scared. But even the hardest men, who have never been tortured, will change their minds after *real* pain. Porter has received his first bullet wounds. He knows what to fear now....Imagine if we put the tip of a revolver between his eyes. Young people often feel immortal...until they are hurt badly. I have made John Porter...moldable."

* * *

8:59 p.m. PST

When Alred was eighteen years old, she tried alcohol for the first time. The taste surprised her...she thought it would be good. Her older friends laughed when she drank the clear liquid, shushing one another as if someone could hear them doing what they shouldn't be doing, when in reality the parents of the friend whose liquor cabinet they had raided had been gone for days on a second honeymoon and weren't due back from the green hills of Ireland for another week. They'd never be caught; there wasn't a chance.

As the night progressed, Alred remembered the sinking flame in her chest. Her head throbbed as if she had a headache, but there was no pain. There was, however, the mild experience of flu symptoms after a time, her head swimming one way and then the other. Someone had lubricated the connection between her spine and the base of her skull.

She laughed with her friends, but felt a grayness around her, unspoken echoes she could never later explain. Then came the sickness. The running. The embarrassment of making a mess in the cream-carpeted hallway. The accusations and bawling out her friend gave her, along with all the guilt of what would happen next—how could they clean it up right before the parents returned. And all this in an unfeeling haze.

Alred remembered the desire to cry, the tears coming all the way to the bottom of her eyelids...but refusing to come out. She was so sorry for it all. Yes it was true, she couldn't "hold her liquor." Yes, it might have been better if she "hadn't come over at all." But she couldn't cry. She chose to show no emotion. No sincerity in her words. Forced apathy.

She drove home inebriated and stupid with a "Don't Drive Drunk" sticker on the back of her Plymouth. She'd never drink again. She hated herself and her friends. But as time passed she hated herself for making the choice....

Stumbling from her car toward Bruno's cafe, Alred had the same sensation she'd suppressed so many years ago. She knew the fire inside her had to be heartburn, but she couldn't explain the dullness surrounding her head. She didn't understand why the world had gone foggy, when she knew the air was clear. Why couldn't she cry...when she felt it rising inside?

Well, she'd never wept in public and rarely at all—proud of her control over emotion. But she wouldn't be able to let it out now if she wanted to. It was the same as so long ago...

And Alred couldn't stop thinking of her dead dog, Dorado, who'd run away never to return.

This had nothing to do with pets.

She'd look for Porter and take his approach to life, drowning herself in a few cups of the old man's hot chocolate.

Her dog was dead.

"Alred!"

She stopped, but her head continued to sway, filled spontaneously with synapse-destroying poison. Her eyes dug through the dark of the alleyway that bent between the cafe and another building and then behind Bruno's place.

"Back here!"

It was a shouted whisper.

Sighing with a drunk groan, Alred was thankful she was on friendly terms again with Porter. But she wished he'd stop all this spy vs. spy garbage. Didn't he understand no one could do anything to him if he stayed in a populated area? Bruno's would suit, but *inside* was where all the people were, not behind the place.

"Hurry up!"

She took a step into the alley. Her head rocked on her soft neck. Her mind seemed lighter, her brain somehow warmer than normal.

Then Alred felt a hand against her, holding her away from the alley. But there was no one there, no one keeping her from walking alone into the darkness, away from the streetlights, away from the populated area where she was headed. It was as if all the molecules that made up her figure began leaning in the opposite direction, attempting to keep her out of the darkness.

Was she losing her equilibrium?

She'd found Ulman. Finally. But now…

Putting a hand to her forehead, she closed her eyes and leaned against the cold wall. "Porter," she said, not loud enough for him to hear, however, "I…think I'm in shock. I need to sit down." "Alred!"

"All right!" she said, throwing her body against the current.

Weaving to the end of the alley crowded with rolled debris that looked like discarded carpets, garbage cans in perpetual use, and heaps of broken tiles and forgotten paint cans, she came out behind Bruno's where there was little room but for the rubbish and the dark.

Something moved among the filth. "Where are you," she said, not afraid to talk out loud. She tried to examine the cans, the soaked boxes, the plastic bags with nifty ties that were already busted open to wait for the scavengers flying around Stratford. Opposite the back of Bruno's, an ancient chain-linked fence protected an older wooden fence rising some seven feet behind the first. The rear door to a '70s style hair salon pinched off any other exit from the darkness. The black wall hugged Bruno's building. Some useless two by fours were piled up against it, as far as she could see. Large boards leaned against the black wall behind her, which climbed another two stories. There was no light.

"Porter?" she said, squinting, though it didn't help.

Alred could barely make out the details and frankly had little time to do so.

"Turn around…slowly." It wasn't Porter's voice.

Alred did as directed and stared into the face of a dark-skinned man with a Latino accent. For all she knew, the voice could have been faked. She'd left all normality last semester. "Where's John Porter," she said.

"I want the codex!" said the man before her. He lifted a hooked knife that had been there in the dark, but which she didn't see until it came within inches of her face. "I know about the ancient book you got from Mrs. Ulman. She was stupid to lie. Now it's gonna cost her. But not until you pay."

"You're going to kill her," said Alred, her lips quivering.

Alred saw the gun go off twice in her mind, Dr. Ulman falling to the blacktop.

She felt the blood rushing through every part of her figure, every appendage. The surge was powerful and her legs were ready to dart for the exit of this hidden hole in the city. But she'd never make the alley before he did, before he—

"No talking!" His voice was a hiss as he closed in on her, pushing her backward with the knife point. "You're gonna give me the codex, or you'll tell me where it is, and all this will be over! Understand?!"

"I haven't understood any of this from the beginning. Did you kill Dr. Ulman?" she said, seeing the gun go off over the hood of the Crown Victoria. Again, the flare of light like a silent sun, there and gone, there and gone again. If this was one of the assassins who'd murdered her favorite professor a short time ago, she would definitely not leave this alleyway in her bodily form. Guns with silencers....

But why the knife?

"Who said anything about him?!! I said you're gonna give me the codex, now let's have it!!!" Alred could see him trembling with adrenaline.

She smelled the twisting rot of tossed meat and wet salad thrown out days ago, and she wondered if it was the man's breath. He was no professional. Not like the others. He wore a sweater with a pattern she couldn't make out in the dark. A goatee hung lazily around his mouth. His eyes were full of shiny darkness, and she could make out no white. He wasn't like the others.

But he could kill her just the same.

"How much longer do you wanna stay alive? Huh?!?" he said, tilting his head with a jerk.

"I don't have it," she said, backing up a little more, feeling the wall close behind her, the discarded waste at her heels.

"I'll end all your troubles here and now, little girl! Now talk to me!!!" he said, taking another step at her, jabbing the blade in the air.

"I said I don't have the codex!"

"You wanna be in the hospital like your friend?!!" he said.

Alred stopped, her heart sinking. Her head rocked without weight as she collated his words and examined the data. Hospital? Calmly, she said, "Porter's...got it hidden away somewhere. He won't even let me see it."

"You just don't understand me, woman!" he said, pointing the cutting edge at her chin. "I'm supposed to kill you and make it look like a mugging! But you're Snow White and I'm the hunter, got it?! I don't have anything against women, and I wanna get outta here!!! You tell me—"

Pinching her lips together into a twisted knot, Alred reached quickly with both hands for the fist holding the blade before her.

His words still caught in his mouth, the assassin went silent as Alred grabbed the pinkie side of his right hand and swiveled it over up and left with a jolt.

The knife disappeared.

Slamming her left elbow into his right elbow as he screamed against the hyper-extension of his arm, Alred forced the man to the frigid ground in one second. As the blade chattered against brick and stone, she released him just in time to pull herself upright and drive the pointed tip of her shoe into the center of his chest.

He yelled a painful moan as Alred started for the alley.

But another man stood in her way, a shadow in the blackness. She could make out the dark suit coat with sharp shoulder pads, perfectly pressed, and the raven-colored turtleneck beneath the blazer, the slick hair, the hard gaze, and of course the raised 9 mm Smith and Wesson, silencer already screwed in place.

The new assassin shook his head and glanced at the writhing thug on the ground. "Figeroa, you fool." He looked up. "Good evening, Ms. Alred. Let me assure you that I *never* underestimate women."

With his thumb, he pulled on the black hammer.

It locked into place.

He smiled without another word…and pulled the trigger.

Chapter Twenty-Five

9:06 p.m. PST

"Harvey Goodwill is a professional eliminator, Peter…" said Andrews with a tight grin.

In a quiet hall, wide enough for a compact car to drive through, Peter shook hands with Harvey, a short man who looked nothing like an assassin. What little hair the man had was dirty blond, and he stood in a simple olive-colored suit with brown shoes. Energy coursed through him, making his movements jittery and quick. He smiled like an old pal at a high school reunion. But he had the frigid eyes of a killer.

"Pleased," said Goodwill.

Peter's lips didn't move. His voice box barely shivered as if frozen in sub-zero temperature.

"Harvey is one of our friends."

The words were a code, the meaning: *He is with us and party to our secrets.*

"Of course, that's not his real name," said the old man. "He's not as sloppy as your man, Polaski. No one notices when Goodwill comes and goes. Excellent for our operations. Mr. Goodwill has served the needy by killing in most European countries and many of their colonies. He's as nonchalant as a taxi on Manhattan Island and as careful as a software engineer," said Andrews.

"What's he for," said Peter, the air dusty and cold around them. He smelled cedar.

The old man smiled. "Mr. Porter is being held in the North Bay Police department, is he not?"

Peter nodded.

"You will direct Goodwill there in order to accomplish one goal." Andrews lifted his chin.

"We want Porter killed before he discusses KM-2 and 3 in the federal courts," said Peter.

"Now you're thinking like one of us, Peter. We will expect a summary of the proceedings."

* * *

The bullet left the chamber, creating a burst of light and a painful chirp which echoed in the tight space behind Bruno's cafe.

Alred felt her heart stop.

It started again when she realized she was still standing. Her eyes closed and snapped open accordingly.

Figeroa's twisting form fell limp against the ground.

No way to escape this guy, Alred thought, staring at the man in black through the reeking darkness. She tried to examine his clothes and recognized them to some degree. This man could have been either of the two who'd murdered Ulman.

Wisely, he stayed near the alley entrance, his gun sturdy in his hand at chest level. "It would be such a simple thing to kill you."

"But a complete waste," she said. "I already told—"

"I heard you. And if you're lying—"

"What happened to Porter," Alred didn't move. This man had just killed the thief behind her. If he'd slain Ulman as well, he would most likely not hesitate to execute her. But what else could she say? Alred refused to be beaten.

"Bullets hit people who get in their way. Now, you're going to help me—"

"I'm not doing anything for you."

The man sipped liters of cold air. He pushed his bottom lip against his top, and sucked on his left canine. "All right." He lifted the gun to arm's length.

A screen door came out of the back of Bruno's. The weak metal smashed into the assassin, turning the gun away and shoving him over.

A jaguar in the shape of a man followed the screen, lunging at the man with the weapon. Fists drummed like hail into the killer's face until he tumbled into the ripped bags of reeking refuse.

The gun disappeared among the garbage piles.

When the man in black failed to rise, Bruno whipped around to face the student. One of the front tails of his button-down shirt had come free of his pants. The old man fixed it while the chemical rush gave his eyes fifty years of youth. "You okay?"

Alred looked at the second assassin, unmoving, his head lost in the rubbish. Stepping away from the corpse, warm water floated up between her eyelids as she glanced at Figeroa's body.

Rubbing his worn and tender knuckles, Bruno said in a husky voice, the softest she'd ever heard from him, "Get out of here, girl. I'm phoning the police, an I gotta hunch you don't wanna be here when they arrive."

She stared at the old man, attempting uselessly to decipher reality. But nothing made sense. Why would anyone kill so much over an archaeological find? Is this what Stratford feared? No professor could afford all these hit men, no matter how strong the lust to steal the glory Ulman deserved. Someone wanted KM-3 bad. But how could they know about it?!? Nevertheless...Porter *couldn't* be right about all this.

"Go!" said Bruno, moving to the cafe's rear door, hidden in the dark. He shot her a serious look.

Alred left the alley, thinking about predator shadows and hospitals. She wondered what Porter had faced and what had resulted....

* * *

May 3
11:57 a.m. PST

"Alred! I didn't think you'd be my first visitor," said Porter. He looked around the white room with red brick walls, thankful he could smell Alred's sharp perfume instead of the sanitized hospital he'd been in the last couple days, or the dirty earth scent of his new cell.

Squinting, Alred said, "You haven't spoken with a lawyer?"

"Not yet. Guess they're booked. Or no one wants to work my case."

"You don't know what I had to do to find you, Porter," said Alred, pulling her overcoat tightly around her, though there was enough heat in the room to make a man think he had a fever. "How could you be in jail!?"

"My mom always said I had a knack of getting into things," he said into the microphone through the glass sheet separating them. There was enough room at the top of the pane to slide his fingers through to touch hers. But the cameras would see, the guards would freak, grab him, strip him, and arrest Alred. Not that she would slip her fingers over the glass to meet his anyway. Porter longed to feel the warmth of someone. But he couldn't call his family, especially his mother, so he phoned no one. And Alred looked beautiful for some reason.

"I didn't want to believe it when they said you'd been shot. In the abdomen? How are the wounds," she said, pointing with her chin at his shoulder. Porter's right arm hung in a sling.

"Sometimes I think there are people out there who just don't like me," Porter said.

Alred smiled.

"You one of them?" he said, his eyes sparkling, but his smile nodding downward.

"If only you could read—"

"Ah!" said Porter, lifting a hand quickly. His eyes flickered toward the microphone standing like a perched cobra about to strike.

Alred grinned without emotion as she looked at the table.

"It's a terrible thing to have something you wanna tell someone, isn't it? When you can't utter a word?" said Porter. They were no doubt being taped.

"You realize we've lost any chance of graduating," said Alred.

"Sacrifice is an important part of life. Build's character," said Porter, but the thought hurt inside. "There must be opposition in all things. We've walked into places angels don't even talk about."

"I'm not so easily defeated," said Alred.

"Oh really?" said Porter with a sigh. "You saying that for your own peace of mind? Because you don't want to think you've moved your last chess piece and admit the game is finished?"

Alred smashed her lips together, but kept her eyes relaxed. She looked at Porter. "Isn't there a Mormon prayer to help you out in court? May 5th is just around the corner."

"I was baptized on that day," said Porter.

"Well it will definitely be the day you begin your new life."

"Am I guilty?" said Porter.

Alred stared at him. "Of many things. We all are. Plato quoted Socrates as saying everyone breaks the law just shy of the degree at which they might get caught."

"I didn't realize you read the classics?" said Porter with a grin. "What happens when these laws we're supposed to follow are set by God?"

"You're the faithful one. Why do *I* sound like the optimist?" said Alred.

Porter scratched the back of his head. "It can't get much worse than this."

"They could nuke the building," said Alred.

Smiling, Porter said, "And I'd turn around and find myself in a happier place."

Alred let her head fall to the right. Her red hair fell in quick waves from behind her ear. "You don't think you're headed for Hades?"

Leaning back in his chair, Porter rubbed his eyes with one hand. He sighed at the white ceiling and coughed into his left fist. "Have you come to discuss my beliefs? We have missionaries outside of prison walls who are more than happy to tell you about the afterlife."

"I came...because...I knew you were alone," said Alred. "You're hurting."

The light in Porter's face faded and red pain took its place. "You know me so well?"

"You'd love it, you know," she said, insinuating the new codex.

Porter lowered his chin to his chest. "I was on top of the world before I met you."

"Tell me one thing, Porter." Alred leaded close to the microphone, looked him hard in the eyes, and whispered with sincerity on her face like a painting of a lonely girl. "How can someone with your intelligence...honestly believe that a god exists?"

Porter focused on her pupils. "Alred, how is it that someone with your investigative capabilities and strategic learning skills does *not* put two and two together and realize that all I've been saying is accurate?"

"I really don't see your church as much different than any other," said Alred, pushing the soft auburn behind her ears. "I went weekly to Catholic mass long ago, and all I saw were formulas filling in blanks when answers weren't present."

"You would bring all this up when I'm at my weakest," Porter said. He sighed and sniffed, rubbing his nose with the back of one finger. "Do you know why Mormons are called Mormons?"

"Porter, I think I know why you've been hunted," said Alred.

"Would you be offended if I—"

"And I think it has nothing to do with religion."

"Pardon?"

Alred studied him for a moment before opening her mouth again. What was she seeing? "I was attacked twice...by armed men insisting I give them—"

Porter lurched forward but kept his voice down. "You were what?!?"

"Porter," said Alred with solid smoke in her eyes, "I know for a fact now that Ulman...is...dead. I've seen—" Alred looked at the microphone, "—terrible things."

Sitting with his mouth hanging loose, Porter put the picture together in his mind. She's seen...what. Ulman? Dead? Alred was attacked? After Porter was shot and charged with illegal possession of foreign artifacts? All while she's been hiding KM-3? "And this has nothing to do with my church?"

"I did some checking," she said, reaching into her black bag. "This kind of activity is not unheard of."

"You're suggesting...what?" said Porter.

"Remember Dr. Peterson at Ohio State? He publicly revoked his statements connecting Ulman's find and the Old World—"

"When!" said Porter, leaning upward.

"There was no date," she said, sliding the pages face-up toward the glass.

Pressing his fingers against the transparent wall as if it helped him speed-read, Porter hummed the growl of a faraway muscle car.

"I pulled it off the Internet. Peterson reminds his associates that many scholars have made the same mistake with past archaeological finds. He even cites a stela which members of the LDS church reportedly associate with the Book of Mormon. Here, on this page."

"I see it," said Porter with a heavy weight in the back of his throat, but he didn't need to focus on the image and writing, for he knew it well. "Stela number five from Izapa." He looked sharply into Alred's green eyes. "That 'tree of life' stone has more than one hundred and fifteen arbitrary connections to an extremely detailed scene described in the first and second parts of the Book of Mormon. Peterson can't use that as proof of—"

"Nevertheless, he has," said Alred with a sigh. "My point is Dr. Peterson refuses to note any more correlations with the Middle East. He has completely changed his testimony on the subject."

Porter slapped the tabletop, looked to his right, then back at her. He felt the pressure in his veins but tried to relax, fearing his excitement would draw the officer who'd led him into the room.

"Peterson even suggests that he'd been fooled by Professors Ulman and Albright into thinking the site in Guatemala to be much more than it actually was."

Shaking his head, Porter laughed without humor.

With her eyebrows high, Alred put the papers back into her portfolio. "Think now," she said with a voice as controlled as it had been on the day they'd first met. "We know Albright died of a heart attack."

Porter opened his mouth.

But Alred raised her voice. "The authorities are unified with that decision. We know Dr. Wilkinson was murdered, but there is no direct evidence to link him to Ulman's find. And Ulman...only recently—"

"I know," Porter said, covering the microphone as if it stopped his thoughts.

Staring at him in silence while he banged the logical facts against his predisposed brain, Alred pushed her lips into the tight red ball she often made. "They want the codex all right," she said, relaxed. "But they are little more than modern-day grave robbers."

With a grin, but still no light in his eyes, Porter said, "You've seen too much Indiana Jones. Nobody steals ancient artifacts anymore."

Alred squinted at him. They both knew he was wrong and only lying to himself...and the microphone.

Porter rubbed his forehead. "Did you know St. Basil pointed out long ago that with all the importance of the sacraments, the exact instruction and liturgy were *never recorded* by the original apostles?"

Folding her arms, Alred said, "Never thought about it." Her face shouted, *Who even cares?!?*

"Why do you suppose that is? While the word for word blessing of the bread and wine are given in the Book of Mormon?" said Porter.

Alred clenched her teeth together. What was this? Another desperate attempt by Porter to claim reason for this semester's insanity? He'd made the greatest mistakes of his life, to her knowledge. He'd never attain the positions for which he had worked so hard and so well. He had nothing left but his religion, that which has throughout history been sought by poor souls when hope was feared to be lost. She had to listen. To humor him. To give him this last moment before the blade met the chopping block, publicly ending his existence forever.

"There's only one other place I know of where the words of the bread and wine sacrament have been written down, and that's on an ancient Egyptian Coptic Christian manuscript called *the Gospel of the Twelve Apostles* discovered in 1904. Funny thing: it's exactly the same prayer. That means archaeological evidence suggests Joseph Smith had an English copy of a sacred invocation, which he then placed in the Book of Mormon, a hundred years before the rest of the modern world possessed it.

"I never said it before, but the *Popol Vuh* tells some specific stories that are found only in the Book of Mormon. Nowhere else that I know of can you find those stories. But the *Popol Vuh* wasn't converted from Mayan into Spanish and published in a common tongue until 1857, about thirty years *after* the Book of Mormon was translated into English. Now anyone can pick up a copy of the *Popol Vuh* in English for under twenty bucks."

"I'm sorry Porter," said Alred, attempting to be as sincere and open as possible. "I won't fill your head with delusions. I have to be honest. You're just not convincing me of anything. I need proof that what you are talking about is real. Why aren't there any more solid, undeniable texts? If the Book of Mormon really is an account of some of the ancient inhabitants of the Americas, why are there no more books confirming the idea? What happened to them all?"

"Alred," Porter whispered, "you know better than I do. All the Spaniards—Father Diego de Landa was a Franciscan friar who tore down Mayan temples, destroyed sacred shrines, and tortured the natives when he caught them worshipping in the fashion of their ancient ways. When he found in the village of Muna some who were able to translate the old writings in their possession, de Landa had their cache of twenty-four books, bound in jaguar skins, all burned! After tormenting thousands of Mayans, de Landa returned to Spain, then came back to the same people in the New World to rule as their bishop. There is also a strong tradition describing what are often called the *Golden Books of the Mayas*, fifty-two gold plates with engravings which relate the entire history of the Mayan people. Now, what would soldiers do if they found a book made of gold? You ask me what happened to the records of the Americas? White man happened. It's an old story."

"I know about Diego de Landa," she said, nodding.

"Then why are you here, Alred?! Tell me the truth," said Porter, knowing her words would be painful to hear, but utterly necessary.

Staring at him for half-a-minute without speaking, Alred considered her options.

This *had* gone on long enough.

"You know I hated the project from the beginning," she said.

He nodded.

"I stayed with you…because I had to find out what happened to Ulman."

"That's it?" said Porter.

"It's all over now, Porter. And you know I won't sacrifice my standards about our judicial system when we come to court."

"At least you have *some* standards," Porter said, his face sagging. He eyed her, a mask of solemn thought changing his features to look like some ancient prophet contemplating the end of the world as seen in a vision. "Alred…you have…held the proof…in your hands."

"But I've had so little time to study the codex."

"A religion is something we analyze for a lifetime. You may figure it all out, Alred….But will it be too late?"

"Can your faith get you out of jail?" said Alred with eyes on the base of the microphone. She ached for him, sitting alone and trapped behind the bullet-proof glass. He had nothing. There was no one to feel for him. No one who would dare care. Didn't he realize his words were pushing her out to the room? He needed her! Whoever hunted him would surely use Porter's family if he pulled them into the picture. Who's to say *they* haven't already? She looked into his gray eyes. "You're gonna be tried for illegally possessing the archaeological treasures of a foreign country. And they'll use me to testify against you. You're a Mormon, so I'm sure you'll understand my honesty when I tell them…that everything they suspect…is true."

"Truth only hurts when it ought to," Porter told himself with a sting, a twisted smile, and a pale face.

Chapter Twenty-Six

May 4
2:35 p.m. PST

"Porter," said Clusser, drumming his fingers together and leaning forward, "What's going on?" The weight of the situation drew his dark walnut-colored face into a mass of ridged sobriety.

"Where have you been?!?" Porter said, adjusting himself in his seat and looking around the tight room with no cameras, no microphones, and no glass walls.

"Do you know a man by the name of Gerard Jasper?" said Clusser looking at his fingers.

"You realize how long I've been in here?!?"

"Don't worry about that."

"I'm getting buried alive in bureaucratic sand! Pounding on the inside of my coffin won't help at all after a few more days. Don't you think this trial is going to court a bit *too* fast?"

"What do you know about the legal system, Porter. If you want help, you'll give me answers. I want to know what you think happened to the man you wrote me about, Christopher Ulman. I want to know where this ancient document, KM-2, is hidden."

Porter's face flushed. "I don't have it anymore. It's back in Stratford's possession."

Clusser ran his fingers through the butched curls of raven hair hugging his slightly balding head, which tilted to the right. He grimaced and sighed together. "You remember Koishi-san? Tall Japanese? Skinny as a starving man? Do you recall that last day he met with us, how through his cigarette-stained teeth he told us in his own language, '*Even if I find the truth, I will not change?*"

"Yeah, Koishi," said Porter, his mind drawn back to Japan behind closed eyes.

"I *never* understood that," said Clusser. "Why would anyone *choose* to dodge the facts when they *know* they are valid and *will* have the greatest impact on their temporal lives?"

"I couldn't figure him out myself."

With solid eyes holding his old missionary companion in place, Clusser said in his naturally deep voice, "Well I don't have a clue as why you would do the same stupid thing!"

Porter pulled his head back. "I've never heard you talk this way."

"I've never been so worried about a friend as helpless as yourself! I know it's not your nature, but I want you to *listen* to me, Porter."

"School's changed me, Clusser," said Porter, his voice weak but serious. He looked at the dark tabletop between his fingers.

"I hope so. You're in real trouble."

"You said not to worry about it."

"Someone shot you with two .40 caliber Smith and Wesson, 180 grain, jacketed round nose bullets from less than ten feet away and then disappeared. Was it a punk?"

"No."

"I didn't think so. My guess is, you were meant to live."

Porter's mouth opened, but there was no power to fuel his voice box.

"You're hiding the codex. You know I recognize your motives. I've read the articles about Dr. Ulman's find. I've even examined your incomplete doctoral thesis."

"How did you get that?!" Porter said, his head popping like a jack-in-the-box.

"You probably think you're doing our church a service, but you've forgotten the Twelfth Article of Faith," said Clusser, putting his hands together.

"Why memorize them if you've always got 'em with you," said Porter. "What are you insinuating."

"You memorize everything else, Porter," Clusser said with disappointment on his face. "I'm talking about the article that says, 'We believe in…obeying, honoring, and sustaining the law.' You think the prophet would sanction your possession of KM-2 in violation of our legal system? Everyone knows you have it."

Drained of hope and power, Porter sagged into the back of his chair. He said nothing and fought back the wetness behind his eyelids. He sniffed the musky scent of Clusser's cologne on the lukewarm air. Porter didn't recall Clusser ever wearing any form of scent. He'd changed. "You're…with them."

Clusser lifted his chin and squared his jaw. "If you mean the law? Yes."

Porter sat quietly. The room otherwise smelled slightly of coffee left by the former occupants.

"But that's not what you're thinking," said Clusser.

Porter leaned forward and whispered. "I…was…shot, Clusser. Do customs agents normally do that?!"

Clusser looked into his briefcase, withdrew a file, and pulled out a picture. "Let me ask you again. Do you know this man?"

It was a candid photo. Porter recognized the face. Clean, hair perfectly set in place, untouched by the bad weather around him. Icy eyes making the blue-gray sky behind him look sunnier. The man wore a long overcoat of some suede-like material, navy in color. A suit underneath with a solid burgundy tie against a pressed white shirt.

"You never said anything about him. Friend of yours?" Porter's last words bit with a bitter tone.

"Gerard Jasper," said Clusser.

"No…this guy's name is Arnott."

Clusser's face lost all emotion and regained it again…in about a millisecond. "*Peter* Arnott?"

"I guess. He works at Stratford University."

Clusser smiled his white teeth. He tilted his head again, but there was no glow in his eyes. "No he doesn't. Is this the man who shot you."

Porter waited, of course well-aware of the answer. "No."

"Then who did."

Porter paused. "I don't know his name." He couldn't very well say he was shot by Joseph Smith! It was obviously a pseudonym.

"You've gotta work with me on this, Porter!"

"I'm going to be tried for an international crime in a Federal court, right? For what, stealing Ulman's merchandise."

"You got it. Look…by law you have the right to say nothing here without legal counsel—"

"Clusser, I need your help! I told you, the University took KM-2 away from me!" Porter said, leaning into his friend's face.

"Stratford strictly states that you, John D. Porter, are in possession of the codex." Clusser stopped with his mouth open. His probing eyes dug deep into Porter's brain, scanning for the facts Porter couldn't explain.

Porter half-hoped Clusser would find what he needed and say nothing. But the throbbing silence ached. Clusser stared until Porter moved to speak for the sake of killing the quiet and salvaging their friendship.

But Clusser's words were faster. "You don't trust me anymore."

"Only because you refuse to believe me when I'm telling you the truth," said Porter, sitting back slowly.

Clusser swished his tongue in his closed mouth. "You think I'm with those who tried to kill you. I'm not. But unless you help me figure out what's happening here, one thing's for sure: your middle initial stands for *Dead-meat*. Either in the courtroom…or outside it."

"Thanks for the confidence," said Porter, folding his arms.

"They don't want you alive, Porter." Clusser added, "You were involved in the incident at the library, weren't you."

"How did you—"

"The librarians made a list of the odd conglomeration of books you'd left on a table. It's amazing the police didn't trace them to you."

"I never checked them out."

"How many students at Stratford would have a mixture of Mayan, Hebrew, and Egyptian texts and dictionaries spread open in one place? It was in the report, but never followed for some reason."

"I can give you one. *They* didn't want the police involved." Porter crossed his legs under the table, then loosened his limbs as he realized he was hugging himself—a common sign of insecurity and an attempt at psychological self-defense.

"The night librarian was given three hundred-dollar bills by an unrecognized man to step out for a coffee. The librarian came forward with the guilt-ridden truth. So if you were the only one in the library… you broke the window to get off the second floor. It was your blood the officers typed."

"And you can't see why I'm in here now? They want to destroy all evidence of Ulman's find."

"And *they* killed Dr. Ulman," Clusser said for him.

Porter nodded.

Leaning forward, Clusser said, "The nebulous *they* won't hold up in court, Porter."

"If *they* got into Stratford, who's to say they wouldn't gain control of the codex after the judge is through?"

"So you do have KM-2."

"No! I'm saying a 'what-if!'" Porter was slipping up. He needed help, but was afraid to open his mouth anymore. He wiped his face with both hands. "What does Arnott have to do with all this, then."

The FBI looked silently through the transparent air, thick with dust visible in the bright beams from over their heads. "I shouldn't say anything."

Porter slapped the table. "Yes you should! Comp.!?!"

"Don't call me that. We haven't been missionaries for years." Clusser groaned as their eyes held each other in a silent bond full of crackling electricity. "Raymond Polaski, the suspect in the Wilkinson murder, came forward. He said he was hired by a man called Gerard Jasper. Polaski said, however, that he heard a number of people call Jasper a different name: Peter."

"Then you have your proof! Polaski can testify and—"

"Polaski shot himself while in Police Protection."

"Really," Porter said in disbelief. "Do people in safe houses usually have access to guns?"

"We don't know how he obtained the weapon. But with Polaski's information, I was able to find out a bit about this…Peter Arnott."

"False name," Porter said with a dull voice. Reality was crumbling around him. With innocence, he looked at Clusser. "You're FBI. You told me agents handled cases in their own areas, never chasing them personally across the US like in the junk novels, but transferring the info and responsibility to whatever office is closest to the relative location."

Clusser stood and looked with dark eyes at his one-time companion.

Porter licked his lips. "You have no jurisdiction here."

With a flat smile, Clusser said, "Just came to help a friend." He turned to the exit.

"Where are you going?"

The agent stopped and looked back. "Porter…you're not lying to me….I need to know."

Porter shook his head.

"Then I'm off to the bat-cave. See you in court."

* * *

May 5
8:40 a.m. PST

Well, the tuna was a little old, but Harvey Goodwill munched away without noticing. He'd waited in his beat-up '92 Mustang for over two hours, watching for his mark, one John D. Porter, to show his face.

It would be an effortless assassination.

Goodwill's mark had a rather simple face with no peculiarities, the kind of kisser Goodwill wanted for himself—Porter would make the perfect killer! The student's hair was flat and dry brown, his eyes a haze of plain gray. Even when Porter smiled there wasn't a glow. At least not in the photographs. Goodwill memorized the snapshots before tearing them into the toilet of a motel with no name.

Goodwill had taken easier men down, like the rich fellow of many years who'd been feeding his own organized criminal unit enough funds to make them immortal and beyond reach. That man had never openly posed as a crime lord, and therefore never suspected that anyone knew of his existence. He'd lived in obscurity behind electronic defenses and more than ten angry rottweilers that chewed on whole tires for fun. That guy was a sip of soda. He never awoke from his sleep, and the doctors blamed his death on his yellow liver.

This Porter job wouldn't be much of a bother at all. It would be over within an hour. Goodwill would be on a Greyhound to Florida before eleven o'clock, reading the sports page and chewing on apple skins.

He smiled at the thought.

The plan was basic. One man on the outside: the hit man. One on the inside: the point man. The point man went by the name *Red Rover,* while Goodwill was known only as *Sunshine.*

Goodwill waited and watched as Red Rover took care of all preliminary operations. Someone made the stupid jurisdictional decision to put Porter in a small bus for the trip to court.

The point man had already checked: there was no one else but the driver on board, one Jackie Golb, and he was a competent officer. Golb wasn't a US Marshall, which was out of the ordinary. And normally, a second Marshall accompanied the driver while transporting a prisoner aboard a bus. These intentional errors in propriety amused Goodwill. Who knows, Goodwill's employers may have had a hand in setting up this folly. The lax attitude on the part of the administrators would become a point of contentious debate during the investigation that would inevitably follow the assassination. The officers would yell at each other while Goodwill put up his heels and spent his well-earned bucks faraway.

Goodwill took another bite of his sandwich as he replayed the rest of the scenario in his mind. He'd designed it. Of course it would work.

Red Rover, also a excellent officer with a heretofore perfect record, would ask Officer Golb where he was headed. The driver would tell him. The inside man would reply that he had orders to report to the Federal courthouse as well and would playfully be kind enough to "escort" the bus. It was an unnecessary offer, but it would help Golb relax. Not that Porter was a particularly corrupt individual liable to escape, or even to make the attempt, but this way Golb wouldn't have much to think about besides driving.

A small remote-controlled relay had been placed in the line of the radio power cable in the bus. It was a simple device, which Goodwill called a *Snubber*, for lack of another term. When activated, the Snubber opened the circuit, resulting in an absence of power to the device the electricity was supposed to operate; i.e., no radio. If Golb had a phone on his person, it wouldn't matter. It would all be over moments after it began.

Red Rover would then get into his own car when the bus driver looked ready to go. He would radio Golb to confirm the green light and give the naive man a feeling of bland normality. Immediately, Red Rover would hit the remote to the Snubber, killing the driver's radio. No smoke. No nothing. Golb wouldn't realize for a moment he'd been cut off from the real world.

Goodwill pulled a green apple from his bag and began skinning it with his teeth, chewing the epidermis like gum.

The next part the inside man would play would make him appear completely innocent of the crime about to occur. It would result in Red Rover's patrol car pulling to the side of the freeway. He would later report a string of carefully crafted fables followed by the verbal admittance that he "was unsure of what he saw and what *really* happened."

Porter would be found dead, the driver also executed. The authorities would come and spin their mental tires until they ran out of gas.

The case of John D. Porter's death would go nowhere, because there would be no leads to follow.

Worse case scenario: By some devilish miracle, flaws were found in Red Rover's story.

Fine. Regardless of Red Rover's moves, the assault on John Porter would never go further than the helpful officer.

Beneath a worn copy of Andrew Boxleiter's, *Natural Contagions*, a 10 mm semiautomatic—which had been taken from the evidence locker of this very police building not one day previously—rested on the smooth passenger seat of Goodwill's Mustang. (The thief was already unknown.) Before catching his Greyhound, Goodwill would drop the gun in a parcel to be picked up by a courier dubbed *Guy Smiley*, who would keep it. And in the case of mishap, Guy Smiley would plant the pistol in Red Rover's apartment—just as a precaution. Of course all legal conclusions would have to admit that the patsy Red Rover had committed the murder himself. He would be the necessary scapegoat for the greater good, the fall guy…

And Goodwill would be at a Reggae concert on the beach.

He bit his sandwich with a new lust. But the taste hadn't changed, and the lettuce was getting soggy, turning to strings in his mouth.

Of course, the assassin took twice as much care not to get caught by his current employers in a similar backstabbing. He took every precaution, including the name by which everyone identified him. In fact, Goodwill had had so many names, it took effort to remember the one his parents had given him at christening.

Like a squirrel suddenly aware of an approaching rattlesnake, Goodwill sat up. He lifted the spy-glass to his face and eyed the crowds coming out of the building.

Four officers talking to each other.

Ah!

Red Rover.

The crooked policeman laughed and slapped another officer in the shoulder.

The driver, no doubt.

It didn't really matter if Jackie Golb had been replaced at the last minute. The plan was so devised as to rebound from possible changes. No job could be more professional.

The inside man shoved his hands up and pointed with his thumb at his own squad car, parked near the front of the mini-bus. So nonchalant. Maybe a little too overdone, but no matter. Red Rover was really a procrustean jingoist in embryo. His kind were very useful, but not often smart, which made them expendable.

This assignment would be no big deal. But Goodwill was a perfectionist in this kind of work. At first, it had been to stay alive and invisible in the wake of a murder. Now he took pride in his skill.

He saw his mark appear. Excellent!

John Porter. Hair slicked back—just rushed from the shower? His eyes stared at the heels of the officer in front of him. Porter looked ragged, even though he was wearing a Pierre Cardin. Where had he gotten the costly apparel? One last gift from his arch-enemy, Erma Alred, the red head who planned on frying him with her testimony? Didn't matter. He'd be all set for burial when the cops caught up with his corpse. Porter's head bobbed, tired, slightly bowed. Was it really him?

The ex-graduate student looked up and in the direction of the sun. Hasn't seen that for a few days, has he, Goodwill thought. Even through the forced smirk, it was definitely John Porter. He disappeared behind the back of the bus.

Swiveling the mini spy-glass to the right, Goodwill lined the cross hairs on his point man lumbering satisfied to his police car. The bus driver boarded as the other officers loaded Porter through the rear door of the larger vehicle.

Red Rover opened the door to his car and slid inside as Goodwill smiled. He watched as the inside man lifted the microphone to his standard 800 megahertz radio and spoke while adjusting his rearview mirror to see the bus driver. The point man was getting a lot of money for this. Red Rover smiled while he spoke, as if Golb sat in the car there with him, then he put the radio down and picked up his cellular.

Goodwill put down his half-green/half-white apple and lifted his phone before it rang. "Hello Sunshine!" said Red Rover with a melody. "All's set. Porter's on the bus."

"Were we not leaving two hours ago?" Goodwill said in a calm voice. "What was the delay."

"...I think we were waiting for Porter to get dressed. Maybe the judge called and—"

"Never mind. Cut the radio," said Goodwill.

"...Done."

"Let's go," Goodwill said, starting his car. Like a caged lion, the Mustang roared before going into gear. He put his foot against the accelerator, pulled the wheel to the left, and felt his back sink into the seat. The car darted into traffic before the authorities could move their vehicles to the gate. Goodwill would make his way to the freeway and toward the Federal courthouse an hour away, allowing the bus to slowly overtake him—an old FBI trick; People who were being tailed never suspected the cars ahead of them.

Goodwill stayed on the freeway for more than thirty minutes before allowing the bus to pass him. He sped up and slowed again into sight repeatedly, but otherwise kept his distance and phone silence.

John Denver finished three in a row on *Easy Listening K102 FM* when Goodwill let Red Rover ease on by. Sliding on his leather racing gloves, the assassin watched the wheels of the point man's automobile with amazement and child-like fascination, but forced no eye contact with the overexcited cop inside.

As Sting began "Shape of My Heart" from his 1993 album *Ten Summoner's Tales* with a skillfully plucked guitar in a lonely dance, Goodwill watched the bus through the side of his left eye until it sped past his car.

When the singer put words to the music, Goodwill hit the gas again casually, forcing himself up to the side of the patrol car before the end of the first verse.

As the second stanza played with the tune, Goodwill lifted his copy of *Natural Contagions* and took the weapon snugly in his gloved hand. Though Goodwill preferred the peace and cleanliness of a 22 pistol when assassinating a mark, today's weapon was a superb instrument of choice: a Colt Delta Elite loaded with hollow point 10 mm 180 grain Black Talons. At this distance, it was precise and powerful enough to stab through thick rubber spinning at seventy miles an hour. The bullets could blow holes in metal walls and tear through bus seats. A fearsome, ugly tool, streamlined black with pristine care and beautifully stocked with enough shells to do the job five times. It would do well. And the silencer was already screwed into the barrel. The extension was really unnecessary, but would add to the confusion.

He rolled down the window with confidence, only faintly aware of his rising heart rate. A casual glance informed him of Red Rover's hands tightening on the steering wheel. But at sixty-five miles an hour…

Goodwill smiled at Red Rover. Then he stuck the nose of the 10 mm out the window and pulled the trigger.

No sound came from the gun. But the squad car's right front tire exploded rubber and immediately swerved directly into traffic.

Goodwill's mustang slowed as the police car swung in front of him.

Red Rover overcorrected, pulling his car to the left.

As the point man spun for the shoulder, and Golb slowed to fifty-five with the rest of the traffic, Goodwill drove along side of the bus.

He pulled the trigger twice.

Both right wheels of the bus shattered into rubber shrapnel. Opposed to Goodwill's expectations, the vehicle lurched immediately for the left shoulder as if about to topple onto its right side. But it hit the center divide just after Red Rover and magically stayed upright.

Goodwill yanked his Mustang to the left side of the freeway. As dumbfounded commuters passed by at forty-five miles per hour, the Mustang slammed into reverse and sped backward toward the bus. With a smile, he imagined Golb shouting into his dead radio, "Eleven ninety-nine! Eleven ninety-nine!" uselessly attempting to tell the outer world he needed dire assistance.

No one would stop to help; they'd all be in shock and out of sight before considering it. Everyone else would see the police car behind the small bus. But if anyone had noticed the first officer out of control, they might quickly phone the authorities with their trusty portables. That meant one thing: viable time would soon be gone.

Goodwill pulled his parking brake without looking forward. He eyed Golb, or his replacement, only to see him with his head down, unmoving against the steering wheel. That could mean anything.

Goodwill jumped out of the rumbling Mustang while Sting moved through the chorus of "Shape of My Heart" for the second time.

The long-barreled pistol hung at Goodwill's side as Red Rover came around the rear of the bus.

"Stupid fool!" said the cop holding a head wound that Goodwill couldn't care less about. "*Who* you trying to kill!?!"

Goodwill lifted his gun at the bus as he came to the skinny door on its right side. The door was slightly opened, which meant the driver must have hit it, and he obviously hadn't done so intentionally. Goodwill expected Golb to be ready with an aimed Colt in his shaking hands.

"You told me you'd done this sort of thing before!" said Red Rover, coming closer. "I could have a concussion! *I'm bleeding!*"

Looking through the glass with a glance before instantly pulling away, Goodwill made sure a bullet didn't wait with his name on it. But Golb—it was Golb—hadn't moved, and his right arm hung limp over the dash, his hand bent painfully around and upward. He might already be dead.

"You listening to me…*Sunshine*?!" said the dirty cop. "Or am I just too elementary school for you?! Hey!!!"

Goodwill didn't look at the slowing traffic, where someone might see enough to feel inspired to call in for sure. He had less than thirty seconds.

He didn't bother looking at Red Rover.

But as he pushed at the concave-bending door with the tip of his silencer, Goodwill heard the hammer of a pistol clicking in Red Rover's swaying hands.

Oh, the drivers were getting a show now, weren't they! Some adventurous citizen was likely to turn his car on Goodwill if they could see his own gun from a far enough distance. But what were the chances of that? Goodwill imagined everyone's fingers going to their cellular phones now. If not to summon extra cop cars, then at least to inform their friends! They'd probably wonder if they'd see all this on *America's Most Wanted* this Saturday.

But no time!

Goodwill saw the microphone from the radio hanging limply by the accelerator.

At least Porter was trapped.

"I'm talking to you, Sunshine! And you'll listen because I still *am* an officer and *can* take you down right now!!!"

Goodwill smiled and lowered his weapon. The grin faded as his eyes turned cold on Red Rover. "Put that away. We have work to—"

Red Rover let his gun sag to his side as he pointed at his head. "This isn't a war wound you know! I expect compensation for—"

Beside the forty-mile-an-hour traffic, Goodwill's Colt Delta Elite made almost no sound as it jolted twice in his quick hand.

Red Rover fell, silenced forever.

No time.

Goodwill pushed himself into the bus as traffic slowed to thirty-five—it was amazing no one collided!

He balanced his pistol at breast level and kept his sharp eyes on Golb, who still didn't move. Rising into the bus, he looked back at the empty seats. Porter was either out-cold, dead already, or playing hide and seek. But then, what else could the poor boy do?

With his eyes turned down the length of the short bus, Goodwill pushed his fingers just under the corner of Golb's jaw. He barely felt a pulse. The man would live; no need to kill him. His story would be obscured by shock and unconsciousness. Golb might not have even seen the Mustang.

"John Porter!" said Goodwill finally to the hollow bus. "This gun can shoot clean through these seats so you might as well show yourself. If I wanted to kill you, there is nothing you could do about it. Better come quietly."

The words were true. But then, Goodwill had every intention of murdering John D. Porter. And the assassin would be back in his Mustang before Sting was finished.

Chapter Twenty-Seven

11:49 a.m. PST

Porter had already been in the courtroom for far too long. He baked in the hot lights from above while sweat rolled along his backbone and into the gray slacks of his suit, which Clusser had been kind enough to bring him.

Pushing an index finger and a thumb beneath his glasses to rub his eyes, the judge looked just as comfortable as Porter.

The courtroom was modern and shining as if just built. The dark wood still held its unweathered original lacquer. The ceiling was so high it took effort to realize it was even there. The odor of perspiration and roses hung on the air.

Porter's hands trembled before him, so he smashed them together and glued them to the tabletop. For some reason, his head continued to bob downward as the debate continued. He had to force his chin into the air repeatedly. This would only make him look guilty, no doubt, and that was the last thing he wanted.

His bullet wounds ached only slightly, though he'd been taking Tylenol for some time now. Porter had refused the Vicodin the doctor ordered because he knew it would hinder the workings of his mind. Desiring to be fully attentive with regard to everything, Porter decided to live with the greater discomfort so any further attempt to kill him would fail.

He expected the attempt, unless his enemies thought it best he rot in prison. Surely a Customs crime such as this would not put him away for life, even if he was found guilty.

But his mind wondered anyway.

Porter hadn't quite understood the ride to the courthouse. He remembered being led to the back of a small bus. The door was opened, the driver was a given a thumbs up by the officer holding Porter's right elbow, then he was led quickly back into the building as the bus pulled away. Clusser's partner, another FBI agent in a classic suit of dark blue with near-invisible pin stripes, had told Porter from the beginning of the trip that he was to remain silent. They never took the handcuffs off his wrists sitting on his lap—never even bothered to loosen them, though Porter was sure Clusser would have, had Porter been permitted to ask.

On the way to the Federal courthouse, the two agents seemed overly intent on eyeing the mini-bus and wrecked cop car on the left side of the freeway where vehicles were causing a traffic jam. Porter thought he saw the agents stare at each other with deep telepathic eyes at that time. If it wasn't for the rear view mirror, Clusser, who was driving, never would have told Porter there had been a phone call the night before—an "unrecorded" threat on Porter's life. The more peculiar part of the experience was the way Clusser smiled into the mirror with that same fake expression he'd always given Porter when they served together in Japan. The unfeeling grin had one meaning: his last words were lies. In Japan, he'd used the performance in jest. But Porter knew Clusser was telling him the call wasn't real or had been fabricated by *someone* to save his life.

So why had the bus looked so much like the one Porter was to have boarded, but only had been taken to and from? Porter suspected that the bus, the call, and his private trip to the courthouse in the back of an FBI-mobile had all been instigated by Clusser to save Porter's life.

It had been a long ride with no more words. But Porter wished he were back in the car now.

A microphone stared at Porter from the table before him.

The Jury, sitting like lost statues watching a funeral, didn't matter at all.

Sitting up in his high-backed chair, the Honorable Judge Carole Panofsky, a heavyset man with a Jewish/New York accent, gazed repeatedly at Porter as though the student were little more than another file in his briefcase. The judge's opinion was irrelevant also.

How many times had Porter testified to individuals concerning the truthfulness of the Book of Mormon and the restored church of Jesus Christ and they would not hear? The truth wasn't in question today.

How often had Porter seen the inside of a courtroom with all its holy proceedings? In movies, hundreds. On TV, thousands...probably more.

It was all a game, like most things in life. Play your pieces right and....

The best lawyer would always—

Porter pinched away his swelling pessimism, squeezing his eyes shut. It had been a rough semester—to say the least. Graduation was an issue he might as well never ponder again....But that pain refused to wander.

In this corner, representing the United States Government, stood the Prosecuting Attorney, Ed Comer. Six foot, six inches, Comer smiled with the flat gaze of death. His motions went smoothly, and his voice hardly rippled, even when Porter gave him the run-around.

Well, what else was Porter to do! Tell them he'd found *The* Book of Mormon written in the original text?!? Unless they translated it no one would be able to tell otherwise! And everyone knew that translators argued endlessly as to the correct meanings in ancient documents. Frankly, Porter didn't know what he had anymore. KM-3 wasn't the issue, and no one seemed to know a thing about it. The trial dealt primarily with Porter's apparent theft of other stolen artifacts, possession of archaeological objects owned rightfully by the government of Guatemala. Porter didn't believe the Central American country had anything to do with this investigation, but they really were leaving him in the dark.

Answer this question.

What about this?

How do you explain that?

That's how it went. It was confusing and there was little more so far. No one wanted to know the *real* facts behind all the commotion. Porter wished they'd just let him talk!

Weighing in at a frightening 112 pounds, dressed in a well-pressed Ralph Lauren Polo suit and never letting go of his Gucci pen, which incidentally was gold-plated, Porter's Attorney continued to nod and grin at his client, telling him with badly hidden lies that everything was going exactly in the direction he wanted it. John Sowerby was his designation, and he buddied up quickly with the Mormon because of their first names. Bottom line: Porter knew Sowerby would get his pay whether Porter won or lost.

The weight of the trial rested on the words of those called to the stand.

The room stunk worse than when Porter had entered hours ago… before the recesses. But only Porter noticed.

Judge Panofsky, who probably didn't want this trial to last too long, mumbled to his over-weight court clerk and wrote him words Porter would never read.

Comer, the Prosecuting Attorney, leaned in. "Once again. John D. Porter, did you or did you not put—"

"I haven't even seen that figurine before. And why isn't my lawyer *defending* me here?! I told you! I don't know how it got into my car, but I sure would be interested in getting my hands on those *obviously Egyptian* objects now," Porter said.

Comer pulled his slicked head back, a relaxed—almost tired—expression on his face, and looked at the jury and then to the judge. "Interested enough to steal it?"

"I don't think I have to answer that question. Of course I wouldn't steal it."

Comer went to his desk and picked up yet another file as someone coughed like a choking boar in the small audience. Porter was surprised more press hadn't arrived. Normally they loved to point out crimes committed by members of the LDS church. Maybe the thought that a Mormon might have found and stolen proof that his church really was true had been too unsettling to print; too much like "*National Enquirer*", lacking credibility.

"What does the *D* stand for, Mr. Porter…in your name?" said Comer, perhaps attempting to pull the case into a more comfortable arena.

"Determined," said Porter.

Comer smiled. "To lie?"

"Are we joking around here? If so, I have a few things I'd like to say."

The Prosecuting attorney shrugged audibly, glanced at the judge, at the jury, then back at Porter as if everyone could see how ridiculous this trial really was. He tightened his blue eyes. "Your simple unwillingness to cooperate will drown you in this court, Mr. Porter."

"I'm following legal advice, saying nothing that might sound incriminatory," said Porter. "Besides, if I told what I really know, it would only make everyone angry."

Comer grinned again. "What's that."

"I've been set up for a fall."

"You're wrong, Mr. Porter....That only makes us laugh."

Porter smiled. There was nowhere to go. He would be fried here, in this chair, and Porter knew it. He could put up a fight, but it would only lead to further pain and humiliation before the end. Yet he couldn't simply sit and take the blows. Not after all that had happened. Without moving, he could feel the simple pulse of his heart in his stomach wound. He listened to the throbbing as his eyes glazed over. Were the doctors sure he was ready to handle a courtroom? Maybe they wanted suspected criminals out of their hospital as much as the jail wanted new prisoners. Clusser was right, Porter didn't know anything about the legal system.

Walking up to the witness stand with his eyes on the ground, Comer put his hands in his pockets. He had an easy job, and Porter realized the man needed to finish this. Attorneys are paid by the case, Porter thought, which meant that if this trial ended, both Comer and Sowerby could move onto another.

"Mr. Porter," Comer said, looking up. He examined the student with honesty in his drying eyes. "Do you have KM-2."

"You asked me that before," said Porter without enthusiasm. He hated lying, but he didn't have to do so with this question. Of course he didn't have KM-2. He didn't even have KM-3, really. But that should have been the question. Why hadn't anyone brought up the latter document? Didn't they know? Someone did! Kinnard had personally held photos of Porter looking at the third codex just after KM-2 was no more.

"For the record," Comer said, lifting his hand.

Another odd thing: How had Alred fallen between the cracks. She'd been little more than a witness so far. Why had all the blame fallen to Porter? Someone was trying desperately to bury him, one way or.... Actually, Porter didn't want Alred involved. She'd had enough of this tribulation already. "KM-2 was returned to Stratford University on the twenty-ninth of April."

"Did you return the document," said Comer, walking closer to the jury.

"No—we've gone over this," said Porter. He knew that if the Prosecuting Attorney pushed further, Alred would get involved. Porter didn't want to drag her down with him anymore.

"Who then?"

Porter froze. Direct question. No way to dodge it. Porter's brain went numb. "I beg your pardon?"

"You have *my* pardon! But not the judge's yet. Who returned the artifact to Stratford University? Be consistent Mr. Porter, your words are being recorded."

Porter looked at the man typing each word with what looked like a very old calculator the size of a shoe box. They still used those in the computer age? Porter gazed into the audience, but wouldn't lock eyes with the red head. He found Clusser's patient gaze. The missionary companion from years ago simply nodded as if to say, *"The truth man! Tell him."*

"Erma Alred."

Comer's eyebrows lifted. "Are you sure of that?" The attorney was calm and drew himself up with a quiet breath. Porter wondered if Comer thought the defendant was resorting to fictionalization.

"I was furious about it!" Porter said. It was emotion. But logic was fleeing fast. He tried to buckle down but would only know how well he'd battened the hatches when next he had to speak, which was immediately.

The attorney scratched his low forehead. "Is that an affirmative answer?"

Porter breathed. "Of course."

"Ms. Alred did not return it at *your* behest?" said Comer, looking in Alred's direction.

"No."

With his narrow nose, Comer pointed at Porter while putting his hands in his pockets. "You wanted to keep it. Didn't you Mr. Porter. Be honest."

Silence. The inset lights hidden in the high ceiling shined an almost orange light down on the menagerie of words. It was a trap of army ants, brawling with little movement, biting with their voices, all ready to jump in Porter's direction and maul him to death. Clusser stood against the dark wood wall in the rear of the courtroom. An American flag hung limply on a pole between him and the two doors with an exit sign glowing red letters of escape. And yet Porter knew he wouldn't make it much farther than the high wall around him and the platform elevating him near Judge Panofsky's seat. The floor, a black marble mirror, reflected the lights above. Porter felt it all close in around him, tighter, smothering him. He had to speak. Everyone was listening and the judge would only move faster away from thinking Porter was anything more than another crooked man in his court. "I wanted to keep KM-2, but that doesn't mean—"

The prosecutor spoke over Porter's words. "If you had a choice, you would keep it. Let me ask you again, Mr. Porter, are you sure Alred gave the document to the University? Were you there at the time? Do you *know* for certain that the hand-off occurred?"

With eyes looking earnestly into the seated crowd for help, Porter at last let them settle on Alred. She sat in a business suit, gray from the shoulder pads to the edge of the knee-high skirt. Her mouth was small and red, but her eyes said nothing for or against his answer. She would expect the truth in this case. And yet *she* still had KM-3 and really should be as guilty as ever they might find Porter.

When Porter opened his mouth…he said nothing.

"Mr. Porter," said Judge Panofsky, his voice deep and somehow refreshingly cool, but also as chilled as the icy metal of a stabbing knife. "Answer the question please."

Like a robot on automatic, the words came from Porter's mouth in a near mono-tone. "Alred gave KM-2 back to Stratford University." His white face laced with a thin layer of liquid glaze, his thin lips quivering, all his visible emotions shouted the ghastly reality. Alred would sense it. Clusser would notice. The jury…the judge…the Prosecuting Attorney….

Porter had no idea what had *really* happened to KM-2.

* * *

3:56 p.m. PST

"Ms. Alred, allow me first to acknowledge that no charges are being brought upon you. However, you are under oath to tell the absolute truth. To do otherwise will result in grievous consequences."

"Do you expect me to lie, Mr. Prosecutor?" Alred said with raised eyebrows and a strong face. She looked relaxed in her gray suit but sat with statue-like posture, looking over the courtroom from the witness stand for the second time. She could smell the judge's Afta lotion.

Comer smiled at the ground and waited as if reconsidering his approach. "Ms. Alred...how long have you worked with John D. Porter."

"Approximately one month."

"And you both used the foreign document termed KM-2."

Alred lifted her chin. "Correct," she said, though Porter had dominated the handling of the manuscript from the beginning.

"How would you describe Porter's attachment to the document," said Comer.

Alred took a long breath through her petite nose. Her green eyes shimmered without emotion. "Porter has been...highly intrigued with KM-2. Perhaps—"

"Obsessive?" said the attorney.

With a sharp gaze, Alred answered his question, while silently making it clear that she would not allow herself to be cut off again. Her voice picked up in volume, but not in pitch. "Anyone who knows Porter's eccentric attitude toward his studies might deem him obsessive about anything in which he involves himself."

Turning away, Comer said the words in a calm voice, "Intrigued! Eccentric! Obsessive!" so they would be noted and run through the judge's mind again.

"He had good reason for excessive enthusiasm concerning KM-2," said Alred.

Comer looked up with fake intrigue emanating from his face. "Tell us why."

"Stratford University offered Porter an ultimatum: Complete a doctoral dissertation by May 21 or fail out of the University. Only a few weeks ago, the aforementioned deadline was moved to May 5; today. Obsessive, yes. Porter has worked as hard as I have, if not more so, in order to make the due date. Now, because of this legal run-around, neither of us will get our Ph.D's. All the work for nothing. When we could have proven to be Stratford's best doct—"

"Ms. Alred, did you give Stratford University the document, KM-2, at Porter's behest?" said Comer, looking at the ground. The Prosecuting Attorney likewise would not allow this Federal Court to be treated rudely.

Her mouth still open, Alred shifted her thoughts to answer the question. "I took the codex from Porter's office as soon as the board asked for it."

"You mean Mr. Porter didn't keep KM-2 in a safe, glass cabinet, or locked drawer someplace? An important relic like that, which could make or lay waste both of your doctoral theses? Or did you both have keys to a common lock?"

Alred surely must have realized her answer could be the bite on a hook Comer would use to reel her into the same cage Porter now found himself. But in this case, the truth would prove to be the best shield. "Porter stored the codex in an air vent so it couldn't be stolen."

"Why," said Comer, his hands again in his pockets.

Alred's quick words sounded yanked from the middle of a lecture she may have given to a freshman class. "Perfect hiding place. The dry air wouldn't hurt—"

"No, why did Porter *hide* KM-2 in a vent? Why did *you* go and fetch it when...the University called for it?" The end of Comer's sentence sounded like playful words of appeasement rather than acknowledgment of the event.

Alred let a myriad of thoughts spin noticeably in her head as she waited for her mind to bring forth the best reply. The facts were plain enough, she thought, and the trial shouldn't be focused at all on KM-2. It was as if the Prosecutor had an agenda unrelated to the possibility that Porter was engaged in some form of theft or illegal possession. But she chose to dart away from the subject in order to steer the congregates from realizing the existence of KM-3. "After all of the sacrifices we've made to complete our time at Stratford, I knew that what the board required—the return of Ulman's codex—would be emotionally trying for Porter. I made the decision for him."

Comer cocked his head to the side, went to his desk, lifted a clip board, read a note, dropped it, turned back to Alred, and said, "Who is on this board?"

"Five people called me to work with John Porter on Ulman's find. Four of those professors were…present when I returned the codex," said Alred.

"Who."

"Masterson, Goldstien, Kinnard," Alred took a breath, "and Arnott."

"Why do you think they requested the return of KM-2?" said Comer, glancing to his desk to be sure his assistant scrawled the names on a legal pad.

Alred lifted herself again, balancing her shoulders before speaking. She chose her words carefully. "I assumed they came to the realization that the University had not procured the codex through proper means. If so, Stratford students should not have been dealing with KM-2, and they had been treated unfairly. Also—"

"What—" said Comer, thinking without listening to Alred's words. He quickly amended his minor show of amateur behavior. "No, go ahead."

"Also," said Alred, irritation clear in her powerful voice, "it seemed to me that some of the professors may have been wary about certain deaths possibly connected with the aforementioned codex."

"Whose deaths?" said Comer, making up for stepping on this would-be attorney's small feet.

"In his office, Dr. Wilkinson was found with his own letter opener protruding from his back. He was one of the five on the board, but dead before the meeting in question. Dr. Christopher Ulman would never make a name for himself as a hidden archaeologist selling stolen goods from one of the world's greatest finds. *He* found it. Now he's *disappeared* and the only explanation is his death. Whether in North America or outside of the States must be based on future investigation. Dr. Albright of Ohio State University, who coined the term *KM* while in Guatemala…is also dead."

Comer waited, regearing his thoughts. "How do we know you gave this ancient document to this board, Ms. Alred. Stratford University pressed the issue this morning that Porter still has KM-2. Porter had other figurines in his car," Comer said as if his last sentence ended the debate.

Calmly, Alred set her hard eyes on the attorney. "Someone is obviously lying. I recommend interviewing the four men I mentioned who were present when I returned the codex."

The prosecutor pulled back and smiled at Alred's strength. He turned away and focused on his attack plan. "How would you describe your relationship with Porter."

Alred thought for a moment. Such an interesting question. She would have answered it differently after each week since she'd met Porter. Had Comer asked three weeks ago, Alred would have done her best to make sure Porter would hang. Now…how exactly did she feel? "We…get along," she said. "We are friends. We worked together with different agendas regarding Ulman's find. I suppose I found myself mostly at odds with Porter. But I respect him…as a scholar."

Comer touched the fingertip of his right index to his lips. He removed it to say, "Do you think he is capable of murder?"

Alred seriously considered the question as the Defense Attorney jumped with the words "Objection! My client's not on trial for murder."

Then she said, "No I do not."

* * *

May 6
3:06 p.m. PST

Standing with his right hand raised, Dr. Masterson said, "I swear to tell the truth, the whole truth, and nothing but the truth, so help me God."

Chapter Twenty-Eight

"Have a seat," said Mr. Comer. "Dr. Masterson, you know John Porter and Erma Alred?"

"Very well," said the tight-skinned old man with the smile of a skeleton and the wise eyes of a deadly king. He was dressed in a new suit, which he had likely bought for the occasion. Comer smiled.

"Dr. Masterson...did you ask them to return KM-2 to the University?"

"I did not."

"Why did they have it?" said the Prosecuting Attorney.

"Dr. Kinnard, overseeing Porter's doctoral studies, gave Porter the codex while under the misunderstanding that it had come into his hands in a legal fashion." Masterson sat back in the chair as though he were a doctor or psychiatrist accustomed to adding his professional expertise in the trials of criminals. He did his best to look comfortable on the stand.

Comer kept his head down. He glanced back at Mr. Sowerby, the Defense attorney. The young man had done little to help Porter and no doubt would only make a fool of himself when he questioned Dr. Masterson. Porter had kept his forehead in his hands since the beginning of this session. He didn't know how lucky—or unlucky—he was to have his trial progress so quickly. He wasn't wanted for murder, so he didn't face a cold chair somewhere. But Porter looked as guilty as a wet boy caught naked near a pond and accused of skinny-dipping.

The Prosecuting Attorney had to get this over with. It was an embarrassing trial, and after interviewing three of the four professors who were supposedly present when KM-2 was returned to the school's hands, it would all be finished. "Did Alred or Porter ever return KM-2 to Stratford University."

"Not to my knowledge," said the old man with little enthusiasm. He looked as if ready to spout a great discourse he'd prepared the night before, but fortunately saved his exuberance for the classroom.

"Did Alred give the codex to you, Dr. Masterson?" said Comer.

"Certainly not."

"One last question, Dr. Masterson." Comer lifted a legal pad. "Does a Dr. Arnott work at Stratford University? Do you know this man?"

Masterson squared his shoulders and looked the attorney right between the eyes, but not directly into the pupils. He took a powerful breath. "No."

* * *

3:18 p.m. PST

Comer put his palms together as if praying, touching his fingertips to his chin. "So, Dr. Goldstien...you're saying you never sat in a room with Kinnard, Masterson, and Arnott as KM-2 was brought into your presence by Erma Alred."

Goldstien smiled, wiped his hands on the left and right pockets of his hazel blazer, and looked in Alred's direction. "I would remember if *she* came into a meeting with us!" He flaunted his interest in her, for he wasn't the one on trial. He knew his smile would detract from the focus of the question. His words would be recorded, and that was the important part. "As for the KM-2 codex...never saw it. I don't know this Arnott fellow you're talking about." He quickly added with a raised finger, "If Ms. Alred is saying she brought us the codex, I would enjoy going along with her story. But I fear she has fabricated her testimony in order to serve John Porter's best interests."

"No...further...questions...."

* * *

3:26 p.m. PST

"Dr. Kinnard, you've heard the story so far." The Prosecuting attorney looked at Judge Panofsky, whose eyes wandered across pages on his desk and glided to the high windows hidden on the east side of the courtroom. "I mean the fable," he said with a raised voice. Kinnard noticed each of the lawyer's movements and flinched—not enough for anyone else to notice, surely—as Comer looked again into the witness booth. "Who is telling tales? That is for you to help us conclude."

"I'll do my best," said the professor with a gruffness in his throat. Kinnard had heard the other testimonies. In fact, he'd been present from the beginning, eyeing Porter's wimpy defender, Alred's steady focus and terrible silence, the judge's decision already determined behind the thin spectacles.

Kinnard had received the same phone call from Arnott which had altered Masterson's and Goldstien's testimonies. It was a simple message following a short salutation. Like a conscience, Arnott told him Alred had never returned KM-2 to the University. And *Arnott* didn't exist. Arnott explained that the authorities would not find a "Peter Arnott" in any database, so to even mention him would sound like a falsification of testimony.

Porter was dying and didn't have a single opportunity to fight. Kinnard blamed himself. He had presented this paranoid eccentric with the ancient manuscript that could have made him famous. No. Kinnard blamed John Porter, who should have had his dissertation prepared long before the last semester of his seventh year at Stratford. No. He blamed Ulman, the oaf with the knack for trouble who'd finally found a way to collapse a small corner of the world. Ulman had probably gotten killed before he could even see the damage.

But it had been Kinnard himself who'd perpetuated the problem when he could have stashed KM-2 or given it to Masterson, who should have received the book in the first place. Porter had really been an innocent who'd gotten in the way and hung on for dear life because his was otherwise at an end. A snare yanked Alred into this.

A worse trap would snatch both students into judicial oblivion, while Kinnard himself pulled the lever.

What other choices were there? Suicide? Who wanted this codex and all its relations buried anyway? Would they kill Kinnard if he explained...what really had occurred? Would the University oust him since he did not stand with his fellow academics? Would the papers be involved in this? What about his family; what would they wonder as they read,

DR. TROY KINNARD OF STRATFORD UNIVERSITY
DEFENDS MORMON THIEF,
THUS LOSES TENURE!

"We need to know the truth," Comer said through the fog of Kinnard's thoughts. "First...who is Peter Arnott?"

Pause. "I don't know."

"Well, we'll get back to him in a moment. Tell me, did Erma Alred return KM-2 to Stratford University on thirty April?"

The cue. Kinnard's lines had already been well-rehearsed before stepping into the courtroom. There wasn't a trial going on, but a play! Kinnard had never auditioned, but had a part so vital that the director, Peter Arnott, stood with his arms folded and his face gray in the back of the brown room right where the professor could see him best.

Kinnard looked at the great double doors with armed officers standing like cast iron ushers and couldn't push away the feeling that *he* was on trial and not John Porter. Would Kinnard make it through those doors after his testimony? How far, before he was stabbed in the back, shot with poison darts, or—

No, they would get him later. Blow up his car? Too dramatic. Poison his orange juice tomorrow morning? They wouldn't spend the money. Their revenge would be worse than death. Kinnard would lose credibility, watch his job fall away. Perhaps they'd even find a way to revoke his credentials....

"Dr. Kinnard?' said Comer.

Looking into the Prosecuting Attorney's caffeine-charged eyes, Kinnard opened his mouth a crack and drew in the warm air of the courtroom. He tasted the scent of the leather chair beneath him as he shifted his weight. He folded his fingers together on his lap and squared his shoulders. His chin lifted and fell, eyes jumping to Masterson's cold gaze, back to Arnott who never moved, both young gargoyles carved out of flesh. Closing his eyes, Kinnard heard the squeak of Judge Panofsky's bottom against his seat.

Comer didn't restate the question or call the professor's name a second time. For only a flashing moment, Kinnard saw in the attorney's eyes the minute concern that Kinnard was about to overthrow the entire point the Prosecution pushed for: that the meeting mentioned by Porter and Alred had never occurred. The insinuation could also then be deduced that Alred was as guilty as Porter, at least in her attempt to lie in a Federal court of law.

Leaning into the microphone, Kinnard said, "I…I can't answer the question at this time."

"Answer the question," said Judge Panofsky.

Kinnard kept his mouth near the microphone as he turned his face to the judge. "I'll have to utilize the fifth amendment."

The courtroom rumbled, and Comer laughed lightly at the professor as if Kinnard didn't know how real courts ran beyond the boundary of the media.

Kinnard looked at Masterson, whose eyes darkened into shady pits.

Arnott lifted his body from the far wall and headed to the door as if he were only going to the bathroom.

Kinnard felt the skin on his face cool, all the moisture evaporating suddenly.

The double doors shut again, and the professor imagined Arnott, the devious shadow posing as a professor and who knew what else, walking away from the courtroom, a cellular in his hand raised to his head. It was an unspoken eulogy of sorts, but only a dream at the same time. Arnott signed the papers verbally. For what? It didn't matter. Kinnard's simple insistence to say nothing told the world that more was happening than Comer suspected. That was bad enough.

At the same time, Kinnard heard Comer say, "No further questions, then. But stick around professor, I may have something else in the near future."

Before standing, Kinnard realized that he himself might be implicated in this crime. After all, who gave Porter KM-2? Who first received it illegally? The codex never came from Stratford University, but from Ulman to Kinnard in clearly illicit fashion. Mailmen smuggled Ulman's prize unwittingly and handed it right to Kinnard, who said nothing about the transaction until after passing the object on to the man on trial today. What if Kinnard did so with full realization and intention of sneaking the manuscript around in order to bring it forth properly at a later date and be one with Porter as the discoverer of this rare and magnificent, world-changing codex. Motive: fame and money. And Kinnard wouldn't have had to do the dirty work. And if anyone was arrested, Porter could play scapegoat.

If Arnott used this ploy, Kinnard would have few defensive possibilities.

He lowered his mouth to the microphone again. "There were many meetings in which I sat and discussed Porter's Kalpa Codex with Masterson and the others."

The rumble of the room turned to a hush as Comer froze with his back to the witness. He turned around. "I'm sorry?" said the Prosecuting Attorney before managing his thoughts. With licked lips, he said, "Dr. Kinnard, did Alred return the manuscript as mentioned, or are you telling us something irrelevant to this case. I said I had no more quest—"

"Alred gave it back," said Kinnard. "I was there. So was Masterson, though he says otherwise. And Dr. Goldstien sat right next to me. Arnott…I don't know who he is, but he doesn't teach at Stratford. Masterson introduced him to the students as a professor working there with us."

Comer looked for only a few seconds into Kinnard's eyes.

What could Kinnard lose now? They would no doubt attempt to entomb him with the scenario he'd already predicted. It was Kinnard's words against his colleagues', and Kinnard would end up looking as dirty as the two graduate students. But it didn't matter. He knew his account was accurate.

Kinnard's eyes moved to Porter, who looked at his supervising professor through tears…or was it just the lighting….

Comer turned his focus on the judge. "I said I had no further questions." He turned away.

Sowerby stood and approached the witness stand with a pale grin.

The facts of Kinnard's testimony meant little now. Everyone knew where he stood. Kinnard wouldn't waver anymore.

* * *

May 7
10:14 a.m. PST

"Ms. Alred," said Comer, smiling at the ground. "You insinuated on the fifth that Stratford University recalled KM-2 because—possibly!—of the deaths of persons involved with the discovery. Do you honestly believe Porter's life was really ever in danger?"

Alred tightened her eyes on the Prosecuting Attorney. She had yet to figure out the man's new ploy. Whether or not that actual meeting happened, wherein she gave KM-2 to Masterson, who then passed it on to Arnott before her eyes, was irrelevant. Comer, as a representative of the government had a job to do. Porter had to be found guilty of the charges brought before him. They had already long discussed the Egyptian figurines found in Porter's car. It was a settled issue, one which Porter himself would not deny to be factual, as he hadn't been in contact with his automobile since he was chased from the library. No one could prove, however, that Porter stole the artifacts from Stratford or even Mrs. Ulman, who had been subpoenaed, but never came to court. But even Porter would not dispute that the figurines were found in his automobile. So where was Comer going with this question?

"I believe there are people who are willing to kill for the codex," said Alred. Of course, after seeing Ulman die in a parking lot and then being attacked by two men herself, her words were understatements that were necessary at present. She wouldn't risk exposing that she currently possessed KM-3 by noting those traumatic instances.

"Murder…for religious purposes?" said Comer, tilting his head.

Alred leaned her head back. Grimacing inside, she cursed all religions. Nothing came with more disfavor to her mind. The aunt after whom she'd been named had died a faithful fanatic at Jonestown. The rest of her living family had a peculiar fear of God, one she would never understand.

Porter's fire would not go out. The more persecution, the better. He'd shine like a sun in this courtroom if Comer didn't drop this.

Of course the Prosecution wanted Porter to go nova. When emotions got involved, people lost all sense of logic. Alred wanted to look over at Porter, to shout out a warning. It was a trap, and no one would fall harder than the eccentric Latter-day Saint in the room. But she kept her eyes sturdy and rethought the question—*why would people try to murder Porter?* "For scholarly reasons."

"We're talking Indiana Jones here, aren't we?" said Comer. He turned to the judge and jury, but didn't bother looking at them, keeping his eyes on the black ground instead as he slid his hands into the pockets of his dark slacks. "Will you be telling the court that this *killer scholarship* is normal among the *highly educated*?"

Alred didn't blink. "Everyone who has ever been directly connected with the study of Dr. Ulman's find in Guatemala is dead now. Only one individual I know of, other than Porter and myself, who has placed his own hands on comparable portions of the relative discovery is still alive, and he has sharply turned his back on the project…as if it were never found."

"Really," said Comer. "And who is that?"

"Dr. Alexander Peterson of Ohio State University. Porter chose to stand alone."

Comer smiled and squinted his eyes as if playing along with this new revelation. "Who would organize such devious acts?"

Alred set her jaw, looked around, then locked eyes with the Prosecuting Attorney. "I believe the *man* in question…has been here in the courtroom today. You know him by the name of Peter Arnott."

"*Has* been here?" said Comer, glancing once at all those watching the proceedings.

"I no longer see him at present," Alred said, realizing how much this probably sounded made-up. "I am sure Dr. Kinnard will concur with my statement."

Comer nodded, pushing his bottom lip against his top teeth. Walking over to the jury, Comer pondered thoughts Alred could not discern. Had she led him down a blind alley, or was she walking the path he'd devised during the recess? He looked at her again. "Ms. Alred. You are a specialist in…"

"Ancient Mesoamerican Archaeology, but I am also well-read in numerous ancient American cultures."

"What relationship does Mormonism have with ancient Mesoamerica?" said Comer.

"Objection," said Sowerby.

Judge Panofsky put his mouth to his microphone. "Mr. Comer, will you state the relevance of your question before carrying us into a religious trial. I hate those."

"Your Honor, according to the *Encyclopedia of Mormonism*, published by the Macmillan Publishing Company in 1992." Comer lifted a brown leather-bound notebook from his desk and read his words aloud. "Members of the Church of Jesus Christ of Latter-day Saints, otherwise known as Mormons, believe a number of Israelites settled somewhere in America in approximately 600 BC. The Book of Mormon specifically describes these people and their approximate 1000 year existence, with an included supplementary book describing another group who came from the Old World to the New just after the fall of the Biblical Tower of Babel." Comer looked up. "John Porter is a Mormon, and I suspect would therefore be more interested in Central American archaeology because of his religion than for scholarly reasons."

"Objection overruled," said the judge, looking at his desk. "Proceed."

"Ms. Alred, based on your knowledge of Ancient Mesoamerica and your personal contact with Mr. Porter, would you say the defendant made *no* religious connections with Dr. Ulman's discovery?"

"I do not feel inclined to say such a thing," Alred said, her eyes relaxed but her head growing hazy. She prayed inside that the Prosecutor would turn the discussion away from religion, then sighed with inner embarrassment for *praying* at all in any form.

"Porter is a specialist in Ancient Near Eastern Studies," said Comer, looking back at his notes. "In your *expert* opinion as a doctoral candidate in Ancient Mesoamerican Archaeology, Ms. Alred, what relationship does ancient Arabia, Egypt, or Israel have with America?"

Alred moved her tongue around in her mouth before speaking. "None."

"On what basis do you make this decree?" said Comer.

"Archaeologists refute claims that anyone came from the Near East to the Americas in ancient times," said Alred. She felt her conviction tearing away at her inside. After all she'd studied personally, in Dr. Ulman's papers, KM-2, and especially KM-3, there ached the constant possibility deep inside her that the connection really was clear. But everything else, all her schooling, every measure of her logical mind told her to ignore Ulman's finds—they only confused the truth.

"Tell us why then was a *scholarly* young man like John D. Porter, a specialist in Near Eastern Studies, given the ancient manuscript dug up by an American Archaeologist from Stratford University." Comer stopped his slow pacing.

"Porter believes there is a connection from both sides," she said. "This does stem from his faith and more precisely from the Book of Mormon. He has used numerous Mesoamerican texts to back up his claims and has found KM-2 to be the greatest of all, expressing the heretofore undiscovered evidence linking the Old and New Worlds. He *is*...motivated by his religious standing.

"I do not concur with these ideas," said Alred for her own peace. "The bottom line is that both Porter, a Near Eastern scholar, and myself, a Mesoamericanist, were commissioned by Stratford University to complete a project which would result with our Ph.D's, following our dissertations given on the fifth of May. As does Porter, I have a full Fellowship and am therefore...*paid* to do exactly what Stratford asks. This was a *paid* assignment. Porter had more at stake than anyone else relative to KM-2. I do not believe he sought money or even fame from this study, but very much hoped to earn his degree and bring to light what he would deem as more evidence that the Book of Mormon is what it claims to be. Due to a technicality, this excellent student who is on trial today wouldn't graduate without the KM-2 project. As I said, Stratford took KM-2 away at the last moment, dissolving all possibilities and inadvertently disposing of our work."

Comer grinned. "And you believe this."

"I have no religious convictions—"

"You think some underground religious freaks might try to kill the both of you, just as you see others murdered for—"

"I see two Ph.D's stolen from the hands of worthy students, and a university that is attempting to—"

"Why can't you see what is going on here?!?" said Porter standing suddenly and speaking fast as one thump of the gavel echoed through the room. "Archaeological evidence in any good textbook confirms the dates suggested in the Book of Mormon, which was written years before our modern information had been found, gathered, and compiled.

"Both modern studies and the Book of Mormon describe a society which lived at the same time and died in the Middle Preclassic period of Mesoamerican history.

"Both sources accurately present us with a new civilization that sprang suddenly out of the Middle Preclassic period, ran for one thousand years, ending with major social catastrophes and changes culminating in the end of the Early Classic civilizations.

"While scholars for decades have called the Mayans a peaceful people, the Book of Mormon describes tribes and kingdoms at constant war with one another. Now archaeologists confirm the description—the Book of Mormon proving to be accurate again. New art filled with armed men and tangible evidence of widespread cannibalism in and around Teotihuacan in the North and Mayan lowlands in Guatemala and the Yucatan begin exactly at the same *time* as the record of Mormon—describing the same situation—purportedly ends.

"As the Book of Mormon prophesies, in the years following its last pages, as Alred and any competent ancient Americanist will confirm, all major population centers completed a shift from theocratic governments to secular lifestyles. The old ceremonialism was done away with. Mayan and Mesoamerican stones were defaced for reasons archaeologists are unable to give. And from the Middle Classic period on, religion became a means to secular ends just as it too often does today.

"I could cite to everyone in this room, the *Popol Vuh* and other ancient Mesoamerican documents which describe scenes from the scattering of people from a mountain—your Tower of Babel, Mr. Comer—to the great flood found in the Bible. Parallel stories. I could bring to your attention the *Annals of the Cakchiquels* translated for the first time into French in 1855 and into English in 1885, or the *Title of the Lords of Totonicapan* translated into Spanish in 1834 and then English in 1953. Shall I refer you to the painted walls of Bonampak in Chiapas, Mexico, which by the way made it onto the cover of National Geographic a few years back? Wasn't brought to white man's attention until the middle of this century. *All* of these relate detailed Book of Mormon stories.

"The Book of Mormon, which first came to light through Joseph Smith *in 1830*!

"The KM codices found by Dr. Ulman coincide with these finds and more particularly with the Book of Mormon.

"Think, now. No one wants these things to reach the ears and eyes of the citizens of the world. Can you imagine what would happen if *irrefutable proof* came clearly pointing out that the Mormons have been professing a religion which is in fact the true faith of God, taught for more than a hundred and fifty years all over the Earth?!? Are you ready to change your lives in the case that occurs?! Can't you see why people have conspired to cover up the assignment I received from Stratford University—including the University itself?

"They made a serious mistake in giving *me* the codex in the first place. And all I've done is what I was told by them to do. The truth is there. I don't need to prove it. But...I did not steal...KM-2, nor the *ushabti* figurines which were placed in my car."

Alred looked at Porter as if she'd been hit with a blast of cold air. In a short moment of silence, as Porter took a breath, she saw him buckle slightly under the pressure of all the eyes on him. Why had no one told him to sit down? Why hadn't the bailiffs grabbed him or someone gagged him? No one spoke with such clear words in a court, for what he said would affect everyone in the room.

Porter's tone lowered and his voice slowed, but he remained on his feet. "As a judge, you know that lack of evidence is *not* proof. Those who cover up the facts in order to say they aren't there don't understand this. You've heard this case. I gain nothing by possessing Ulman's artifacts if they are illegal. Does it further my education? Will the theft make my church seem *more* authentic in some way? If the finds are illegally held, the ecclesiastical authorities of my faith could never bring them forth as artifacts proving the truths I've explained because to do so would be to the detriment of the church.

"It is up to you to decide my motives for committing the crime the prosecutor suggests. All I know is, I won't get a degree after doing the work assigned. Because KM-2 is gone, I have only my notes and my word as proof now. And that's as good as fiction in the religious community of scholars."

The air was spiced with Porter's sweat, and Alred thought she smelled it cooking on the hot lights hidden in the ceiling. She lowered her head, shocked at the audacity of the preceding comments.

Surely everyone felt the pressure, the questions unasked, the weight of one man's religion different from the world's smashing like a flood of rainwater over the wall of a dam.

The judge removed his glasses as Porter slowly sat down. "John Porter…I am not prejudiced against you or your church. Do you understand me. You will not stand up and speak in that manner again in my courtroom."

Porter nodded humbly.

Comer went to his assistant and whispered something which the younger fellow quickly scribbled. It could have been nothing; an attempt by the Prosecutor to look as if he had the case in his pocket.

"No more speaches are to be made. I want these questions settled fairly and succinctly. Mr. Prosecutor," said the judge, focusing his spectacles with his fingertips, "your compound questioning will not continue in my presence. I've put up with you long enough and expect you to give time to each witness before proceeding with further inquiries, are my words simple enough for you?"

Alred's eyes floated onto an old man approaching the barrier behind Porter's chair. Dressed in fine tweed, he smiled and handed a small envelope to Porter's attorney, which Sowerby opened. As the gentleman proceeded out of the courtroom, the defense lawyer withdrew a small sheet of paper, which he read and handed to Porter.

Comer started casually back for the witness stand and the judge.

Porter read the note. The color in his face turned to sleet, and his eyes focused on something beyond the courtroom walls. Then with tombstones in his gaze, Porter looked right at Alred and never removed his eyes.

Chapter Twenty-Nine

John Sowerby considered himself to be a good attorney, but couldn't shake the feeling his client was lying to him. Porter so often ran away from direct questions, he looked guilty to everyone. But even Sowerby could say nothing after Porter's bold spiel. He hadn't dared to yank his client back into his seat—not that the poor student was paying for his services, but Porter had his own agenda and was intent on keeping his attorney in the dark. Whatever.

The words in the note had no meaning to John Sowerby. Porter looked down at the paper again, as Alred stood to leave the stand. Sowerby ran the words through his mind. What was it, a psalm from the Bible? He'd never gone to any form of Sunday school, but had really enjoyed the Bhagavad-Gita in junior college.

Mr. Porter,

"He that findeth his life shall lose it: and he that loseth his life…shall find it" (Matthew 11:39).

Your only friend,

—J. Smith.

Judge Panofsky spoke without looking up. "We will take a one hour recess, after which time, gentlemen, I hope you will prepare your final arguments." The gavel came down with one crack and everyone stood to depart.

When Alred, studying the ground, came within earshot of Porter, the student called her over with a clearing of his throat.

Sowerby packed his briefcase as if he hadn't noticed.

Before she could comment on anything said so far in the courthouse, Porter grabbed her by the elbow and drew her close.

He whispered into her ear.

Alred immediately pulled away as though she'd just been propositioned. She stared at Porter as if he'd already been shipped to the crazy house. Porter pulled her again and whispered into her left ear for a longer time.

Sowerby felt someone brush up behind him and stay. He turned to see a large African-American with hard eyes looking down at him. The man wore a dark gray suit and a green paisley tie which looked slightly out of date, and he held a file folder in his left hand against his chest.

"Who is that," said Alred behind Sowerby. There was just enough seriousness in her voice to tell Sowerby that at least she cared about who was talking with Porter's lawyer.

"Batman." Porter spoke with the same gravity. "I hope."

"Stan Clusser, FBI," said the agent, raising his identification with his right hand. He gave Sowerby the folder without looking at his old missionary companion. "Call me to the stand and ask me these questions after the recess. Take the steps you need to reach this goal."

"I'll have to look them over first and meet with the Prosecuting Attorney," said Sowerby, fighting to keep a hand on some semblance of dignity.

"You do whatever is necessary," said Clusser. "Memorize the file."

One eye shot to Porter and Alred, and the agent pushed into the small crowd behind him.

Sowerby huffed in indignation, then looked at his client.

Porter raised his eyebrows while tilting his mellow face downward. "I trust that man more than I trust you," he said to Sowerby.

"Well...you've gotta have someone on your side." Sowerby let his smile show the sarcastic bitterness.

Alred walked away shaking her head at both of them.

Staring at the empty judge's seat, as Sowerby packed his black briefcase, Porter said, "You have a piece of paper?"

Sowerby handed a sheet to him and watched his client sit and scrawl out the date: *May 7, 1997.*

"What's that, a journal entry?"

Porter looked at his attorney with obvious anger in his eyes. "Yeah."

Sowerby lifted a hand, finished gathering his things, and turned to chase after Mr. Comer. But as he did so, he gazed over his client's shoulder at Porter's first written words:

I, John D. Porter, have done at last that which I thought I would never do.

Sowerby didn't want to read anymore.

* * *

12:02 p.m. PST

The recess was not nearly long enough, and Porter still had a vast amount of questions. Sowerby was in a bad mood and didn't seem to care about Porter at all anymore. Porter thought that even Sowerby wanted him to fry in the legal pan. But the truth came in the form of Clusser's script. Questions filled the page, and Sowerby no doubt realized he would do little for this case; it was all in the care of the FBI now, though Sowerby would never understand how or why.

Porter watched the skinny attorney stand and call Agent Stan Clusser to testify. Mr. Comer had already been briefed and had no problem with a member of the FBI stepping forth.

Porter wondered what the Prosecuting Attorney intended to do after his verbal explosion. Well, Porter had said his peace. He felt good about it and would stand behind his words to the end, while at the same time he wondered when that end would come.

The next act of the play had begun. A few preliminary questions: Tell the court who you are, what are your credentials etc.

Sowerby did his best to look like he'd invented the questions himself. "Agent Clusser, in your opinion as a field operative of the Federal Bureau of Investigations, has a crime been committed?"

Sitting tall in the leather chair, Clusser gave a powerful, "Yes."

"Will you tell us what has happened?"

"I will. On the twenty-second of March, an object of archaeological significance, the property of Guatemala, illegally entered the United States."

"You are referring to KM-2?" said the attorney.

Clusser's brow lowered as he nodded, and Porter suspected the attorney wasn't sticking to his lines. "That artifact was then passed to two graduate students attending Stratford University."

"Who," said Sowerby.

"John D. Porter and Erma Alred."

"Do you suspect Porter and Alred *knew* they had an illegal object?" said Sowerby.

Porter bit the inside of his cheek as he saw Clusser tighten up. Sowerby didn't want to play the game. Porter trusted his missionary companion, but he was quickly losing faith in his attorney who had helped him little so far. For a second, Porter even wondered if the lawyer had already been bought off by those who'd tried to kill him. But he couldn't continue thinking that way, because the next question might be, who else in the courtroom had been swayed by the secret combination pushing for Porter's destruction?

The FBI agent's eyes darkened. Porter knew his companion wasn't the best at hiding his feelings. That's what made him a good missionary. Porter wondered how he could possibly be a good field operative for the government if he couldn't lie well.

"Agent Clusser?" said the attorney.

"I do not know to what realization the students came concerning the legality of their work."

"But you have sat in court since the beginning, haven't you? Listening to the testimonies?" said the attorney.

"I have."

"Did you hear the statements made by Ms. Alred and the accused that Stratford University *assigned* them both to the project?" said Sowerby.

Clusser nodded. "The research was directed by a man known to some of the faculty and the students as one Dr. Peter Arnott."

Sowerby tilted his head. "Are you giving credibility to Dr. Kinnard's testimony that there *was* a person named Peter Arnott? Dr. Masterson and Dr. Goldstien deny there even was such a man."

"Of course," said Clusser. "Peter Arnott *does not exist.*"

"Excuse me?" said Sowerby.

"If it will please the court," said Agent Clusser, "I will point out that the FBI has a classified file on the man called Peter Arnott. We did not until recently. However, the man has been identified with one Gerard Jasper, a pseudonym for someone currently under investigation."

Sowerby stopped breathing. Porter eyed his attorney closely, trying to discern his thoughts, his true motives, and whether or not he would continue with the outline in his hand.

Clusser didn't wait for the Defense Attorney to speak. He turned to the judge. "Your honor, I have reason to believe this entire crime has been orchestrated by outsiders who may be involved in a number of illegal activities presently being studied by the FBI. I am not, however, able to reveal any more at this time in a public court. Nevertheless, I have brought an edited file on this 'Peter Arnott' which may evidence enough to show that the defendant has been caught in the crossfire of a highly organized criminal operation.

"A connection with Arnott may also implicate Stratford University or some of its colleagues to such a degree that I would assume Dr. Masterson and Dr. Goldstien might wish to…amend their testimonies based on clearer memories revived by photos of Mr. Arnott. And of course, Stratford will then have to reconsider the possibility that two of its students may have been…mistreated. I believe you will find there is not enough evidence to convict the defendant, but that crimes have been committed, and the perpetrators are still out there."

"I…have no further questions," said Sowerby, moving to his seat while glancing at the Prosecuting Attorney.

Judge Panofsky lifted his eyes to the Prosecution. "Mr. Comer, would you like to question the witness?"

Comer spoke with his assistant for a few seconds before standing. "Your honor, the State wishes to review the new information before deciding whether or not we have a case with which to continue."

* * *

2:17 p.m. PST

Porter met Alred outside the courthouse, his eyes looking all about for the old man he knew only as Joseph Smith. He saw a newspaper salesman, bent with age and malnutrition, but dressed in a flashy orange vest so that both pedestrians and cars would spot him from far enough away to get their change ready. A woman with too much makeup and jewelry waited as her orange-brown chow sniffed a skinny fern held up by a wooden stick in a hole cut in the sidewalk. A quiet menagerie of folk passed the courthouse, people who had little else to do with their retired days.

"I got back as soon as I could," she said, wiping her nose with her finger.

"It's over, Alred," said Porter with a sigh.

"Well, you're on the outside, which is good. What did I miss?" The wind pushed at the back of her auburn hair.

Porter looked up at the long line of double doors on the granite building. Crows bellowed overhead. He thought he heard a child yelling somewhere, but hadn't seen one. "Stratford made an official statement."

"What." Alred licked her lips.

"They admitted the responsibility for Ulman's codex falling into our possession. They are willing to hear our dissertation arguments and give us our degrees based upon work accomplished."

Alred nodded at the ground. "What about Dr. Kinnard? Will he be charged with—"

"No, the FBI is conducting a manhunt for Peter Arnott. All the blame has fallen on him." He smiled a sigh, but knew things really hadn't ended. There were too many loose strings. Would *they* still come after him? Would they kill him simply for the trouble he had become? Or would they run, hide for years before taking their revenge...just to be safe? They would get their doctoral credentials, but would they live free enough to use them?

"Porter...did we do the right thing?" she looked up at him with passion in her green eyes.

Porter beamed down at her. "I'll tell you everything at Bruno's. Meet me at five?"

She nodded, then reached into her pocket and handed him a small slip of paper as Clusser came up behind him.

As Alred marched down the concrete steps, the FBI agent sagged loudly, "You're a lucky man, Porter!"

"Why didn't you say anything about *them*?" Porter said with a bite in his voice.

"The court knows enough," said Clusser, relaxed. "They've learned the FBI is searching and has reason to believe your case was only a fraction of the big game."

"You let the whole issue skid by!" said Porter.

Clusser put his hand on Porter's shoulder to steady him. "They will always exist, Porter. You know that. This little case wouldn't touch them. If I gave the court too much information, it would only announce that one lone LDS man who works for the FBI has spotted *them*. Let me handle this."

Porter threw his hands up. There was no more he could do about it. "What if the judge learns of our relationship."

"He will," Clusser said with a glow with no grin. "That will prove only that I had motivation to find you innocent. That's not a crime, if the facts are present, and there are plenty."

Clusser stuck out his right hand. "So long, John Porter, you're a good man."

Porter took his hand like a clamp, tears rising under his eyeslids. He hated partings. "Take care of that wife of yours. Easy come, easy go, they say!"

Clusser smiled. "You don't know anything about the wiser sex." He eyed Alred, almost around the corner of the office building beside the courthouse and into the parking lot.

"I still have time to learn," said Porter, ignoring his gaze.

"Not by my standards!" said Clusser. As he strode down the steps in a different direction than Alred went, Porter had the terrible feeling their relationship would remain the same for years to come.

Porter realized he had no way to get home, and it was a long drive. But there was no worry. Porter started for the parking lot after Alred, who wouldn't get to her car before he caught up. Nevertheless, he pushed his feet at high speed down the courthouse stairs while slipping his hands into his suit pockets.

"John Porter?" said a man with a microphone as Porter moved down the sidewalk, his eyes scanning ahead to make sure Alred's car wasn't pulling out of the lot too quickly.

Spinning to see the reporter, the student slammed into the old man selling newspapers.

"Mr. Porter, congratulations on your case! May we ask you a few questions?"

A cameraman appeared with a beautiful Japanese contraption hanging around his neck while his right shoulder was armed with a larger camera with a Channel 12 logo in blue and pink on the side.

Though slightly flattered, Porter asked forgiveness from the newspaper salesman, and looked back to the parking lot around the side of the building. "I've gotta get my ride," said Porter as the news anchor started in with inquiries as to how he'd felt in the courtroom, and whether or not he truly believed the Mormons were right about the end of the world, and when exactly would that finale come, and—Porter really wasn't listening.

The old man swore at them and moved away.

Porter kept walking as the jabbering reporter stepped in front of him, lowered the microphone as said, "Then one shot! Please, just a picture! Sandy, get over here!!!"

The cameraman came around in front of Porter and put the black machine up to his eye. The inquirer in a flashy yellow shirt stood beside Porter as the camera snapped three times.

"Now just one with the courthouse in the background," said the professional annoyance as Porter spoke.

"No, I really need to go."

"Last one, I promise!" he said, waving energetic hands. He stepped beside Sandy and looked at Porter and the background. "This is good!"

Porter sighed and quickly turned to see where they were in relation to the front of the courthouse, which was still somewhat in view around the brick office building. He grinned a fake curve of teeth which Clusser would have been proud of.

The flamboyant newsperson, a little man with the microphone swinging from some kind of hook on his belt now, waved his arms. "No, a little right. Right, Mr. Porter, please, thank you that's beautiful. Now back, back...Good! Now Sandy!"

Just behind him against the curb, Porter heard a van door roar open on metal wheels as he concentrated on his smile. Four hands grabbed and yanked his body like it was a cloth doll. The world disappeared, and the dark interior of the van grew crowded as Sandy and the reporter jumped in. The door closed while someone struck Porter across the face twice.

When the van started moving, Porter realized he was pinned and not just dazed. His head exploded with a flash of light as they threw him against the side of the empty automobile. His arms bent backward, and he screamed out, struggling against—what—he could not tell. He heard the screech and bellow of duck tape being pulled from the roll. They bound his wrists together as the reporter hit him and said, "Sorry for soiling your suit."

"You gotta be insane snagging me in front of a Federal courthouse! The whole planet probably saw you!" said Porter, his eyelids fluttering, his hands raised to ward off further attacks. He felt the tape tear at the skin on his forearms, his heart pumping so fast and hard it hurt. They yanked him around, and Porter hit metal again with his chin.

Leaning his face close to Porter's, the reporter said, "Do you think we would have picked you up right there if others were watching?"

"What about the old man selling newspapers!" said Porter, his eyes only beginning to adjust to the darkness. "And the old lady walking the dog!"

"They are *our* eyes, Mr. Porter," said a voice from the passenger seat in the front of the vehicle.

Porter whipped his head around. Against the blinding light of the windshield, he could clearly make out a man looking back, a face filled with darkness.

"Peter Arnott!" said Porter.

Arnott turned to the reporter. "Excellent work Mr. Goodwill."

The assassin leaned again to Porter's face and whispered. "I've never missed an opportunity to kill a mark I've been hired to hit. You would've been my first loss."

* * *

It felt like a ski mask, but it didn't matter what it was. Porter fought claustrophobia and couldn't see a thing. They drove for hours, or so it seemed. No one said a word, and when the car finally stopped, Porter felt Harvey Goodwill grab his shoulder and come close enough to kiss his right ear.

"The cold sensation against the back of your neck is the icy muzzle of a lovely 10 mm Colt Delta Elite handgun," said Goodwill. "We will escort you into a building, into an elevator, and into a room. You will say nothing, or you will be shot and buried in the cement of some new construction site. I have every reason to kill you for free, Mr. Porter. I fear no one. I suggest…silence."

They wanted him alive. It was Porter's only comforting thought. But his heart went into overdrive, and he pictured himself jumping off a building and into the tops of a brittle tree to escape. Stupid. He could have killed himself. But that was passed, and things had grown worse. If he tried to run now, it would definitely be the end.

It hurt when they tore the tape off his wrists. They never removed the ski mask. Would anyone see him, his head covered as he entered the building to which Goodwill alluded? Would they suspect anything nasty? Call in the police? Or would they be as dirty as the men who grabbed him? Porter would never be sure.

Finally, the short trek by foot ended as Goodwill had described.

Porter heard a door close. No one spoke. Goodwill released him. But the room reeked with the sensation of cold eyes and old breath.

"Thank you, Mr. Goodwill," said an aged voice some ways away. It was a big room, with a ceiling low and soft enough that Porter heard no echo. In fact, as he thought about it, he heard nothing but the tick of a clock on an unseen wall. No cars outside, though when they had left the van he had no doubt he was in the middle of some city. Porter could hear his own heart pumping, and that worried him. He stood still as ancient stone in an Egyptian desert.

"Take off the mask, Mr. Porter."

The light was bright as Porter pulled the hood from his head. He saw an expensive room with pictures of presidents and other prominent political figures along each wall but the one filled with windows covered by shades. Porter tightened his eyes on numerous faces from the dusty past he'd studied throughout his college career.

Was that Herodotus?

And that one Solon?

Thomas Jefferson?

A long table dominated the room, with high-backed chairs running around it. In each seat sat a man who easily should have been retired. They all looked at him through coarse webs of wrinkles. But they held themselves up with metal skeletons hidden beneath their flesh and atrociously expensive suits.

The one at the far end, whose features were difficult to see, spoke while the others listened. "You've failed us, Peter. We have confirmed that the FBI has quite a file on you at present. It's only a matter of time before they track you down. You're a liability now."

"I brought you John Porter," said Arnott without showing signs of stress. "I brought you the codex."

"You have brought us, if only slightly, beneath the microscope of the ever searching Federal Bureau of Investigations. We can live with this. We can make up for your mistakes. We've returned from worse conditions in the past. But you must pay for your crimes."

Arnott looked at Porter, and Porter saw all the blood drain from the pseudo-professor's cheeks. "I still have assets to give."

"You are a lie, Peter. You are a bad one. Goodwill, please escort him into the next room," said the old man as the assassin's black pistol lifted. The tip of the barrel bumped Arnott lightly against his cranium. "We will speak again in a moment."

Porter watched Goodwill lead Arnott to the door.

Arnott said nothing, but kept his head high, his shoulders level, his eyes as unshaken as possible. But both Arnott and Porter knew he was a dead man.

"There are two kinds of people in this world, Mr. Porter," said the old man at the end of the lengthy slab of cherry wood. "The successful and the unsuccessful. I'm sure you will agree that the difference between the two is that successful people *do* things they do *not* necessarily enjoy. Yet some things need to happen...for the good of the whole."

In a moment of silence, Porter felt the old man's eyes examining him from afar. As his eyes adjusted to the lighting, he realized the room was actually dimly lit from the ceiling. Then the gentleman said slowly, "Tell us the location of KM-*3*. We know you have it, and we understand your motivation behind keeping it."

"You want it destroyed," said Porter, not hiding anymore. They recognized the truth as well as he did. But Porter couldn't understand their motivations.

The old man at the far end of the table lifted his chin. "The rest of the world will thank you."

"I will never give it to you. You'd better kill me now."

Everyone smiled. Some even laughed lightly.

"We do not intend to make you a martyr, Mr. Porter. We won't fuel your passionate religious flame. But there must be a balance in the world. The codex cannot come to light."

"Like the Dead Sea Scrolls," said Porter. "Were *you* the ones behind their suppression?"

The old man kept his hands under the table. He didn't move at all while speaking. "You realize the scrolls of Qumran are trivial compared to KM-3. Their ambiguity among the professionals is an adequate shield protecting the Earth's population. I do not intend to bribe you either, Mr. Porter, but we are willing to pay a worthy sum to take possession of your precious Mesoamerican codex."

"So you can do what you will with it?"

"Don't play hero, Porter. Your life is nothing. No one will notice or even care when you are gone."

"I matter to you," said Porter, his lips trembling.

"Two million dollars," said the old man as others watched for Porter's expression. "I've attempted to explain the value of KM-3. It has nothing to do with religion."

"Right."

"The price is negotiable, Mr. Porter. We are prepared to discuss the manuscript's worth in relation to *your* needs. And I am sure you recognize our resolve to purchase the document. You may choose not to sell. You have your agency. But you also must be aware that we will be obliged to kill you if you decide not to do business with us. What figure do you put on the codex?"

Smelling the freshness of the recently cleaned carpet, Porter imagined himself on a plane to Hawaii. A degree, a vacation, and all the money he would need for the rest of his life…it was all being laid before him. Like the kingdoms of the world placed by Satan before Christ in the first book of the New Testament. Yet this was different. This was what Porter longed for. Peace at last. Every stumbling block had dropped in his path, and all would be taken away instantly if he demanded it. They offered him power, not just money. They put him in a position to request anything. And he had the firm feeling they *would* comply. But could he ever revoke the truth, the testimony he'd given in court, the experiences he'd had, and the knowledge in his heart?

With wet lips, Porter said, "You know others will eventually seek out and find Ulman's site. Albright's article was enough to plant that seed of curiosity."

The old man smiled. "You don't know how easy it is to hide these things. You see…there has been a most unfortunate occurrence in the Highlands of Guatemala recently. There appears to have been a battle between drug lords in the area."

"In Guatemala?!?" said Porter, realizing the lie.

"Rafael Madrigal threatened to blow up the entire plantation of his *competidor*, Antonio Janés. But Janés purchased the local anti-government guerrilla militia to intercept Madrigal's powerful weapons. Regrettably, the army caught up with Madrigal's men just outside of a little-known village in the Highlands…called Kalpa by the natives—You've heard of it."

Porter ground his teeth and twisted his lips, his face growing red with anger while his heart melted with hopelessness.

"No one survived," said the old man, leaning forward, pushing his unseen ribs into the cherry wood. "No modern Quiche Mayans, no guerrillas…. The explosion may have provoked the 6.8 scale earthquake and recent lava flow mentioned in this week's paper. Did you read the incoherent story? Only a short mention really. After all, who cares about a small band of Indians in the mountains of Central America? Who cares about rotting archaeological sites?"

Porter tried to steady his breathing. He was powerless to even stop the gentleman's words.

"The entire area is buried again…by the hand of our sweet Mother Nature." Relaxing back into the leather chair, the old man sighed. His words lacked no measure of force. "Now…where is KM-3."

"I already gave it to Salt Lake City," said Porter, wiping the wetness from his eyes. He tried to not think about those innocents, murdered in order to keep the past in the past.

"You lie badly."

"I tell the truth much better," said Porter. "Alred did it for me during my last minutes in court. I have the proof in my pocket. She was the one who had KM-3 during the whole trial. Actually, I understand she gave the codex to an old friend for safe storage. I told her to send it away, though it was the last thing she would have expected of me. In my pocket I have a certified mail receipt. It won't take long for you to figure out who received it, I'm sure."

"Andrews," said the man at the end of the table.

One old fellow nearest Porter stood casually, walked to Porter and reached a hand into the pocket Porter indicated with a glance of his eyes while speaking. Andrews read the markings. He nodded to the gentlemen that Porter's words were accurate.

"What does that mean?" said the man at the end of the table to another member of this secret board.

Joseph Smith leaned forward, curling fingers together in his relaxed fashion. His voice, deep as always, shifted in pitch as he pointed his face from the fellow at one end of the table first and then to Porter standing alone at the opposite end. "KM-3 is in the hands of the Mormon church now."

Andrews sat down.

Smith looked at Porter with incalculable thought in his eyes.

Others stared at the table in front of them, their old brows rising and falling, their dry lips mumbling, their hands shifting.

Porter wondered if the time to die had come at last.

The room filled with wave after wave of thick silence.

The air conditioning shut off with a jump.

The quiet boomed louder than thunder.

"Then it's over," said the man at the far end.

Shaking, Porter ran multiple scenarios through his mind. What next? Should he sprint for the door? Was he dead already? Would they kill Alred and anyone who knew anything about the codex to cover all their footprints? Would they carry their covert works on to other members of the church? Leaders of the LDS faith?

First things first. If anyone would die, it would be John D. Porter. After a long pause, Porter finally said, "What about me?"

Squinting his colorless eyes, the old man at the end studied Porter...for a long time...before deciding.

Chapter Thirty

7:16 p.m PST

"You have a nice day now," said Bruno as Alred and Porter left the cafe. Porter felt the gaze of the boxer with ancient wisdom in his eyes. He smiled and waved.

Outside, the sun touched the horizon, lighting the world with a blaze of electroplated gold.

Alred frowned.

"You've done well, Mr. Porter," said an old voice.

Porter looked behind him as the man with the British walk stopped. It was Joseph Smith, leaning on his cane as the jasmine-scented wind tugged at the bottom of his gray overcoat.

"You stayed alive."

"No thanks to you," said Porter, pushing a hand through his brown hair. He held his suit coat at his side in a tightening fist.

The gentleman smiled. "Actually, *all* thanks goes to me, but I require none. I told you. I have my own reasons for messing up their little game."

Alred looked at the man in silence. Porter had explained everything from the beginning, so she knew this had to be the *Joseph Smith* Porter had described. Porter glanced at her, squinting with curious eyes at the gold-lit man east of where they stood.

"I still don't understand anything about you," said Porter. "I want answers."

Smith smiled and blinked slowly. "Some things are best left unknown. You lost the codex, but some ancient documents aren't meant to be in the hands of scholars. Those belong in the possession of prophets who don't need them for proof of their religion...but use them for spiritual profit and learning. Sometimes the only way to keep something is to lose it."

"Your message," said Porter, referring to the scriptural note in the courtroom.

"Congratulations on your doctoral dissertations." He looked at the two students as the evening wind cooled between them. The old man's grin faded, but Porter could not discern why. Smith turned as if he still had much to do and walked down the sidewalk to nowhere.

"Why did *they* let you go?" said Alred, watching the old man in the long coat. Three twelve-year old boys shot out of an alley in front of Smith and disappeared across the street.

Porter shrugged. "I can't track them down. I'd be killed the moment I got close." He put his cold fingertips into the pockets of his slacks. He licked his lips. "In ancient times, a community just to the west of the Dead Sea in Israel believed we were all...living 'through the dominion of Belial.'"

"Who?" said Alred. Porter looked at her through tight eyes. The sun blazed a bright yellow and orange behind her and yet many thousands of miles away. The sky was a swirl of pink, florescent purple, glowing gold, and low clouds valiantly holding their shimmering whites.

The cool wind blew right into Alred's face, holding back her red hair, but she kept her green eyes opened. The air was sweet.

"Our time will come, Alred. But right now...we are meant to have trials," said Porter.

"You never stop, do you." Alred shook her head and grinned. "I guess I'll miss that someday." She turned into the sun and started walking, looking back. "Good-bye, Porter."

Porter stood with his right hand in his pocket, a sinking sadness in his throat as she left him at last.

Alred whipped around suddenly, but her feet kept moving. "Wait a minute. You never told me your middle name."

Porter glowed. "D," he said with a wide grin. Then he moseyed away.

About the Author

A historian obsessed enough to do the work for an MFA in Creative Writing on top of a master's in Education, James Steimle is the award-winning author of "Pearl of Great Price" and "The Happy Dog and the Lonely Cat." While he has written multiple volumes on developmental theory and many books for children, he is also the author of *Interference*, *The Room That Wasn't There*, and *The Ghost People*.

Visit him online at www.steimle.us.

www.ingramcontent.com/pod-product-compliance
Lightning Source LLC
LaVergne TN
LVHW091642100826
845152LV00006B/128/J

* 9 7 8 0 9 8 4 1 6 0 0 0 6 *